His Small Shadow

His Small Shadow

Sue Hallett-Martin

Matador
9 Priory Business Park,
Wistow Road, Kibworth Beauchamp,
Leicestershire. LE8 0RX
Tel: (+44) 116 279 2299
Fax: (+44) 116 279 2277
Email: books@troubador.co.uk
Web: www.troubador.co.uk/matador

ISBN 978 1780882 932

British Library Cataloguing in Publication Data.
A catalogue record for this book is available from the British Library.

Typeset by Troubador Publishing Ltd, Leicester, UK

Matador is an imprint of Troubador Publishing Ltd

Printed and bound in the UK by TJ International, Padstow, Cornwall

"Time is for dragonflies and angels. The former live too
little and the latter live too long."

James Thurber, *The 13 Clocks*

For Venetia and for Maurice

PROLOGUE

Today he will do it. He has decided. His parents have never allowed him to go to the lake with the other boys, so he has never actually swum, but he is sure it will be easy – gliding through the dark water like a fish, slipping down through the weed. He can hold his breath for a long time now. He has been practising.

He peers down into the pool. At first he can see nothing in the blackness but his own feet, two pale fish floating at the ends of his legs. But if he leans over as far as he can and stares really hard and long and screws up his brain, he can see right down to the bottom, where colourful fish and strange creatures swim in and out of swaying weed, and treasures lie hidden maybe…who knows?

When his head gets too dizzy he sits up for a while, fingers the hard knotty wood of the log, listens to the sounds of the valley, the water, trees and birds, all talking in their quiet, summer voices. In winter the stream chatters loudly as it runs and jumps on the far side of the bend, but today it only whispers as it slides round rocks stained red-brown like old blood. He gazes up into the trees, where long paths of sunshine slice through the archway of leaves above his head. Between them the air is cool, green, dancing with gnats and butterflies. He tries to catch them when they come close. When he opens his fingers, they are always empty.

A dragonfly lands only inches away, resting beside him on the fallen tree. He studies each section of its long, blue-black body, the intricate pattern of its wings, as delicate as cobwebs. Bulbous eyes, blue and shiny, seem to look at him. A tiny mouth works at something he cannot see. His throat catches with excitement. He sits motionless as he ponders how to catch it, hardly daring to breathe.

The watery crack of rock dropping onto rock makes him start, sends the dragonfly skimming away to the other side of the stream. He tuts and glares along the tree trunk at a small figure crouching barefoot in the shallows, hands full of gravel and stones. His brother is trying to make a dam, trying to fill the gap beneath the log. The water is clever. It always finds a way through, however large the rocks he heaves into place, however many heaps of gravel and mud he throws into the spaces.

The pool turns slowly under its dusty surface, draws him back down into the darkness. Of course *he* can't come. He's just a baby. He couldn't hold his breath for long enough and would just as likely drown and then there would be an almighty fuss. No, he must do it on his own. He will do it today.

❧

He has taken off his clothes and is sitting on the log, ready. *He* wanted to know why, of course. Because I'm hot. You can as well, if you like. Don't tell Mother. So they are both naked – one on the log, one in the shallows building, always building.

It looks very deep, the pool…and dark. His heart begins to thump in his chest, his hands grow sticky as they grip the rough bark of the tree. He can't stop now. He has waited all summer for this. His feet slip further and further in, the icy water sending shock waves through his body as it slides over his hot legs. Suddenly his hands lose their grip and he is in the pool, over his head, gasping, kicking, thrashing with panic…water in his mouth, in his eyes…can't breathe… *help*…

His feet feel rock. He stands up, coughing, heaving air back into his lungs. He laughs with relief and sobs with disappointment. After all the waiting and hoping, the water is only as deep as himself and is full of rocks. No swaying weed. Or fish. Or treasures. Nothing.

He looks over to the shallows. *He* hasn't noticed. He isn't even looking. He is lying on the wet gravel, face down, hitting the stones with his hands and his feet. What is he doing? There is hardly any water there – he can't be trying to swim. Is he cross because his dam is no good and the stream has won again? He shakes the water from his eyes and ears and calls out. Get up, get up! He doesn't understand. Something is wrong.

PART ONE

Kent, October 1863

CHAPTER 1

Cecily trudged along the narrow winding lane which led from her home in the small town of Wittenbury to the village of Blackford some five miles away. A fine drizzle blew in sheets across the sodden brown fields towards her, soaking her hair and face, which was already wet with tears. She made no effort to keep her skirts out of the mud or to dry her eyes and nose. Harry, her brother, walked beside her, struggling with her heavy carpet bag. She couldn't look at him. She was too angry. Instead she addressed loud sobbing complaints about her misfortune and the cruelty of her parents to the dripping woodlands through which they walked and to the heavy sky. Harry listened silently, only interrupting once to hand her his handkerchief. When she had finally run out of tears and accusations he spoke quietly, kindly.

"Listen, Cecy, they do care about you, you know. Mother may not appear to, but that's just because she's too tired and busy and has too many of us to think about. They feel this is the best thing for you."

She rounded on him, shaking her head. "That's all very well for you to say. You're a *boy*. You can do no wrong. How can you say Mother cares for me when all she does is scold me? And you'll never have to polish the silver or iron a stupid apron. I don't want to go, Harry, and it isn't fair of them to make me." She pulled damp seed heads from the long grasses and flung them away from her.

1

"I know you don't want to go, but you'll soon get used to it. It'll teach you how to manage a home – you *will* have one of your own one day, you know. You can't go on as you do, always making a mess of things and then becoming so upset if you're corrected. It'll teach you to be more patient and work at things until they're right. You're lucky to get this position, Cecy. It's not far from home. And the Reverend Hopwood's a kindly man. Goodness knows, he must be kind or daft to be taking *you* on. You should be grateful, you know."

She stopped in the middle of the lane, standing in his path and glaring. "I'm *not* grateful, I'm not! We're not *poor* like Eliza's family. I don't understand at all why I have to go."

Harry sighed, pulling at her arm. "Come on, Cecy. We've miles to go yet." She followed reluctantly, scowling at her feet.

He continued, "No, we're not poor, but we're not rich either. You know that. Try to see another point of view apart from your own, dear. Mother will be glad of a few extra shillings for the little ones' clothes and boots."

Cecily was silent for a while, but to be asked to see things from her mother's point of view was too much. She burst out, "And how could they send me away without even telling me what was going to happen?"

Harry took her hand and squeezed it. "I can see that it was a shock for you, coming home from Grannie's to find your bag already packed…"

"It *was* a shock, it was horrible!" She began to cry again.

"Don't cry any more, Cecy. Mother didn't do it to be cruel. She was just frightened of the fuss she knew you would make, and thought if you had no time to think about it, it would be easier for everyone."

"But she and Father knew I wanted to be a teacher. It's so…" Another sob caught at her throat. "…so unfair."

Harry paused, before responding quietly, "We can't always choose what we do."

"But Miss Finch always said I was the best reader in the class and wrote the best compositions. Why *can't* I be a teacher?"

"Cecily, you know as well as I do that Father can't pay the fees for the college. Besides, they would never have you. The compositions may have been fine, but it was a miracle that Miss Finch could read them at all, your handwriting is so bad!"

She sniffed loudly and wiped her eyes. She was not yet ready to concede that he was right.

The pair continued to argue for several miles. The light was beginning to fade and by the time they could see the outskirts of Blackford village the lamps had been lit in several cottages. When they reached the large Georgian Rectory, set back from the village green and next to the church, they were both tired. Cecily's stomach was churning with nerves. They found the tradesmen's entrance at the side of the house and rang the bell.

A tall, plump, red-faced woman ushered them into the kitchen with large, flapping hands. "Oh, here you are at last, Cecily. I'm Mrs Norris, the cook. You'll answer to me most-times, when you're not with the mistress. Come in, come in… and you, young man. It's a nasty, mizzlin' afternoon to be sure. Come and get them coats dry by the range."

Later in the evening, after Harry had been given supper and had set off for home, and Cecily had tried to eat, but could not force the food past the lump in her throat, Mrs Norris showed her up a narrow wooden staircase to a tiny attic room and left her to unpack. Now she stood in the doorway unable to face the cold emptiness of the room, a small candle trembling in her hand, tears running down her cheeks once more and dripping from her chin. She could make out two small beds side by side under the eaves. One had clearly been slept in – the other maid, she guessed. She hadn't yet met her and couldn't remember her name. At least they had a bed each; the first time she had ever slept in a bed of her own. This thought cheered her a little and she forced herself to step inside the room and shut the door. Placing the candle on top of a small chest, she dried her face and nose and, finding two empty drawers, unpacked her clothes, hairbrush and two precious books. That done, and the light of the candle being too dim to read by, there was nothing left for her to do but lie on the bed and resume her weeping. When, by half past nine, there was still no sign of her companion, she got into her nightdress, climbed into bed and cried herself to sleep.

∞

Her sister was calling her. She was running through the town, along roads which never quite went where she expected them to. Her throat ached with a terrible feeling of desolation, although she didn't know why. She became increasingly desperate to find a familiar road, to find her sister and her home.

"Cecily, wake up. If we're not downstairs in ten minutes we'll catch it good 'n proper."

She opened her eyes and a cold blast of memory swept through her, as chilling as the air in the dark attic room. The ache in her throat turned immediately to tears, but she bit her lip hard and sat up in bed. Through the gloom of the candlelight she could see a girl, a little older than herself, taller, more womanly, washing her face at a wooden stand. She was pretty, with dark eyes and lashes, her black hair dangling down her back in a long, thick rope.

"What should I wear?" Cecily's voice wobbled alarmingly.

"Those are yer clothes there." The girl pointed to a grey dress, white apron and cap hanging behind the door. Her exasperated eyes met Cecily's. " 'urry up, will you? Yer goin' to make me late. Mistress told me to see to you today, though goodness knows I've enough to do already."

4

"I can't remember your name."

"I'm Edith. Edith Penton." Several minutes of silence followed as Edith dressed and Cecily began to wash.

"I 'ave to go now, Cecily. You'll 'ave to come and find me in the breakfast room."

Edith bustled out of the room with the self-important air of those who are old hands in a job and closed the door behind her. Cecily stared after her. Unable to stop the tears spilling from her eyes, she felt herself begin to sob and knew that she must stop now or lose control completely. She splashed her face with the icy water in the bowl and dried herself roughly with the sleeve of her nightgown. The scene from the previous day, when her father had given her the awful news, came flooding back as she dressed, the shock of her mother's harsh words hitting her once more with the force of a physical blow:

"Oh, for heaven's sake, Cecily, stop that snivelling. What did you expect? Did you think you could live here forever, with nine of us in the house? It's time for you to go and there's an end of it."

Mercifully, the sound of her mother's voice, even just a memory, had its usual effect on her and she began to feel the terrible sense of abandonment give way to indignation, quickly growing into rage. She was grateful for the strength the anger gave her to struggle into the ill-fitting dress, whose previous occupant had clearly been a good deal thinner and taller than herself. She pinned her thick chestnut hair under the starched cap as best she could and surveyed the result in the mirror on the wall by the door. A pale oval face with dark brown eyes stared back at her. The dress looked ridiculously tight. She had been teased at home lately for becoming something of a dumpling. She had grown breasts and at the same time had found that her thighs were no longer skinny, nor her hips and arms. Puppy fat, her mother had called it, sticking up for her for once. She was yet to gain the height that would, in her mother's words, spread the fat about, so the dress was also far too long. It would have to be shortened or she would break her neck on the stairs. Despite these shortcomings, there was something about the sight of herself in uniform which filled her with unexpected pride. She had spent most of her fourteen years wanting to be older, and now suddenly she was. With one last look in the mirror, she picked up her skirt, took a deep breath for courage and ran down the stairs to try to find Edith.

❧

Cecily's first day in service passed in a whirl of duties. As she lay in bed that night, unable to sleep despite her exhaustion, every muscle in her body ached and her mind was in turmoil. The faces of both Mrs Hopwood and Mrs Norris were indelibly printed there, the cook's shining red from the heat of the range, her brow deeply creased with frowns, the mistress's pale and pinched with disapproval. They had scolded her from the beginning of the day to the end, calling her "slapdash" or "thick-thumbed" or "cack-handed" or "like a bull in a china shop" or "worse than useless." She had tried her best with each new task – filling the coal scuttles, emptying and polishing the grates, lighting the fires, making the beds, emptying the chamber pots, dusting and polishing the furniture, brushing the carpets, beating the rugs, cleaning the lamps, polishing the silver, peeling the vegetables and endless more – but had accomplished nothing to anyone's satisfaction. Only Edith had shown any kindness, whispering instructions behind her hand, correcting her mistakes when no one was looking.

She was used to constant criticism from both home and school, but it still stung her cruelly. As she lay in the dark, listening to Edith's soft breathing, she remembered being scolded even as a tiny child for falling over and running into things and people and the bafflement she had felt when she was made to promise to be more careful next time, for how could she do that, when she had no idea how the accident had happened in the first place? Memories of school flooded back, too – the frustration and humiliation of trying, but being unable, to make her writing follow the beautiful curves and lines she was required to copy, of producing embroidery which looked as if it had been chewed by a mouse and pictures which were completely unrecognisable. Teachers seemed to be whispering in her ear once more, telling her that she would never be good at anything. Her mother, too, was there, with looks of exasperation and loud tuts at her efforts to iron a shirt or polish the grate.

She put her fingers in her ears and shook her head. No, she wouldn't listen to the unkind voices in her head – they would only make her more miserable. She would think of Harry and of what he had said to her on their walk. His gentle strength and calmness always helped her to see her problems differently, and she trusted him to tell her the truth. He had promised her that she *would* get used to life here, so she must hold onto that thought and banish all others. She forced herself to conjure up some happy pictures in her mind – of the two of them playing together as children, and of their many companionable conversations as they grew older. Gradually they had the desired effect. Her breathing slowed and deepened and, as exhaustion finally overcame her, she slipped into a deep and dreamless sleep.

CHAPTER 2

It was a Wednesday morning towards the end of October. Alfred had woken late and was standing beside the open window of his bedroom dressing quickly, taking deep breaths of crisp air to clear his head. He was pleased to see the pink glow of sunshine on the fields across the lane. Rain-sodden grass shone with heavy dew and lakes of mist filled the hollows. It was the first day without rain for nearly two weeks. A good day to start work on the school porch.

In the distance a door slammed. He heard the sound of heavy boots walking up Stonefield Road from the hamlet. The men would be there before him if he didn't hurry. He flung his jacket over his shoulders, ignored the sight of his unruly sandy hair in the mirror and strode quickly from the room, down the stairs, past the kitchen door, which seeped delicious smells of bacon and new bread, and out into the large cobbled yard. Most of it was still in deep shadow, but the wet roofs of the stables, sheds and workshops which surrounded it glistened in the sun. He slipped into his tiny office and sat down at his desk, watching through the window as the gate in the far wall opened and three of his men walked in. They stood together for a while, Jimmy, the apprentice, yawning and shuffling his feet, Reg and Bill talking in low voices, their breath appearing in clouds. All three were well-wrapped against the cold in caps, scarves and heavy jackets. He wondered whether they had a problem he should be dealing with, but after a few minutes they dispersed. Jimmy disappeared into the stables. The others took timber from the carpenter's workshop and stacked it in the yard, then gathered tools and materials from various stores. When the apprentice re-appeared with Horace, their large, grey horse, harnessed to a long cart, they began to load up.

Half an hour later, when he could see that they were almost ready, Alfred walked out into the yard and stood in the corner in the first patch of sunshine to strike the cobbles, his face breaking into a smile.

"Morning, lads," he called, "and a good one, thank goodness, after all the rain we've had this past week. Are you set, Reg?"

"Just the barra' to load, Mr Nicholson, and then we'll be off," replied the oldest of the three. He turned to the apprentice. "Look lively, Jimmy lad, we don' 'ave all day."

Alfred opened his mouth to say something else, but stopped when a small, familiar figure appeared at the doorway of the house on the far side of the yard. Her face, already made severe by her greying brown hair pulled tightly back from a centre parting, was contorted by squinting into the sun and frowning with annoyance at the same time.

"Alfie, Alfie." She waved at him urgently.

Reg and Bill exchanged looks. Alfred, noticing, frowned and turned away from them, his long legs carrying him in a few quick strides across the cobbles to his mother's side. He took hold of her arm and guided her back into the house. With the door safely shut behind them, he took a long breath to steady his voice:

"Mother, please. How many times have I asked you not to call me Alfie in front of the men? Did you see the way they looked when you called? I have a hard enough job to win their respect after they've worked for Father for so many years…"

His mother tutted. "Really, Alfie. If you want to earn their respect you could start by dressing like a gentleman, rather than one of the men. Look at you! You have a perfectly good coat hanging virtually untouched in your wardrobe and you wear that dreadful old jacket. Your father paid good money for you to mix with the sons of gentlemen at school, but it seems to have had no effect on you whatsoever."

He looked down at her, knowing he would never tell her the real effect of school days spent with boys who had viewed him with the same scorn they felt for the children of their servants. She reached up and tried to straighten several untidy locks of hair which had fallen across his forehead.

He moved his head away. "Mother… "

She ignored him and continued, "And why you insist on working in that ridiculous tiny shed you call an office, when you could be inside in the warm study your father used, I shall never know."

"I've told you before, I like to be near to the men. I can see everything that's going on in the yard and the office is quite adequate for my needs. Now, I'm sorry, I don't want to be rude, but I do need to get on. Did you come out to say anything in particular?"

She looked aggrieved. "I only came to tell you that you have had no breakfast and it's after eight o'clock. Annie needs to clear away."

"I'm sorry, I woke late and I haven't time to eat now. Please give my apologies to Mrs Dawes. Tell her I'll eat in the kitchen later so that Annie can get on with the clearing up. I must speak to the men before they go." He gave her a small smile, opened the door before she could respond and walked back out into the yard. He rejoined the men, who were now sitting on the raised seat at the front of the cart, Jimmy in the centre holding the reins. The horse shook its head and snorted with impatience to be off.

"Remember you have to pick up the bricks from Taylor's on your way, Reg," Alfred said.

"Yes, Mr Nicholson, I'll remember. We shan't be buildin' much of a porch without 'em!" Reg gave a small chuckle at his own joke, then paused expectantly. "Shall we be off then?"

"Yes, lads, off you go. And I shall be over this afternoon to see how you're getting on."

The cart rattled out of the yard. He watched it negotiate the gateway, then closed the gate and wandered into the carpentry workshop, where he sat on a bench for a few minutes, his elbows on his knees, stroking his beard and moustache, and staring at the wall of tools in front of him. Then, with a long sigh, he pushed himself upright and walked back to the house.

❧

The cart turned right out of Stonefield Road and into Blackford Lane. Once safely out of view and ear-shot of the yard, Bill leant behind Jimmy's back and poked his father in the arm.

"What a mother's boy, eh, Pa?" He imitated Mrs Nicholson's high-pitched tone: "Alfie! Alfie!" He laughed and dug Jimmy in the ribs. Jimmy kept his eyes on the road, twitched the reins and said nothing.

"Mind yer manners, boy," Reg warned. "That's yer master yer talkin' about." Bill looked away from his father, rolled his eyes and shrugged his shoulders at a group of cows gathered in a gateway. The men sat in silence, rubbing their hands against the cold and watching the familiar landmarks pass, the long ridge to their right, dotted with farms and small patches of woodland, and the high hedges to their left. They listened to the sounds of the sheep and cows and a few autumn birds and felt the roll and bump of the cartwheels beneath them.

"I feel sorry for the lad meself," Reg continued after a few minutes. "'E's a quiet one, bit reserved like. I reckon it's lonely for 'im, stuck 'ere with the business to run. I remember 'im as a young 'un. 'E weren't never interested in buildin' nor carpentry nor nothin' like that. Not like 'is younger brother. 'E were only a nipper, but put a few tools and a lump o' wood in John's 'ands and 'e'd make a box or a toy in no time."

"What *did* 'appen to John Nicholson, Pa?" asked Bill. "I've never got Ma nor no one to tell me. They say it's not to be spoken about or some such nonsense."

Reg rounded on his son sharply. "That's 'cause it's not for the likes of us to talk about our betters' business. Mind that big nose o' yours, Billy boy – it'll get you into bother one o' these days."

"All right, all right! I was only askin'." Bill huffed and turned away.

To emphasise the point that there would be no more discussion on the subject, Reg pulled a piece of paper from his inside jacket pocket, unfolded it and began to study it carefully, occasionally making marks on a plan and jotting numbers around its edges with a stubby pencil whisked from the bush of curly white hair at the side of his head. The only other conversation of the whole journey was a heated one about the proper loading of the bricks at the brickyard. An hour later they rattled into Blackford and came to a halt outside the tiny village school.

Reg jumped down from the cart. As he walked up the steps to the school, the front door opened and a tall young woman stepped out into the bright sunshine. He noticed both lads staring and fidgeting. She was strikingly attractive, in an unconventional way. Her fair, wavy hair was tied in a soft knot at the back of her head. Her face was pale and rather long, but her eyes were a beautiful blue, framed by dark lashes and eyebrows, and set off by the cornflower blue of her dress. Her figure was slender, but shapely. It would certainly have met with his approval when he was younger. She looked at them with a direct, cool gaze. Jimmy and Bill pulled at the peaks of their caps and looked at their feet in some confusion. Reg, at fifty three, was less daunted and greeted her respectfully with a nod of his head.

"Mornin', ma'am. You'll be the new school mistress. I'm Reg Barton, come to build yer new school porch."

"Ah, Mr Barton, I'm pleased to meet you. I'm Emma Fielding. How do you do?" She held out her long, fine fingers. He hastily wiped his fat, mucky ones on his jacket before shaking hands. They disappeared inside the building, leaving the others to collect their senses and unload the cart.

※

By the time Alfred arrived at the school later in the afternoon, considerable progress had been made in preparing the patch of ground in front of the door, ready to start building the new walls.

"It's looking good, lads," he called, as he climbed the steps. "Any problems, Reg?"

"Not at the moment, Mr Nicholson. The ground's wet, o' course, but it's well drained up 'ere – we'll 'ave no problem with the footins, so long as we don't get too much more o' the wet stuff. I think we'll be able to start layin' bricks t'morra, sir."

"That's good. Well done, lads. I'll just go and speak to Miss Fielding, to make sure she's happy with everything so far."

He knocked on the large door, which opened directly into the one small classroom. The young teacher sat at her desk at the other end of the room, a silent queue of children standing beside her, holding their slates ready for her inspection. The rest of the class were quiet, too, copying from the many lines of beautiful copperplate writing on the blackboard. Even the youngest children, who looked like babies to him, sat still and silent, waiting for one of the older ones to help them. From previous visits he remembered them as a rather noisy, unruly bunch, barely under the control of the elderly school master. He wondered how she could have so effectively subdued them in a few short weeks.

As he entered the room the silence was broken by a great scraping of boots and benches as the children rose to their feet. She stood too, smiling confidently as she bowed. Something in her directness unnerved him. He bowed awkwardly in return.

"Good afternoon, Miss Fielding. I'm Alfred Nicholson."

"Good afternoon, Mr Nicholson. I'm pleased to make your acquaintance. Children, Mr Nicholson has come to build us a new porch, where you will be able to leave your dirty, wet coats and boots. Say good afternoon."

Alfred smiled, embarrassed, as the class chorused their greeting.

She went on, "Now class, sit down and get on with your work, while I talk to Mr Nicholson. If you have finished what is on the board, then you may draw the flowers on my desk. I shall leave the door open. I don't expect to hear a single whisper!" Her fierce gaze swept the four rows of faces and all but the older pupils in the back row bent quickly over their work to avoid her eyes. She turned to him.

"Come outside for a moment, where we can talk, Mr Nicholson."

He followed her through the open door and down the steps into the road.

"Well, we meet at last," she said. "I've seen you in the choir at church, of course, but I don't believe we've ever been introduced."

"No, we haven't. I'm pleased to meet you, too, Miss Fielding. Unfortunately, choir duties mean I usually stay on for a short Eucharist after Morning Prayer on Sundays and don't have the opportunity to greet friends. I've come to make sure everything is all right with the building works. I realise the arrangements had all been made before your arrival here. I hope you find them satisfactory."

"Yes, they're quite satisfactory. Thank you for asking."

"Well then, I shall leave you to your charges. Reg is an excellent foreman. Please speak to him if you have any concerns about the work and he'll let me know."

"I will, thank you."

He could think of nothing more to say and gave a small bow. "Well… Goodbye then, Miss Fielding."

"Goodbye, Mr Nicholson."

He stood untying his horse from the railing, watching her climb the steps and disappear into the school. He had seen her and Mrs Fielding in the congregation, of course. It was impossible not to be aware of newcomers in such a small community. But he hadn't really *noticed* her. To be honest, he didn't really notice any women. Not these days. He used to, before his father died – the girls in the village, and Molly, who had lived with her aunt in his father's cottage on the other side of Stonefield Road. A quiet girl. Not beautiful exactly, but interesting. He used to think of her when he was supposed to be adding figures in the ledger – her hazel eyes and the way she had smiled at him when he went with Reg to collect the rent. And at night, though it wasn't her eyes that he thought of then, but the shape of her breasts beneath her dress and the curve of her hips. He knew he shouldn't, for it always ended in the same, shameful loss of control and afterwards he felt unworthy of her. Perhaps that was why he had never summoned the courage to ask her to walk out and then his father had died and that was the end of that small dream. From then on the business had taken all his energy. He didn't want it to, but that was how it was. And she had moved away, to marry a bank clerk from Wittenbury, so it was said. He sighed, thinking suddenly of all the work he had to do on the new plans before supper tonight. He kicked the horse into a canter, quickly passing the green and turning down the lane for home.

❧

That evening he and his mother sat alone in the gloomy dining room that ran along the north side of Stonefield

House. The room always seemed to him to smell of mildew, even in the summer, and was perishing in the depths of winter, however many logs were thrown onto the fire. He was telling her of his plans to build a new street in Wittenbury. He had begun enthusiastically, explaining what the houses would be like, all the details he thought might interest her – the deep sink and tap in the scullery, the south-facing drawing room overlooking a long garden, the latest style of range for the kitchen. But the expression on her face as she gazed from the other end of the long oak table across the remains of their meal towards him, but not really *at* him, soon sapped his will to continue. Her eyes had dimmed and he knew she wasn't listening. She wasn't even thinking about him. It had become worse since his father died, but it had always been the same. She wasn't interested in him. He was the wrong son and the right one was gone, though she had never said as much of course. His voice trailed away. After a moment or two she noticed the silence and blinked several times, as if trying to bring herself back to the present.

"Alfie, I'm sure you have it all in hand and it will be a great success, but do tell me how you got on this afternoon. What did you think of her? Did you like her?"

"*Her,* Mother? Who do you mean?"

"Oh don't pretend you don't know who I'm talking about, Alfie – the new school mistress, of course."

Alfred gazed into space, trying to conjure a picture of Miss Fielding in his head, then looked back at his mother, who sat expectantly, eyebrows raised.

"Well? Alfie? Did you hear me? Did you like her?"

"Oh Mother, I don't know. I really have no idea about women. She seemed pleasant enough, I suppose."

"Well, at nearly five and twenty years of age it's about time you did have some idea about women. I spoke to Miss Fielding at church on Sunday. Her mother has been unable to make calls because of ill health, and is finding life in

Blackford terribly quiet after Wittenbury. They are both in need of some stimulating company, so I am planning to invite them for afternoon tea – as soon as Mrs Fielding is fully recovered, of course. I hope you will help me to entertain them, dear."

Alfred suddenly felt flustered and didn't answer. Instead he excused himself and left the room. The thought of entertaining Miss Fielding unnerved him somehow, he didn't know why, and his mother's excessive interest in her irritated him. He went into the drawing room, a smaller, warmer room, cluttered with his mother's treasures – ornately carved chairs and small tables, each covered with vases, pictures and ornaments. At the far end of the room stood his own beloved Broadwood piano, which had been his father's before him.

He sat down on the piano stool and looked up at the photograph of Alfred Nicholson senior, which hung on the wall above. The photograph had been taken two years ago, on his father's 60th birthday and just a few weeks before his brain haemorrhage and slow, distressing decline. Kind eyes looked back at Alfred out of a long, gentle, serious face, much like his own, but deeply creased from years of outdoor work. What would his father say now if he knew how restless he was feeling and how frustrated at his mother's complete lack of interest in his world, in him? It wasn't that he felt inadequate or incompetent in his role. He had spent several years working with his father, watching him deal with the many aspects of running the small building business. In fact he felt quite pleased with how things had been progressing recently. If the plans for the new development in Wittenbury were finalised soon, as he had every hope that they would be, the business would be able to grow. It was that he felt so alone and dissatisfied. All his life he had been moving towards this point, when he would own the business, run it his way. But he wasn't even sure that he wanted it. Had never been sure. It was just there, using all his energy. Taking his life.

He looked again into the familiar eyes and tried to imagine his father speaking to him. Nothing came into his mind. No helpful words of comfort or advice. But then his father had always been a self-contained man and Alfred remembered that it was more his quiet acceptance than any words that had comforted him as a boy. And his piano playing. The joy of sitting beside him on the piano stool as he played well known songs and tunes, all from ear, and even classical works which he had somehow memorised from the recitals he loved to attend at the church.

Alfred reached inside the piano stool for a well-used book of Mozart sonatas. It fell open at one of his favourites, Number 11 in A Major. As he played, his restlessness began to seep away, dissolving like mist over the fields in the sunshine. By the time he had begun the second variation it had lost all form and power and his heart felt freer again.

CHAPTER 3

Cecily ran through the driving rain across the road from the butcher's to the baker's, her hood and cloak pulled tightly around her and her eyes on the ground, trying to avoid the largest of the puddles. It seemed to her that it had rained non-stop since her arrival in Blackford. Last week wild storms had stripped the gardens of the last of their colour. Everywhere there was a feeling of heaviness, as if the clouds were weighing on the villagers' shoulders. Even so it was a relief to breathe the fresh air. She hardly ever escaped from the house, there being no need with tradesmen calling each day. But today the Reverend had upset all the plans by bringing two unexpected guests back for luncheon and emergency supplies were needed. She pushed open the door and stood panting and dripping on the sacking Mr Hill had spread in the doorway in a vain attempt to stem the flood which poured in with every new customer. The conversation between the two elderly women ahead of her in the queue was one she had heard repeated by almost everyone who had called recently at the tradesmen's entrance of the Rectory.

"Lawk-a-mercy, but this rain will drive us all into the asylum," exclaimed one.

"It will that," agreed the other. "I've never seen anything like it, not in all my sixty-seven years. We shall be needing to build ourselves an Ark soon, if it don't let up. I don't think I've seen the sun for more than two weeks…have you, Mr Hill?"

"No, indeed, Mrs Grant," replied the baker, as he handed the old lady a small, brown loaf. "Nor have any of us, more's the pity. It dampens the spirits as well as the shoes, that's the trouble."

Cecily agreed silently. Everyone in the Rectory seemed to be in a dreadful mood, especially Mrs Norris and the mistress, and she seemed to be bearing the brunt of it. Patience and resignation did not come easily to her, but since her arrival a few weeks before, she had made superhuman efforts to accept her situation. Her dreams were shattered – even Harry thought she would never teach – so she must make the best of it now. But with the constant criticism from her superiors, her determination to be good and not make a fuss, wavered. Maybe the weather *was* to blame. Whatever the cause, it was making her miserable, that she did know. She decided that what she needed was a heart to heart with Edith. Their growing friendship was one of the few compensations of her new life and, like Harry, Edith always seemed to be able to say something helpful, to calm her when she was agitated or upset.

Later that morning the two maids sat at either end of the large, scrubbed oak table in the centre of the kitchen, peeling vegetables. The air was full of steam from the suet pudding boiling fast on the range and the two high windows ran with condensation, while the rain battered on them from the outside. In contrast to Edith's well-ordered work space, Cecily's end of the table was a mess of scattered vegetables and peelings, a good proportion of which had fallen on the floor. She was frowning with concentration, her face flushed with effort. She pushed a stray lock of hair from her eyes and looked at her friend.

"Edith?"

"Yes, Cecily?"

"Do you think it's this bad weather that makes the missus speak so snappy to me all the time? You should've heard her this morning, going on about the finger marks on the silver and the soot on the rug and Lord knows what else…" Her actions with the vegetable knife grew more violent with each word, until Edith cried out in alarm,

"Cecily, look what yer doin', you'll cut yer fingers off!"

"Oh, don't you start on at me as well. The missus and Mrs Norris between them, they never stop. I can't get anything right most of the time."

"I just don't want you to cut yerself, that's all, and you know you'll be for it when Mrs N gets back if those veg aren't chopped 'ow she likes 'em."

"I know, I know, I do try, but nothing ever seems to come out how it's supposed to, even the blinkin' veg." Cecily smiled wryly at her friend and shrugged her shoulders.

Edith put down her own knife for a moment. "Mrs N says the missus was a different person when she first married the Reverend – 'appy and kind, not snappy at all. Mrs N says it's too many babies what've done it – three babies in three and an 'alf years, and twin boys to boot, and now expectin' another one. A desperate woman, that's what she says our missus is and that's why she bites our 'eads off all the time."

Cecily pondered poor young Mrs Hopwood's fate for a while, and tried to feel some sympathy for her, as Mrs Norris and Edith clearly did.

"Well I don't see as that's any worse than what my Ma has had to put up with, but there again, she can often be snappy herself."

"Mrs N says the missus was an only child and not used to children and that's why she's taken it so 'ard. I don't know, Cecily. Some of it's you as well, you know. Mrs N gets cross with you too – all the time in fact. I mean, look at those carrots – she told you to peel 'em carefully, but you've taken off 'alf the carrot with the skin. I know exactly what she's goin' to say when she comes in."

Cecily winced, knowing Edith was right and anticipating the scene when Mrs Norris returned in a few minutes from her meeting with their mistress. She looked across the table at the carefully chopped and peeled parsnips and potatoes Edith had produced, and at her friend's concerned face. She sighed and turned back to her work.

A few minutes later the door flew open and the large figure of the cook ran into the room. Cecily could see immediately that Mrs Norris was in her usual state of panic that luncheon would not be prepared in time, filling the kitchen with her huge bosom, her great, flapping hands and her contagious anxiety. Throughout the rest of the morning Cecily cowered as the cook nagged and clucked, her round cheeks, already hot from the stove, now doubly flushed with frustration. From time to time she burst out impatiently, "Oh my goodness, where was you when God was givin' out fingers and thumbs, Cecily?" or some other cutting comment.

Cecily had learnt to reply meekly, "At the back of the queue, Mrs Norris," or to say nothing at all. She could not agree with Edith that a kind heart beat beneath all the cross words. For Cecily the cook was as difficult to be with as her own mother, and she was always relieved to be released from the kitchen to work elsewhere in the house.

On this particular morning Mrs Norris seemed more panicky than usual, which in turn made Cecily nervous and, as a result, even more clumsy. The consequence was that she knocked over a jug of custard, spilling the contents onto a resting joint of beef, only minutes before luncheon was due to be served. All three stood for a moment in shocked silence, staring at the disaster on the table. Cecily looked at the floor, her face burning with shame. She then had to watch, helpless, as the others rescued the situation as best they could. She could not help hearing the cook's mutterings that "something must be done," and a wave of anxiety swept over her as she wondered what the "something" could possibly be.

❧

When lunch was finally served and cleared away, (the beef having been washed, sliced and re-heated with gravy), Ada Norris left the kitchen and climbed the large central staircase to the nursery on the first floor. She wasn't sure exactly what she would say to Mrs Hopwood, but she knew she must say something. Things could not go on as they were. As she stood outside the door she thought, not for the first time, how inappropriate it was for her young mistress to be caring for her own children. The sight which met her eyes, as she knocked and, hearing no answer, entered the room, confirmed her view and filled her with concern.

It was a large L-shaped room, light and airy, with windows on two walls. Ada remembered it as the master bedroom of the house, when she had first arrived some twenty years ago. The unusual step of converting it to a nursery was a concession granted by the Reverend Hopwood to his new and heavily pregnant wife, who did not want to spend her time incarcerated in a gloomy attic room, far from her husband and the life of the house. She looked around. Toys, wooden blocks and books were strewn all over the floor. A fire burned low in the grate and on the rug in front of it sat Charles and William, the two and a half year old twins. They were unusually quiet, she thought. As she stepped closer, she understood why.

"Oh no, my lovelies, no, no, you mustn't do that," she cried loudly and ran to take the scissors from Charles' small hands. Immediately, little Edward, who had been sleeping in his cot in the foot of the L at the far end of the room, woke with a wail. She hurried to pick him up. As she brought him back sobbing to a chair at the fireside, she noticed the sleeping figure stretched out on a tiny bed under one of the large windows. It was Mrs Hopwood. Her eyes remained tightly shut throughout all the commotion, her still face deathly pale against the dark hair spread on her pillow.

"There, there, my lovely," whispered Ada to the baby as she rocked him in her arms. She looked at the little boys sat in front of her on the rug. "Dear, dear, dear...now what we goin' to do with you?" Two pairs of identical blue eyes looked back at her, wide with the anxious realisation that they had done something wrong, but not knowing exactly what. Ada ruffled their hair and tried to cover the glaring gaps in their baby brown curls.

"Well, you're very clever boys to be cuttin' with scithers and only two years old, I'm sure. But there's nothin' for it, m' dears, we'll have to tell Mamma." Still holding the baby, she walked over to the sleeping form. The two boys followed her.

"Mrs Hopwood, ma'am, please wake up," she said, gently.

"Mamma, Mamma." Charles began to tug at his mother's skirts and William at her hair. The latter did the business and she woke with a cry, holding her head.

"Mrs Hopwood, are you ill, ma'am? Should I call the Reverend or send for a doctor?"

"Oh Ada, what are you doing here?" Mrs Hopwood sat up and held her forehead as if she felt faint. "No, no, I'm not ill. It's just that I'm so terribly tired and sick. I know it will pass, but I can hardly bear it. I feel worn down, Ada. And this weather is so awful. We've been cooped up here for days and days at a time. The poor children... "

"You shouldn't be here alone with the kiddies, ma'am, really you shouldn't. I know it's not me place to say, but..." Ada's voice trailed away as she realised she had spoken out of turn.

Mrs Hopwood sighed heavily. "No, Ada, really. I appreciate your concern, but I can manage. Thank you. I will take Edward now." She stood up and took the baby, looking down at the boys as she did so.

"Oh my goodness, whatever have you been doing, boys? Oh you naughty, naughty children. I have told you so many times not to touch Mamma's scissors. What will your Papa say?" Mrs Hopwood sat down heavily on the chair in front of the fire. She looked as if she might cry, and Ada felt that she could not possibly burden her now with her concerns about Cecily. She stood silently waiting. In a little while her mistress drew herself upright.

"Well, Ada, what did you want to see me about?"

"I'm frettin' about Cecily, ma'am. The work's hard for her and I'm not sure as how I can properly help. I don't think she's happy, Ma'am."

"*She's* not happy?" Ada was unnerved by the speed of Mrs Hopwood's transformation from depression to righteous indignation. "*I'm* not happy, Ada! The girl is worse than useless. I can hardly think of a single task that she has been able to complete to my satisfaction. When she has cleaned the fireplace, there is more soot left on the rug than ever there was in the grate. The silver she has polished is covered in thumbprints. Her ironing worsens the appearance of clothes rather than improving it. Her sweeping merely moves dirt from one place to another." She bounced the baby on her knee to emphasise each point. The recollection of each new misdemeanour sent both her voice and the baby slightly higher, much to the baby's delight and Ada's alarm. She realised that her mistress was merely pausing for breath, gathering strength for a second onslaught on poor Cecily's efforts, and decided that she must speak quickly on her behalf.

"She does try hard, ma'am. I can't fault her tryin'. And she's where she's meant to be most-times – apart from her first mornin,' 'course. I believe she's a good girl, ma'am…I hope she'll get better at her jobs in time."

"That's as may be, Ada, and I don't wish to treat her harshly, but something must be done now."

Ada looked anxiously at her mistress, covering her mouth with her hand as she realised that the consequence of the conversation might be much more serious than she had intended, but knowing there was nothing more she could say.

Mrs Hopwood stood up. "Please ask Cecily to bring the perambulator to the front door. That, at least, she should be able to accomplish without mishap. Come along boys. We shall call on Grandpapa and Grandmamma and see what they have to say about your new hairstyles."

CHAPTER 4

At four o'clock in the afternoon, Clementine Hopwood walked back from her parents' house along the road beside the green, already as dark as midwinter with the heavy cloud and rain, and turned in towards the Rectory. She was feeling fortified by her mother's sympathetic attention and by her father's remarkable ability to amuse the children, which had given her two hours of respite from the usual exhausting chaos of her life. She opened the heavy front door, hung her wet cloak in the hall and entered her husband's library, determined to sort out the unsatisfactory domestic arrangements at the Rectory once and for all.

She stood in the doorway looking at her husband, who sat at a large desk in the centre of the room. She sighed with half-resigned irritation at the disorder which surrounded him. Covering the floor and every available surface were piles of books and papers. Walls of shelves on three sides of the room were crammed untidily with books of every size and colour. Against the fourth were glass display cabinets filled with dead butterflies, moths, tiny stuffed birds and mammals, insects and spiders, all gathering dust, because he would not allow the maids to touch them. She had long ago given up trying to sort out the room, just as she had stopped commenting on his brightly patterned waistcoats with non-matching, threadbare jackets and mess of curly, grey hair. She watched him for a moment, while he scribbled furiously on the paper in front of him, holding a book in his left hand and glancing back and forth at the three others open on the desk. He was completely unaware of her presence and she wondered, not for the first time, why she had married this rather short, round, elderly man. She coughed quietly.

David Hopwood looked up over the wire spectacles perched on the end of his nose and smiled.

"Ah, Clemmy. How lovely you look – the bloom of motherhood I dare say. And speaking of motherhood, where are my precious boys? You haven't left them alone, have you dear?"

"No, of course not, David, they are with my mother and father. As for blooming, I'm actually feeling quite unwell. I've come to ask you if we can have a serious talk about my health and the domestic help I now need."

"Ah…well…my dear, that might be a little difficult at the moment. I have just now embarked on a most important passage on the life cycle of the Common Blue damselfly – often mistaken for a dragonfly you know. I should much prefer not to stop now I am in mid-flow. Could we speak a little later, perhaps?" As if to illustrate the point, he surreptitiously scribbled a few notes as he spoke, glancing down at them and up at Clementine with a curious nodding movement, which suddenly irritated her beyond endurance.

"*David*," she said, more loudly and forcefully than she intended. "This really cannot wait. I beg you to come into the drawing room with me now, where we can speak without distraction."

"Yes, yes, my dear," he murmured, hastily removing his spectacles and standing. "Perhaps you do look a little pale. Yes, yes, of course we shall speak. Here, take my arm." She allowed him to guide her out of the room and to pull up a chair for her by the large, stone fireplace in the drawing room. He sat himself close by and, leaning forward, took both her hands in his own.

"Now, dearest, tell me what is troubling you."

Clementine had found herself disarmed by his kind and gentle manner on numerous previous occasions. It was, after all – in answer to her own question – why she loved him and had married him. Once again she found herself weakening under his tender gaze. This time, however, the recollection of her embarrassment in front of Ada strengthened her determination to stay firm.

"David, I can no longer look after the children on my own. I have only managed up until now because Mother has helped me, especially when the babies were tiny, but she's not as young as she was, and I don't want to have to ask her here again when the new baby comes."

She paused to gauge the effect of her petition. Her husband was still listening intently, his eyes full of concern. She decided to play her trump card.

"And I'm so tired and ill at the moment. I'm worried that one of the little ones will have an accident because I can't watch them properly. Today I fell asleep and they cut off each other's hair with my sewing scissors. If Ada hadn't come in it might have been much worse – they might have cut off their dear little fingers or worse. Who knows what might have happened? So I've come to say that I need a nursery maid, David. I can't go on without one."

Her husband looked into her dark eyes, which had begun to swim with tears, and sighed.

"Clemmy, my dear, I'm so sorry to see you so tired and troubled. I've neglected you and the children, I can see that. But you do know that we can't afford a nursery maid, don't you? I have explained to you before that my income is modest and I'm afraid there is no prospect of that situation changing in the near future. We can barely afford the servants we have now."

"I have a plan," she replied. "I want to dismiss Cecily and to replace her with a nursery maid." She saw him frown and draw back ever so slightly, but decided she must press on. "Cecily is ill-suited to domestic work and hasn't settled well. Edith is very capable and I'm sure can manage the extra duties."

David Hopwood sat silent for a moment before

replying, "I'm unhappy to hear that Cecily hasn't settled, my dear, but I shouldn't want her to be dismissed after such a short time. I'm particularly anxious to support her family after hearing from the Reverend Tidy in Wittenbury how her father is now a reformed character, who comes each week to church and hasn't touched a bottle of liquor for several years. It will be a bitter blow to them if we send her back home, for she will surely stand little chance of securing another position."

Clementine was tempted to retort that he should surely want to care for his own family more than for that of some reformed drunkard in Wittenbury, but she stayed silent.

He went on, "Besides, my dear, didn't we agree that our children should not be brought up by servants in the customary way, but by those who know and love them most, and who can best teach them in the ways of our Lord and guide them through this life?"

"Yes," she replied quietly. "We did. At the time I was very young and didn't really know much of life and its difficulties. One of the things I most admire about you, David, is that you don't care at all about what others think of you, but try to do what is right. I was much impressed by your belief that we should raise our children ourselves, rather than to follow convention. However, since then God has blessed us with three children in as many years and another to be born in the spring. My view has changed. I don't propose to relinquish all my parental responsibility, but simply to share it with another, carefully chosen woman."

"Couldn't Cecily fulfil the duties of a nursery maid, my dear? After all, she comes from a large family and has several young brothers and sisters."

"Certainly not. She is only fourteen. I can't leave my children in the care of another child, especially not one as incompetent as Cecily. No, David, I want to advertise for a mature woman, to start as soon as possible."

They remained sitting quietly. Finally she withdrew her hands from his, stood up and kissed the top of his head.

"Dearest husband, I know that you care for us all and want only what is best for us. I shall leave you to consider what to do. My health and happiness are in your hands."

⁓

The next day at ten o'clock Cecily was summoned to the Reverend Hopwood's library. Some five minutes later she reappeared in the hallway, ashen faced. She ran through the house to the back stairs and up to her small attic room, threw herself on her bed and lay, sobbing helplessly, her world destroyed for the second time in less than two months. Sometime later she heard the door open and Edith come in.

"Cecily, whatever is the matter?" Edith spoke quietly, sitting on the bed and stroking Cecily's hair.

For some time Cecily could not catch her breath to speak.

Finally she shuddered, "I'm to be dismissed, Edith."

"Dismissed? No, Cecily, that can't be right."

Cecily nodded, tears still streaming down her face.

"It's true. Reverend Hopwood spoke so kindly and gently and seemed so sorry, but he says they must have a nursery maid and so I must go. He's given me till January to try to find a new position, but how shall I do that? No one else will have me. I know I haven't been so happy here and the work's hard and I'm not good at it, but I've tried so hard, and might have got better, and now it's all for nothing." She began to sob again. "I can't go home, Edith. I can't. They don't want me there, Mother said so. What will I do? I don't know what I'm goin…" Her last words were lost as she was overcome with sobs once more.

The two young girls sat in silence for some while longer, Edith holding Cecily's hands as she wept. Eventually Cecily dried her eyes and reluctantly allowed herself to be led back down to the kitchen. Mrs Norris was the last person she wanted to see. It could surely be no coincidence that now, only a day after the custard disaster, she was being dismissed. She felt sure it was mainly the cook's doing. As they walked through the door, she was surprised, therefore, to see Mrs Norris looking quite upset herself. She was even more shocked when the woman, who usually did nothing but scold her, came towards her with arms outstretched. She found herself enveloped in the comforting softness of an enormous chest and there she stayed, sobbing once more, until she had run out of tears.

CHAPTER 5

Alfred sat watching the rain drops running down the window of his office. From time to time he looked at the page of figures in the ledger in front of him, then back out into the yard at the rivulets cascading across the roofs and over the sides of the gutters, his forehead furrowing deeply each time he looked at the numbers on the page. He ran his hand through his hair, then stood up, sighing heavily and drumming his fingers on the desk as he tried to make a decision. Finally he opened the door to the yard, poked his head out into the driving rain and called loudly across to the open door of the carpentry workshop opposite, "Reg. Can you come across and have a word for a moment?"

"Right you are, Mr Nicholson," came the distant reply. Reg appeared in the doorway a moment later, shaking the raindrops from his hair and brushing sawdust from his apron.

"Reg, sit down." Alfred moved a pile of papers from a second chair in the corner of the tiny room. "We have a problem, with all this rain – I'm sure you must be aware."

Reg nodded, looking with concern at his master, but saying nothing.

"I have reluctantly come to the conclusion that I can't keep paying Bill to tidy the sheds. I'm going to have to lay him off for the rest of this week or until this weather clears up and we can finish the school porch and start the roof work on the dairy at Kingswood Farm. I'll pay him for all the work he has done up until this evening, of course. I'm really sorry, Reg. I know you rely on his income, but there's nothing else I can do. This awful weather has gone on for so long now; it's played havoc with the work schedule. But it can't go on much longer and if we can only finish the roof of

32

the porch, we can get on with completing the inside. Meanwhile I'm also tendering for a piece of indoor work in Blackford. If we get the job, we shall be starting that next week, unless a miracle happens and the skies clear of course, in which case we'll finish the outstanding work first. Either way, hopefully, there'll be work for Bill again next week."

Reg cleared his throat. "It *is* 'ard, for 'im and for us, Mr Nicholson. I won't say it ain't. But I do understand, sir. These things 'appen – we can't order the weather we'd like, more's the pity. Shall I tell 'im or shall you, sir?"

"I'll tell him. Send him over in a minute. Now, there's one more thing. Tomorrow morning I've got a meeting in Wittenbury and I'd like you to come with me. I've got the pattern book for the houses and we're going to look at it with Mr Miller from the town council. I'll see if Mrs Dawes can wrap us up some bread and cheese. We'll be leaving at nine o'clock and I have every intention of staying away from here until at least half past two."

Reg's eyebrows rose quizzically.

"Don't ask me, Reg – I couldn't possibly explain."

"Right you are, Mr Nicholson, sir. I'll be there. No questions asked!"

Alfred drew aimless patterns on the corner of an invoice as he waited for Bill. He was dreading tomorrow. Mrs and Miss Fielding were coming to Stonefield House. He knew that a tea party was not something to be frightened of, yet every time he thought of Miss Fielding his stomach knotted. She had been in his mind a great deal since their first meeting – while he was on his daily walks along the lane and when he was alone in the office trying to do planning work. He found himself studying her in church each Sunday, snatching quick glances over his hymnal when he was sure she was looking elsewhere. Before he had hardly noticed her, yet now it seemed as if her presence in church attracted his attention like a lone light in a dark landscape. He *had* to look at her. There was no doubt in his mind that he found her very attractive, even beautiful. He felt he could while away hours just gazing at her face. Yet there was something about her which unnerved him, too. Her cool, authoritative manner, perhaps, he wasn't sure.

As Bill's large shape passed the window, Alfred felt impatient with himself. Here he was thinking about her again when his mind should be set firmly on the business. He stood up to greet the young man.

❦

The following morning Stonefield House was buzzing with activity. Annie was charged with beating every rug and polishing each piece of furniture in the hall and drawing room. She must also dust every ornament and picture in the drawing room and find new homes, on already over-crowded surfaces, for those now standing on the small tables, which would be needed later for tea cups and plates. Mrs Dawes, who came in each morning to prepare luncheon and whatever was needed for a cold supper, must also find time to make biscuits and cake, a demand which sent her grumbling and muttering around her kitchen all morning long. Mrs Nicholson paced in and out of the rooms, moving ornaments from where Annie had put them to other places and finding dust on surfaces which the maid had only just polished. When she finally retired upstairs to work on her outfit and hair, those downstairs breathed a sigh of relief.

Alfred was pleased with himself for having had the foresight to create a cast iron excuse for being away from the house for the morning. He had promised his mother that he would return in time to greet their guests, however. He and Reg drove back along the lane, eating Mrs Dawes' picnic luncheon and discussing the plans for the street they now had permission to build. He was glad of Reg's company to distract him from the thought of his imminent meeting with Miss Fielding, a thought which unsettled him increasingly the nearer they got to home.

At three o'clock precisely he stood at the gate of Stonefield House, waiting. The rain, which had continued all morning, had finally stopped and he was gazing up at the sky, hoping that the patches of blue appearing briefly between the fast-moving clouds might herald a more permanent change in the weather. He heard the clatter of hooves and wheels and looked down the lane. A small hooded carriage, driven by a young boy, came into view, rounding the corner and coming to a stop in front of him. Two women sat above him, Miss Fielding looking tall and graceful, and her mother, also tall, with piercing blue eyes which told of a time when she, too, must have been attractive. He could see that they were both elegantly dressed under their warm bonnets, gloves and cloaks, and he regretted refusing to change into his morning coat and waistcoat, as his mother had urged him to do. Miss Fielding smiled as she took Alfred's hand to climb down. He felt himself turn hot and found it difficult to return her gaze.

The afternoon passed excruciatingly slowly. He sat beside Miss Fielding, both of them on hard, upright, ornately carved chairs, which seemed to him to emphasise her tall elegance and his gawky awkwardness. He did not know how to sit or where to look and so fixed his attention on the two older women, who sat opposite on the small sofa. They dominated the conversation, discussing the hardship of widowhood and the latest articles in the "Englishwoman's Domestic Magazine". His mother chattered on enthusiastically, pointing out various family heirlooms and objects of interest, while Mrs Fielding responded politely, but perhaps a little coolly, he thought. He and Miss Fielding were given relatively few opportunities to join in the conversation, a blessing for him, in his current state of agitation. She turned to him occasionally, smiling, to ask a question about the house or the business or the church choir. Each time he answered, but then could think of nothing sensible to ask her in return, so that their conversations quickly lapsed back into silence. They sat quietly sipping tea and eating small cakes, she apparently confident and composed, while he fiddled nervously with the teaspoon in his cup, stirring repeatedly and unnecessarily until his mother glanced at the cup and back at him with a fierce look of disapproval.

After a while he stopped listening to the mothers' conversation and instead began to study Miss Fielding as closely as he was able via his peripheral vision, becoming fascinated by the soft, pale texture of the skin of her neck and the wonderful deep, golden light of the low autumn sun coming through the window behind her and shining through her fair hair. When his mother addressed him directly, suggesting that he play the piano, he startled visibly, taking a moment to collect himself before walking over to the instrument. Once he had begun playing, he felt grateful for the restorative effect of the music on his breathing. His relief when the guests left was profound, though tinged with a strange longing, which left him slightly on edge.

❦

Emma and her mother sat silently in the carriage on the journey back to Blackford. Emma looked out into the darkening countryside, deep in thought. She turned to speak to her mother, but saw that she had her eyes closed and decided to wait. Later, as they sat eating supper in the dining room cum parlour of the tiny schoolhouse cottage, the idea, that had grown like a small seedling in her mind for several days now and blossomed suddenly as she had sat listening to Alfred Nicholson play the piano, would stay in her head no longer.

She took a deep breath, leaned across the small dining

36

table and, looking her mother in the eye, stated boldly, "Mamma, I have a proposal to make."

"Yes, my darling, what might that be?"

"I wish to marry Alfred Nicholson."

Her mother's fork stopped mid-way to her mouth. She put it down on the plate with a clatter and began twisting her hands together in her lap, her face crumpling into a worried frown.

"Oh dear, oh dear, no, darling girl, I don't think that would do at all. What would your father have thought? No, oh dear – a clergyman's daughter to marry a *builder* – a *tradesman*. I don't think…"

Emma had expected this objection and had armed herself with an irrefutable reply.

"Father would have wanted me to be *happy*, as I'm sure you do too, Mamma." She spoke gently and paused, looking intently at her mother, daring her to disagree, knowing she could not. "You know how difficult it has been for us since Father's death and how grateful we have been to the Reverend Hopwood for securing my position and this cottage for us both."

"Yes, yes, of course, my darling. We are very grateful, *very* grateful, and I know it has been hard for you being the breadwinner now, and having me so dependent on you. And teaching those children…yes…it must be so difficult. A nice little girls' school in Wittenbury would have been so much better, but…" She looked at Emma with a sad smile. "Beggars can't be choosers I suppose. Oh dear, if only your Father had been more careful with money. But…there we are…no use crying over spilt milk, as they say." She gave a nervous little laugh and continued twisting her hands in her lap, the cold meat of her supper lying untouched on the plate in front of her.

"No use indeed, Mamma, and that is why we must now be *practical and sensible*." She enunciated the last three words slowly and deliberately. For her poor mother their standing in the community was everything, especially in their present circumstances, but for her it was different. She had to make her understand.

"I don't wish to remain in this situation for a minute longer than is absolutely necessary. As you say, the teaching is difficult. The children have no more inclination to learn than…than donkeys. And we're living in this tiny house, as if we were…well, as if we were peasants ourselves."

Her mother opened her mouth to protest, but Emma silenced her. "It's true, Mamma. Look around you." Their eyes swept the tiny room together. Her mother looked stricken and remained silent. Seizing her advantage, Emma went on,

"So you see I need to marry *soon* – and someone with wealth. I believe Alfred Nicholson is the ideal man, Mamma. He is kind, intelligent, well-mannered. He can provide well for me and for you, too. I've made enquiries in the village. He's well thought-of and his business is successful. Really, I can't see how you can object to him. So…will you give me your blessing and support me?"

A long pause followed. With a look of weary resignation, her mother eventually replied, "Well…if you put it like that, dear child…of course…yes, you shall have my blessing." She smiled weakly. "I have to admit he seemed a pleasant enough young man, though he hardly said a word throughout the whole afternoon."

"That was because you and Mrs Nicholson did enough talking for us all."

"Oh not me, dear, surely? Mrs Nicholson was quite over-inclined to chatter, I grant you, but not me. She did go on so about those dreadful ornaments. I'm sure I didn't know what to say."

"At least she *has* ornaments, Mamma, whereas ours went under the auctioneer's hammer some months ago."

"Yes, dear, yes, I know. Please don't remind me." Mrs

Fielding's eyes became watery. She sighed and got up stiffly to clear away the plates. As she did so, her face brightened for a moment. "But…Emma darling…how can you be sure that Mr Nicholson returns your feelings?"

"Leave that to me, Mamma. Now, how long should we wait before we return the Nicholson's kind invitation, do you think?"

CHAPTER 6

Throughout the week after the tea party, Alfred's thoughts returned again and again to Emma Fielding, when he should have been sorting out the increasingly worrying financial situation in the company. His feelings about her were confused, oscillating between a strong desire to see her again and an equally powerful anxiety at the thought of being with her. When a letter came for his mother inviting them both to take tea with Mrs and Miss Fielding at their cottage in a few days' time, he knew he could not go. He gave his apologies, excusing himself on the grounds of a pressing business engagement. He could see that his mother was furious and steeled himself for the inevitable argument over luncheon.

As soon as Annie had poured the soup into their bowls and left the room, his mother leaned forward, fixing him with a determined look. "Alfie, about Emma Fielding…"

"Oh no, Mother, please." Alfred grimaced. "I really don't want to discuss this with you again. I have explained why I can't go. I'm sure they will be pleased to see you without me."

She looked at him sternly. "No, Alfie, I'm sorry, but I insist that you listen to me. Eligible young women like Emma Fielding do not appear very often in a tiny community such as ours. When they do, they must be snapped up – *snapped up*, dear."

Alfred sighed. "Mother, we've had this conversation several times before. I'm only four and twenty. There's no need for me to marry for several years yet. Besides, the business occupies my every waking hour. I would have no time to give to a wife, let alone any children who might come along."

"Children, yes, you should be thinking of children, Alfie. It's not good that you must run the business alone and children would one day help and support you. You don't want to be as elderly as your father was before we had you and…" Her voice trailed away and she looked at him, dismayed.

He hesitated before speaking again. "Why may we not talk about John, Mother? I've never dared to ask before, but I'm a grown man – the head of this house now – and I still know nothing about my own brother – what he looked like, what sort of a child he was. Was he like me?"

He regretted the question as soon as it was out of his mouth. For a moment there was no sound or movement in the room except the long, slow swing of the pendulum behind the glass of the longcase clock. She looked up at him, her face pale, her eyes brimming. Her reply, when it finally came, was barely audible.

"No, he was not like you…not like you at all. You take after your father. He…he was like me – dark brown eyes and hair. Such a beautiful boy…my Johnny…"

A voice in his head spoke clearly: stop there, that is enough. But he didn't want to stop. They had spoken his name at last and now he needed to know more. "Mother, I'm sorry, I know perhaps I shouldn't ask, but…what…what did happen to John?"

He started as she pushed back her chair with a sudden movement and stood looking at him, eyes burning with reproach, cheeks drained of colour, her chest heaving with shallow breaths. After what seemed an age, she walked unsteadily from the room, a handkerchief pressed to her eyes, leaving the door wide open behind her.

He stared at her empty chair. A wave of shame rose from somewhere within him, stealing his breath, leaving him as bereft as a small child who believes he has committed an unpardonable crime and will never be loved again. Why was she so upset…angry even? Did she believe he was somehow to blame for what had happened?

Without warning, images and sounds he had kept hidden from himself for many years came rushing, unbidden, into his mind: this room, dark and chilly, silent except for the sound of knives and forks on plates and the same slow tick of the clock, the air thick with everything that wasn't said; the empty chair beside him; his father at the head of the table, looking up at him, trying to smile, failing; his mother turning away when he spoke as if she couldn't bear to look at him, hot shame rising through him, just as it had today.

A rustling noise in the doorway broke into his thoughts. Annie entered with a tray. She glanced at the untouched bowls of soup, at his mother's empty place and his stricken face.

"Oh…I'm sorry, Sir…shall I come back in a bit?"

He tried to give her a reassuring smile. "No…Thank you, Annie. Please give our apologies to Mrs Dawes. We have both lost our appetites, but we shall have the meal re-heated at supper time. I don't want it to go to waste."

She cleared the bowls and hurried from the room, leaving the door ajar once more. He sat motionless for a while, watching raindrops slide down the window panes, then stood wearily and walked back to his office.

❧

Later, when the rain had eased, but before it was completely dark, he gave up on the planning work he had struggled with all afternoon and took himself out for a walk along the lane. His loss of concentration, which had begun with Miss Fielding's visit and gradually worsened as the days had gone on, was now complete. He had achieved nothing. He walked briskly, breathing in the cold, damp air to clear his head. Beyond the hedges the fields were disappearing fast in a sea of mist, the trees and farm buildings reduced to vague, dark outlines as the light began to fail. Above his head twigs and branches dripped. A lone blackbird called noisily, always the last bird to fall silent before the long nights of autumn and winter.

Thoughts of his mother and brother went round and round in his mind. Whatever had happened to John, she seemed to believe that he was in some way responsible. Could it be true? He tried desperately to remember, but his mind refused to step over the edge of remembering, turned away in panic as it had when he was a child. And she would never speak of it. They would continue as before and it would always be there. *He* would always be there, in her face, her thoughts, a shadow between them, not a figment of his own childish jealousy as he had always assumed, but the shadow of his guilt.

His heart felt sick and heavy. Telling himself that he could not be blamed, as an adult, for something that had happened when he was a small child, had no effect. If only he had his father's steadiness, his faith in God and people and life. But he didn't. Though he took after his father in appearance, in temperament he was like her – anxious, fretful, always wanting things to be different from how they really were. This was how he was. He was weak. He couldn't change himself.

His feelings for Miss Fielding were another example. For weeks he had thought about her, watched her in church, longed to see her even, but when the opportunity to be with her had arisen, he had backed away, terrified. He wasn't sure if he was in love, or just infatuated by her beauty and her strength. It didn't matter. She would never want him. Now more than ever he knew that he was not worthy of her.

As darkness fell, he turned around and walked back to the house, letting himself into the yard by the gate and crossing to his small office. He lit a lamp and sat down heavily, taking a deep breath. He must pull himself together. He had a business to run. Men relied on him for their livelihoods. His mother relied on him. He was no longer a child – he was a man and must behave like one. Whatever his mother's feelings for him, whatever had happened in the past, he must love and protect her.

He spoke out loud, his voice weary, but stern. "Come along, Alfred. Enough of this now. It's time to get on." He opened the pattern book, dipped his pen and began making notes on the blank sheet in front of him.

❧

School had finished and the last child had mercifully left the premises, taking its noise, dirt and difficult behaviour with it. Emma stood in the schoolroom, surveying the rows of desks and benches crammed into the small space and smelling, still, the musty odour of damp wool and farm boots. This was her favourite time of the day, when the room regained some peace and sense of order. She turned to the blackboard and began writing up the next day's lessons. As she wrote the last easy addition for the little ones and began the next column of multiplication sums for the older children, she sighed with weary depression, knowing that many of the slates she looked at tomorrow would be an indecipherable mess of incorrect calculations.

She asked herself, as she often did at this time of day, what possible purpose there could be in educating the children of labourers, who had no ambitions themselves beyond labouring, whether back in the fields with their parents or in the new factories that had sprung up in Wittenbury and neighbouring large towns. She knew that the school had been built by the previous incumbent at the Rectory, a wealthy, but misguided, philanthropist, who believed that God had told him to bequeath all his wealth to the parish to ensure the education of its illiterate peasant children in perpetuity.

"What a waste of good money," she muttered aloud, thinking of her own father and his generosity to others, which had left herself and her mother in poverty. Immediately she felt ashamed. What would the Reverend Hopwood think of such an attitude? What would her dear father have thought?

Sadness replaced shame then, as she remembered how enthusiastic she had been in the beginning, determined to be a good teacher – firm, but kind – and how she had tried hard to see something of worth beneath the uncouth speech of the farm children, their offensive manners, their filthy hands and greasy, nit-ridden hair. But the reality of keeping them in order and teaching them had taken all her energy and goodwill. There was none left over for actually *liking* them.

In a different situation she might have grown fond of some of the small girls from the village, the ones who worked hard and were no trouble and who reminded her a little of herself as a child. But the boys…no, she couldn't like the boys, with their incessant fidgeting and rough, noisy play. Nor the older children, who were becoming more difficult every day, not openly defying her, not yet, but producing work which they knew would try her patience to the limit, responding to her chastisement with sullen looks, barely audible tuts and sighs. She had not yet used the cane, but the dreadful weather had made the class more restless than usual and she had come close to it on several occasions recently. Instead she had sent them outside to run around in the driving rain, the cold and wet quelling their boisterous behaviour more effectively than the stick would ever have done.

She finished the column of sums and began a handwriting exercise on the other side of the black board – a poem about autumn, by John Keats. Though she knew its beauty and meaning would be lost on the children, it would at least keep them occupied for some time. As she wrote, she chided herself for her unhappy thoughts and decided to think about

45

Alfred Nicholson instead. As her mother had pointed out, he *had* seemed shy and quiet at the tea party, but this was no bad thing, for he did not seem the kind of man to try to dominate her, which she knew she would be unable to tolerate. Moreover, he was clearly musical, an attractive quality. She could still hear the music in her head, and see him there on the piano stool, even as her hand moved automatically across the blackboard. She had reached the third line of the poem – "Conspiring with him…" – when her mother burst through the door, waving a letter.

"Hello, Mother. What *is* the matter? I'm just finishing my work here and I shall be home in a few minutes."

Mrs Fielding was breathless from her climb up the schoolhouse steps. "Oh dear me…I can't breathe…oh dear, I must be getting old," she gasped.

"Sit down here, Mamma. Now, tell me, what was so important that it couldn't wait until I got home?"

"It's this letter, dear." Emma thought she could detect a gleam of triumph in her mother's eyes, now she had recovered her breath. "*He* is *not* coming."

"He is not coming? Who's not coming where?"

"Mr Nicholson is not coming to tea on Saturday, dear. Mrs Nicholson will come, but she apologises on his behalf and says that he has an important business engagement."

Emma fought to hide her disappointment. "Oh…well, never mind, you will enjoy your conversation with Mrs Nicholson, will you not?"

"I suppose so, dear, though I thought her taste a little…a little common, compared to ours. But what about you, dear? You have set your heart on Mr Nicholson and now he's not coming. Don't you think it strange that he claims to have a business engagement on a Saturday afternoon?"

"Not at all. I'm sure it happens all the time in his line of work. Now please go home, Mother dear, so that I can finish my work here. I shall be back very soon."

Mrs Fielding rose stiffly from the low bench and walked to the door, struggling to fit her wide skirt between the rows of desks and benches. "Don't be long now, my darling. I shall have supper ready for you."

Emma turned back to the board. Her hand seemed heavy now, a deep weariness spreading through her as she wrote the last few lines. That done, she tidied the books on her desk, then crossed the room to the door, turning back to look at the classroom, which was growing dark. She sighed deeply, locked the door behind her and, walking past the half-walls of the unfinished porch, descended the steps to the cottage. As she passed through the garden gate, she saw a young boy standing on the doorstep, about to knock at the door. She recognised him as the Reverend Hopwood's boy, who had been kindly loaned to them last week, along with the carriage, for the trip to Stonefield House.

"Hallo, Peter," she called. "What brings you here?"

"I've a letter for you, Miss, from the Reverend." He handed her a decorated card, pulled at his cap and ran off towards the Rectory.

She let herself into the cottage, took off her cloak and hurried into the parlour to sit by the lamp. As she read the card, her face relaxed its anxious frown. She called in the direction of the scullery, "Mamma, come and look at this. We have an invitation from the Reverend Hopwood to his Christmas Recital. I expect we shall see Mr Nicholson there."

CHAPTER 7

At the beginning of December autumn ended abruptly and winter arrived. Overnight the wind turned into the east, blowing away the clouds and rain, replacing them with cobalt blue skies, whole days of sunshine and frosty nights. Each morning, as they woke in their attic bedroom, Edith and Cecily were greeted by air so cold that they could see their breath. They put on as much of their underwear as they could under the bedclothes before venturing out of bed. Washing was reduced to a quick splash on the face. Once wrapped in dresses and shawls, they set about trying to breathe some warmth back into the house, clearing and lighting the fires and stoking the kitchen range.

The rest of their day was now dominated by preparations for the social event of the parish year – the Reverend Hopwood's music recital evening, traditionally held at the Rectory on the last Saturday before Christmas. Both girls enjoyed helping the Rector in the drawing room, putting up the decorations and the Christmas tree, to be dressed later by the children. For Cecily it was a welcome distraction from miserable thoughts about being sent home in disgrace.

Other tasks were more mundane and less helpful in taking her mind off her problems – hours spent in the scullery, up to her elbows in the large sink, working her way through piles of pans, plates and bowls, or sitting at the kitchen table mixing, chopping and beating ingredients for the elaborate buffet supper Mrs Hopwood had ordered. When she was alone she couldn't help fretting about what her future would be. Her father no longer had his own tailoring business, so he wouldn't be able to find her work (even if she could sew, which of course she could not). She had often wondered what had happened to him. No one would talk about the "bad times" when he had lost the business and she had been too young at the time to understand what was going on. There had been arguing and shouting and her mother had cried a great deal, that much she did remember, and she knew they had once been a more prosperous family than they were now. She supposed she would have to stay at home to help her mother with the housework and the younger children. Perhaps she would replace Dorothy, who came in for a few hours each day to help with the laundry and the cleaning – that would save the family a little money. But how could she bear to be at home all day long at her mother's beck and call? She would never do anything right – it would be awful. She would rather work under Mrs Norris any day.

Cecily and the cook spent a lot more time alone together now, while Edith worked in the dining room on all the delicate tasks, such as polishing the silver and cleaning the glass and china. She found Mrs Norris much less alarming than she had done a month ago. Far from pleasing her, however, this novel state of affairs had become something else to make her fretful. Late one night, as the maids lay shivering between their icy sheets, waiting to warm up so that they could sleep, she tried to explain to her friend how she felt.

"It's a funny thing, you know, Edie."

"What's that Cecily?"

"Well, Mrs N's really nice to me now. She doesn't seem to mind when I don't do things quite right. Even the missus seems less snappy."

"Don't complain, girl. The missus 'as been on at me all mornin' 'bout all the things that need cleanin', and if I don't 'urry up it won't be finished in time, and what will everybody think if they 'ave to eat off dirty china and drink out o' dirty glasses and sit on dusty chairs and so on and so on. She's in such a two an' eight about this blinkin' party, just think yerself lucky she's not been on at you as well."

"I'm not complaining. Well, not really. It's just I wish they hadn't been so horrid before. I'm sure it made me worse, Edie. I haven't broken or spilt anything for ages and Mrs N even said I'd made some quite good pie crusts yesterday. I could've got better, you know, if they hadn't been on at me all the time, I know I could. It just seems unfair, that's all." Her voice cracked and tears began to well in her eyes.

Edith reached across from her bed to Cecily's and gently touched her friend's hand. "I know, Cecy. Try not to think about it, dear. It don't do you no good at the end of the day – just makes you miserable. Mrs N said the notice 'as gone in the paper for a new nursemaid, so there's nothin' to be done 'bout it now. She said it's only on account of the Reverend bein' so kind that they've kept you on till after Christmas – you could've been gone by now."

"I know." Cecily sniffed, wiping her eyes with the sleeve of her nightgown. "The Reverend told me that he's written to my father. The new woman will start in the middle of January and that's when I have to go."

The two girls lay quietly in the dark for a while, both heavy hearted at the thought of Cecily's imminent departure. As their bodies began to warm up, bringing the possibility of sleep at last, another thought jolted Cecily back into wakefulness.

"Edie?"

"What now?" Edith yawned. "It's time to sleep."

"I know, I know. Just one more thing. The Reverend asked me if I'd like to go home on the Sunday after Christmas and stay until Monday morning. It's kind of him, and I would like a little holiday, but I'm frightened about seeing my parents again. I don't know what they're going to say about all this. Would you come with me, Edie? I know you can't get back home to Rochester till the summer, so it would be a little holiday for you too, if the Reverend and the missus say you may. I'd like you to meet my family. Mother won't be horrid if you're there *and*…you can meet Harry!"

Edith propped her head up on her hand and smiled at her friend.

"I'd like that. Thank you. Now let's go to sleep, shall we?"

❦

The maids were up an hour earlier than usual on the day of the musical evening. By eight o'clock all the fires were lit, the kitchen range cleaned out in preparation for a final burst of cooking and all the downstairs rooms given a sweep, beating, dusting and polish. They had eaten their own breakfast and were now in the dining room with Mrs Norris, the three servants standing in a row facing Mrs Hopwood. She sat on a dining chair, looking exhausted, her face pale and her hair coming loose from its usual careful arrangement at the back of her head.

"Is everything in hand, Ada?"

"Everythin' so far, ma'am. The meat pies and fruit pies are all done, the jellies and blancmanges, the mince pies, the cold meats, the cordials and the cakes." Mrs Norris counted off each item on her fingers. "I think we can finish the rest this mornin' and after lunch, ma'am."

"Remember, it's just a light luncheon today, Ada. We'll have the soup and fish, but no dessert – there will be plenty of desserts later. Now…tonight…" Mrs Hopwood gave the maids detailed instructions for each part of the coming evening. "Is that all clear, girls?"

"Yes, ma'am." The two girls bobbed slightly.

"Cecily, I don't need to tell you how important it is that you don't spill or break anything this evening. We are expecting more than thirty of our most esteemed parishioners, so please don't let me down."

"No, ma'am. I'll do my best."

"Hmm…Let's hope your *best* is better than usual. Come along then everyone, let's make a start."

Make a start? Cecily thought indignantly of the three hours' work she had already done, but curtsied again politely, and left the room.

⁂

The day passed in relentless, exhausting activity for the maids. At half past six they stood by the front door in clean, starched dress aprons and caps, hair newly brushed and pinned, their heads spinning and their legs aching. As soon as guests began to arrive, however, their tiredness was quickly forgotten in the excitement of seeing familiar figures of the parish walking into the hallway dressed in their most extravagant outfits.

"Lord, Edith, do you think they'll all fit into the drawing room? Did you see Mrs Hill's dress? She'll take up two chairs on her own!" whispered Cecily, as the matron in question swept through the drawing room door like a great white cloud on a blustery day.

"Ssshhh, Cecily," hissed Edith, " 'ere comes the curate, and the schoolteacher and 'er mother."

"Ooh, I think he's so handsome, don't you?"

Edith had no chance to reply as they took cloaks and bonnets from Mrs Fielding and her tall, attractive daughter. The young curate, Mr Roberts, smiled mischievously at the maids as he handed over his coat and hat. They both blushed, suppressing their giggles as they hurried off to put the coats in the cloakroom.

Edith was called into the drawing room to serve drinks, leaving Cecily alone to greet the guests. She was determined to enjoy the role of hostess, curtsying and smiling cheerfully as she opened the door. She recognised a few parishioners from her occasional excursions into the village: Mr and Mrs

Gilbert, the butcher and his wife, both round and rosy, on account of all the meat they ate, she thought, and looking distinctly uncomfortable in their formal attire; Mrs King, a widow who kept the general store, and her spinster daughter, both dressed in drab Sunday outfits – how shocking, to have made so little effort; and Mr Winslow, the middle-aged, portly and heavily whiskered postmaster, with his young, thin, unhappy-looking wife – what a dreadful life for a girl so young, living with such an unpleasantly fat old man – she would never let such a fate befall *her*. She noticed that the tradesmen and women of Blackford greeted her politely, but not as warmly as when welcoming her as a customer. Tonight they like to see themselves grander than they really are, she thought. A number of other couples arrived, whom she did not recognise, more important folk, whose long faces suggested that they were clearly anticipating something of an ordeal this evening, and who did not appear to notice that she was there at all.

The last guests to ring the bell were a small, severe-looking elderly woman, accompanied by a tall young man with a mop of sandy hair. The man looked at Cecily as he gave her his hat, his gentle face responding warmly to her generous smile. A strange feeling of recognition, quite unlike her giggly response to Mr Roberts, filled her body. She became flustered and dropped one of the old lady's gloves. The woman clicked her tongue with annoyance as she swept across the hall into the drawing room, the man following close behind. As she walked back to the kitchen, Cecily decided that perhaps he reminded her of Harry – yes, his kind eyes were just like her brother's – that's what had unsettled her. Opening the kitchen door, she was immediately swept up into Mrs Norris's whirlwind of panic and all thoughts of young men were forgotten.

CHAPTER 8

Alfred walked into the drawing room of the Rectory and looked around. This was the third year he had attended the Reverend Hopwood's Christmas recital, and he was always impressed with the transformation of the Rector's otherwise modest home, which he achieved for the occasion. The large square room, with its high ceiling and two long windows, draped with heavy, velvet curtains, glowed warmly with many lamps and candles. Boughs of holly and ivy, intertwined with scarlet ribbons, were laid along the mantelpiece over a bright coal fire, a wreath of greenery and berries hanging from the looking glass above. A large Christmas tree, decorated with candles, sweets, fruit and paper decorations, stood on a table in the corner facing the door. He sought out the grand piano, which had been moved into a central position on the back wall. Rows of chairs were placed in a semi circle facing it, many of them already occupied by the great and the good of Blackford village and the surrounding hamlets. The few wealthy parishioners who had condescended to put in an appearance had seated themselves on the larger chairs at the front, no doubt to show off their fine outfits. Casting his eye over the assembly, he regretted agreeing, this year for the first time, to play a solo piece. He was quite comfortable in his usual role as an accompanist, but solo playing was much more daunting, his fingers having a disconcerting tendency to tremble uncontrollably. He found two empty chairs at the back of the room.

"Shall we sit here, Mother?"

"Oh no, dear. I have just seen Mrs Fielding and her daughter at the side of the room...there...look. There are two chairs beside them." Without waiting for his response, his mother hurried over to Mrs Fielding and greeted her enthusiastically. Looking back at him, she beckoned anxiously. He looked at Miss Fielding, who stood beside her mother, talking to the curate on her other side. Her hair fell in soft, fair curls around her face, the green silk of her dress perfectly complimenting the pink of her cheeks. Her eyes seemed to dance in the lamplight and an unpleasant sensation filled his chest at the sight of her obvious enjoyment in the company of the curate. He took a deep breath and crossed the room to join them. They broke off their conversation to greet him, Miss Fielding bowing and smiling with her usual confident directness. His pleasure at the sight of her quickly grew into a blush as they exchanged greetings. He was relieved when their conversation was cut short by the Reverend Hopwood's loud, jovial voice directing them to take their seats. Despite his mother's attempts to arrange the seating so that he would be next to Miss Fielding, Mrs Fielding's equally obvious manoeuvrings won the day and he found himself between the two older women, with Miss Fielding next to her mother on one side and Mr Roberts on the other.

Alfred sat through the first half of the evening struggling to master his nerves. He wasn't sure what bothered him more, the thought of playing his piece or of talking to Miss Fielding over supper. Twice he was required to accompany female singers, which helped to calm him, especially as they both sang well, filling his veins with the familiar pleasure of melody and harmony intertwined. There followed a number of instrumental items of varying musicality, then a string quartet comprising Mr Johnson, the verger, playing cello, Mr Roberts viola and two men, whom he recognised as tenors in the church choir, playing first and second violin. They had chosen to play the first movement of Beethoven's Quartet in G major, a challenging piece for the most competent of musicians. The young curate, he could quickly see, was the only one with any real mastery of his instrument. Alarmingly, the piece came almost completely apart on several occasions and the tuning was so bad that it was extremely difficult for him not to wince. When the players finally reached the last bar, the audience applauded enthusiastically, unable to hide their relief that the ordeal was over. He clapped heartily with the rest, his anxiety lifting with the realisation that his own contribution could not possibly be worse than this.

The Reverend Hopwood rose to his feet.

"Thank you for that fascinating rendition, gentlemen." His eyes twinkled with amusement as he bowed in the direction of the four embarrassed string players. "And now, the last item before we retire to the dining room for supper – our most talented pianist, Mr Alfred Nicholson, will play one of Mr Chopin's fine Nocturnes for us – his Nocturne in E flat major, I believe. Thank you, Mr Nicholson."

Alfred bowed and sat down at the piano. He took a long, slow breath and began to play, shutting out all other thoughts and giving himself completely to the music. The piece rose and fell like a song under his fingers. The room became utterly still, listening intently until the very last note died away. He stood to acknowledge the applause and smiled with relief as he bowed. Several of the less refined women in the audience looked misty-eyed, including the young maid who had greeted him earlier, now standing at the back of the room by the door, dabbing her eyes with her apron. Emma Fielding looked directly at him, clear-eyed as always, but her face alight with a warmth which seemed to transform her beauty into something softer and more approachable. Returning her smile, he moved forward to speak to her, his desire to be near her finally overwhelming his anxiety. Two steps was all he managed on this new, confident journey, however, before he was again thrown into a state of agitation and dismay. For, as the applause died away, the curate offered her his arm and she, smiling apologetically at Alfred, took it and left the room.

He returned to his mother who flapped her hands with anxiety.

"Alfie, Alfie, hurry up, dear. We must catch up with Miss Fielding so that we can sit with them at supper."

"I think Miss Fielding is with the curate, Mother."

"No, no, he's just being gentlemanly. I'm sure there's nothing in it at all. Come along now, before the tables all become full." She took his arm and propelled him towards the dining room.

The room was crammed with five small tables, around which Blackford's parishioners were fussing and jostling in an effort to sit with the neighbours they liked, while keeping well away from those of whom they disapproved. The long table, normally in the centre of the room, but now pushed against the wall, was laden with dishes and platters of food, all elaborately and colourfully decorated so that the overall effect was of a summer border in the garden. At the far end of the room was another table, which was set apart from the others both in distance and in the quality of the linen and tableware set upon it. Here sat the Reverend and Mrs Hopwood with the important guests of the evening – Mr Grange, a wealthy farmer and landowner, and his wife and daughter, Doctor Tucker, with his wife, and Mr Downs, a solicitor and widower.

"Oh no," exclaimed his mother as she scanned the tables anxiously. "The Fieldings' table is full already. Oh Alfie, what a shame. I had so hoped we could sit with them. I thought they would save places for us, didn't you?"

"Not at all, Mother. Now please don't fuss." Alfred found them seats at a nearby table with the baker and his wife and Mrs King and her daughter. The Reverend Hopwood stood and the room fell silent.

"Heavenly Father, we thank Thee for this food. Bless it to our strength and to thy glory. Amen."

"Amen," came the chorus.

"Ladies and Gentleman," the vicar continued. "I apologise

for having insufficient servants to serve you all at table. Please take your plates and help yourselves from this splendid feast. The maids will be pleased to fill your glasses with cordial. Let battle commence!"

Alfred had lost his appetite. He took enough for himself to appease his mother and filled her plate with everything he knew she liked. On his return to the table, the young maid, who had greeted them earlier, arrived with a jug of cordial. After filling his glass, she hesitated beside him for a moment.

"Mr Nicholson?" she asked.

"Yes?"

"I'm sorry, sir, I probably shouldn't speak to you at all, sir, but I just wanted to say how much I loved your playing. It was the most beautiful piece I've ever heard. It made me cry!"

"Thank you…er…what is your name?"

"Cecily, sir."

"Thank you, Cecily, I'm glad you enjoyed it. It's one of my favourite pieces." He looked up at her young, flushed face and smiled. She bobbed a curtsy and hurried away.

Alfred was happy that his playing had brought pleasure to some people this evening. He looked over to Miss Fielding's table. She had been touched by the piece too, he was sure, and it pleased him, though he wasn't sure why, to think that she appreciated good music. She glanced in his direction and smiled at him, before resuming her conversation with Mr Roberts. She really is beautiful, he thought. I could look at her forever. He turned to Miss King, who was not beautiful, and chatted politely until it was time to return to the drawing room for the rest of the recital.

⌒⌒

Late in the evening, Emma and her mother said goodnight to Mr Roberts, who had accompanied them across the green from the Rectory, and shut the door of the cottage. They stood in the tiny hallway, taking off their cloaks and bonnets. Emma could see that her mother could barely contain her excitement.

"I know what you are thinking, Mamma, but it's no use you getting your hopes up."

"Hopes up, dear? About what, pray?"

"About Mr Roberts, of course. You are hoping that he and I may soon develop an understanding."

"No, no, no…well…perhaps I am. Is that so very wrong of me?" Mrs Fielding walked into the parlour and sank wearily into a chair. "He seems such a pleasant, respectable young man, and handsome, too, you must admit, with those dark eyes and dark curls. He may not be wealthy, but he has a steady income, which may hopefully grow one day when he is given his own parish. Best of all, Emma dear, he seems very anxious to pay you attention. I'm sure we can expect him to call on you one day soon."

Emma sat down in the chair opposite her mother.

"Mamma, I'm not interested in Mr Roberts. You know perfectly well why."

Her mother frowned, opened her mouth, then closed it again. She spoke after a long pause.

"I'm not sure that you are behaving wisely, dear. It's not as if Mr Nicholson has made you an offer. He barely spoke to you this evening, in fact."

"That's because you made it very difficult for him to join our circle. Don't imagine I didn't realise what you were up to, Mamma, both in the recital and over supper. I didn't appreciate your interference, I have to say."

"Interference? Emma…really…how could you say such a thing? You know I only want what is best for you." Her voice began to wobble.

Emma fought to keep the irritation from her voice. "You're tired, Mamma. Why don't you go to bed?"

"Yes, perhaps I will. What a shame, and I thought it was such a lovely evening, too." Her mother stood up, sighing loudly, and retired to the bedroom, taking the one small lamp with her.

Emma sat in the dark, her jaw set with frustration. Scenes from the evening played and re-played in her mind – her mother's maddening manoeuvring, thwarting every opportunity to speak to Alfred Nicholson, and her ridiculous fawning over the curate. She tried to recall the beautiful piece Mr Nicholson had played, but irritation kept displacing the music. After a long while, she managed to calm herself enough to think. Her choice had nothing to do with respectability or with attraction. No, it was simply a matter of security. The thought of one day becoming the sad, poverty-stricken old lady her mother had become terrified her. As Alfred Nicholson's wife, she might one day be a wealthy woman, free of this terrible fear. As Mrs Roberts, she would not. The choice was obvious; indeed there was no real choice. Her mother would never understand her feelings, however, that was now very clear. There was no point in trying to explain any more or in hoping for her support.

She sat for a little while longer, listening to the fast tick of the clock on the mantelpiece and the scuffling of mice in the roof space above her head. Her anger had subsided, leaving her exhausted and needing to sleep. Sighing heavily, she got up to go to the bed she reluctantly shared with her mother.

❧

Alfred drove the carriage slowly. The light of the new moon and the carriage lanterns were barely adequate for negotiating the heavily rutted lane. He could just make out the dark outlines of the hedges and the trees, the occasional farmhouse and the brickworks as they passed. The frosty air was very still, amplifying the sound of the wheels and the horse's hooves on the road, and the occasional lonely hoot of a tawny owl from woodland across the fields.

His mother, seated in the carriage, wrapped in many layers of rugs, was exhausted and silent. After ten minutes of plodding, he heard the sound of gentle snores and sighed with relief. He could not have tolerated her chatter, as he had been forced to do on the journey to Blackford earlier in the evening.

As he had anticipated, John's name had remained unspoken between them since their unfortunate lunchtime conversation, but instead of the strained silence he had dreaded, their conversations were now dominated by her constant speculation about the Fieldings' circumstances and praise for Miss Fielding's appearance and accomplishments. He suspected it was a diversionary tactic on his mother's part, designed to push John to the back of both their minds. Normally it would have driven him to distraction, but now he listened and said little, grateful to feel on safer ground with her again, grateful, too, to be distracted from the wave of shame which still swept over him whenever he looked at her and thought of what had happened to his brother. Tonight was different, though. Tonight he was in turmoil and knew he might not be so controlled if he heard a single word more from her on the subject of Miss Fielding.

Emma Fielding – the name went round and round in his mind, while images of her talking to Mr Roberts and, worse, walking on the handsome young curate's arm, were far more vivid in his mind's eye than anything he could see as he travelled along the dark lane. He was shocked at the strength of his feelings, at this terrible longing to feel her leaning on *his* arm. Yet he had allowed a combination of his own nerves and her mother's obvious dislike of him, to prevent him from getting close to her. He could not understand his own weakness and indecision. He only knew it left him feeling angry, worthless and hopeless.

The horse's pace slowed right down. When it stopped in a gateway to eat the grass, he made no attempt to move it. His mother slept on and he climbed down, leaning on the gate and watching the dark shapes of the sheep moving in the field. Out of the confusing and painful jumble of feelings assaulting his body and mind, frustration gradually rose to the surface and overwhelmed the rest.

"Get a grip on yourself, man," he whispered fiercely to himself. "Just do it, for heaven's sake. If she won't have you, then she won't, and there's an end of the matter. Nothing can be worse than this damned torture – nothing."

He picked up the reins, whispering in the horse's ear, "We must snap her up, Horace – *snap her up!*" and jumped back onto his seat.

CHAPTER 9

Emma sat at her desk in the schoolroom, stitching a new sampler to show to the children before they began their own version in the new term. "The Lord is my shepherd, I shall not want," it said. She did not feel she could agree wholeheartedly with the sentiment it expressed, but she knew it would win the approval of the Rector and the diocesan inspectors.

It was the Monday after the music evening and school had finished for Christmas. The room was empty and quiet, except for the distant swish of paintbrushes as Jimmy and Bill whitewashed the inside of the new porch. The stove wasn't lit in the holidays, leaving the air perishing. She had a rug over her knees, a heavy shawl around her shoulders and fingerless gloves to keep her hands from seizing up completely. The embroidery could easily have been done at home in the warmth of the cottage, but the atmosphere of her own exasperation, together with her mother's stubbornness and anxiety, threatened to suffocate her. She had left straight after breakfast this morning, breathing in the sharp morning air with relief as she closed the door behind her.

The repetitive movements of the sewing helped to steady her as the morning wore on. She knew she would have to resolve matters with her mother soon. She wondered what her father would have said about the whole sorry business. His benign, detached presence had been the rock on which her childhood had stayed secure despite her mother's ever-changing moods and constant demands. Although she understood the bare facts of her mother's life, including the terrible loss of three of her four infants, still she could not forgive her for not being what she had needed, and for becoming, instead, an obstruction to what she most wanted. Where her father had supported her to go to the small local girls' school in Wittenbury, her mother had objected, wanting to hire a governess for fear of the influence of less desirable children. Where he had understood her desire to be a teacher (how foolish that seemed now!) and had been willing to pay for her to go to training college, her mother had been desperate to keep her at home. She needed him here now, to speak sternly to her mother and smooth the way between them, as he had always done when he was alive.

She put down the sampler and stretched her arms and neck. It would be time for luncheon soon and she would have to go back to the cottage. As she stood to peer out of the high window, her heart jumped in her chest at the sight of Alfred Nicholson riding up to the school steps and tying his horse to the railing. When she heard his voice in the porch, her usual calmness completely deserted her and she found herself flinging off the rug and shawl and smoothing her dress. There was a quiet knock on the classroom door.

"Come in…" Her voice was soft and high, lacking its normal confident authority. She cleared her throat as his head appeared around the door. "Oh…good morning, Mr Nicholson."

"Good morning, Miss Fielding."

Emma thought that he looked uncomfortable too, as he stood by the door fiddling with his jacket buttons, looking alternately at her and at his feet as he began to speak. "Er…I've come to check on the lads. I hope everything has been completed to your satisfaction. They've…um…they've just finished the whitewashing and the pegs and the shelves will go up this afternoon. Then we'll be off. I'm so sorry…of course… that the work has been so protracted due to the weather. I…I do hope it hasn't inconvenienced you too greatly."

Emma found her own anxiety lessening in the face of his nervousness.

"No need to apologise, Mr Nicholson. It has been an exceptionally wet autumn. The important thing is that it's finished now and will be ready for the new term. Your men have done an excellent job, for which I'm very grateful."

"Oh good…thank you."

They stood in silence for a moment. He didn't seem about to leave and Emma didn't know whether she should invite him to sit down.

"I enjoyed your piano piece very much on Saturday," she ventured instead.

"Oh…yes…thank you. It's very kind of you to…" He gave her an agonised look and suddenly started forward. "Miss Fielding…"

"Yes, Mr Nicholson?"

"I have…I have a question I must ask you, but…but I beg you please not to reply immediately." He seemed to be trying to summon strength from somewhere. He drew himself upright and looked straight into her eyes. "I realise that we… that we don't know each other very well yet, and that I have been very…very remiss in that respect. I should very much like to put that right. So, I have come to ask you if you will consent to…" He paused, apparently struggling for the words he needed. "…if you will accompany me to an organ recital at St Peter's Church in Wittenbury next Saturday afternoon… with your mother, of course, if she would like to come."

Emma opened her mouth to reply, but he put his hand up.

"Please, I beg you…please wait just a moment before you say no!"

She stood looking at him for a moment, her eyes bright with amusement.

"Can I speak now?"

"Yes…yes of course!" He looked embarrassed.

"I was going to say yes!" She laughed. "I cannot speak for Mother, but I shall be delighted to come."

"Oh…oh good!" Alfred laughed too. They stood smiling awkwardly at one another for a moment. "Will it be convenient if I call at two o'clock?"

"That would be most convenient. Thank you."

"Well…er…good day, then, Miss Fielding. I shall look forward to Saturday." Alfred smiled and bowed.

"Good day, Mr Nicholson."

She stood for a while staring at the classroom door, unable to fully absorb this astonishing turn of events. When she heard the sound of hooves on the road outside, she ran from the classroom, through the porch, and stood on the top step watching as Alfred rode past the last of the cottages on the green. He pulled up his horse at the signpost and turned to look back at the school. She waved and he raised his hand in reply, grinning broadly, before turning down the lane and disappearing behind some trees. She turned back to the school, her face alight with excitement, and noticed, for the first time, Jimmy and Bill sitting in the porch on the newly constructed bench, eating their bread and cheese. They pulled at their caps politely as she walked past, but she couldn't help noticing the exchange of amused looks between them. Well, let them laugh, she thought. I don't mind. I'm happy.

She collected her embroidery and left the schoolroom. Taking a deep breath, she opened the cottage door, praying that her mother would have recovered her spirits and be in a more reasonable frame of mind. She walked into the parlour, calling out that she was home.

∽

Alfred turned the horse into the lane and kicked her into a canter. He was normally a cautious rider, but today a surge of energy drove him to ride faster and harder than he had done since he was a lad. The strong body of the horse moving beneath him and the cold wind blowing on his face and through his hair added to his exhilaration, so that he found himself wanting to shout out. Instead he laughed, with relief, and at his own foolishness.

A couple of miles later, at the top of a short rise, the familiar landmark of Kingswood Farm came into view. Knowing that he was now almost home, and still much too full of unspent energy to face his mother, he turned left onto a bridleway which skirted the farm and led up onto the ridge on the far side of the valley. He trotted slowly through a small wood, enjoying the patches of sunshine that appeared between the bare trees and the sound of the horse's hooves crunching on piles of leaves still crisp with frost. Turning right into a narrow lane at the top of the hill, he cantered again for a short while before stopping at a gateway, where he left the horse tied to the gate and walked into the field, up onto the highest point of the ridge.

From here he could look down into Blackford Lane and all the familiar landmarks on either side. To his right was an untidy patchwork of small fields and hedges. Stonefield Hamlet nestled in the valley to his left. Smoke blew sideways from the chimneys and each garden was festooned with Monday laundry, flapping in the strong east wind. At the top of the track, the weatherboarding of Stonefield House shone white in the sunshine, contrasting sharply with the red brick of the houses nearby. Annie was in the garden taking in the sheets and he could see Reg walking across the yard and into the carpentry workshop. His mother was no doubt dozing in the drawing room after luncheon.

This was his world – his life – and as he stood and surveyed it, he felt calm and content. All the restlessness and anxiety of recent weeks seemed to have blown away on the ride between the village and this beautiful spot. He felt a new certainty that this was where he was meant to be, doing what he was meant to do. His old longings to be…well…he had never known exactly *what* he wanted to be, just something more than a builder...seemed foolish and wasteful to him now. He felt fortunate. He had found a beautiful woman, who, to his astonishment, might want to be with him. The business was on a firm footing again and by next Christmas he would begin to reap the fruit of the new venture in Wittenbury. Then perhaps he could marry. If she would have him. And the house could become a home again, with a family to fill the sad, quiet spaces he and his mother now inhabited.

The sky remained clear and cloudless, but at the thought of children he suddenly shivered. No...not now. He would not let him spoil this moment. He swung his arms vigorously to banish the cold and strode back down the hill to the gateway and his horse. It was time to tell his mother. She would be thrilled.

CHAPTER 10

Cecily was grateful for the frantic busyness of Christmas week, which gave her little time to dwell on her misgivings about her imminent visit home. By the time Sunday afternoon arrived, however, her nervousness had provoked Mrs Norris several times into scolding her for excessive banging and clattering of plates and pots. Eventually lunch was cleared away and the girls escaped through the back door and across the green. They set off briskly down Wittenbury Lane, each clutching a small bundle in one hand, and with the other holding their hoods tightly round their faces to try to keep out the biting wind and stinging flakes of snow, which had just begun to appear.

"Oh, I thought we were never going to get out of there," exclaimed Cecily. "Mrs N does get on my wick sometimes! Every time I thought we were finished, she found me three more pots to wash! We're late now. I wrote that we'd be home by four. They'll worry, with this snow."

"It's not snowin' too much – look, it's not really settlin', is it?" said Edith.

"No…let's hope it doesn't get worse." They walked on for a while, talking quietly, both struggling a little for breath as they climbed the steep hill through Cornbrook Woods. At the top of the road, as they left the trees behind them and began the winding descent into the next valley, Cecily burst out:

"I do feel strange about going back, Edie. My stomach's all churned up like one of Mrs N's batter puddings!"

"But you've been lookin' forward to seein' the little ones again…and your big brother."

"Yes, I know…but Mother and Father…I think they

may be really angry with me for losing my position. They haven't said so…in their letters…but I'm sure they will."

"You don't know that, Cecily, and I'm with you, don't forget. Let's talk 'bout somethin' else to take yer mind off it. I know…Mr Nicholson! Tell me again 'bout when you talked to 'im at the recital."

"Oh no, Edie. Don't be silly! Why would I want to talk about that again?"

"'Cos you're sweet on 'im, that's why!"

"Edith Penton, stop it! Course I'm not sweet on him. Don't be so daft. He must be ten years older than me at least. I just said he reminded me of Harry, that's all."

"Yes, but you go red every time you say 'is name!"

"That's because you're embarrassing me. Stop it, Edie, please."

They walked on in silence for a while. Despite her protestations, Cecily had to admit there was a grain of truth in what Edith had said. She had thought about him a great deal over the past few days. During the Christmas services and this morning she had found her attention drawn again and again to the back row of the choir stalls and to the features of his gentle face. She had been so absorbed in trying to work out why it was that she found them interesting (she wouldn't allow herself to use the word 'attractive') that she had lost the thread of the service several times, receiving sharp nudges from Edith when she failed to join in the responses. Then there had been the excitement of a Boxing Day visit by Mr and Mrs Nicholson to an afternoon of family carol singing. Just a few friends and Mrs Hopwood's parents. Everyone around the piano, including the children and the servants, with *him* playing, of course. She couldn't take her eyes off him. And she was sure he had smiled at her, more than once. Her legs had gone funny and she had blushed furiously, burying her head in her hymn book before Edith saw. She thought of him at night, too. The image of

70

him playing at the recital came back to her clearly, his expression so intense, his long fingers producing such a wonderful sound. She was still unsure whether her tearful response had been to the music, or to the sight of him, or both. Whatever the reason, she had been deeply affected and was finding it difficult to shake off the strange, unsettled feeling she had been left with.

She sighed. Edith took her arm, chiding her gently.

"Come on, you old silly. Don't sulk. I was only teasin'. Tell me all about yer brothers and sisters."

"I've told you about them before."

"I know, but tell me again. I want to get all their names right. Do it from the youngest up."

Cecily rolled her eyes. "Oh, very well. First there's Ernest, but we call him Ernie, who's nearly three and he's the baby. Then there's Sam who's seven now, I think, then Margaret who must be nine or ten…I can't remember. Then Tom, Frances and me, we're all really close, and last of all Harold… Harry."

" Is 'Arold much older than you?"

"For goodness sake, Edie, you can't call him 'Arold! Say 'Harold' with an aitch else my parents will think you're really common and so will he."

"Oh Lor. I can see I shall 'ave to mind me Ps and Qs in your 'ouse. All right then…*h*ow old is *H*arold."

"He's eighteen – nearly four years older than me and much too young for you!"

"What do you mean, much too young? I'm only sixteen!"

"But a man should be much older than the woman. Two years isn't enough!"

"Now who's bein' silly? First of all Mr Nicholson's too old, now 'Arold, I mean *H*arold's, too young. Make yer mind up! And who says I'm interested in your brother, anyway, Miss Nose in the Air?"

Cecily laughed and walked the next few yards with the

mincing walk and elevated nose of an upper crust lady.

"Now tell me what they're like, yer brothers and sisters. What's little Ernie like? Is 'e a dear?"

"Well, he was when I left, but I expect he's grown now and got naughty. Frances is a goody-goody. Mother and Father praise her to the skies and I want to cut up her perfect samplers and spill ink on her beautiful pieces of writing."

"You're jealous, Cecily Carpenter!"

"No I'm not! Anyhow…then there's Tom, he's naughty, but I like him better and…oh Edith, look…"

"What? What am I lookin' at?"

"That man down there by Cornbrook Farm. Look…it's Harry!" Cecily dropped her bundle in the middle of the lane and ran towards the figure that had just appeared around the far corner, hardly visible in the failing light and thickening snow. She waved and shouted his name as she ran, jumping into his arms with a cry of delight when they met. He laughed and spun her round.

"Little Cecily! My goodness me, but you're tall and thin! In just three months…I can hardly believe it!" He gave her a big kiss on her cheek and put her down. "And this must be Edith."

Cecily had forgotten Edith completely. She turned back to her friend, who had picked up the abandoned bundle and walked slowly to meet them.

"Oh, sorry, Edith. This is Harold, my brother."

"I've *h*eard a lot about you, *H*arold," Edith said, smiling mischievously.

Harry returned her smile, a little too enthusiastically Cecily thought.

"I'm pleased to meet you, Edith," he said. "Unfortunately, we shan't have long to get to know one another as it happens."

"You've got all evening, Harry. Isn't that enough?" Cecily regretted her slightly sharp tone as soon as the words were out of her mouth, but Harry didn't seem to notice.

"I'm afraid you can't come home, Cecy."

"Can't come home? Why ever not?"

"Ernie has the whooping cough. Two other children in the street have it, too. Mother is frightened that you could take it back to the little ones at the Rectory."

"Oh no! Poor little Ernie…Poor Mother – she must be so worried. Oh dear…Is he bad with it, Harry? Not bad like Frank?" Cecily began to cry. Harry put his arm around her shoulder.

"He's holding his own at the moment, dear. Don't cry now. Come on. Let's start walking back to Blackford. This snow is getting much worse – look, it's settling fast on the road now."

Cecily was distraught and had to be helped along between Harry and Edith. Images of Frank came flooding out of a dark corner of her mind, where she had kept them locked away for three years: his poor little body wracked with coughs and heaving for breath, and their mother, heavily pregnant with Ernie, sitting beside him weeping and helpless. He was just three; she never forgot *his* age, or the date on which he had died. Now she was convinced that Ernie was going to die too, and nothing the others said would comfort her.

"But I want to be at home with him. I may never see him again," she cried. "And I want to help Mother – I'm sure I could be a comfort to her now."

"You can't, Cecy. It wouldn't be right. Now come on, try to stop crying and walk a bit faster. We shall all perish of the cold out here soon." Harry spoke firmly and exchanged an anxious look with Edith as the snowstorm worsened. They were still a mile and a half from Blackford and it was now almost completely dark. The wind blew fiercely towards them, plastering them with large flakes of snow and forcing them to walk with their heads right down, looking only at their own sodden boots. Cecily caught the worried tone in her brother's voice and made an effort to calm herself. They walked on in silence, their footsteps muffled by the deepening snow, until they reached the outskirts of the village some thirty minutes later.

Harry stopped at the signpost at the edge of the green.

"I must leave you now, ladies, if I'm to get back before the lane fills up with snow. We'll send word as soon as we're able, Cecy. Try not to fret, dear. He's a strong little lad and we're all praying for him. I've been glad to meet you, Edith. I hope we'll meet again soon, in less worrying times. Goodbye!"

He gave Cecily a quick kiss and turned back along the road. She began to sob once more as she stood watching him disappear into the whirls of snow. Edith took her arm and propelled her the last few hundred yards to the Rectory.

⤬

Ada Norris couldn't believe the vision before her eyes as two snow-covered figures burst through the kitchen door at four o'clock. She had worried about the girls as she had watched the snowstorm worsen outside the window, but had comforted herself that they would soon be safe in Wittenbury.

"Gracious heart alive, but look at the pair o' you!" she cried. "What are you doin' back here? Oh, you'll catch your death o' cold. Quick, take off those wet things...no, don't put 'em on the chairs...look, we'll hang 'em on the horse in front o' the range. Come and sit over here and get warm... Oh, but whatever's the matter, Cecily? Why are you cryin' now?"

She could see that something serious was amiss. She fussed around the girls, finding dry shawls and making tea. Cecily hung her head and said nothing, the occasional tear dropping into her lap. Eventually Ada appealed to Edith to tell her what had happened. When the distressing tale had been told, she drew up a chair beside Cecily and took the maid's still-cold hands between her own.

"Goodness, Cecily," she said gently, "I was sure someone had already died. Now look at me, my dear." She waited until the maid was looking her full in the eye. "He's not dead, and the chances are he'll be as right as rain in no time. It's a horrible illness, as you know, dear, and I'm very sorry indeed to hear about your other little brother. But most kiddies get over it, you know. My three did, and so did you. Now, you've to stop cryin', 'cause it's not doin' you nor us no good, and certainly not little Ernie, is it?"

Cecily shook her head.

Ada went on, "So dry your eyes and blow your nose, Cecily, and then we'll have some bread and cold meat and some cold rice puddin' for afters. Girls, set the table now, while I just go and tell Mrs Hopwood that you're here and not at home. Then it's an early night for the pair o' you, and a little extra sleep tomorrow, too. You wouldn't have been back till eight o'clock, after all, so just make sure you're downstairs before that clock strikes eight."

❦

Ada went to find Mrs Hopwood in the drawing room, where the family usually gathered for an hour before the children's supper. The Reverend Hopwood answered her knock. She couldn't see her mistress, only her master sitting on the large rug in front of the fireplace, the baby on his lap and the twins beside him, all engrossed (including the Rector) in building towers of blocks.

"Oh, Reverend Hopkins, please let me help you, sir. Shall I take the baby?"

"Ahh, Ada, you are shocked, I can see. You assume, like most of society, that the male of our species is incapable of protecting and amusing its young, even for an hour or two."

Ada had no idea what he was talking about and so said nothing.

"But you are wrong," he went on. "We are quite safe and happy, aren't we, boys?"

The twins looked up at him.

"Look, Papa," said Charles, putting another block onto his wobbling tower.

"Marvellous, Charlie. Yours is almost as tall as Papa's… You see, Ada, we males are not as helpless as you imagine us to be. Did you know that a male stickleback builds a nest for the eggs, and cares for them and the young fry?"

"Er, no sir, I didn't."

"Admittedly such examples in nature are quite rare. Nevertheless, I can assure you that I'm quite capable, even in my advanced years."

"Oh, sir, I didn't mean to say…" Ada said, alarmed.

"No, no, Ada. You were being of kind assistance, as always, but it's not needed. The boys and I have a regular playtime from three until five each afternoon now, while their dear mamma has a much-needed rest, and we have had no mishaps so far. No more hair-cutting, eh, boys? In fact it is most enjoyable and I have been happy to relinquish some visiting duties to Mr Roberts, who is more than capable of taking my place for a few weeks…Did you come to see me about anything in particular, Ada?"

Having worked for the Rector for more than twenty years, Ada should have been used to his eccentricities by now. Still, she found herself so taken aback that she couldn't immediately remember why she had come.

"Did Edith and Cecily get off all right in this snow?" he asked, when she didn't reply.

"Cecily…oh, yes, sir…I mean no. That's why I've come… to tell you about Cecily, sir."

"I hope there hasn't been an accident. They weren't going by carriage, were they?"

"No, no, Reverend. Cecily and Edith are as right as rain, though a little wet and cold. But they couldn't stay at her home – her little brother has whoopin' cough. I'm sorry to say there are several cases in Wittenbury, sir. I thought as you should know, sir."

Ada had remembered with alarm, as Edith had told her about little Ernie, that all three Hopwood children had attended a large Christmas party at the home of the vicar of St John's in Wittenbury, just a few days before Christmas. She suspected the Rector was thinking of this too, as she watched him put his arms more tightly around little Edward.

"Thank you, Ada." His voice had completely lost its usual playful tone. "Kindly watch the children for a minute or two while I go to speak to Mrs Hopwood."

Ada took the baby on her lap as the Rector left the room. She stroked his fat little hands and silky soft cheeks. This is how it is with little ones, she thought, remembering her own three children, now long-grown, as infants – nothin' but worry and work.

❧

Cecily and Edith were sent off to bed early, but neither felt ready to sleep.

"Will you read to me, Cecy?" asked Edith. "Some more of 'The Old Nurse's Story' – we'd just got to the bit where she'd 'eard the old organ playin' and nobody wanted to talk 'bout it and we're thinkin' it must be a ghost. It'd 'elp keep yer mind off yer worries, wouldn't it?"

Cecily had enjoyed reading to her friend on many previous nights, ever since she had discovered that Edith could hardly read. It was fun to discuss the different characters and their lives, and to wonder what might happen next, like gossiping about folk from the village. She loved Mrs Gaskell's books in particular, and had brought her only two precious copies with her from home.

Though she didn't have much heart for ghost stories tonight, she knew that Edith was right and that it would help her to stay calm. She found the book under her bed and brought the candle close. Edith slipped quickly into bed beside her. They pulled the covers up round their necks, shivering as the temperature in the room fell to its lowest so far this winter. The skylight above their heads was now completely covered with snow and the water in the jug had grown a thin crust of ice. The cold and dark seemed an appropriate setting for the creepy tale. She began to read from the beginning of the last paragraph where she had left the story a few nights ago:

"As winter drew on, and the days grew shorter, I was sometimes almost certain that I heard a noise as if someone was playing on the great organ in the hall."

Edith snuggled up closer, grinning with anticipation. Despite herself, Cecily found all thoughts of Ernie slipping away as she took them both into the Gothic delights of the old Manor House and the strange characters who lived there.

CHAPTER 11

Clementine Hopwood felt that she would go mad with anxiety. The heavy snowfall on Sunday night had continued intermittently for two more days, cutting off all communication between the Rectory and the world beyond the village. She had no way of knowing whether any of the children from the tea party at the vicarage in Wittenbury had succumbed to whooping cough, but a terrible foreboding, which sat like a sickness in her stomach, told her that they had. She could not bear to be away from her babies even for the two short hours of her afternoon rest and dismissed David's exhortations to go and lie down. Distress overwhelmed her every time she remembered how often she had longed for a nursemaid to take the children away and look after them. She wondered if God was about to exact a terrible punishment for her lack of submission to her husband's wishes about their care. She found herself feeling relieved that the nursemaid whom she was to have interviewed yesterday had not arrived, presumably unable to travel in the snow.

"If only my little ones can stay well, I will look after them, Lord," she pleaded. "I'll not complain of tiredness or of being bored or irritable. I shall be happy just to be here with them."

Every minute that she was with the children she spent studying their beloved features for signs of illness. No amount of reassurance from their father that their complexions were a healthy pink and their small bodies full of normal two-year-old energy helped to calm her. When, exactly a week after Christmas Day, the twins simultaneously produced runny noses and slight fevers, she had to be restrained from running

79

along the snowy road to Doctor Tucker's house herself.

David helped her back upstairs to the nursery.

"Clemmy, my darling, come and sit down, do. You cannot possibly go out in your condition and Cecily will get there much more quickly. Now, calm yourself, dear – it's not good for you or our new baby that you should become so agitated. I'm sure the doctor will tell us that it is just a cold. See… they are playing quite happily."

She looked across the nursery at her baby, who sat happily playing with a rattle in his cot, and at William and Charles, who were both trying to climb onto the rocking horse, each shouting loudly "Mine turn, mine turn," into the face of the other. As if sensing the anxiety in their father's voice, they both fell silent and turned to look at their parents with questioning eyes. Clementine knew she must try to hide her fears for their sake and brushed away the tears which had begun to spill from her eyes.

"Come and listen to a story with Mamma, my darlings," she said, her voice brittle with the effort of cheerfulness. "What shall we have?"

The boys left the horse and clambered onto little stools, one each side of her chair.

" 'Now White," they cried in unison. She wiped their noses and found the story in the large book of fairy tales, which lived permanently beside her chair and which was in constant demand. They both leaned over her lap, pointing excitedly at the engravings.

"Doors, doors!"

"Yes, *dwarves*, my darlings, the little men are called dwarves. Now let's start at the beginning…"

The story progressed. Snow White was just about to knock on the door of the strange little cottage in the woods, when a real knock on the nursery door brought Clementine to a sudden halt, her heart thumping in her chest.

"Good morning, Mrs Hopwood. Good morning

Reverend," boomed the large, red-faced, white-whiskered doctor as he strode past Cecily, who was holding the door, into the nursery. Clementine had always felt that Dr Tucker was unnecessarily loud in the face of others' adversity, but now she felt relieved at the size of his presence, which somehow reassured her of his ability to cure her children.

"Well, well, what do we have here? Two naughty boys, causing your poor mamma to fret and worry. Well, we shall soon put a stop to that. Come here, boys."

The doctor scooped the terrified children from the safety of their mother's skirts and sat them side by side on the edge of the nursery table. He peered into their eyes, pushed a wooden stick into their mouths to look down their throats, exhorting them to say "aah", listened to their chests with his impressive new stethoscope and generally prodded and poked them until they both began to wail. Clementine jumped up to comfort them. The doctor motioned to her to stay sitting, and beckoned to David Hopwood, who had been watching the examination anxiously from his wife's side. The two men spoke quietly together, standing with their backs to her, so that she was unable to hear what they were saying above the noise of the crying. David then picked the boys from the table, one under each arm and carried them back to the hearth.

"Come along, my dear," he said to her gently, lifting her by the arm and guiding her to the door.

"But, David, I must stay here with the children. What does Doctor Tucker say?"

"Let me take you down to the drawing room, Clemmy darling, and I will tell you there what he has said. It wouldn't be a good idea to talk in front of them, would it?" He led her downstairs and left her briefly in a chair by a window while he went to find Cecily. She stared out into the snow-filled garden, tears streaming down her cheeks. It must be the worst. She knew it. She had known it all along.

Cecily ran upstairs to the nursery as the Reverend had just asked her to do. She had no idea why she had been summoned, though she knew something was wrong with the twins after her urgent errand through the deep snow to the doctor's earlier. She knocked and walked into the room. Dr Tucker was sitting at the table, writing in a notebook. He looked up, fierce blue eyes peering at her from below bushy white eyebrows.

"Cecily?" he barked.

"Yes, sir." She gave a timid little curtsy.

"Come over here, girl. I need you to listen carefully. What do you know about whooping cough?"

Cecily's heart leapt in her chest.

"Oh…I…I…" she stammered.

"Don't hum and hah, girl. Do you know anything or not?"

The doctor's rude tone suddenly made her feel rather indignant. She drew herself upright.

"I have had it…and my brothers and sisters, sir. It starts with a cold and then you get a terrible cough and it can be hard to breathe. My little brother died, sir. He got pneumonia."

"Yes, indeed, and that is what we have to prevent here. And you are going to help. These two have just a slight fever and a cold at the moment. Perhaps it will come to nothing. Let us hope so. However, the number of cases in the district has been rising every day, so we have to assume the worst, I'm afraid. They are to be kept warm at all times – extra flannel underclothes, and on no account expose them to the cold air. A light diet – I have asked for the cook to be instructed – and plenty of fluids. I am to be informed as soon as there is any change, is that understood, girl?"

"Yes, sir, of course."

"Very well, then, I leave them in your charge. Mr Hopwood seems to think you are capable – I hope he is right." He snapped his notebook shut and strode from the room.

Cecily stood by the door where he had left her, her heart pounding. What did he mean, leave them in *her* charge? She looked over at the two small boys, who sat miserably on the hearth rug, pressed against each other for comfort, one sucking his thumb and the other twiddling his hair with anxiety. The thought that they might become as ill as little Frank had done, and that she might be expected to help look after them, sent a wave of panic through her body, leaving her giddy and sick. She thought of Ernie and felt even more ill. Her knees wobbled beneath her and she sat down heavily at the table.

In his cot at the far end of the room little Edward was tiring of his rattle. After a few minutes his grizzling deteriorated into full-blown crying, which in turn set the two boys wailing once more. Still no-one else came. She looked from the baby to the boys, now all crying heartily, and back again. Something in their helplessness seeped through her panic and into the future mother in her. She couldn't just leave them like this. Taking a deep breath to calm herself, she walked across the room and picked Edward from his cot. She held him to her breast and talked quietly in his ear, as she had seen her mother do countless times, and as she herself had done with the babies at home, when she had been left in charge.

"There, there, Edward. It's only me, Cecily. Shush, shush… no more crying now, there's a good boy. Come on then… let's go and see your brothers shall we?" She carried him over to the hearth and sat down in the large nursing chair Mrs Hopwood always used. She cast around for something to distract him. On the floor lay a story book, open at a page depicting Snow White knocking on the door of the seven dwarves' cottage. The illustration was beautifully detailed and everything looked real enough to touch – the dappled leaves of the forest trees, the diamond patterns on the tiles around the windows of the cottage, the vivid colours of the garden flowers and Snow White's long, black hair, brilliant in the sun's rays, which shone like beams from heaven into the clearing. How she would have loved to own a book like this as a child. She settled the baby on her knee and picked the book up reverently.

"William, Charles," she said softly to the still-weeping children. "Would you like me to read you a story? Look… here's Snow White…she's knocking on the cottage door. Do you know what's going to happen next?"

There was a momentary lull in the wailing.

"Doors," said Charles in a watery whisper as he pulled himself up from the floor to look at the picture.

"Doors!" said William, joining him.

"Doors?" She settled them both on the small stools beside her chair.

"Doors!" echoed the children, much more loudly, impatiently turning the page and showing her the next picture, of the scene inside the cottage.

"Oh, *dwarves*! Yes, of course, the seven *dwarves*!" She smiled with relief at the two small children, who looked back at her, large-eyed, still sucking and twiddling, but quiet now. She turned back a page and began:

"Snow White knocked on the door of the tiny cottage…"

⌘

Two more stories and six nursery rhymes later, she was just about to embark on "Hickory Dickory Dock" when the nursery door opened and the Rector walked in. He surveyed the scene in front of him and smiled.

"Ah, Cecily, well done. I somehow knew you would have the magic touch."

She looked down at the baby, who had fallen asleep in her arms, and the twins, pressed up close to her, one on either side, eagerly awaiting the next item of entertainment. Not so much magic as hard work, she thought. The boys ran to their father, who bent down to ruffle their hair.

"Cecily, your mistress would like to talk to you in the drawing room. I will watch the boys for now. On your way, please go to Mrs Norris and ask her to send Edith up with some milk for the children – we must keep your strength up, mustn't we boys? Strong little soldiers, that's what we need you to be, eh Charlie? What do you say, William?"

By way of an answer the children grasped at his hands and pulled him across to the hearth.

" 'Tory, 'tory," they chorused.

Cecily got up from the large chair to make way for him, moving gingerly with the sleeping infant in her arms. She carried him carefully to his crib at the other end of the room and laid him down, gently covering him with a quilt and brushing his fine, blonde baby hair from his eyes. Her master called to her over his shoulder as he disappeared under a heap of squirming children on the chair.

"Ask Edith to bring more coals for the fire as well."

"Yes, sir, I will."

She left the room and stood for a moment on the quiet landing, her back to the nursery door, trying to absorb something of the events of the last hour. She looked unseeing over the banisters, down the stairs and into the hallway. Her hands shook as she contemplated the task she seemed to have been given. I don't think I can do it, she thought. I'm not old enough, or sensible enough – I'll make a muddle of it like I do everything else. But…if they need me…then… oh dear… She took a deep breath, blowing it out through puffed cheeks, grabbed the banister and forced her feet down the stairs, though her legs felt again as if they had lost their bones.

She delivered her message from the Reverend to the kitchen and received a stern telling-off from Mrs Norris when she began to cry with anxiety.

"No, we'll have none o' that, Cecily." The cook held her firmly by the shoulders and looked fiercely into her face. "Stop cryin' now. This is your chance to show 'em what you can do. You've looked after small children at home – you've told me so yourself. You're *more* than capable. Dry your eyes now, and off you go." She felt herself propelled by the shoulders towards the door, which was shut firmly behind her.

Standing outside the drawing room, she scrubbed away any traces of tears with her apron, then smoothed it frantically when she realised what a mess of creases she had made. She knocked and, hearing a faint reply, walked in and curtsied to her mistress, who sat limply in a chair by one of the large windows. Mrs Hopwood turned a pale, tear-streaked face towards her. She was shocked to see such obvious distress in someone she had thought capable only of short-temper and head-biting. She must really love those children, she thought, and felt suddenly ashamed of her own fuss and cowardice.

"Cecily, come over here." Mrs Hopwood spoke weakly. "Has Dr Tucker spoken to you?"

"Yes, ma'am."

"Then you will know that you are to care for the little ones until this snow clears and a proper nurse can be appointed. I'm forbidden to enter the nursery on account of my condition." There was a long pause. Mrs Hopwood looked out of the window and struggled to master her voice as tears filled her eyes.

"This is very hard for me, Cecily. I feel so anxious for the children. You know that I haven't always found your work to be satisfactory and I'm extremely reluctant to leave them in your care. But...I've been persuaded that you have some experience, which Edith does not have, and that you have a kind nature." She paused again, before looking up at Cecily with an agonised expression.

"So…there we have it…what can I do? I have to put my trust in you. I beg you to care for them as if they were your own. Cherish their dear little souls, do everything the doctor tells you and come to me as often as you are able to tell me how they are. I shall be waiting. I'm sure no other thought will occupy my mind until they are safely well again." Mrs Hopwood broke down into sobs.

Cecily suddenly felt nothing but pity for this tortured, young mother. With it came a new strength flowing through her – a new confidence in her own ability.

"I will look after them, ma'am, I really will. Don't you worry now – I'm sure they'll get well."

Mrs Hopwood, unable to speak, her face covered with her hands, nodded and motioned her to leave.

She tiptoed from the room, closing the door quietly behind her, then lifted her skirts and ran up the stairs to the nursery. All the strength, and more, had returned to her young legs. Mrs Norris believed she was not just capable, but *more* than capable. Well, perhaps she was.

CHAPTER 12

As a child nothing had pleased Alfred more than to open the curtains on winter mornings to discover that the world had been transformed overnight. Today he looked out at the rounded white tops of the hedges, the tree branches bowed with the weight of their load and the drifts half filling the lane wherever it was exposed to the full force of the north-east wind, and clicked his tongue with frustration – another heavy fall overnight and the sky threatening again. It would be impossible to get to the recital in Wittenbury today.

He scratched his beard and ran his hands through his hair, turning back to the washstand. As he poured the jug of hot water into the bowl, he looked at himself in the mirror and grimaced at what he saw – an unremarkable face with blue eyes still puffy with sleep, unruly hair and an unkempt beard which had strayed well beyond its usual permitted boundaries. The elation and confidence he had felt a week ago was seeping away rapidly with each day he spent away from Miss Fielding. Looking at himself, he found it hard to believe she might really want to be with him – she was so beautiful and elegant, and he was…well…just ordinary, certainly not handsome. He set about the hair on his neck with the razor. I have to see her, he thought. Perhaps he would walk to Blackford this morning. Would she be happy to see him? He couldn't feel sure, but he hoped so. In any case, it would be better than another morning sitting huddled over the stove in the bitterly cold office. Work was always a bit slack between Christmas and New Year. The men were largely doing house-keeping work or carpentry and needed little supervision. He could easily catch up later.

The decision now taken, he completed his toilet carefully, dithered uncharacteristically about his clothes and finally went down to the dining room for breakfast. His mother greeted him anxiously.

"Oh Alfie…all this snow. What will happen about the recital? I'm afraid you won't be able to go. What a pity, just when everything was going so well between you and Miss Fielding."

Alfred took an egg and some toast from the sideboard and sat at the other end of the table. He found it best not to answer his mother immediately, since his replies to her comments about Miss Fielding had a habit of coming out more sharply than he intended. He cut the top off his egg and buttered his toast slowly, before smiling at her.

"Don't worry, Mother. I'm sure there will be many more opportunities for us to meet. I'm going to spend the morning up in the store, sorting through some of father's old tools, which really aren't up to the job any more. I'll take some bread and cheese up with me, so I won't need lunch."

He felt guilty about the lie, but couldn't face the fuss she would make about the risks to his health of the walk in the snow nor the inevitable questions about Miss Fielding over supper. It was easier if she didn't know.

After breakfast he gathered heavy outdoor clothes and boots and slipped into the yard while his mother was occupied with her morning meeting with the servants. He ducked quickly into the carpentry workshop, where Reg and Bill were busy making window frames for the new houses. They both stopped and lifted their caps.

"Good morning, lads. What a morning, eh! It was a good job we got that load of timber in last week, wasn't it? We could be stuck here for days with this lot."

"Mornin', Mr Nicholson. Yes, we've plenty to be gettin' on with."

"Don't mind me, then − carry on. I'm just off to

Blackford. I'll put all my gear on here, out of the way of everyone in the house."

"Will you be takin' the 'orse, sir?" Reg looked concerned, a frown knitting his bushy brows into one.

"No, no, Reg, the snow's much too deep. It would be dangerous – he might step into a pothole or into the ditch. Have you seen it in Blackford Lane? Some of the drifts are more than three feet deep! It was quite a blizzard we had last night."

"It certainly was, Mr Nicholson. We 'ad to dig ourselves out the door this mornin', didn't we, Bill?"

His son nodded and laughed.

"But I wouldn't fancy goin' nowhere beyond the 'amlet meself, sir. 'Ave you seen the sky? It'll snow again for sure before the mornin's out," added Reg.

"I know, I know. I just need to sort out some business there, but if there's no sign of me by nightfall, you'll have to come along the lane with shovels and see if you can dig me out! By the way, Reg, I don't think Mrs Nicholson will venture out of the house today, but if she does come looking for me I am up in the store and can't be disturbed. She would worry if she thought I was out in this."

"So shall we all, sir, if you don't mind me sayin' so."

"Don't worry about me. I'll be back soon after lunch, I expect."

He pulled on his hat, gloves and heavy coat and slipped out of the door into the yard, where nearly twelve inches of snow covered the cobbles. He strode through the gateway and into the lane, his breath hanging around his head in clouds and his eyes already smarting from the cold. The foolishness of the venture registered only lightly as he struggled around the first of many snowdrifts a few hundred yards from the house. The snow reached the top of his high boots and dropped down unnoticed onto his stockinged feet. He felt energetic and strong. In less than three miles he would be with her again.

In winter, when the sky was overcast, the parlour of the school cottage was dark, even at midday. Emma sat at the small table next to the window, the only place she could see clearly to write a letter to Aunt Harriet. As a child she had spent several weeks each summer in Kingston-upon-Thames with her father's sister. Her aunt had always understood her far better than her own mother and she remembered those summers with wistful fondness. Now she was trying to explain her feelings to her aunt, while struggling to avoid a petulant, complaining tone, which she knew would not be well received. Putting down her pen, she looked over at her mother, who sat by the small fire working a piece of embroidery. She, too, was clearly finding it difficult to see, and was holding the material very close to her eyes while at the same time leaning down to catch the light from the flames.

Since Emma's triumphant return home from her meeting with Alfred at the school a week ago, her mother had slid into a decline. Not quite capable of producing a real illness, she had nevertheless succeeded in becoming pale, listless and shrunken. She refused all but the smallest portions of food and all diversions, preferring to sit in her chair with her sewing for hours at a time. Her white hair, once fair and lustrous like Emma's, was pinned severely beneath a black lace cap. A deep frown line was etched between her eyebrows. Her face wore a permanently aggrieved expression, which dulled her eyes and puckered her mouth.

Emma sighed heavily and looked out of the window, rubbing away the condensation on the tiny panes with her handkerchief and peering cheerlessly out at the snowy green. She didn't like snow at the best of times – it was impossible to walk outside without her boots and dress becoming soaked and filthy – but now she felt imprisoned by it, locked in the cottage with her mother, with no possibility of a long walk in the fresh air to relieve her taut nerves or of escaping to the school room, which was now too cold to be habitable. Even teaching seemed attractive in comparison. She found herself longing perversely for the new term to start so that at least time would not hang so heavily and she would have some occupation to divert her thoughts. To compound her misery, the one event she had been looking forward to all week was now almost certainly cancelled. No carriages had entered or left the village all morning – a journey to Wittenbury would be impossible. There had been no word from Mr Nicholson, but then perhaps the post was disrupted. She would brave the snow and find out. She wrote for a few more minutes, then sealed her letter.

"I'm going to the post office, Mamma," she said brightly, a tone she had adopted recently in a vain attempt to lighten the mood in the cottage.

"Very well, dear," came the barely audible reply.

Her mother's passive agreement with everything she said, while at the same time oozing silent disapproval from every pore in her body, was much more difficult to deal with than a good argument, which would at least have provided some distraction. Repressing her desire to tut, she left the room and dressed with difficulty in the narrow hallway. She was just reaching for the door handle when a loud knock startled her. Perhaps Mr Nicholson has come, she thought. She wasn't sure whether it was likely that he could manage the journey in the snow, but she hoped he might still want to see her, even if the recital was cancelled. She opened the door.

"Oh, Mr Roberts…" She was aware that her face betrayed her disappointment. "Er…I apologise, I was expecting someone else." She bowed hastily. "Good morning."

The curate lifted his hat, returned her bow and smiled graciously. "Good morning, Miss Fielding. I've come to see if I can be of any help in this terrible weather." He spotted the letter in her hand. "Perhaps I could post your letter for you to save you getting wet and cold."

"Oh...thank you...that is kind, but I need the fresh air..."

Her mother appeared and pushed past her to the doorway.

"Mr Roberts, how lovely to see you! Do come in and take a cup of tea with us and warm yourself by the fire. Emma, take your coat off, dear, and show Mr Roberts into the parlour while I make some tea."

"Well, thank you, Mrs Fielding, but...I don't want to be any trouble. I think Miss Fielding was hoping to..."

"No, no trouble at all, Mr Roberts. Emma can post her letter any time. Do come in now — we're letting in all the cold air. Take Mr Robert's hat and coat, dear."

The curate stamped the snow off his boots and followed Emma into the parlour, while her mother bustled off to the scullery. Emma drew a third chair up to the small fireplace and the two young people sat down together, the curate warming his hands near the flames. She didn't know what to say. She was angry with her mother for pushing them together yet again, but was aware that the situation was not his fault, and thought that she should at least try to be pleasant. In the event, he made it easy for her. He launched into an amusing appreciation of the recital, re-telling the story of the dreadful string quartet with self-deprecating humour. She found herself laughing and began to relax, despite herself.

Her mother seemed to be taking an excessive amount of time to make one pot of tea, but reappeared eventually with a tray laden with tea pot, cups and Christmas cake. Emma was astonished at the transformation in her appearance. She had changed her black lace cap for a white one and re-arranged her hair into its usual softer, more flattering style. Her eyes were bright and her cheeks rosy. The effect was of a completely different woman from the one who had sat so dejected by the fire only half an hour ago.

"Milk and sugar, Mr Roberts?" asked her mother, once

she was settled in her chair. "And you will try a slice of my Christmas cake, won't you? Emma and I have hardly made any inroads into it and it won't keep forever. Besides, I always think one needs to eat well in this sort of weather, to ward off the cold, don't you?"

"Yes, I do indeed, Mrs Fielding. Thank you, I would love a piece. But no sugar, thank you."

"You're sweet enough, I daresay." Emma cringed as her mother giggled like a schoolgirl. The conversation returned to the recital and then inevitably, to the weather. She had to admit he was easy company, confident in conversation, with a keen sense of humour, which set them all laughing several times. He was attractive, too, and managed to look well-groomed even in his dull clerical garb. She found herself reluctantly drawn to his large, dark brown eyes. He's bound to be popular with the women of the parish, she thought, then quickly took herself in hand and turned her mind to Mr Nicholson. It was such a pity that it hadn't been him at the door.

Twenty minutes later, the tea and cake had all been consumed. She was amazed at the large slice her mother had tucked away.

The curate rose to his feet and thanked his hostesses warmly.

"Please let me know if there is anything I can do to help you while this inconvenient weather lasts," he said, as he made for the door. "Thank you again for your kind hospitality. I shall look forward to seeing you both at church tomorrow."

"Yes, indeed, we shall be there. Goodbye, Mr Roberts. Emma will see you to the door, won't you dear?"

"Of course, Mamma."

Emma followed the curate into the hallway, feeling embarrassed as they stood too close together in the narrow space while he put on his coat and hat.

For the first time he seemed a little awkward. "I hope

you will permit me to call again, Miss Fielding."

"My mother and I are always pleased to see you, Mr Roberts." Her heart was beating fast, but she kept her voice as neutral as possible and gave a shallow bow. "Goodbye."

He looked a little taken aback, but took his leave politely and set off down the path towards the green.

CHAPTER 13

The walk to Blackford should have taken Alfred less than an hour. When he turned onto the road which circled the green, the striking of the church clock told him that it was more than an hour and a half since he had set out. It had been a much harder walk than he had anticipated and, despite the freezing temperatures, he was now sweating profusely with the effort of wading through the deep snow. For long stretches of the journey his had been the only footprints in a pristine river of white, which wound through the countryside, almost indistinguishable from the fields on either side. In some places the drifts reached the tops of the hedges and had been blown into fantastic shapes by the wind. Only when he passed farmyards and cottages was the way made a little easier by others having trodden parts of the lane before him.

The school was only a hundred yards away now. He looked over to the cottage, and, as he did so, saw the front door open and a man in a black hat and fashionable grey overcoat walk down the path. The visitor glanced in his direction and raised his hat. It was Edgar Roberts. Alfred raised his own worn, brown hat in reply and stopped. He supposed the curate had been visiting Miss Fielding. It was a disturbing thought, but one he couldn't dismiss, for Roberts had certainly seemed anxious to pay her attention at the recital. He looked down at his sodden boots and trousers and became embarrassed at the contrast between his own bedraggled appearance and that of the handsome young cleric. He never had been any good at dressing well or making himself attractive. His mother nagged him about it constantly: Brush your hair, Alfie. Put your shoulders back. Sit up straight, dear, don't slouch like a working man – you are a *gentleman*. Do you have no better shirt to wear than that, Alfie? Recently he had thought perhaps she was trying to re-create the better-looking child she had lost. But for himself, his appearance had never interested him or seemed important – until now. He dithered in the road for a minute, then turned round abruptly and headed back the way he had come. When he reached the turning to Stonefield he stopped once more and leaned wearily on the signpost. He couldn't face Miss Fielding while he looked like this, yet he couldn't face the journey home again without seeing her either.

He stared dejectedly across the green. It was deserted now. A few tracks of footprints crisscrossed the central area and marked the routes from villagers' homes to the shops; there was no other way of telling where the green stopped and the roads began. The huge old yew tree, which stood near the centre, touched the ground in several places, so weighed down were its branches. A few hungry-looking jackdaws hopped around the door of the baker's. Wisps of smoke rose from the chimneys. Otherwise there was no sign of life. He shivered; he should keep moving.

In the far corner, at the junction of the road to Wittenbury, a thick plume rose from the forge. His spirits rose a little. George would give him a cup of tea and somewhere warm to eat his bread and cheese before he headed back. He struck out across the wide expanse of snow, past the church and the Rectory and the two other large houses of the village – the doctor's and the solicitor's. The forge was a long, low building, set back from the road, the blacksmith's house half hidden behind it. Today the door was shut fast, though normally it was left wide open to let out the excessive heat. Alfred banged hard on the huge knocker and, without waiting for an invitation, walked in.

His old friend was bent over, holding a small piece of metal with a pair of long tongs in the white hot centre of a large heap of burning coals. "I'll be with you in a minute," he called without turning round.

"It's all right, George, it's only me."

"Alf, me old friend, what brings you 'ere on this snowy mornin'?"

"It's a long story...I'll tell you when you're done."

The young man pulled the metal out of the fire and took it over to the anvil, smiling at his visitor on the way, his face scarlet, smeared with soot and sweat.

Alfred perched on the edge of a chest of metal scraps. He sighed with relief as the wall of heat from the fire enveloped him, making his feet and legs steam. "There can't be many horses needing shoeing in this weather, are there?"

"No, no one's been out this mornin'. I'm just makin' nails. Can't 'ave too many nails!"

"Where's your father?"

"Oh, I told 'im to stay indoors. I knew there wouldn't be much to do. 'E's gettin' a bit old for this game – a bit stiff in his 'ands now, though 'e won't never admit it." The young blacksmith continued working as he talked, bending and breaking the red hot metal with pliers and striking it this way and that with a large hammer, until he was holding a large, perfectly formed nail in the tongs. He dipped it, hissing loudly, into a bucket of water, then dropped it onto the pile of nails he had made earlier, wiped his hands on his apron and came over to shake Alfred's hand.

"It's good to see you, Alf."

"Good to see you, too, George. You're looking well." George always seemed to him to exude an enviably vigorous masculinity. He wasn't a large man, but his small frame was packed with muscle and energy. His face, surrounded by short dark hair and a neat, thick, black beard, was animated, his eyes bright, as if eager to make the most of everything life had to offer.

"I *am* well – very well indeed, thankin' you. But you're

lookin' a bit…er…what can I say…a bit *ropy*. You didn't walk 'ere through all this lot, did you?"

"I did, yes…" He grinned sheepishly.

"What in 'eaven's name for? It's goin' to snow again, y' know. You'll be stuck 'ere if you're not careful." George looked deep into his friend's eyes, then laughed. "Oh I see! It's a woman. It surely is. No one in their right mind'd walk three miles through all this lot. 'E's in love! At last! I thought it weren't never goin' to 'appen! Well, well. Let's 'ave a cuppa and you can tell George all about it."

Alfred laughed, too, at being so easily found out and at the absurdity of the situation as his friend would undoubtedly see it. He started to relax. George had an easy manner in the company of women, the result of living in a house full of sisters, and was now happily betrothed to a very pretty maid from the doctor's household. He was certain to give Alfred some good advice. The blacksmith put a battered, black kettle onto the fire. Alfred got out his bread and cheese and the two settled down for a heart to heart in the warmth of the forge.

❧

A while later George sat with an uncharacteristic frown knitting his dark eyebrows.

"Well, what do you know – Alf in love with the school teacher!" He paused for a moment, scratching his head. "Alf…er…I may be speakin' out of turn and I don't want to put you off, you know, not now you've finally embarked on a bit o' courtin', but…are you sure she's your sort? The kiddies at 'ome say she's…well, a bit *fierce*, shall we say. Our Ellie's frightened of 'er, to tell the truth. I 'ad it in mind that you'd end up with a quiet, gentle sort o' girl, like our Phoebe, for instance."

George and his sisters had been trying to persuade Alfred to walk out with Phoebe for years. She was the eldest of the family, a lovely girl. Of course his mother would have disapproved, as she disapproved of his friendship with George. She had never understood why he had made no friends amongst the doctors' and lawyers' sons of his small private school and instead chose to spend time with the son of a common blacksmith. But it wasn't for social reasons that he had never taken to Phoebe. He couldn't say why.

"Miss Fielding is a very strong woman, George, I know that…but that's part of what I admire about her. I can't explain why I have feelings for her or why I've never fallen in love with Phoebe. Does anyone understand love? I just know that I long to be with her."

"Well…that's fair enough, my friend." George smiled at him. "Then she must be the woman for you! And that bein' the case, we need a plan. I think you're wise not to see 'er lookin' like you are – puttin' it bluntly, you're worse turned-out than Cedric."

Alfred laughed. "That's a bit rough, George – comparing me unfavourably with a pig!"

George's eyes twinkled. "Just bein' honest, my friend. You need to get yerself over to Fred's and get a decent 'air cut and shave. But that'll 'ave to wait for another day and it'd be a good idea, given old Roberts' interest, to do somethin' today…" George thought for a moment, then stood up and clapped him on the back. "Come on, we're goin' to make a quick visit 'ome, then you've to be off back to Stonefield as fast as those skinny legs'll carry you. Look, it's snowin' 'ard again. What did I say?" He pulled open the door and the pair hurried through the whirling blizzard to the small house behind the forge.

❧

The respective moods of the occupants of the school cottage underwent something of a reversal following the visit of the

100

curate. Emma sat pushing the food round her plate at luncheon. She considered herself a steady person, with her feelings well under control, yet she could not deny that she had found Mr Roberts attractive. But she didn't *want* to find him attractive. It was Mr Nicholson she must love. She was upset with herself for her weakness and with Mr Nicholson for not coming to see her today. The rational part of her mind knew that it was probably unreasonable to expect him to wade through the snow to Blackford. Nevertheless, she felt that if he truly loved her, that is what he would have done.

Her mother, on the other hand, was quite restored to her former self by the visit, and was tucking into her ham and potatoes with relish.

"Mr Roberts is such a nice young man, isn't he, dear? And he did make me laugh. Perhaps he shouldn't describe Mrs Hill's dress in quite that way, but…oh dear…it was amusing."

"So you have said, Mamma. Several times, in fact. Yes, he is an amusing man, though, I agree, he shouldn't be so disrespectful to his parishioners."

They continued eating in silence, Emma forcing herself to finish her food so as not to attract attention.

Her mother looked out of the window. It was snowing hard again, the snow blowing almost horizontally across the green.

"Well, we certainly can't go to the recital now, dear. I can't say I'm sorry. I never did like the organ."

"You didn't have to come, Mamma."

"Of course I did! What would people have said if they had seen you there alone with Mr Nicholson? Have you heard from him?"

"No, but I doubt if there's any post. I would have found out if I had been able to get to the post office this morning."

"You can't go now, my darling! Look at it out there – it's a blizzard! You would be lost! Buried!"

"I hardly think so, as it's barely two hundred yards to the post office. You do exaggerate, Mamma. However, I have no wish to get soaked and frozen, so I shall post my letter tomorrow."

When the meal was finished, and her mother busy in the scullery, Emma sat back down at the window and began to read while there was still enough light. She opened the book – Mr Dickens' latest novel, "Great Expectations", kindly leant to her by the Rector's wife – and tried to lose herself in Pip's complicated world. A little while later she was distracted by a shadow passing the window. She jumped up and ran into the hall just in time to see a letter addressed to herself drop onto the mat. Wrenching open the door, she was about to call out, when she realised, from the height of the retreating figure, that it could not be the man she was hoping to see. She closed the door again quietly so as not to alert her mother, picked up the letter and took it back to the table by the window, where she hid it under her book until she heard the click of the bedroom door. Her mother had gone for her afternoon rest. Thank goodness. She tore it open impatiently, her eyes quickly scanning down the lines of careful handwriting.

So he *had* come! And if Mr Roberts had not been here she would have seen him. Yet again her mother had managed to get in the way of what she wanted. She tutted with exasperation. At the same time she felt happy that he *had* wanted to see her and had indeed made a supreme effort to get to her. She read and re-read his closing line – "I am filled with longing to see you again. With fondest regards…" *Fondest* regards. Emma was not by nature a ditherer, or plagued by indecision. These words were enough to sweep aside her momentary lapse in certainty about her feelings. In her mind Mr Roberts quickly became nothing but a rather superficial, vain young man, who was rather too pleased with himself, particularly in relation to young ladies. Mr Nicholson, on the other hand, was steady and true. He did love her. And she was sure that she would grow to love him.

However, this battle with her mother was tiresome. It was always the same. Her mother was too cowardly to stand up to her in a face to face disagreement, but would undermine her whenever she had the opportunity. She had no doubt that she herself would win in the end, but she really needed an ally. She had made very few friends in the village – there had been little time for socialising, what with moving into the cottage and establishing herself as a teacher. She looked at her book. Mrs Hopwood had been kind, though. She had visited several times and invited Emma to take tea with her twice. Recently the poor woman had been unwell – yet another baby expected, so people said – and she hadn't seen her. But perhaps she could call at the Rectory tomorrow. Yes, that was an excellent idea. It would get her out of the house and might provide her with the support she needed. Mrs Hopwood would be happy to receive her, she was sure.

CHAPTER 14

Cecily lay in the dark nursery listening to the children's snuffling and coughing. She was grateful that their colds had not stopped them from sleeping soundly, but knew that they would wake up all too soon and that she would have no rest then until they were back in bed. The makeshift bed she was lying on was hard and lumpy. She tossed from one side to another, but couldn't get comfortable. The more tired and desperate for sleep she grew, the more wild her imagination became, creating dreadful scenes, all involving coughing, choking children. When the fantasies started to include small, white coffins being carried from the house, she knew she must stop. Mrs Norris would scold her roundly for such morbid thoughts and tell her to think of something nice.

She cast about in her mind for a while until the thought of Christmas at home came to her. Festivities in their cramped house in Wittenbury weren't elaborate as they were at the Rectory, but it was always a happy time. They had their own traditions, which were guarded fiercely by the children and reproduced faithfully year after year. On Christmas Eve the house was decorated by the older ones with holly and ivy cut from hedgerows on the outskirts of the town. Christmas morning began with the walk to church, followed by dinner at midday with goose and an enormous pudding full of sixpenny pieces. There was a small tree in the parlour where everyone who was old enough placed a gift to be chosen later in the evening by each child or adult in turn, blindfolded and giggling after being spun around many times. Then came the best part of the day, when her mother played the piano and they sang Christmas carols. Her father and Harry had lovely bass voices. She and Frances could sing well, too;

Frances did the descants and she the alto line. Even the little ones joined in, quickly remembering the choruses. The effect was as pleasing as a trained choir, filling the small room with a huge, joyful noise. 'See Amid the Winter's Snow' was the family favourite and very apt at the moment. She began singing it to herself in her head and could soon hear the rest of her family joining in. After the first verse she had to concentrate to remember the words and became increasingly muddled until, by the third verse, she had lost her place altogether and had to start from the beginning again.

She didn't remember falling asleep, but the next thing she knew was the sound of small feet landing on the floor and padding across the room, together with, "I go wake up Papa." It was still pitch dark, but she could hear sounds of life in the house, so it must be after six o'clock. She dragged herself awake. The twins had recently moved into their own bedroom and were used to taking themselves next door to their parents' room first thing in the morning. Now they were back in the nursery, one at either end of the bed under the window, and must not be allowed out. She got up stiffly from her mattress on the floor and felt for the lamp and matches on the mantelpiece. With the lamp alight, she could see that it was William who was awake and who was now at the door, trying hard to turn the handle. She went over to him, scooped him up and took him back to his end of the bed.

"Sshh, Will. You have to stay here with me today. Papa will come to see you very soon."

He began to whimper. "Mamma, want my mamma and papa."

"Sshh, now, don't cry. Here's rabbit, look." She tucked him under the blankets with the knitted rabbit Mrs Norris had made for each of the boys when they were born. William's was looking careworn, its body flattened and one button-eye missing, but its presence had an immediate comforting effect.

He stopped crying, put his thumb in his mouth and lay looking up at her with large, puzzled eyes. She sat next to the small bed on the floor and stroked his head for a while, before finding her clothes and getting dressed.

Little Edward slept behind a curtain in the foot of the L-shaped room and was still quiet, thank goodness, but the light of the lamp, together with his brother's fidgeting, soon woke Charles and she realised that it was pointless to postpone the beginning of the day any longer. She consulted her pile of instructions from Mrs Hopwood. These had arrived yesterday afternoon and evening, brought up in instalments on sheets of closely written paper by an apologetic, but slightly amused Edith.

"It's a good job you're a good reader, our Cecily. I don't envy you wadin' through this lot. It must be a very complicated business lookin' after babies, that's all I can say. My poor ma didn't have no instructions as far as I know. Per'aps that's why we didn't turn out too clever!"

The sheets set out in detail what should happen at every moment in the children's day: when and how they must rise, wash, dress, eat, play, rest, undress and sleep. Cecily could understand that her mistress was desperate, and, being unable to be with the children herself, this was the only way she could relieve her anxiety. However, it made life extremely difficult. She quickly realised that the twins had no intention of fitting into the routine set out for them. It was not that they were wilful or disobedient. In fact they were, especially William, sensitive children, who were keen to please and who would usually do what she asked them to do. They were also, however, highly distractible and could never sustain their good intentions for more than half a minute at a time. And there were two of them – if one was where he was supposed to be, then the other was not, and the first would soon go off to join him. It was impossible!

When Edith brought the hot water, Cecily set about

trying to get the twins washed and dressed. They wriggled and fidgeted and slipped from her lap. It was like trying to hold on to ferrets. She was anxious to have them dressed quickly before they got cold in the chilly air and called to Edith, who was tending the fire, to help her.

"Lord, don't ask me. I don't know nothin' 'bout little kiddies."

"Just sit there, Edie, and hold him tight – don't let him go. I'll do the rest."

She deposited a child on her friend's lap and between them they managed to wash, dry and dress him in the many layers of flannel and wool as per the mistress's instructions. When the second was also dressed, Edith breathed a sigh of relief.

"Goodness, rather you than me, Cecy. These little nippers don't seem at all poorly to me – much too lively for my likin'. I'll be glad to get back to the kitchen for some peace and quiet. I'm off to get you some more coal. Breakfast'll be ready soon."

"Bekfast! Bekfast!" called the boys, running after her as she left the room.

"Breakfast will be coming soon. Come over here, boys – let's find you something to play with." Cecily shut the door firmly, lifted a box of tin soldiers from a shelf in the alcove beside the fireplace and steered the twins onto the hearth. She watched them for a moment. Their colds were still all too obvious, but seemed no worse than yesterday. She knew that whooping cough could start with just such a mild phase, which might go on for more than a week. They would just have to wait and see. She quickly pushed away the beginnings of anxious thoughts.

"Now…time to sort out your little brother."

Edward had been awake for a while, roused by the noisy washing and dressing at the other end of the room. It was fortunate he was such a passive child, she thought – happy to sit in his cot babbling to himself. His baby chatter was beginning to turn into whimpering, though, and she knew he would need his breakfast very soon. She picked up the next sheet of her mistress's instructions and began to read. After only a few seconds she was distracted by the chaotic scene all around her – the wash bowl and spilt water on the table, nightshirts on the floor, unmade beds and her own nightclothes and makeshift bed still not tidied away. She flung the piece of paper back onto the pile, muttering, "I haven't got time for this," picked up the wash bowl and hurried to the far end of the room to find Edward.

The arrangements for the baby were difficult. The doctor had forbidden Mrs Hopwood to look after him, even though he had no symptoms, in case he later became ill too. So he was to be kept in the nursery, but separated from the twins as much as possible. This meant keeping him behind the curtain, for it was thought that the physical barrier would help to prevent the spread of the disease, but how she was to achieve this in practice, she had yet to work out. The master had promised to help whenever he was able, but he was a busy man with an ailing wife, household and parish to attend to.

In the event, the baby proved much easier to manage than the boys. With the distraction of a small wooden giraffe to hold, he was happy to be washed and dressed on the table by his cot and she was pleased to see how quickly she managed to get him into his warm layers. She then stripped his bed of most of the bedding, filled it with animals from the Noah's Ark and settled him back behind his cot bars, so that she could clear up the mess in the room and lay the table for breakfast. There he stayed, mostly playing happily, but occasionally pulling himself up and shouting for attention, which she gave him by playing a quick game of peep-bo from behind the curtain, until breakfast arrived.

In the dining room Clementine's breakfast lay untouched in front of her as it had done for the last few days. Her dear husband chided her as usual, and for his sake, and for the sake of the baby inside her, she forced down some porridge and a little scrambled egg.

"I shall call in to the nursery after breakfast, my darling, so that I can reassure you that all is well before I go to see Mrs Gregory."

"Oh, must you go to her, David? You know I shall be pining here all morning without you. I can't keep my mind on anything except the babies at the moment and the time goes so slowly. It's agony to be kept downstairs when they need me and I feel so desperate to be with them."

"I know, I know. My poor love. I'm so sorry that this is all so difficult for you. But, yes, I must go I'm afraid. She's dying, poor woman and hardly anybody to care for her in that cold, cheerless house, except her old servant. It's a terrible thing to be dying in this weather, Clemmy. People who might have visited from further away are prevented and she is quite alone most of the time. There's no hope at all, Dr Tucker says. I won't be very long."

He looked out of the window.

"It has snowed again. Yesterday's tracks are quite covered over."

"There will be no chance of the nurse coming from Wittenbury today, then? Oh dear…do you really think Cecily can look after them properly? I'm so anxious that she might forget something important. You know how scatter-brained she can be. Did she read all the instructions I wrote for her?"

"I'm sure she did, dear. You really mustn't fret so about her. She is an intelligent girl and very sensible when it comes to looking after small children. She is also kind, but firm, and seems to have kept them in order. No one has cut off anyone else's hair, or any other part of their body, as far as I know."

"Oh David, how can you joke about something like this?"

"I'm sorry, dearest. I'm only trying to cheer you a little. I think it's very bad for you and the new baby that you are so anxious, though I know it's only because you are such a dear, sensitive soul. But we must have faith in our loving Father God, Clemmy, and keep hopeful as we are commanded."

Clementine looked down shamefacedly. She knew he was right, but found it hard to feel as certain about Godly matters as David obviously did. Her faith fluctuated depending on her feelings and circumstances. At the moment she couldn't understand how a loving God could possibly visit horrible diseases upon precious, innocent children. She had tried to pray many times since yesterday, but had felt only a cruel emptiness, as if she were talking to herself. She looked up at him and tried to smile.

"I know you're right. I will try to hope, as you say I must. But will you *please* go up now and see how they are?"

"Of course I will." He got up from his chair and came round to her, kissing her tenderly before leaving the room.

She brushed away a tear and let out a deep, shuddering sigh. The baby wriggled and kicked. She stroked her round abdomen, feeling grateful that at least he or she was safe.

❧

Sometime later she was sitting by the fire in the morning room trying hard to concentrate on her sewing – a new cotton bonnet for the baby with fine embroidery and lace trimming. It was hard to imagine that the weather would ever be warm enough for it to be suitable, but with the baby expected at the end of April, she had hopes that spring might have arrived by then. Sewing was not her favourite occupation, but she had to admit that it helped to soothe her nerves and while away the endless hours. She was thinking of her parents, who would want to know the latest news and might perhaps call on her this afternoon. She had just decided that she would send Edith with a note, when the maid appeared at the door.

"There's a visitor for you, ma'am – Miss Fielding, the school mistress. Shall I bring 'er in?"

"Oh, I don't think I can receive visitors today, Edith. Please give her my apologies and say I am unwell."

"Very well, ma'am." Edith turned to leave.

"Oh no…wait. Yes, perhaps I will see her. A short visit might do me good. Show her in, will you."

"Very well, ma'am."

Clementine was aware that she had let herself go in the last few days and was torn between the need to hide herself away and to have some distraction from her worries. She hastily tidied her hair. She felt mortified when Miss Fielding appeared in the doorway looking lovely in a dark green dress, her waist tiny, her eyes bright and her cheeks glowing from her walk across the green in the snow. Her own body seemed shapeless and huge in comparison. She decided to stay sitting as she greeted her visitor. They sat on either side of the hearth, exchanging pleasantries for a while, chiefly bemoaning the awful weather and the everyday difficulties it caused. She made light of the children's illness when Miss Fielding enquired after the family's and her own health. She didn't trust herself to talk about them without weeping and didn't know the school teacher well enough to want to reveal such painful feelings. The conversation moved onto the health of their respective parents. Miss Fielding suddenly leant forward and burst out, with a vehemence that startled her for a moment,

"Oh, Mrs Hopwood, I…I wonder if you may be able to help me. It's a delicate matter, but…I've no one else in the village I can confide in."

Clementine was surprised to see this normally confident young woman looking so uncomfortable. She gave what she

111

hoped was a sympathetic and reassuring look. "Oh dear… Please tell me, if that would help."

"It's my mother. I mentioned that she hasn't been herself lately and I'm afraid she blames me for her ill health."

"Blames you? What could you have done to make her ill?"

"Well…" Miss Fielding hesitated, apparently searching for the right words. "I don't quite know how to put this…I have an interest in someone she disapproves of."

"An interest? Ahhh…that is difficult for you. Do I know the lucky man?"

"Yes, Mrs Hopwood, you do. He was at your Christmas recital and played the piano most beautifully – Mr Nicholson."

"Oh yes, he's done work on the house on a number of occasions and sings in the choir. My husband speaks very highly of him." Now Clementine was leaning forward too. Despite herself, she was intrigued to find out more about this love affair. She remembered noticing that Edgar Roberts seemed to pay the schoolteacher a lot of attention at the recital. The curate would surely be a much more suitable match for the daughter of a vicar? She checked herself, aware that Miss Fielding had come hoping for the support of a confidante, not a judge.

"And… er…Mr Nicholson. Do you have reason to think he returns your…*interest*?"

"Yes, I do. He asked me to accompany him to a recital, which has unfortunately been cancelled on account of this wretched weather, and he has written, expressing most fond feelings for me. But my mother feels he is unsuitable and has interfered on several occasions to come between us."

Clementine was silent for a moment. She had never encountered such a problem in her own short life. Her parents had been happy to give their blessing to her marriage. Perhaps they might have had secret misgivings about David's advanced years, but they had never given any indication if they had. She didn't really know what to say.

"I can see that must be hard for you."

"It is *very* hard. Of course I do love Mamma dearly, but she can be so trying at times!"

Clementine was shocked that Miss Fielding was criticising her own mother to someone she barely knew. She would never dream of doing such a thing. Not that she would ever have wanted to. Her mamma was nothing but a blessing in her life – she wouldn't know how to live without her. She thought perhaps she should try to elicit Mrs Fielding's point of view on the matter.

"Do you know what your mother's objection is?"

"Oh, she feels that Mr Nicholson is beneath us, being a tradesman."

"And you? This isn't a problem for you?"

"No, it is *not*, Mrs Hopwood! And that's why I've come to pour my heart out to you, because your husband is well known for valuing people in other ways than mere social rank. I hope perhaps he may be able to help me to persuade dear Mamma that this…this understanding between us will not be the disaster she assumes it will be."

"Oh…I see…" Clementine was taken aback at the boldness of the request. "Well…er…of course I can't speak for Mr Hopwood now, but I can talk to him later if you wish, though I can't imagine that he would want to interfere in a family matter such as this."

Miss Fielding looked a little deflated. "I only imagined perhaps a little word from him might resolve the matter. Mamma does admire him. She misses my father terribly, and Mr Hopwood has been so kind to us. But, of course I shall leave it to your good judgement to decide whether you should speak to him. I know he's a busy man and you, too, of course, with the children. I can see I've tired you, now. I shall take my leave. Thank you so much for listening to my troubles. I hope I may call again?"

Clementine, though unsure whether she wanted to involve herself in Miss Fielding's 'troubles', was nevertheless grateful for the distraction the conversation had brought her from her own, much more pressing ones. On balance, she thought, another visit would be welcome.

"Yes, of course. Please come again soon. I'm sorry that I'm unable to return your call, but this weather keeps me a prisoner here, I'm afraid."

Miss Fielding stood to leave, taking Clementine's hand in her own. "Goodbye, Mrs Hopwood. I do hope you will keep well. I shall look forward to seeing you again."

Left alone again, Clementine sat for a while, her sewing untouched in her lap, mulling over the conversation. Miss Fielding was certainly a bold woman and seemed determined to get her own way. She didn't think she could possibly have acted knowingly against her parents' wishes in anything as important as her marriage. But then again, the necessity hadn't arisen, and how was she to know how she might have felt if they had tried to thwart her? Perhaps Miss Fielding's and Mr Nicholson's was a grand passion, something else she knew nothing about. Well, it couldn't hurt to mention it to David. He would consider it in his usual wise, detached manner and could decide for himself whether to intervene.

With a start she realised it was a full fifteen minutes since she had thought about the children. A guilty lump rose in her throat. The poor darlings! She picked up the bonnet and needle and took herself in her mind back up to the nursery where she belonged.

CHAPTER 15

Cecily had never learnt to swim. She had tried once, at the lake in the woods on the edge of town, one blisteringly hot day when she was eleven. She had followed Harry and his friends and watched them from the trees as they dived and splashed in the inviting, green water. It looked so easy, the boys' bodies as sleek and graceful as fish. But when she tried, wading into the water up to her waist, launching herself towards the middle of the lake, her feet stuck in the mud and weeds, her arms flailed and her dress caught around her legs. The terror of the water filling her mouth and nose returned to her sometimes in nightmares. It was the only time she could remember Harry shouting at her as he dragged her onto the bank. So much in her life had been like trying to swim. Only learning to read had come easily to her, if you didn't count thinking and talking. Everything else was a struggle of fingers and thumbs and legs and arms, which went their own way, and not where they were supposed to go. Until now. Now she felt different. Now she was swimming with the rest, feeling for the first time the joy of accomplishing tasks with the gifts she had been given and doing them well.

It was not that life in the nursery was easy. Her day continued in much the same hectic, chaotic way in which it had begun and she quickly realised that looking after three little children was a great deal more tiring and challenging than any amount of sweeping, dusting or ironing. But somehow it all came naturally to her. Despite her earlier misgivings, she was able to stay calm and to deal with the many small disasters which occurred without getting angry or agitated. Everything got done and the children, though they missed their mother, were remarkably happy, given that they were ill and cooped up in the one room all day. Playing on the hearth, immersing herself in a world of animals and castles of wooden blocks, or of princesses and witches in the stories they loved to hear, came easily to her. She felt she belonged with them and they in turn responded to her playfulness and affectionate nature with an immediate, warm attachment.

At the back of her mind the constant, nagging anxiety about their illness still lurked. There was little time to consult her mistress's instructions and the logistics of trying to keep the baby behind the curtain might have defeated her if he had not been such a contented little chap, who mercifully still needed both a morning and afternoon sleep. She had some help from Edith at mealtimes and bedtime and the master dropped in occasionally for a few minutes, in addition to his usual afternoon playtime with the twins, giving her a chance to sit with Edward or to catch up on chores. By the end of the day, when the children were all asleep in bed and the nursery tidy and quiet, she felt exhausted, proud and relieved. A whole day had passed and they were all still breathing.

At seven o'clock Edith was sent up to sit in the nursery. The mistress was waiting for an account of Cecily's day and of the condition of the children. She felt the old, familiar anxieties returning, fearing that it might be all too obvious that she had not followed the meticulous instructions she had been given. She went down to the drawing room and knocked nervously on the door. The reassuring voice of the Rector answered.

"Ahh, Cecily, our young nurse. Come in. What a marvel she is, my dear. The nursery is so well organised and the children so content you would think she had been in the profession for years."

Mrs Hopwood looked unconvinced. She sat by the fire, her face pale and tired, her hands restless in her lap. Cecily found it difficult to look into the dark, anxious eyes which were fixed upon her.

"Cecily, come here and tell me about the children. How are they? Is their fever any worse? Did they eat their supper and drink their milk?"

"Well, ma'am, they…"

"What about Edward? Does he show any signs?"

"No, I don't think so…"

"Did you put them in the double flannel underclothes as I instructed?"

"Yes, ma'am I…"

"Is it warm enough up there? It's always been such a problem heating that room, especially for my darling at the far end behind that horrible curtain. I can't bear to think that they might be cold." Her voice became unsteady. Cecily felt awkward and sorry for her at the same time. The Reverend put his hand over his wife's.

"Clementine, my darling, Cecily understands how anxious you are, but she can't answer so many questions! Cecily tell your mistress as much as you can about how well the boys are doing."

"Yes, sir. Er, well…" She paused, choosing her words carefully. "William and Charles still have their colds…but their fever is only slight, ma'am, and they have eaten tolerably well, I should say, and drunk all their milk. They didn't like the tonic the doctor sent, but they took it with a spoonful of honey to follow. They've played with their toys with only a little squabbling and listened quietly to lots of stories. And, yes, they've been well wrapped up as you instructed and the room is warm… The baby is well, ma'am. He's a cheerful little soul and he's been no bother at all, to tell you the truth."

Mrs Hopwood seemed to relax just a little. The Rector patted her hand again.

"So there you are, my dear. You see, it *is* as I described. All is well in the nursery. Now, I think we should let Cecily go to eat her supper, don't you?"

The young mistress sighed. "Yes, of course. Off you go then, Cecily. I shall expect a full account tomorrow at the same time." Cecily curtsied and hurried from the room. She ran to the kitchen and burst through the door. Thank goodness Mrs Norris was there – someone she could talk to who would understand and be able to give her sensible advice. She flopped down at the big table, almost too tired to eat the supper set out for her, and poured her heart out as the cook sat beside her preparing apples for stewing the next day. After five minutes of listening with sympathetic nods and knowing shakes of the head, Mrs Norris put down her paring knife and gave her a firm, motherly look.

"Well you've had quite a day and no mistake. And it sounds to me as if you've done as well as anyone could expect and you should be proud of yerself. But that's enough talkin' now, dear. I haven't cooked this lovely lamb for you to sit lookin' at it. You need to eat to keep yer strength up. There'll be plenty more to say another day, I'm sure. Come along – eat up! I'll tell you about *my* little ones while you're eatin'. Goodness, that was a long time ago now! Well…my Lily, she was a proper little madam, I can tell you, but if ever she was poorly she was as good as gold – took her medicine without a murmur – not like the boys! Now, when they all got ill with the whoopin' cough…she must have been just two, I think…"

Cecily listened and ate. Mrs Norris's matter-of-fact and sometimes humorous account of her family's troubles, with its happy outcome, was just the tonic she needed. By the time she had finished her pudding her eyelids were drooping. She was ready to go back upstairs, make up her lumpy bed and say goodnight to Edith. If the children slept, she would not be staying awake tonight.

In the drawing room the Hopwoods sat quietly beside the fire. He was engrossed in a weighty theological text, his glasses slipping slowly down his nose, his free hand ruffling his hair into a wild mess. She tried to read; a light-hearted novella was all she could manage these days, but even that was too much for her agitated mind to concentrate on. She envied her husband's ability to stay calm and rational in a crisis, and to turn his mind fully to his work, even while he remained as concerned as she did about the children's health. As the romantic entanglements of the fictional characters could not keep her attention, she turned her mind to real life and Miss Fielding's odd request. She wondered what it was about Alfred Nicholson that made the school teacher so determined to marry him. He was an unremarkable looking man, pleasant enough to talk to, but rather shy and quiet. There was his undoubted musical gift, of course, which she supposed might make him interesting to some people, though not to her personally. And he had a successful business. But...the building trade? It wasn't the most glamorous of professions, was it? Miss Fielding, in contrast, seemed to her to epitomise elegance and good breeding. It was very strange. Still, there was no accounting for taste and no doubt her own marriage had set village tongues wagging. She had discussed Miss Fielding's problem with David over lunch. As usual, he had refrained from critical comment, but had assured her he would give it some thought. She knew she shouldn't interrupt him, but her ability to wait patiently was quite exhausted by the end of the day.

"David?"

He continued reading. "Yes, dear?"

"Did you have a chance to consider Miss Fielding's difficulty?"

He took off his glasses and looked at her, his eyes twinkling.

"Yes, I did. In fact I have made several decisions which I hope may help to settle the matter." He replaced his glasses and went back to his book.

"Well? Surely I may know what they are?"

Off came the spectacles once more. "Why would you want to know, my darling? You're not usually one to enjoy romantic intrigue."

"Oh, David, don't tease me. Of course I enjoy romantic intrigue. In fact it is just the diversion I need at the moment."

He laughed. "Very well. If you insist! I will tell you my little plan…"

❧

In the morning life in the nursery became both simpler and more complicated. The first sound Cecily heard when she woke was the baby's voice, croaky and congested, crying from his cot. One look at him, even in the dim light of the lamp, told her that he was ill. She quickly roused the Reverend, who sent Edith for Dr Tucker. His diagnosis was the same as on his previous visit. It could be just a cold or it could be the whooping cough. Whatever it was, the baby must be kept warm, dry and well-nourished, but there was no point now in isolating him from the twins. After examining all three children thoroughly, the doctor left the room with the Reverend. Their grave expressions and low voices sent a shiver through her body.

The next few days were even more challenging for her. Edward was feverish and fractious and needed her attention when he was awake. The twins were coughing more and were also more irritable and less inclined to play happily for any length of time. She was grateful that the Rector was spending extra time with them, usually reading to the twins, or getting on the floor with the soldiers or the Noah's Ark animals. Mrs Norris came whenever she could spare a few minutes, always bringing something tasty to tempt the boys to eat. If the baby was awake she would hold him, rocking him gently and singing or talking to him quietly. Cecily envied the calming effect the cook had on him, for he would often fall fast asleep in her arms. Edith came frequently, with meals, coal and hot water, but preferred to leave child care duties to Cecily. Between them all they kept the children amused, fed and comforted.

The outside world seemed distant, almost dreamlike to her now. She had few opportunities to look outside the windows, but whenever she did the same wintry scene greeted her. The weather continued bitterly cold. On a few fine days some snow had melted from the roofs and trees, causing huge icicles to form under all the eaves, but then the sky darkened once more and fresh snowfalls undid the good work of the sun, blocking the roads and paths all over again. She had seen very few carts and carriages around the green and was surprised, therefore, when Edith came in one morning with a letter for her.

"I didn't think there was any post at the moment."

"The post boy walked all the way from Wittenbury. 'E says they've been out clearing as much as they can, though as fast as they shovel it away the blinkin' stuff falls out the sky again. 'E said it may 'ave been posted a few days ago and 'e apologises for the delay. Come on then, open it!"

Cecily would have preferred to have opened her letter in private, but hadn't the time or energy to argue. She scanned the few lines quickly. They were from her mother. When she reached the bottom of the letter she put her hand over her mouth.

"Oh no!"

"What, Cecy? What's the matter? It's not Ernie is it? I saw it didn't 'ave black edges so I thought it must be all right. Oh dear, I'm so sorry…"

"No, no, don't worry, it's not Ernie. Mother says he's a

little better and they have every hope that he'll be quite well soon. No, it's that…oh dear, Edie, this is awful…"

"What's awful? Oh dang, I wish I could read!" Edith's hands flapped with frustration.

"Edie! The children!"

Edith put her hand over her mouth. "Oh, sorry… But I can't stand mysteries. Tell me what it says… *please*."

"Mother says I've to go to Whitstable to live with my Great Aunt Ellen when I leave here. She's my father's aunt. She lives on her own and needs a companion. She's willing to take me, Mother says, and I should be grateful. She's ancient, Edie, at least eighty by now, I should think. She's never married, 'cause she's too nasty, I'm sure. I've only seen her twice, but we were all terrified of her. Tom said she looked like a witch and barked like a dog. Mother never had a good word to say about her before, but now of course she's my 'dear, kind Aunt Ellen.' Lord, how can I be *grateful*? It'll be awful!" Her eyes began to fill with tears. Edith patted her gently on the arm.

"Poor you, Cecy. I shouldn't like to be shut up all day with a crabby old lady, I must admit. And it's a long way from Blackford, too. I'd so 'oped we could stay friends now we've got to know one another."

Cecily sat down heavily on a chair by the fire. Edward, whose fever seemed improved this morning, was cruising round the furniture, holding on with one hand and experimenting with letting go for a few seconds, before clutching at the nearest support again. He tottered from the low shelf beside the fireplace to her chair and grabbed onto her skirts. Without thinking she reached down for him and settled him on her lap with a toy. She played with his blond curls and stroked his chubby hand while she watched the boys, who sat in front of her on the hearth, squabbling over the pieces of a jigsaw puzzle.

"I don't want to leave the children now, either, Edie. I'm

fond of them and I think they are of me. It will be terrible to think of someone else looking after them."

"Well, let's not think 'bout it yet, eh? The Missus hasn't even interviewed the new nurse yet, 'cause she's stuck in Wittenbury. There's something good come out of all this snow, anyway! I've got to get back now, Cecy. Try not to fret, dear. Think 'bout little Ernie – that's such good news, ain't it? I must go and tell Mrs N. She'll be so pleased. I'll see you in a little while."

Cecily put the baby back on the hearth rug and sat down with the twins to help sort out the jigsaw before the argument turned into a full scale battle. Edie was right of course. She should be delighted that her little brother was going to be all right, not fretting about herself. Looking at the boys and picturing him at home on the floor with his puzzles brought more tears to her eyes. She reached out to separate a bunch of little fists fighting to hold on to the two remaining puzzle pieces.

"There, Charlie, your piece goes there to make the little boy's hat. That's it. And what about yours, Will? Shall I help you? There, it's finished now. What are the children doing in the picture? Can you see?"

"Play with hoos."

"Hoops, yes, good boy, Will. And what else? What are these?"

"A birdy!"

"No, it's not a bird, Charlie, it's a kite, on a string – look. It flies in the air and you hold the end of the string to stop it flying away."

"I want play kite!"

"So do I, Will. It would be fun, wouldn't it? But we can't today 'cause of all the snow. Maybe in the summer when it's warm." She sighed. Kite flying was the last thing she was likely to be doing this summer.

The children wandered off to find something else to play

with. She watched them for a few minutes. Was it her imagination, or were they all a little better today? For the first time a surge of hope filled her – perhaps they really did just have colds. Hope turned to distress as it gradually dawned on her that if the children got better, she would no longer be needed in the nursery. She brushed away another tear, impatient with herself for thinking such self-centred thoughts. Edward crawled over to help her as she began putting away the puzzle pieces. She smiled at him as she gently removed a piece from his mouth and put it in the box. Of course she wanted them to get better. She loved them now.

But what was to become of her? Harry believed that there was a purpose in everything that happened – God's will, he would call it. Well, she was blowed if she could see the purpose in being sent to look after a dreadful old lady, doing work she had been given no talent for, when all she wanted was to be here, looking after these children, using the gifts she *had* been given. But then God's purposes had always been beyond her. She couldn't accept things the way Harry could.

She shrugged and tried to sigh away her frustration. Life goes on, her mother had said, as she had picked herself up after Frank's death and numerous other setbacks. So it would go on for her too, and she would have to go with it, whether she wanted to or not. She *knew* that, though accepting it was a different matter. Best to try to enjoy the few days she had left, then. She reached for the book of fairy tales.

"Shall we have a story, boys?"

CHAPTER 16

Alfred didn't know what had woken him. Nothing usually disturbed his sleep. He was used to the nocturnal sounds of the countryside – screeching owls, barking foxes, the many voices of the wind in the trees – but tonight something was different. He propped himself up on his elbow, fully awake now, straining to hear. *There* it was, just outside the window, a soft drip, followed by another and then another. He got up and opened the window wide, leaning his head out and sniffing the air. The wind had changed. The air was mild and damp, blowing from the west and promising rain to wash away the snow, which had held his life in suspension for nearly two weeks now. With a muttered "Thank goodness," he climbed back under the heavy covers and settled himself for sleep once more.

It didn't come. Instead images and thoughts began to jostle in his mind, quickly demolishing the peace his dreamless sleep had brought. First came John, his face out of reach as always, no more than a hazy reflection in his mother's sad, reproachful eyes. His mind returned to the old questions like a child picking again and again at a scab on his knee: Why did his mother love him so much less than John? What had he done to deserve those looks? He supplied himself with the answers as he had done countless times before – John had been more beautiful, more accomplished, an easier, happier child, more loveable. Even before his death she must have loved him more. But afterwards…after what had happened… With heavy sighs he turned over first one way and then another, plumping and hitting his pillows, pulling the covers up over his head, pushing them away again, finally resting his head and shutting his eyes, determined to sleep.

After another long interval, still awake, he opened his eyes once more and stared across the room at the dark outlines of the washstand, the looking glass above it and the large oak chest of drawers at the foot of his bed. This had been his father's room. He, too, must have lain awake sometimes in this bed, worrying about the business, his wife, about John. But he wouldn't have allowed himself this self-indulgent wallowing. Alfred chided himself: Stop it now. Things always seem worse in the middle of the night. Think of something else, something pleasant.

Miss Fielding. Emma. He hadn't heard from her since the day he had walked to Blackford in the snow, and hadn't had the courage to call on her again until he could be sure that she really wanted to see him. Even so, at the thought of her, his mood lifted. He prayed for a fast thaw so that the post might get through at last. Only a few minutes later his prayers were answered as the steady dripping of the melting snow was suddenly lost in the sound of heavy rain battering against the window. His heart jumped a little in nervous anticipation. Perhaps there would be a letter in the morning.

He closed his eyes and said her name softly to himself, conjuring images of her face, her hair, her shapely figure standing in the schoolroom and sitting in the golden light of the rectory drawing room. His breathing quickened. He felt himself harden and groaned with a sudden sharp longing to hold her in his arms. His thoughts were quickly out of his control. He was undressing her, touching her, lying with her…No…no… He opened his eyes, placed his hands behind his head and stared at the ceiling, mortified. No…this wasn't what he wanted. He must keep himself chaste for her. Above everything he wanted to be worthy of her. He penned his thoughts like sheep within the safe walls of the church, allowing himself to picture her only as she sat in her pew under the eye of God and the Rector. A beam of colourful sunshine fell from a stained glass window onto her hair and face as she sang. He drank in the beauty of her and smiled. In the darkness his heart gradually slowed, his mind relaxed and he was eventually lulled into sleep by the noise of the wind and the rain.

❧

There was no letter in the morning, but the next day there were two. Annie left the post on the sideboard in the dining room at breakfast time, in full view of his mother. Her face lit up when she saw them.

"Oh good, some post at last! Is there a letter from Miss Fielding, Alfie? I expect you have been hoping for one."

"No, I've been waiting for quotations from suppliers and some final paperwork from the council. It's been a real nuisance, actually. I haven't been able to finalise some of the plans because of the post. So that's what these will be... thank goodness." He felt a pang of guilt that he seemed to be lying with increasing ease these days, though perhaps it was kinder than showing the irritation he really felt.

"Aren't you going to open them?"

"No, I'll take them to the office. I like to be organised with my paperwork, Mother."

"Oh yes, I know. I'm sure you are very organised." She sighed and sat down with her porridge. He took some toast on a plate and headed for the door.

"Where are you going, Alfie? Sit down and eat your breakfast now. A few slices of toast aren't nearly enough. You must eat properly or you will make yourself ill."

"No, I'll be all right, Mother, really I will. I have a lot to be getting on with this morning, now these have arrived. We begin recruiting for the new project in just over two weeks, you know. There's a lot to sort out."

"Oh dear, yes, I'm sure there is..."

"And I shall be here to eat a large lunch with you at half

past twelve. You can watch the potatoes and carrots and steak and kidney pudding as they disappear down my throat and convince yourself that I won't waste away!"

She frowned. "You are teasing me, you bad boy!"

He gave her an apologetic smile. "I know. Now *you* eat your breakfast and stop fretting. I'll see you later."

He reached the safety of his tiny office with relief and placed the letters on the desk. They didn't look like letters from suppliers or the council, but he didn't recognise the handwriting of either. Taking a deep breath he opened the nearest and scanned quickly to the bottom of the page. It was from the Reverend Hopwood – something to do with a summerhouse. He pushed it impatiently to one side and tore open the second. His hand trembled as he found her name. Sitting down heavily on the chair, he began to read. Her handwriting was as beautiful as you would expect from a schoolteacher, and the words, well, to him the words were beautiful too. She was *so* sorry for his wasted journey in the snow, especially as Mr Roberts had only been making a quick call on her mother, but she had been *delighted* to receive his letter. She had been *very* disappointed that the recital had been cancelled and hoped that there would be another that they could attend together soon. He was welcome to call on her and Mrs Fielding *anytime*, although she would of course be teaching in the day as soon as the school re-opened. She returned his *fond* regards. The emphasis was his own, though he was sure that it reflected her sentiments. He couldn't stop the broad grin that broke across his face as he stared through the window at the empty yard.

A full five minutes passed before he could tear his eyes away from the short message and turn his attention to the Rector's letter. The Reverend would like a new summerhouse – he gave approximate dimensions – and hoped Alfred could be available to discuss it with him at 11 o'clock on the 12th January at the Rectory, weather permitting. He looked at the calendar on the wall. Today was the 12th! He pulled his watch from his pocket. It was half past eight already, but if he hurried he could get there. He had work to finish here and must see the lads off on their long-postponed job at the dairy in Moorhurst. Then he would ride to Blackford and call in to Fred's for a haircut and shave, as instructed by his friend, before meeting the Rector. *Then*, he would call on Miss Fielding. His day had suddenly taken on a brighter prospect than any day for…for as long as he could remember. He set off across the yard to find Reg, his heart light and his promise to eat steak and kidney pudding with his mother completely forgotten.

❧

Emma was pleased when an invitation came from Mrs Hopwood to call on her. The dreaded re-opening of the school, postponed because of the snow for over a week, was to take place tomorrow. She had found herself hoping that the outbreak of whooping cough might prolong the closure, a thought she was ashamed of, knowing the distress the illness caused, but one she couldn't help. In any event, the epidemic appeared to have passed Blackford by and this afternoon she must go to the schoolroom to do the preparation she had put off for so long. The visit this morning would be a pleasant distraction from thoughts of difficult children and of her mother. An uneasy truce had settled over the cottage since Mr Roberts' visit, nearly two weeks ago now. He hadn't called again, perhaps sensing her coolness, and her mother had gradually lost most of her regained cheerfulness. They had achieved a certain level of harmony by studiously avoiding the subject of potential husbands, but she was still glad to take every opportunity to escape.

Mrs Hopwood was alone when Emma entered the drawing room of the Rectory. She stood to greet her visitor, smiling broadly. Emma was struck by the complete change in her appearance from their meeting the previous week. Today Mrs Hopwood's cheeks had colour, her eyes were bright and her hair and clothes were attractively arranged, despite her obviously large figure. She took Emma's hand and drew her to a chair beside the fire.

"Miss Fielding, I'm so pleased to see you. May I call you Emma? I do so hope we can think of each other as friends now. And you can call me Clementine. David calls me Clemmy, but actually I prefer my full name."

"Clementine is a lovely name. And may I say how well you look today?"

"Thank you. Yes, I feel so much better than I did when I last saw you. We were so worried about the children then, though I didn't really like to say. We thought they might have the whooping cough, but it turned out to be just a cold! I'm so relieved, I can't tell you how much. And our other good news is that a proper nurse is coming for interview this afternoon, now the wretched snow has cleared, and I have every hope that she may start at the beginning of next week. One of our maids has been helping out, and I've had some difficulty persuading Mr Hopwood that she wouldn't be suitable for the permanent position. I have to admit she shows some natural aptitude, but I feel it's important to have someone with the proper experience, don't you?"

"Oh yes, I'm sure I would want that too." After her teaching experiences these past few months, the thought of having children of her own left Emma cold, but she couldn't confide in the enthusiastic young mother about that particular anxiety.

"Anyway, he bows reluctantly to superior maternal instincts, he says, so the matter is decided…Now, about the small problem you told me about last week."

Emma was feeling embarrassed now about her outburst, especially knowing how anxious Mrs Hopwood had been about her children. "Er...Mrs Hopw...Clementine, I was very grateful for your listening ear, but please don't feel obliged to do anything about that. I think it may have been rather an inappropriate request on my part."

"No, not at all. David is full of compliments for Mr Nicholson. A splendid man and an ideal match, he says. He's happy to be able to help. He's just now finishing a little business discussion and then he will call on your dear mamma. Mr Hopwood has marvellous powers of persuasion, as I have found out many times to my cost! I'm sure he'll work his usual magic."

"Well...thank you. It's very kind of you both to take an interest when you have so much else more important to think about."

"To be honest, Emma, it was a welcome distraction for a few days, when I was in such a state of anxiety...Now, tell me about school and your little charges. Are you looking forward to the start of term? I'm not sure I could work as a school teacher. I don't think I have the patience. Three seems hard work to me...but twenty!"

Emma was acutely aware of her own position, beholden to the Hopwoods in more ways than one now, and didn't want to sound ungrateful or complaining. She painted as rosy a picture of school life and of her own feelings as a teacher as she was able, without telling outright lies. They were discussing the difficulties of teaching embroidery to little girls with little control over their fingers, a safe enough subject, she felt, when the door opened and Mr Hopwood walked in. Behind him, to her surprise and delight, walked Mr Nicholson. He looked as surprised and pleased to see her as she was to see him. She noticed an exchange of mischievous smiles between the Hopwoods.

"Miss Fielding, how nice to see you again." The Rector came forward and shook her hand warmly. Not a man for formal bowing and curtsying, she noted. "And you know Mr

Nicholson already, of course. He is here on business. The Rectory would have crumbled into a state of disrepair long ago were it not for his excellent company."

Greetings were exchanged, they all sat down around the fire and a maid brought in tea. After ten minutes of pleasantries the Rector drained his teacup.

"Now Clemmy, my darling, I believe you are needed in the nursery. Cecily thinks little Edward is cutting another tooth and is a little fractious. He needs his mamma, I think. And I have an errand I must see to on the other side of the green." He smiled knowingly at Emma, who felt herself blushing. "I hope you won't think us rude if we leave you. Please stay and finish Mrs Norris's ginger cake or she is sure to be offended."

The Hopwoods left the room and the two were left standing awkwardly on either side of the fireplace. She noticed he had had his hair cut and beard trimmed. He looked quite presentable, she thought. Not handsome, but a pleasant face, especially when he smiled. They both stepped forward and opened their mouths to speak, then stopped and laughed.

"This is absurd!" He came to her and took her hand. "What a pair of schemers they are! I wonder who put them up to it? I hope it wasn't my mother – I should be so embarrassed if it was! Never mind! We're here together at last and I'm grateful for their scheming. I've longed to see you again – it's been torture with the snow, not hearing from you, Miss... Oh, may I call you Emma?"

"Of course you may, and I shall call you Alfred."

"Yes, please, and not Alfie. I can't bear it when my mother calls me that!"

She began to feel awkward holding his hand and gently released herself.

"Shall we sit down?" She sat down again beside the fire, but he seemed too restless to settle and quickly jumped up from his chair. He knelt in front of her and took her hand once more, looking intensely into her face. She could hardly hold his gaze and left her hand lying limply in his own.

"Emma! How wonderful to be able to call you that! I've dreamed of it many times and of this moment when I would hold your hand in mine."

She didn't know what to say. This wasn't how she had imagined things at all, not this *touching*, this intensity of feeling. She had dreamed of long conversations and of music – he playing, she singing. Of sitting in recitals. And maybe of walks in the countryside around his home, discussing nature or his business. But not this. He was too close. She felt a knot of anxiety building in the pit of her stomach.

Perhaps he sensed her discomfort, for, to her relief, he released her hand and sat back in the chair opposite. He continued to smile warmly and her composure slowly returned. She decided to turn the conversation to something practical and safe.

"I was sorry we weren't able to get to the recital. I love Bach's organ toccatas and preludes. The organist at my father's church often played them and I would sit and listen to him practising. I liked to be there on my own in the empty church, with the beautiful sound all around me."

"I was sorry, too. They are fine pieces. I've often wished I could play the organ. It has such majesty and power, quite unlike a piano."

"Oh, but you play the piano so well. The piece you played at the Rector's Christmas soirée was lovely. I wanted to tell you how much I enjoyed it, but it was difficult to get away from my party."

"Thank you. I'm glad you liked it…" He paused, running his hand through his hair, obviously wondering whether to speak or not. "Er…I hope…I hope you won't feel I'm speaking out of turn, but I, er…I felt that your mother was trying to stop us from talking to each other that evening…

I'm concerned that she may not approve of us seeing more of one another."

"Don't worry, Alfred. Mamma has some strange ideas sometimes, especially where my future is concerned, but she will be pleased that we have met, I'm sure."

"Oh good, good…I wouldn't like to go against her wishes." He leaned forward, looking intently into her eyes once more. She instinctively moved back into her chair, anxious that he was going to reach for her hand again. This time she realised that he had noticed her withdrawal. His eyes lost a little of their brightness and his smile faded momentarily. She hastily moved the conversation onto a positive note.

"I would like to attend another recital with you, if you hear of one nearby. Or perhaps we might ride out together one day, and you could show me the countryside around your home – when the weather is warmer, of course."

"I'd very much like that too. Will your mother want to accompany us, as a chaperone?"

"I shall ask her."

"May I write to you, meanwhile?"

"I hope that you will! And I'll write, too. And we shall see one another at church every Sunday – in the distance!"

"Yes, we will. Oh Emma…"

She stood up quickly. She couldn't bear any more of this intense feeling. It was too much…too soon. She forced her voice to sound bright.

"Well I think I must be getting back to Mamma now. I shall look forward to hearing from you."

She stepped towards the door before he could reach out for her hand and bowed, smiling as warmly as she could manage through the turmoil inside her.

"Goodbye, Alfred."

He smiled and said goodbye, but she couldn't help noticing his concerned look as she turned to leave. She hurried out of the front door and across the green, passing the cottage, where she could see the back of the Rector's head opposite her mother in the parlour, and climbing the steps to the schoolroom. There she sank onto the nearest bench and sat motionless, staring unseeing through the window. More than anything she was angry – angry with her own weakness. Until today he had seemed the nervous one, timid even, while she had been confident, in control of her feelings. Now their positions appeared reversed. It was ironic and very distressing.

After a long while she stood up, walked to the blackboard and began to rub away the arithmetic and writing left there at the end of last term. This new and unsettling anxiety was no reason to change her course. Perhaps it was how all women felt about getting married. Perhaps being close to a man was just something you had to gradually get used to. Her mother had once hinted darkly of an unpleasant side of married life. It wasn't important, she had said, just one of those things to put up with. So that's what she must do. Put up with it and smile. She picked up the poetry book on her desk and rifled through it. This would suffice – a fatuous ditty about snow, by someone she had never heard of. She squared her shoulders and began to write.

CHAPTER 17

The morning was overcast and dark. A biting wind blew unchecked along the station platform and through Cecily's cloak. She shivered, pulling it closer around her. Harry looked concerned.

"Do you want my coat round your shoulders, Cecy?"

She looked at him, her face pale, her eyes swollen from weeping, and tried to smile. At this moment she felt that he was only person in the world who really cared about her.

"I'll be alright, Harry, thank you. It can't be long now till the train, can it?"

"It's late already. Let's just go through all the arrangements again, shall we? Now what will you do at Rochester?"

"I'll look for the London, Chatham and Dover line office, buy a ticket to Whitstable and ask which platform I must go to."

"Yes, that's it…good. And what about at Whitstable?"

She drew a small piece of paper from her cloak pocket. "I've written it down here, look."

He took her hand and looked at her anxiously. "I do wish I could go with you, to see you safely there."

"I know you do, but it would've been too much money. The cart and my ticket must have taken more than my wages for this month, especially going second class."

"Well, old Roly owed Father a favour for some tailoring work he'd done, so the cart was free. But you have Mother to thank for the second class ticket. I know you think she doesn't care about you, but she was insistent. She was very worried that you might have caught a chill, going third."

Cecily was thoughtful. "I do wish I could have seen her and Father and the children before I left. It was all so sudden

– the new nurse coming, and me off, with hardly time to say goodbye to anyone."

"Aunt Ellen needs you there straight away. Her health has taken a turn for the worse, apparently. The doctor wrote and Mother didn't want to argue, though I know she would have liked to have seen you too. But I'm sure you'll be home to visit soon, Cecy. Now, are you sure you'll be all right?"

"Yes, thank you, I'll get there sooner or later. I'm quite grown up and capable now, you know."

"I can see that. You've become a real young woman and no mistake. But I didn't mean so much the journey, as how you're feeling. I don't like to see you so upset…"

She looked down at her boots for a long while and then up into her brother's anxious face, her eyes brimming.

"Let's not talk about it now, or I'll get upset again. I'll write to you, though, to tell you that I've arrived safely and you *will* write to me, won't you, Harry? You hardly wrote at all when I was at the Rectory."

"I know – I don't find it easy to put my thoughts down, like you do, Cecy, but I will try, I promise."

"Don't *try*, Harry – just do it!"

He laughed and put his arm around her shoulder. "That's more like my Cecy – bossy and cross! Oh, I can see smoke, now – the train's coming. Let me have your bag and I'll carry it into the carriage for you."

The two were soon enveloped in a cloud of smoke and steam as the train pulled into the small station. They looked for a second class carriage and he followed her in. She found an empty window seat, finally losing her battle with her tears as he put her carpetbag down and kissed her goodbye. She looked steadfastly out of the window, anxious to hide her misery as others entered the carriage. Harry stood on the edge of the platform, his smile full of loving concern, waving as the train rolled slowly and noisily out of the station. He soon disappeared behind smoke and tears, but she kept her eyes fixed to the same spot, as if she could still see him, long after the station had vanished from sight.

All the events of the morning went through her mind. She saw the children, well now, happily waving goodbye, completely oblivious of the fact that their Ce*cly* would never be coming back to read them a story or tuck them into bed. Edie and Mrs Norris both crying into their hankies. The Reverend shaking her hand solemnly and wishing her well. Mrs Hopwood looking uncomfortable. And now Harry… gone. She had no idea when she would see any of them again. Tears rolled down her face and she made no effort to check them.

After a while the gathering speed of the train and the fast-changing views of the countryside began to filter through her grief and into her consciousness. She blew her nose and dried her eyes and started to look properly out of the window. She had never been on a train before. It would have been far too costly for them all to go on an outing, though her father had once taken a train to Hastings and had returned telling exciting stories of fast, noisy engines, tunnels, bridges and the sea. Despite her sadness she gradually began to enjoy the sensation of travelling fast and of having so many different things to see. It didn't frighten her as she had thought it might. If only she was looking forward to arriving at her destination, it might be quite exciting.

At the thought of Whitstable a sickening dread filled her stomach. She looked at the bag of cheese sandwiches Mrs Norris had made for her early this morning, but couldn't face eating. The cook would be upset with her for leaving them. "You must eat to keep your strength up, Cecily," she could hear her say, and "It's a sin to waste good food." Out of respect for the woman she had lately grown very fond of, she forced herself to eat one sandwich. After a while she felt less queasy and ate another and another, until the bag was empty. When the train finally arrived at Rochester, her stomach had settled and her head cleared, so that she was able to negotiate the change of line without too much difficulty.

❧

Just after two o'clock the London, Chatham and Dover train rolled into Whitstable station. Cecily struggled down the carriage steps with her heavy bag and followed the stream of passengers through the ticket office, out into the town. The dark clouds had lifted and a weak sun was breaking through, brightening the busy street scene in front of her, but not her mood. She stopped outside the station to retrieve her instructions. Nerves were threatening to get the better of her once more. She took a deep breath. The air smelt different. There was a strange new tang, quite unlike the smells she was used to. Perhaps it was the sea. Her spirits lifted a little as she headed down the High Street, past numerous small shops and into Harbour Street where her aunt lived. With a name like that she guessed the sea could not be far away. She promised herself she would go looking for it soon.

Finding the small house was easy, sandwiched as it was between the draper and the butcher. Its front door opened directly onto the street. After knocking three times and waiting for several minutes with no reply, she began to feel awkward standing conspicuously alone on the busy pavement, her bag at her feet. Perhaps she had the wrong house. She checked her instructions. No, this was definitely 23, Harbour Street. But where was Aunt Ellen? She didn't think the old lady would have gone out – she knew what time Cecily was due to arrive. Besides, Harry had said she had been ill recently. Even if she wasn't at home, the servant girl would surely answer the door. She tried looking in the window to the left of the door, but the heavy curtains were pulled almost shut. It all seemed very strange. When her fourth attempt to raise the household failed, she tried the door handle. To her surprise it wasn't locked and she found herself looking down a dark, narrow hallway. She called out. Silence again. Reluctantly, she stepped inside.

The hall was dingy. The once-green wallpaper was turning brown in patches. There were no pictures, only a vase of dead flowers on the shelf below the mirror. She peered into the room to her left. A musty smell hit her – the smell of a room left unused. She wrinkled her nose. Nothing to see here but the dark outlines of furniture. Leaving her bag, she walked down the corridor to another, smaller room, obviously the dining room. Pale sunshine filtered through the window onto a round table in the centre and narrow sideboard against the far wall, each adorned with a vase of dead flowers. On the mantelpiece an old clock, stopped at half past eight, stood silent between two more vases. She walked round the room, her fingers gently brushing the brown stems, curled black leaves and shrivelled blooms, many of which had fallen onto the surfaces and floor. The scene puzzled and disturbed her. Motes of dust and pollen swirled in the sunshine, making her sneeze. She looked through the window into the garden. It was just possible to make out a central path, leading to the privy at the bottom, between a tangle of grass, weeds and winter-brown brambles, but here and there she could see the remains of cultivated plants – roses and several others she didn't know the names of – with a small patch of snowdrops and a Christmas rose blooming bravely in the midst of all the decay. Someone in the house loved flowers, that was clear, but why keep them when they were dead?

She turned away from the window and left the room, finding herself in a tiny scullery and, beyond that, a small kitchen. Everything here was clean and tidy, the wooden tabletop looked recently scrubbed and the range was warm. In the middle of the table a piece of paper stood propped against a teapot. She picked it up:

"To who it may consern.

I cant stay no mor. Sorry.

Jane Hemsley"

She stood for several minutes, the paper in her hand, trying to understand the peculiar situation in which she found herself. Jane must be the servant – *was* the servant – but why had she left? What was going on here? Suddenly the ceiling shook with several loud knocks. She jumped in fright and clutched her hand to her heart. Aunt Ellen! With her pulse racing she returned to the hall and looked up the steep, narrow staircase to the landing above. Every part of her body shouted at her to pick up her bag and run from the house. But where would she go? She knew no one in Whitstable. She had only a shilling to buy stamps and paper to write home – certainly not enough to get her back to Wittenbury. The banging began again, this time accompanied by a thin, querulous voice:

"Jane! Jane! Where the blazes has that girl got to? Jane!"

She took a deep breath and began to climb the stairs, calling out as she went.

"Aunt Ellen, it's me, Cecily. I've come to stay with you."

"Who? I can't hear you! Come up here this minute, Jane. You said you would be here when I woke up. Where are you?"

Cecily reached the landing. The voice came from the room ahead of her, its door slightly ajar. She knocked hesitantly.

"Come in! Come in! For goodness sake hurry up, girl."

She pushed open the door and stood, pale and trembling in the doorway.

"Hello, Aunt Ellen. I'm Cecily."

Her first impression was of standing at the foot of an enormous bed, but she quickly realised that it wasn't the bed that was large, but her aunt who was tiny. The old lady lay facing the door, her deeply wrinkled, colourless face and white night cap the only parts of her visible amidst a heap of pillows and green shawl. She peered towards the door, her eyes screwed up into countless creases, her voice high and agitated.

"Cecily? Who's Cecily? Come over here, girl, I can't see you."

Cecily stepped forward gingerly and stood at the bedside. A gnarled hand flew out from under the shawl, grabbed the walking stick which lay on top of the covers and waved it at her.

"But you're not Jane! Where's Jane?"

"I think she may have left, Aunt."

"Speak up, girl. I can't hear you."

Cecily leant a little closer to the bed and raised her voice. "I think Jane may have left. There was a note in the kitchen."

"Left? What do you mean left?"

"I think she's gone, Aunt. Look."

Cecily tried to show her aunt the piece of paper, but the old lady pushed it impatiently aside.

"Oh I can't see that – take it away! And who are you, anyway? What are you doing here?"

"I'm Cecily, your great niece, Aunt Emily. I'm Richard's daughter – your nephew Richard. You wrote to him saying you would have me to stay. You said I could be a companion for you in exchange for my board."

"Richard you say? Ah, now, he's a lovely boy, though it was a pity he took to the drink. But they say he's a reformed character now. I didn't much like his wife, I have to say. But who are you? Where's Jane? I need her to come up right now!"

Cecily was at a loss. She tried once more.

"Jane can't come, Aunt Ellen. She's gone. But I'm here. Is there anything I can do to help you?"

"Oh I don't know. Everything's in such a muddle. I haven't been well, you know. Who are you, anyway?"

"I'm Cecily, Aunt. Shall I get you a cup of tea?"

"Tea? Is it teatime? Oh…I don't know what day it is, even. What day is it today?"

"It's Monday, Aunt, and it's tea time. I'll go and make some, shall I?"

"Some? What are you on about, girl? I can't understand you. Speak up for goodness sake! And don't call me Aunt – I don't know you!"

Cecily began to panic. She felt like a fly caught in the web of the old lady's confusion.

"I'll go and make some tea, Miss Carpenter, shall I?" She started towards the door, but stopped dead as her aunt let out a terrible screech:

"No! No! Come back here! No you can't go! They all go…they all go. They just want me to die – I know they do. They want to throw me away like the flowers, you see…but I shan't let them, no I shan't. Oh dear…but I'm not well. I haven't been well at all. And I tell them to get the doctor, but they won't, they just want to throw me away, that's what it is, like the flowers, you know…" She stopped, looking up at Cecily with watery, red-rimmed eyes.

"Do you want me to get the doctor, Aunt…I mean Miss Carpenter?" Cecily made a slight movement towards the door again.

"NO! I SAID YOU WERE TO STAY! DIDN'T YOU HEAR ME GIRL?"

Cecily reeled from the force of the old lady's voice, from the shock of her face, contorted and purple with rage, as if from a physical blow. She stood, helpless and shaking, not daring to speak or move, as her aunt tried to sit up in bed, coughing violently with anger and effort. Eventually the spasm passed and she sank back against the pillows once more, her breathing laboured and rasping, her eyes tightly closed. Several minutes passed in which neither spoke nor moved. Then the wrinkled eyelids fluttered and Cecily found herself looking into the face of a different person. Those eyes – monstrous, terrifying, a few minutes ago – were frail and pleading, almost childlike now.

"Would you sit here and read to me…what's your name? Are you a new servant?"

Cecily's voice shook. She felt near to tears. "I'm…I'm Cecily, ma'am."

"Please sit down, whoever you are, and read to me from that book there." Aunt Ellen pointed to a small volume on the chair beside the bed. "He liked flowers, you know, Mr… Mr…Oh! I can't remember his name. But I know *he* wouldn't have thrown them away, I'm sure he wouldn't. He loved them, you see."

Cecily picked up the book and sank onto the chair, grateful to take the weight off her legs, which were still trembling. She opened it at the bookmark and began to read:

> "I wandered lonely as a cloud
> That floats on high o'er vales and hills,
> When all at once I saw a crowd,
> A host of golden daffodils;
> Beside the lake, beneath the trees,
> Fluttering and dancing in the breeze…"

The old woman closed her eyes once more, and was silent as Cecily finished the poem and began another. The tiny figure gradually slid down the bed, disappearing almost completely amongst the bedclothes. Within five minutes Cecily's voice was drowned by the sound of heaving snores. She closed the book carefully and tiptoed from the room.

CHAPTER 18

The light was fading rapidly outside the kitchen window. She guessed it must be about four o'clock. After creeping back downstairs she had found the coal hole, brought coal in for the range and made herself a cup of tea. But that was all she had managed. There was food left in the larder, but she couldn't eat. She crept out to the privy, opening and shutting doors with exquisite care, terrified that she might wake her aunt and provoke another hideous scene. Then she sat at the table, head in hands, struggling in vain to get her sobbing breath under control, her cup of tea growing cold beside her.

She tried to think of some of Mrs Norris's wise words, or even her mother's: "No use crying over spilt milk," or "Every cloud has a silver lining," or "Things are never as bad as they seem," she could hear them say, her mother's voice impatient and cross, Mrs Norris's kind, but equally firm. But they didn't know what the old lady was like, how confused she was and how terrifying when she got into a rage. If her parents *had* known, surely they wouldn't have allowed her to come? There again, Aunt Ellen had always been a difficult woman, short-tempered and intolerant, with a wicked tongue. They had known *that* and still sent her. However hard she tried, she couldn't accept that they cared about her. Her mother had wanted her to go second class, out of the cold, so Harry said. So perhaps she cared for her body, as all mothers had to do. But she didn't care for *her*, for her feelings. And her father was just weak. As a small child she had adored him in his quiet gentleness. She remembered how she had loved to sit on his lap, stroking his beard and tracing the veins on the back of his hands with her fingers. But now she saw him differently. He could have stood up to her mother and kept her at home, but he hadn't. They were both to blame. She didn't know whether she was more angry now, or sad. She fingered the note. She was just desperate to escape, like that lucky Jane.

The room was becoming quite dark. With an enormous effort she roused herself to search for lamps and matches while she could still see a little. As she was lighting the lamp on the mantle above the range, a loud knock sent a jolt of panic through her body. Oh God. *She* had woken up. It would all start again and she couldn't face it. She stood still, the taper still alight in her hand, waiting, hardly daring to breathe, hoping that, if she made no noise, the house might go quiet again. But another knock came, louder this time, more insistent. She realised with relief that it didn't come from upstairs, but from the hallway. Picking up the lamp, she hurried to the front door, wiping her eyes and nose as she went.

A short, middle-aged man in black top hat and coat, a large leather bag at his feet, stood on the doorstep. He lifted his hat, smoothing a few wisps of greying hair back across his scalp.

"Good evening. You must be Miss Carpenter. I'm Doctor West."

His voice was cultured, almost haughty, his appearance an odd mixture of expensive, stylish clothes and distinctly unattractive features. She felt shabby in her travel dress and hoped the darkness would hide her red eyes and blotchy cheeks. She stood aside for him. He put his bag down in the hall next to hers, abandoned since her arrival, and followed her to the kitchen.

"I think I probably owe you an explanation, Miss Carpenter. I suggest you light another lamp and we sit down for a moment."

She felt his small, dark eyes on her as she carried out his instructions. His angular features were accentuated in the lamp light, giving him a disconcertingly foxy look. She looked at him warily as he spoke.

"As you know, your mother wrote asking if you could come to live here in exchange for some light duties. At the time Miss Carpenter senior was already too ill to reply. I felt it was necessary for young Jane to have some assistance, so I wrote back on behalf of your aunt to ask that you should come as soon as possible. Since then, her state of mind has deteriorated significantly, as you have probably discovered for yourself, though her lungs were somewhat improved when I came yesterday…Where is Jane, by the way? Is she upstairs?"

Cecily gestured towards the note. "She's left, sir."

"Oh…" He picked up the piece of paper, looked out of the window into the darkness, frowning and tapping his finger on the table, then got up abruptly. "I see. Well, I can't say I'm surprised. Now Miss Carpenter will have to have a nurse, whether she likes it or not. Either that, or I'll be forced to have her committed." He picked up one of the lamps and left the room with no further explanation. She could soon hear movement and voices from the room above. She sat, motionless, only stirring once to check the range and shovel in more coal. A deep instinct for survival told her that she must stay warm, if nothing else. Twenty minutes later the doctor stood in the kitchen doorway, bag in hand.

"I'm leaving now. There's no immediate danger. A nurse will be with you in the morning. You'll have to manage as best you can until then. I don't think she'll trouble you much. I've given her a sedative and she'll not need anything more to eat or drink tonight. She might wake for the commode, that's all. Follow the nurse's instructions when she comes. And there's money for food in the brown stone jar in the larder. I leave a small sum there each week from an amount Miss Carpenter entrusted to me when she first became ill. I'm sure it will be more than adequate for your needs. I shall call later in the week. Good evening to you."

"But, sir…" He gave her no chance to reply or to ask any of the questions which were whirling in her head, but strode from the room. She heard the bang of the front door with the sickening realisation that she was alone in the house with her aunt once more. Still, at least she had stopped crying. That was something achieved. And he had said that her aunt was unlikely to wake. And a nurse was coming tomorrow. And – she continued to clutch at cheering straws – perhaps her aunt might die soon, so that she could go home. What a truly dreadful thought. She apologised to God for it immediately. In any case, the doctor had said her aunt's lungs were getting *better*. She sighed. No, she must resign herself to a long stay, take herself in hand and try to make the best of things, as the mother and cook in her head were urging her to do. Still too cross to listen to her mother's voice, she had to admit that Mrs Norris *had* cared, and her words of wisdom usually proved to be right.

She remembered the calming effect of the cook's sandwiches earlier in the day and decided to find some food and make a fresh cup of tea. This time she would make herself eat, whether she wanted to or not. That done, she did indeed feel stronger, strong enough to climb the dark stairs to search out a room to sleep in. Of the two remaining bedrooms, she knew the bigger would be needed for the nurse. The other was only just big enough for a bed and washstand, but had the advantage of being further from her aunt's room and of overlooking the garden. The air in the room struck damp and cold, with the same musty, unused smell as the parlour. She carefully carried glowing coals upstairs from the range and lit a fire in the tiny grate. The room warmed up quickly and began to seem almost homely once the bed was aired and her two precious books placed on the mantelpiece. She banked up the range downstairs, bringing more coal up for her fire and a jug of water for the basin. There was no way of knowing the time. Every clock in the house, including the one on her own mantelpiece, had stopped. Well it didn't matter. She was more than ready for bed and for some Mrs Gaskell.

A lump came to her throat once more as she found the place that she and Edith had reached in the story. The attic room at the Rectory suddenly filled her mind, clear in every detail as if she were still there, Edith lying in the bed beside her, snoring softly, and the skylight above her head shining with stars. How she longed to be there! She had been such a baby when she had first arrived in that cold room, crying and complaining, yet how much better it was than this sad, lonely situation. She felt tears welling in her eyes and brushed them impatiently away. No, she wouldn't start crying again. That wouldn't help her in the slightest. She forced her eyes and mind to focus on the words in front of her and to read and re-read them until they began to filter into her consciousness. Within five minutes she was deep in the story; within ten she was drifting into sleep. She extinguished the lamp, pulled the bedclothes high around her neck and let out a long, deep sigh.

❧

A child was crying. She could hear it in her sleep. But it couldn't be one of the twins – it was too far away. It must be Ernie. He was ill. Of course he was! How could she have forgotten? Panic overwhelmed her. If she didn't get to him quickly he might choke to death. She *must* wake up and go to him. Her sleep pressed down on her, a huge weight of water drowning her. She fought to wake, to take a breath, crying out in terror as she felt herself dying, and woke, gasping and shaking. The darkness in the room surrounded her like a blanket, obscuring everything. For several seconds she had no idea where she was. Then she heard it again – a high pitched wailing: "Help me, help me. Please won't somebody help me? Oh, why don't they come? Please! Please help me!"

Her aunt! She sprang out of bed, fumbling for matches and the lamp and pulling her thick shawl around her shoulders. Across the landing the cries began again. She opened the door of her aunt's room. A tiny, hunched figure stood beside the bed, one hand leaning heavily on a violently wobbling stick, the other clutching the back of the chair. She looked as if she might crumple to the floor at any moment. Cecily hurried across the room to help, all fear forgotten at the pitiful sight in front of her. She realised immediately that her aunt had been trying to reach the commode. Her nightdress was soaked, a large dark puddle spread around her feet, and she was whimpering now, and shivering, apparently oblivious of Cecily's presence. Cecily put an arm around her shoulder to steady her.

"Let me help you." She hastily cleared the books and other debris from the chair and guided her aunt to sit down. "I'll find you a dry nightdress before you get any colder."

The old lady looked at her with tearful, childlike eyes. "I'm sorry…I couldn't help it…I don't know how it happened. Mother will be so angry that I've wet myself! You won't tell her, will you, Jane?" She began to cough then, a terrible racking cough that left her heaving for breath and slumped so far over that Cecily feared she would slip from the chair. She must get her dressed and back into bed as quickly as possible. After checking the bed, which was still dry, thank goodness, she mopped the floor with a towel and searched in the chest for drawers and a nightdress. Her aunt had stopped coughing and was watching her, the small, white face exhausted, defeated.

"Let me help you take this off now, Aunt. I've found you a nice dry nightdress to put on." They struggled together for several minutes. The old lady tried to co-operate, but seemed unable to co-ordinate her arms and legs, so that Cecily had to dress and undress her like an overgrown baby. She even found herself talking as she had done to the children.

"There we are. That feels better, doesn't it? We need to get you back in bed, now. Can you stand up?"

A barely perceptible shake of the head told her no. She was forced to heave and push the awkward, surprisingly heavy body back beneath the bedclothes. It distressed her when her aunt cried out, knowing she was hurting her, but there was nothing else she could do without help and the old woman didn't resist. When her head hit the pillows, she closed her eyes and immediately began to snore. Cecily picked up the sodden clothes and towel and escaped from the room. She stood outside the door and shuddered. If this is what happened when you got old, then she hoped she would die young.

Sleep would be impossible now – better to get washed and dressed and go downstairs. By the time she had put the wet things into soak in the scullery and sorted out the range, the sky was beginning to lighten outside the window. A robin called from a tree in the garden, the only bird she recognised among the unfamiliar cries of the gulls. Sounds of morning life drifted from nearby streets. She sat down to a breakfast of bread, jam and tea and had to admit that she was feeling better for her sleep. The nurse would be coming soon. At the very least she would be company and would carry the responsibility for her aunt's care.

The sight that met her eyes when she opened the door at 8 o'clock was exactly what she had been hoping for. In the doorway stood a short, round, dumpling of a woman with wisps of curly, grey hair escaping from beneath her hat, fat, red cheeks and smiling eyes. She was breathing heavily and struggled with her bag into the hallway.

"Hello, duck. You must be Cecily. The doctor's told me all about you. Be a dear, will you, and take this bag. I don't think I can walk another step! I'm Mrs French, by the way.

Mr French's passed away and the less said about him, the better! Now, how about a nice cup of tea?" She peered down the hallway. "Where's the kitchen? I'm parched!"

Cecily led the way, hardly able to lift the bag, which clinked with every step. Bottles of medicine, she guessed. She settled Mrs French at the kitchen table and, at her request, made tea and toast. They exchanged a few pleasantries and she watched, fascinated, as the nurse slurped and gobbled her way through a huge breakfast. As she was sucking the last of the tea off the saucer, a loud banging above their heads made her jump and spill it down her ample front.

"My Lord! What on earth's that? Now look what I've done!"

"That's Miss Carpenter, Mrs French. She'll be wanting her breakfast, I expect."

The nurse flapped her hands at Cecily. "Oh, you'll have to see to her! Look at me! Where's the scullery? I need to wash this off my apron before it stains."

Cecily hesitated by the door. This wasn't quite how she had imagined her nurse. Her nurse would take charge whatever the circumstances, dealing efficiently and compassionately with the old lady, leaving Cecily with the light domestic duties her mother had requested. The real nurse looked at her, still smiling, but with just a hint of irritation in her eyes.

"Well, dear? The scullery?"

"Oh sorry, it's just through here." As she showed the way, the banging started up again, with shouting now, for Jane.

"Go on then, young Cecily! She's waiting for you. I'll be up in a while. But I'm sure you can sort her out. You seem a capable enough girl to me." Mrs French disappeared into the scullery, tutting and wiping her front as she went. Cecily left the room and climbed the stairs with heavy legs.

❧

Late in the afternoon she stood on the shingle at the edge of the water, the sun low in the sky to her left, and gazed out to sea. Behind her a long shingle road stretched back to the shore. She had walked out along it, fascinated by this pathway into the ocean, delighted by the sharp smell of the air, the cold wind in her face and the wide, glittering view. The difficulties of her day were wiped from her mind for a few precious minutes as she watched and listened to the water behind her and in front, the waves rolling towards her and past her in a continuous, rhythmic line. Once or twice the spray wetted her dress, making her jump back, laughing, completely oblivious of the cold discomfort round her legs. Most of the time she was utterly still, the sound of the shingle moving in the waves soothing her like a lullaby.

She didn't know how long she had stood there and would have stayed longer but for a shout from the beach which made her turn to look back. A man was waving. She could only just hear his voice above the wind and waves.

"Oi! You out there! Don't you realise the tide's coming in?"

As she gazed back along the shingle pathway she could see that it had become narrower and that more waves were breaking over it. Picking up her skirts with one hand and her basket of provisions with the other, she stumbled back over the stones. She was farther out than she had realised. By the time she reached the shore she was panting heavily, her shoes soaked by the rising water. The man looked at her disapprovingly.

"You need t' be more careful, young lady. You'll get awful wet walking on the Street at this time o' day!" He walked away, shaking his head, but she stayed looking out to sea, transfixed as the pathway slowly disappeared under the waves in the fading light. Eventually the cold, wet and gathering gloom registered in her brain. She shivered and set off along the beach towards Harbour Street. She was tired now and the walk back, which she had barely noticed as she had set out earlier full of excitement at her first sight of the sea, was a long one.

An unpleasant feeling of foreboding grew as she drew nearer to the house. Disturbing scenes from her day crowded, unwelcome, back into her mind. The all-capable, kindly nurse emerging from her room only when absolutely necessary for cups of tea and lunch, and to bathe the old lady and put her on the commode, her fat cheeks flushed, her eyes unnaturally bright and the smell of her breath reminding Cecily strangely of her father when she was smaller. Her aunt, lying in her room, either confused mad, or shrieking mad, or like a desperately unhappy child, whining and crying. She herself running up and down the stairs, in and out of rooms, until her head pounded with stress and exhaustion. The only bright spot had been clearing the house of dead flowers, replacing them with snowdrops and blooms from the Christmas rose in the garden, some for her aunt's room, but some for herself, too. She had ignored the banging and shouting from upstairs for a few minutes while she cleaned and polished the dining room furniture, arranging the flowers on the table with a feeling of guilty satisfaction. Later, after lunch, when a chorus of snoring had greeted her on the landing, she had seized the opportunity to slip away, her excuse being the need to buy food, her real need being to escape the suffocating atmosphere and breathe the sea air.

It was almost dark by the time she arrived back. Standing for a moment on the doorstep, steeling herself to go in, she thought perhaps she could still hear the soothing sound of the waves dragging through the shingle, back and forth. Whatever happened in this horrible adventure, she had at least seen the sea. She had walked right into the middle of it. No one would believe her at home. But she had.

As she stepped into the hallway a terrible sound swept away the remains of her composure with the force of a huge breaker. From the open door of her aunt's room came the angry voice of the nurse, shouting words Cecily had never heard before, obscenities she assumed, followed by high pitched screams from the old lady. Her heart raced in alarm, but she was not altogether surprised. As the day had gone on she had been dismayed to watch as the nurse had handled her aunt increasingly roughly, as if she were an object to be dealt with and put out of sight as fast as possible. Her growing suspicion that the smiles and endearments were a veneer spread thinly over a hard heart were now sadly confirmed. She understood all too well how irritating and difficult the old lady was, but she had quickly come to feel about her as she used to feel about the frogs and mice her younger brother and his friends would catch and torture. She didn't like them – they made her shudder – but neither could she watch them being tormented. They were small and helpless and she felt compelled to rescue them and set them free. She dropped the basket of food in the hallway, gathered her skirts and ran up the stairs two at a time.

CHAPTER 19

Alfred stared across the dingy room. The beer house was almost empty, just one other pair of men sitting quietly beside the fireplace, smoking pipes and playing cards. When he and George wanted company they went to the Half Moon, a much livelier, more salubrious establishment at the other end of the village. But they liked to come here for a talk – you could guarantee it would be quiet. Tonight the poor light, shabby furniture and filthy floor suited his mood. He was struggling to find the right words and George was waiting patiently. Why could he never explain his feelings, even to himself? He toyed with his glass and took another mouthful of beer before deciding to avoid the real issue and talk about something safe instead.

"How's business, then, George?"

George scratched his head and gave a rueful smile. "Oh, fair to middlin' I should say."

"Only fair to middlin'?"

"Well you know what it's like working with yer old man, don't you, Alf? 'E 'as 'is ideas and I 'ave mine and we don't always see eye to eye. And 'is 'ands are really playin' 'im up, but 'e won't admit it. I see 'im when 'e thinks I'm not lookin', rubbin' 'em and tryin' to straighten 'is fingers. But they ain't goin' to straighten, are they? They're as bent as the nails I used to make when I was a nipper. And it makes 'im slow. Sometimes it's 'ard to get through the work. I want 'im to 'and over his 'ammers and let me get an apprentice in, but there's no movin' 'im at the moment. Stubborn as one of Farmer Trench's mules, 'e is. I shouldn't complain, I suppose. 'E's been a good dad to me and as like as not I'd be just the same in 'is shoes."

"Stubborn as a mule? Yes, I'm sure you would, George!"

"All right, all right! That's enough of me, any'ow. What 'bout you? 'Ow's business at Alfred Nicholson and Company?"

Alfred smiled, feeling on safe ground. "We've had a good week recruiting in Wittenbury."

"Oh yes?"

"Yes, I'm really pleased. I think we've got a good group of men together. I'm particularly excited about one young man – a brickie. He's a really bright spark. I think he'll make a good foreman with a bit more experience."

"That's good. You'll need a good team. It's quite a job, ain't it? Don't it worry you, takin' on that amount o' work?"

"Yes, of course, but I think we've got it all in hand. It's a lot of work, yes, but to be honest it's the least of my worries."

"Ahh!" George raised his eyebrows. "I didn't think you'd dragged me out to this 'ole to talk business. Come on, then, spit it out. Would Miss Fielding 'ave anythin' to do with it, by any chance?"

Alfred looked embarrassed. "I think I may have really upset her, George. She hurried out of that room as if I had the pox!"

George frowned. "I'm a bit lost 'ere, Alf. What exactly are we talkin' 'bout?"

Alfred had forgotten that his friend knew nothing of his meeting with Emma at the vicarage, nearly two weeks ago now. The memory of her anxious face as she sat opposite him, and of her cold, limp hand in his, was so vivid that it seemed like only yesterday. He tried to explain what had happened, finishing lamely, "I don't know what I did wrong, but it haunts me. I've written to her several times and she's replied, and on the surface everything seems to be all right, but somehow I know it's not. It's like torture, George, it really is!"

George raised his eyes to the ceiling. "Good God, man,

157

'ave another beer and stop talkin' like a woman! 'Torture'…
whatever next?" He called for more beers and downed his
own in a few gulps, pushing the other jug towards Alfred.
"Get that down you and listen to me, mate. I think you've
been tryin' to run before you can walk, as they say. I know
you 'ave deep feelins for 'er, but it's much too early for all
that sort o' thing. 'Oldin' 'er 'and? No wonder she took
fright! Some women just don't feel the same as we do, Alf,
and she may be one of 'em. They need to keep their distance.
I can't say as I understand 'em completely. My Sarah was a bit
like it in the beginnin', frettin' 'bout 'er reputation and
insistin' on Phoebe bein' with us whenever we walked out.
She's different now – now we've set a date. I'm sure your
Emma'll be the same, though she's quite a lady o' course –
they're more delicate in their feelins, or so I'm told."

"But what can I do? It's happened now. Do you think
she'll ever trust me again?"

"You'll need to give it time, but it'll come out right in
the end, I'm sure. What you need now is a nice, safe outin',
with plenty o' chit chat and absolutely no touchin'!
Something musical if she likes that."

"Yes, she does. They're putting on the organ recital again
this Saturday. Should I ask her, do you think, and her mother,
as a chaperone? She's written to say that her mother is
pleased that we shall be walking out now, though I'd swear
she didn't like me."

"Sounds perfect to me. An old lady's just what y' need to
cool yer passion!"

Alfred leaned across the table, grinning sheepishly at his
friend. "Thanks, George. I don't know what I'd do without
your common sense. This courting business is a nightmare for
a clumsy idiot like me!"

"Glad to be o' service, my friend. Anytime you need
Aunty George's advice, just let me know." He stood and
clapped Alfred on the back. "It's a bit late for you to call on

'er now, but you can drop 'er a note. Let's go 'ome and we'll find you some paper. We're makin' quite an 'abit of this, ain't we? Perhaps I'll set meself up in business. Let's see, 'Forge Romance' I'll call it – 'Advice and love letters from George, our expert in all matters pertainin' to romance. Very competitive rates.' The girls'll love it – an endless source o' gossip!"

The playground behind the schoolhouse was surrounded by a wall just tall enough to thwart most attempts by small boys to climb it. The surface of the ground was packed mud covered with a layer of loose grit. After rain it was covered in muddy puddles. In the dry it was slippery, the grit lethal to knees and hands alike. Today there were patches of frost and ice still unmelted in the shadows. Emma stood shivering by the schoolhouse door. The sun was weak and the wind icy, blowing through her shawl. She watched the children, seemingly oblivious of the cold and all happily occupied for once. The older girls were playing hopscotch in their half of the yard. The little girls had tried to join in, but had retreated to a sheltered corner to play clapping games when it was obvious they were not to be included. The older boys were rolling hoops. Bobby Bentley, a small, unhealthy child with a deformed leg, was crouching on the ground, apparently keeping a tally of chalk marks on a large stone as boys rolled their hoops from the schoolhouse to touch the wall on the far side of the playground. Cheers went up for each successful attempt. Small boys rushed after stray hoops when they threatened to veer into the girls' area.

Despite the cold, it was a relief to be out of the schoolroom and she was inclined to let them have a few minutes longer as they were playing so well today. It wasn't always such a tranquil scene. The boys would fight frequently.

All their disputes seemed to end in brawling. She only intervened if it became serious, or too many began to join in. Then she would wade into the middle of them, shouting and waving her cane until they stopped. The girls' disagreements seldom became physical, but they would often fall out with one another. One minute they would be walking arm in arm, smiling and laughing, the next standing in an angry huddle, comforting some weeping child, and glaring hatefully at the alleged persecutor. They knew better than to seek help from her. She couldn't abide tale-telling and wasn't willing to waste her precious time and energy sorting out their trivial difficulties. Much better for them to deal with their own problems. That's what everyone had to do in the end, after all.

She watched as several children wandered miserably on their own, or huddled by a wall, trying to look inconspicuous. They were always there, utterly rejected by the mob: the strange-looking, like little Janet Gresham, whose eyes were so far adrift from one another that it was impossible to know how to look at her; and the stupid, like Percy Trench, a huge lump of a boy who could barely speak, let alone read or write, and who spent most of his time on the dunce's stool, much to the other children's amusement. It was sad to see them, so isolated and miserable, but that was life, wasn't it? She couldn't change it for them. She had to try to teach them, which was quite difficult enough. The prospect of producing a deformed or mentally abnormal child herself made her shudder. She would rather stay childless. In fact she would rather stay childless full stop.

At the thought of having her own children, she remembered Alfred and the invitation which had arrived yesterday evening, for herself and her mother to join him at the long-delayed organ recital. Its arrival had sent her mother bustling excitedly to her room to begin planning her outfit. The transformation in her since the Rector's visit had been astonishing. Now she had nothing but praise for Alfred, referring to him as that "pleasant young gentleman of yours". She herself was pleased, but not excited. Since their meeting at the Rectory she had been left with a vague unease in the pit of her stomach, which wouldn't leave her, however sternly she talked to herself about the necessity of this marriage and the good nature of the man whose bride she hoped to be. She had decided her only course was to ignore her feelings and hope they would resolve themselves in time. To make decisions, or change them, on the basis of one's emotions was childish, as childish as the scenes she saw played out in front of her on the playground each day.

Her feet and hands were now so cold they were going numb. She picked up the heavy hand bell at her feet. At its first notes the little ones obediently ran to her, standing in two silent lines in front of her. The rest of the children followed at a slightly slower pace, lips sealed, watching her warily. All apart from Charlotte and Eleanor Adams, the blacksmith's daughters. Ever since school had reopened after the snow, the pair of them had been difficult. Charlotte, a blonde haired beauty with blue eyes which flashed with temper, would be leaving in the summer and had obviously decided she had no further need of school or her teacher. Her rebellion had escalated beyond contemptuous looks, smirks and poor work now. Twice she had been openly defiant and Emma had been forced to cane her to make her comply. Eleanor, only a year younger, and in appearance as similar as a twin, worshipped and copied her sister, her behaviour gradually slipping with Charlotte's from model pupil to sulky rebel. The two girls stood in the far corner of the playground, whispering behind their hands, pretending they hadn't heard the summons. She felt her anger rising and forced herself to sound icily calm as she called across to them.

"Eleanor Adams, Charlotte Adams, line up immediately. How dare you keep us all waiting?"

Charlotte looked across to her and rolled her eyes, then went back to her conversation.

The children at the front of the line were distracted by something behind Emma. One began tugging at her skirts.

"Miss, Miss, there's someone…"

She cuffed the small child across the top of the head, silencing him abruptly, while never taking her eyes from the defiant pair. Being forced into such a humiliating position by common girls made her seethe. She sent one of the infants for the cane. The rest of the children were motionless, utterly silent, every pair of eyes fixed on the sisters. She spoke quietly, her voice carrying easily across the playground in the stillness.

"You will line up now, girls, or I will cane you." Eleanor looked at her sister anxiously. Charlotte shrugged and made no move. Eleanor hesitated, then walked slowly to the line and stood behind her classmates, her face suddenly scarlet and her eyes bright with tears. Her older sister stared defiantly back at her teacher.

"Get over here, girl, and hold your hands out." The child didn't move. Emma's hands began to shake as she gripped the cane behind her back. If she was forced to cross the playground to carry out the punishment, she would have lost, and every child in the school would know it. Her anger and anxiety pushed her on beyond her common sense. She spoke in a voice hardly louder than a whisper,

"Very well. If you refuse to move, I shall send for your father and have him remove you from the school. For good."

As soon as the last two words were out of her mouth a hot wave of panic swept over her. What was she saying? She had no right to permanently remove a child from the school! Only a member of the Board could do that. In a disciplinary emergency she was to send for the Rector, or, if he was not available, the curate. The Reverend Hopwood had been at great pains to ensure she had understood this ruling. His was

162

always to be the final decision. Knowing his soft heart, she was sure no child had ever faced permanent removal. But if the child continued to defy her, she would have to see that her threat was carried out, or lose her authority altogether.

She fought to keep her features calm, her glare as icy as before, though her heart was pounding out of control. The silent stillness of the playground was unnatural and seemed to be lasting forever. She could hear the sound of leaves skating across the ground in the wind. Then the girl moved. She walked quickly towards Emma, stood in front of her, holding out her hands, and looked up into her eyes with a furious defiance. All the anger had drained from Emma at the realisation of what a stupid thing she had done. She hit the child's hands, three whacks on each palm, but her arms had no strength. She doubted it had really hurt. The girl walked to the back of her line, her eyes still flashing, her head high.

The children filed back into the schoolroom and sat with their primers in silence. Only the faint whispers of the smallest infants could be heard as they read to their older partners, that and the ticking of the clock. Charlotte sat isolated from the rest on the floor at the front of the class, sulking, her primer open, unread in front of her. Emma ignored her and sat at her desk, apparently watching the children, in reality staring at nothing, willing the hands of the clock to move faster to release them all from their misery. When half past three finally came, the children could barely restrain their eagerness to get out of the room. Once beyond the walls she heard them erupt into shouting, laughing and over-excited chatter. She sat, her exhaustion profound, almost unable to move. Finally, when the sounds of the children outside had faded away, she left the classroom, leaving her preparation for the morning untouched, and walked wearily back to the cottage.

She excused herself, telling her mother she thought she might be coming down with an unpleasant stomach ailment which had kept several of the children away from school this week, knowing her mother had a horror of sickness and would stay out of her way. The bedroom was icy. It was beyond their means to heat more than one room in the house, so she wrapped herself in the eiderdown and sat down on the edge of the bed. Stupid, stupid woman! How could she have let herself get so out of control? Charlotte was only a child after all, totally powerless in reality compared to herself as an adult and teacher. She sighed, trying to calm herself and think more rationally.

The girl was unlikely to tell her father, knowing that she would be punished again for her disobedience. Eleanor would keep quiet, too frightened of being punished by Charlotte. Other children had no such fear to restrain them, however. It could already be round the village by now – almost certainly was. In her favour, she had always found the parents more than eager to support her in disciplining their children, especially the boys. "Whack 'im as 'ard as yer like," she was urged, "Yer need t' learn 'im oo's in charge." They wouldn't encourage their children to admire Charlotte Adams – quite the reverse. Perhaps they would be pleased she had been put in her place. But were there busy-bodies among the parents who would understand that she had no right to threaten Charlotte as she had, and who might quietly report her to the Reverend Hopkins? It distressed her to think that he might find out that she had disregarded his instructions. He had been unfailingly kind and supportive. Almost like a father to her. The last thing she wanted to do was to disappoint him. She was worried, too, that he might feel it necessary to report the matter to the Board. While she trusted him to understand the circumstances of her misjudgement, she had no way of knowing what view they would take.

She lay down in her eiderdown cocoon, her eyes closed, speaking sternly to herself, as sternly as she would to a naughty, but repentant, child. There was nothing to be done.

She would have to wait and see. Today was Tuesday. On Friday she had been invited to take tea with Clementine Hopwood after the close of school. If she had heard nothing more about it by then, she could probably assume no action would be taken. Till then she would have to pull herself together and carry on as if nothing had happened. The thought of attending the recital on Saturday with Alfred took on a whole new meaning now, and her earlier uneasiness was completely forgotten. If only this trouble would blow over, how wonderful it would be to spend the evening with him. With a perverse desperation she found herself longing to see him, to put her arm in his, even to hold his hand.

There was something else bothering her, though, something which got in the way whenever she tried to think of Alfred. Something at the back of her mind, a vague memory she was unable to access. It related to the incident in the playground, but she had no idea why. When it refused to go away, she forced herself to relive the whole sequence of events several times. Suddenly it came back to her. Tiny Charlie Wilson, tugging at her skirts. Other children at the front of the line distracted by something behind her. Something or *someone*. She sat up abruptly and clapped her hand over her mouth. That was what the child had been trying to say, but she had stopped him – there was someone in the schoolroom. Whoever it was would have seen the whole incident through the open door. She sat on the edge of the bed, the eiderdown slipping from her shoulders, her hand still over her mouth. They could be at the Rectory at this very minute.

CHAPTER 20

Alfred woke suddenly and sat bolt upright. He swung his feet out of bed onto the cold wooden floor, rubbing his eyes and running his hands through his hair over and over. The remains of an unpleasant dream lay around him like a cold December fog, though he could remember nothing substantial about it, only that he had been dreaming of John. He felt shaken and anxious, unable to fully connect with the day ahead. Splashing his face with icy water from the jug, he decided to dress immediately and to go outside for a walk. He crept down through the silent house and out into the lane. It was still almost dark. He walked fast, pushing his feet hard into the ground and swinging his arms vigorously to warm himself and to feel himself real and alive again. Gradually his unease lessened and he began to think about the day. It was Sunday. He had completely forgotten. He could have stayed in bed a while longer, but never mind. It was good to be in the fresh air. The day promised to be a fine one, with the sky burning red behind him and stars still glittering ahead. A hard frost filled his nose with a sharp, metallic smell.

He decided to cut across the field to his right. The ground, churned up in the wet of the autumn by the animals, was now set hard, every ridge and bump pushing painfully through the soles of his boots into his freezing feet. A small group of sheep lay huddled together under the hedge, chewing silently, their eyes reflecting the glowing sky as they followed his progress. He reached the bottom of the field and turned right again, keeping to a narrow path which ran along the edge of woodland. It was a walk he often did in the summer, when he needed peace and time to think. The first rays of sunshine were catching the tops of the trees on the ridge to his left. He kept his eyes there, watching the slowly changing colours on the hoar-tipped branches as he walked. Below the ridge were more fields, then the woods, which disappeared into the valley. He could hear the stream in the distance, rushing with winter rain. In hot, dry spells you couldn't hear it at all. As far as he could remember he had never walked in the valley. One day he must get down there and explore. In the summer, perhaps with Emma. They could take a picnic.

His thoughts turned to their evening together yesterday and he smiled with pleasure. It had been a great success. The mothers had chatted in the carriage, apparently happily, and sat next to one another in the church. Emma and he had been allowed to sit together. She had seemed delighted to see him and, as they sat side by side at the front of the carriage, had talked animatedly about music and books, about her father and her childhood. She had asked him questions about himself, his childhood, his father, the business. Talking to her was easy, so different from their last encounter. She had even taken his arm as they walked up to the church. He couldn't account for her change in mood. He had followed his friend's advice to the letter and kept his behaviour cool and restrained throughout the evening. Perhaps that was all she had needed to free her from her shyness. Whatever the reason, she was a delight – everything he had hoped for – and beneath his composed exterior he had glowed all evening with relief and desire, an exquisite warmth which flowed through him now as he relived each scene, completely washing away any traces of his earlier anxiety.

The evening had been just what he needed to restore his confidence after his embarrassment at the Rectory and to relieve a slight, but stubborn disquiet about what he had seen at the school. He had regretted bitterly his decision to call in to see her and had crept away as she had been about to cane the girls. He couldn't watch that. It was too brutal, too manly somehow. But now he had seen her true warmth, he was able to confirm to himself what he had wanted to believe all along – that the harsh, fierce tone she had adopted was an act, put on out of necessity rather than choice. Obviously her actions were justified given the defiance and rudeness she faced, but after last night he could also see that they did not reflect her real nature or her feelings for the children. They hadn't spoken of the incident. He wasn't even sure that she had known he was there. He was happy to put it behind him and to think of their future life together, now.

The path took him past the back gardens of the hamlet. They were small, with every inch of land used to grow vegetables, and raise chickens, rabbits or the occasional pig. At this time of year everything was looking dead and rotten under its layer of frost, just a few winter cabbages and sprouts still to be eaten before digging must start again in the spring. He enjoyed growing vegetables and flowers himself, though he had little time for it these days. The garden of Stonefield House was large and sunny and could be productive when given sufficient attention. The small orchard at the bottom of the garden was his favourite spot. He had often played there as a boy, under the trees with his soldiers or retreating high into the ancient, gnarled branches if things seemed difficult in the house. He imagined his own children playing in the warm spring sunshine, a boy and a girl, sitting with soldiers and dolls respectively under the blossom-filled trees, while he and Emma tended the garden, he digging manfully, she cutting spring flowers and looking radiant in her blue bonnet and dress. He sighed and smiled again. This smiling at no one was faintly ridiculous. He must make sure he didn't do it where any of the men might see.

He let himself into the house from the yard. A delicious blast of warm air, thick with the smell of newly-baked bread, hit him as he opened the kitchen door. Mrs Dawes was busy preparing breakfast, her sleeves rolled to the elbows, wisps of hair already escaping from her white lace cap as she beat eggs and sliced bread with astonishing speed and energy.

"Good morning, Mrs Dawes. It's going to be a fine day, I think."

"G'morning, Mr Nicholson. Yes, it's grand to see the sun, though there's a fierce nip in the air, too. Breakfast'll be ready at eight-thirty as usual, sir."

"Yes, yes, don't worry, I'm not trying to hurry you. I need to have a wash first. Where's Annie?"

"She's with your mother, sir. I'm afraid Mrs Nicholson's not feeling well this morning."

"Oh. I'll go up and see her."

Worry clouded his happy mood as he climbed the stairs two at a time to his mother's bedchamber. Perhaps she was just over-tired from their evening excursion. He knocked and waited for her call. Annie opened the door.

"Mrs Nicholson's asleep again, sir. I'm afraid she's real poorly. She looks awful flushed and says she's got an 'eadache fit to split 'er 'ead open and a sore throat, too. Should I get Jimmy to go for the doctor, sir?"

Alfred looked from the doorway at his mother's sleeping form. Damp strands of hair stuck to her forehead, which was deeply creased into a painful frown. Her eyelids fluttered restlessly and she made small, moaning sounds. Suddenly he could see that she was getting old and frail and he felt alarmed. She was irritating and stubborn and interfering. He wasn't even sure that she loved him. But she was always there. Now he understood that a time would come when she was not and it shocked him how much he minded.

"Yes, go, quickly. Tell Jimmy to take Horace. I'll stay with Mrs Nicholson." He sat down heavily on the chair beside her bed and took one of her hands in his. She stirred and opened her eyes.

"Oh, Alfie, what a silly old nuisance I am." Her voice was faint and hoarse. "I shouldn't be going out at night at my age, that's the trouble…" She paused, as if needing to gather her strength. "But it was a lovely evening…"

"Yes, it was, Mother, it was lovely. But now we need to think about you and how to get you better. Jimmy's gone for the doctor."

"Oh, I don't want to make a fuss…" She paused again, closing her eyes for a moment. "Oh dear, but my head is bad, and he's such a loud, bossy man."

"Dr Tucker is just the man you need. He's only loud and bossy to keep you in order. He'll be here within the hour." Alfred patted her hand and stood up. "Here's Annie back now. She'll come and find me if you need me. I shan't go to church this morning."

"Oh…but the choir…"

"The choir can manage perfectly well without me for one day. I'm going to wash and eat now, while you rest." He walked towards the door, but she lifted her head from the pillow, beckoning him back anxiously.

"Alfie…I need to just tell you…"

"Not now, Mother, just rest until the doctor comes. We'll talk later."

"In the bureau in the drawing room. The key is on my dressing table." She pointed across the room. "It's time you saw the will…" She closed her eyes again then and appeared to fall asleep. He walked across to the dressing table, hesitated for a moment, picked up the key and left the room.

❧

After the doctor had been and gone, pronouncing it a bad case of tonsillitis which must be prevented from going to her chest at all costs and producing several bottles of noxious cure, and his mother had been made comfortable and had gone back to sleep, Alfred sat alone in the drawing room in front of his father's old bureau, turning the small key over and over in his fingers before opening the lid and looking inside the drawers. Each contained a neat bundle of papers, most of which had obviously lain untouched since his father's death. They bore the stamp of his orderly mind. Letters, deeds, business papers, financial documents, all in separate bundles, sorted in date order. Eventually he found his father's will and under it, his mother's. He glanced through it, but could see nothing unexpected. The business was already in his name, as was the house and the other property. His father had seen to that. His mother's will simply bequeathed him her own small legacy and her personal possessions. Her wedding ring should go to his daughter, if he had one. He returned the will to the correct drawer and was about to close the bureau when a small piece of paper caught his eye. It was concealed beneath the blotter, with just a corner visible, as if someone had been surprised while reading it and had hidden it hastily. He drew it out and held it up to the light of the window to read.

It was a letter addressed to his father, which had clearly been opened once, then re-sealed with his father's seal. He cut it open. It was dated July 16th 1847.

"Dear Mr Nicholson

Further to my previous letter and to your reply of the 16th July, I can confirm that the death certificate gives the cause of death as "heart failure". The secondary diagnosis, which we have discussed, does not appear, nor do any of the other circumstances of the death. I hope this will reassure you.

I should, however, make clear that the infirmity is hereditary in nature. It will therefore become necessary that your elder son is informed of the true reason for his brother's death before he marries.

May I again send my deepest condolences to you and to Mrs Nicholson.

Yours most sincerely,

Dr Adam Tucker."

As he read the page again and again the anxiety he had

woken with enveloped him once more. He sat motionless for a long while, struggling to steady his breath, staring across the room at his father's photograph, the letter trembling in his hand. Gradually his heart rate slowed and he tried to make sense of what he now knew and what was still lost in secrecy. The doctor had said he should be told of the "secondary diagnosis", yet his parents had hidden the truth from him. Why? Why had his father, who appeared to love him and think highly of him, not told him what had happened? Had his father believed he was somehow to blame too? Somehow involved in these "other circumstances"? Did his mother know the whole truth about John's death? After his last attempt, it was unlikely he would ever be able to ask her about it, especially now that she was so ill. He might never know. He slipped the letter into his jacket pocket, closed and locked the bureau and stood up, swaying slightly. Even the floor beneath his feet no longer felt solid.

CHAPTER 21

The wind was blowing so hard today that her skirts and cloak became sails, pushing and pulling at her until she thought she might be blown over. It was frightening and exhilarating, like no wind she had ever felt before. The sea was a grey and white heaving mass as far as she could see. Near the beach the waves were enormous, crashing over each other, over the Street and onto the shore in explosions of white spray and foam. The roar filled her ears and body. It made her want to laugh and shout.

It was heaven to be out of the house again. Throughout her twenty-three days in Whitstable, Cecily had missed her walk by the sea only three times, when the nurse had slipped out to the Duke of Cumberland for the afternoon and evening, claiming her half-day off. Cecily's daily outing was now as essential to her well-being as breathing and eating. Without it she would surely have set off for home on foot long ago, or murdered the old lady, or the nurse, or both. At first she had been worried that it might be the nurse who murdered the old lady while she was out, but Mrs French hadn't dared to lay a hand on her aunt after that first day. She liked to relive that encounter. It made her feel proud and strong and grown-up. She smiled each time she recalled the shock on the nurse's face as she had burst into her aunt's room with a cry of "Mrs French, stop that right now!" Her loud, authoritative voice had erupted from fury and disbelief at what she was seeing and had surprised her as well as the nurse. Mrs French had recovered herself quickly, scoffing when Cecily had threatened to report her to the doctor.

"You wouldn't dare," she had sneered, "He'd never believe you and you'd lose your position."

But Cecily wasn't cowed. She had taken great delight in retorting that she would be only too glad to lose her "position", that, yes, she would dare, and, by the way, she knew that the bottles in the nurse's bag were not medicine. That had wiped the silly smile off her face and there was no more trouble after that first day. The doctor came from time to time and Mrs French put on an extraordinary show of efficiency and care for a half an hour or so. The rest of the time she did her duties, the bare minimum, but she never shook or hit the old lady again.

They avoided each other as much as they could. Cecily helped when the nursing tasks required it and ran the household the rest of the time. Harry would be proud of her, she thought. She cleaned and tidied, washed, shopped and cooked. She had only broken a small vase and a plate to date, and spilt one jug of milk. Without someone watching her every move and criticising, she managed remarkably well, she felt. The silver wasn't polished, the ironing was somewhat crumpled and the grates weren't blacked, but the house was clean and its inhabitants fed. Cooking was her biggest challenge. She had watched and helped her mother, of course, and Mrs Norris, but had never actually cooked on her own. The old lady only really ate bread and milk and beef broth, but even making broth was a mystery. She had taken advice from the butcher's wife next door. They were a kind couple, who seemed truly concerned about her situation.

"It's not right," the large, blood-stained wife would say, shaking her head, "A pretty young thing like you shut up with that dreadful old woman all day." They saved bones and cheap ends of meat for her to make broth and stew and the wife explained simple recipes, which even a scatter-brain could follow. The old lady seemed happy with the broth. The nurse complained that the meat was tough and the stew tasteless. Cecily's sharp reply was that if she didn't like it she could cook for herself. She wasn't the nurse's servant and was

174

blowed if she was going to take complaints from her.

Life had settled into a bearable sort of rhythm of tasks and walks and time with her aunt. The old lady no longer frightened her. Cecily understood that she wasn't in control of herself and ignored her angry outbursts and irritating whining. The rambling, endlessly repetitive conversations were harmless and she was happy to indulge her by nodding and smiling and pretending to be Jane, or whoever her aunt thought she was that day. She read to her from time to time. It inevitably soothed her aunt's agitation and sent her to sleep. She couldn't say she was exactly fond of the old lady, but she did care about her now and wanted to keep her as comfortable and happy as she could.

She walked westwards along the beach for a while, eventually becoming exhausted with the effort of battling against the wind. The lee-side of a small fisherman's hut provided some welcome shelter and she sank gratefully onto the shingle, basking in the relative warmth and calm for a moment, before reaching into her cloak pocket and taking out two letters. Both had arrived this morning. She had forced herself to save them for this moment and now anticipated reading them with delicious excitement.

The first was from Harry. Dear Harry. She knew he hated writing, but he had managed a whole page. She read quickly, enjoying all the snippets of news about home, all the little things that made up life in the family, just as she remembered it. Ernie had been frightened by a fox which had walked, bold as brass, across the back garden. Tom had been in trouble again at school and Father had threatened to strap him (though they all knew he never would). Sam had learnt to read at last, thank goodness, for they had all been worried he was a dunce. Frances had won a prize for her needlework (she rolled her eyes and moved on quickly to the next sentence). Mother was unwell, being sick again – he was worried it was another baby on the way. Good heavens, *another* baby, she thought. Poor Mother. And then his news: he was soon to leave the old firm and begin work for a company building houses in Wittenbury. It was near to home and he really liked the owner – Alfred Nicholson. He seemed intelligent and fair and forward-looking. He hoped he might have a future working for them.

Alfred Nicholson. The name had a strange effect on her, sending her pulse racing and colour rushing to her cheeks, even in the cold air. She was glad no one could see. Harry would be working for Mr Nicholson. Perhaps he might introduce her one day, when she was back home. The fluttering excitement in her stomach grew stronger. How ridiculous. She scolded herself sharply in her mother's most dismissive voice. What a lot of nonsense, girl. Pull yourself together.

She sighed and opened the second letter, recognising the writing from the many traders' orders she had handed over at the back door of the Rectory.

"Dear Cecily,

It hardly seems possible that it is not quite three weeks ago that you left us dear it seems much longer. We are all missing you. Edith is lonely in her little attic room and I have no one at all to scold now. The little boys are missing you too but more about that later.

I do hope you have settled into your new position and that your aunt is treating you well. Have you been to see the sea yet? I would so love to see the sea one day though I suppose I am too old now for such an excitement. Please write and tell us all about it dear. That would be the next best thing for me.

I am not sure I should be telling you this Cecily but as you are so far away it can do no harm I suppose. Edith and I do not like the new nurse at all and are very worried that she is not right for our dear little chaps to tell you the truth.

176

There is something very sour and severe about her. But there we are. We have no say in the matter the mores the pity. Edith is glad Miss Cornwell sleeps with the children for she would not want to share a room with her she says.

Apart from that life here goes on much as before dear. There is some gossip in the village about the school teacher. Mr Gilberts boy said his little brother said she threatened to have one of the blacksmiths daughters taken from the school for good. The Reverend is ignoring it as he always does with gossiping in the village. We always thought she was a bit on the severe side didn't we? Like our Miss Cornwell. Still there is no accounting for taste for the other rumour in the village is that Miss Fielding is walking out with that very nice young builder Mr Nicholson. He seems such a gentle quiet man it seems a very odd pairing to me but as I say there is no accounting for taste not with the young people these days they just do what they please and marry who they like.

Well that is quite enough from me dear. We do so hope you will write to us soon. I have enclosed a stamp for I know you may not have much money to spare. Edith sends you her love and hopes you will send her regards to Harold your brother.

With fondest regards, Mrs Norris."

Cecily leant back against the wooden boards of the hut and closed her eyes, the letter resting in her lap. Her heart was full of feelings, mixed up, unsettling and sad. She could hear Mrs Norris's voice as she read and the sound of it brought tears instantly to her eyes and running down her cheeks. Mrs Norris and Edith and Harry and her family were all so far away. How she missed them. It was like a constant, nagging pain which she pushed down somewhere inside her where it hurt her less, but now here it was, back in her throat and her eyes and her heart, just as painful as on the day she left. But it wasn't just missing them that hurt, was it? Something else

had disturbed her. She re-read the letter and there it was –
Mr Nicholson was walking out with the schoolteacher. Each
time she read the sentence it had the same effect, like a blow
in her stomach. It was horrible. It left her feeling empty and
low. But why? Why should she mind who Mr Nicholson
walked out with? Edith had teased her endlessly about being
sweet on him and she had been irritated by her friend's
silliness. But perhaps Edith was right. Perhaps she *had* fallen
in love with him. Was that possible? She had only seen him
three or four times and had spoken to him only once. You
couldn't love someone you had spent so little time with,
could you? No of course you couldn't. She was being as silly
as Edith. Besides, it meant absolutely nothing whether she
loved him or not. She was a girl, not even a maid now, and he
was a man, a business man, an important member of the
community, in love with a woman of position and class. She
despised her own childish stupidity, especially now, when she
had been proud to be feeling so much more grown up. But
whatever she said to herself, she could do nothing to shift the
terrible feeling of loss which had settled on her. It weighed
her down as she walked back along the beach, barely noticing
the wind and the waves, and stayed with her all evening,
cruelly highlighting her loneliness. Nothing could distract
her. Not her aunt's needs nor her tasks nor the stories on her
shelf. She wept whenever she was alone and fell asleep crying.

❧

Several days after the letters had arrived Cecily overslept. Her
depression had clung to her despite all her efforts to shift it
with stern words and even longer bracing walks by the sea.
She was finding it hard to get to sleep and as a consequence
was waking later and later. This morning it was light when
she opened her eyes. There was a loud banging on her door.

"Cecily! Wake up! What are you thinking of still lying in

bed, girl?" The nurse sounded agitated. "It's past eight o'clock. Come here, quick. The old lady…I'm not sure she's still… Well, you'd better come and see for yourself."

Oh Lord. Had Aunt Ellen died? Having wished for it once, she was now terrified that it might have happened. She flung her shawl around her shoulders and ran across the landing. Her aunt was slumped down in her bed as usual, her nightcap slipped over her eyes and her mouth hanging open in a strange, lopsided way.

"I've tried to wake her to get her on the commode before she wets the bed, but I can't. She hasn't moved." The nurse was nervous, breathless. Cecily was surprised, given that she was supposed to be the experienced one in such matters. She called her aunt's name, but there was no response. She took a limp, bony hand in her own. It was still warm. She remembered reading in a story once that you could tell if someone was alive by putting a mirror against their lips. Her aunt's hand mirror misted reassuringly – she was still alive, thank goodness.

An hour later Cecily sat beside her aunt's bed, waiting for the doctor. Having run halfway across the town for him, she had been annoyed to be told by his maid that he would visit "sometime in the morning." Her protests had been met by the slamming of the large, glossy black door. She looked at the tiny figure lying motionless and silent in the bed and felt sad at the thought of her aunt ending her days with no one to truly care for her, not even her own doctor. Perhaps it was her own fault, for being such a crabby, unpleasant woman, but it still felt sad.

When the foxy little man finally appeared he pronounced her aunt to be dying. He didn't deign to say what she was dying of. He suggested that Cecily should contact her family and make arrangements to return home in the near future. Meanwhile, she and the nurse were to turn Miss Carpenter hourly, wash her and change her bedclothes daily, but otherwise do nothing. There was no point in sitting with her, he added helpfully, for she would have absolutely no awareness now. He would return tomorrow. He did not want to be called out if she were to die in the night. He bade them good day and left the house a full five minutes after he had arrived.

The nurse retreated to her room and her gin and Cecily was left to keep vigil at her aunt's bedside. She didn't care what the horrid little man said, no one should die alone. She would stay here until it was all over.

CHAPTER 22

The air in the schoolroom was thick with the smell of damp wool and wet hair. The mood of the children was subdued, as it had been all last week. The only sounds were the scratching of pens on copy books and slate pencils on slates, the children's occasional sniffs and coughs and the ticking of the clock. The subject of the essay was "My Week", a useful standby for a Monday morning when her imagination failed to come up with anything more interesting. The resultant pieces were usually dull and repetitive, detailing farm and household tasks, family illnesses and playground games which varied little from week to week. Occasionally she was treated to some flight of fancy from one of the small girls, like Freda Johnson's last effort. Freda's week had consisted of visits to London to see the Queen, complete with colourful descriptions of the monarch's clothes and jewels, her parlour and the bread and butter she had eaten for tea. Emma had some sympathy for Freda. The little girl was an intelligent, pleasant child – she hadn't done it to be naughty. Emma remembered writing similar nonsense when she was little, the delight of escaping into a magical world of her own invention. She couldn't let it pass, though, or they would all be doing it. Freda had spent playtime re-writing her week, making it suitably tedious.

The children who were not yet able to write were copying a piece from the blackboard, the smallest children laboriously scratching each letter onto their slates. She watched them for a while. One small, tousle-headed urchin spat noisily on his slate and rubbed his writing away impatiently with his sleeve.

"Timothy Headly, where's your sponge?"

"Don't know, Miss. Lost it."

"Spitting is a disgusting habit, Timothy. Don't let me see you do that again!"

"No, Miss." The child put his head down to hide his shame and set to with his slate pencil again.

Emma liked Monday morning essay time. After the exacting start to the day – the Bible reading and prayers, drill, mental arithmetic and table chanting – it gave her time to sit and think. She had been thinking about *her* week. The first few days had been difficult with her anxious uncertainty over the playground episode, but she had reached Friday with no obvious repercussions and felt increasingly confident that it had all blown over. Clementine Hopwood had said nothing during her visit to the Rectory at the end of school on Friday and had behaved as if nothing were amiss. Surely she would have cancelled the visit if Emma were in disgrace? They had talked mostly of Clementine's concerns for the children, in fact. She was always worrying about her "little ones" as she called them. Emma couldn't help feeling they were rather over-indulged. The latest worry was that the new nurse was proving rather difficult, apparently reluctant to share the nursery with her. Why she should want to be in the nursery at all was a mystery to Emma. Now she had an experienced nurse, she should make the most of her freedom before the next wretched baby arrived.

Then there had been her evening with Alfred on Saturday. Her anxiety in the week had heightened her anticipation of the outing and her pleasure when it finally arrived. He was quite cool and restrained, perhaps because of the elderly chaperones, but that suited her, enabling her to relax with him more than she had ever done. In fact he was so restrained that she had even begun to worry that perhaps she had offended him and that he no longer cared for her as he had done. She was shocked at the perversity of her own feelings, for no sooner had this thought occurred to her, than her reluctance to be close to him vanished and she found herself taking his arm. This see-sawing of emotions was exasperating. She was quite unused to having so little control over her own feelings and couldn't help judging herself as weak and pathetic, as she had so often judged other women.

She glanced at the clock.

"You have ten more minutes, class."

She noticed that some of the boys had stopped writing some time ago, but they knew better than to speak before the half an hour was over. They spent their time picking at their clothes or their noses or the dirt under their finger nails. She was distressed to see how little influence she had had over their disgusting habits. Suddenly the squeak of the door hinge broke into her thoughts. The Reverend Hopwood appeared at the back of the room. The children all turned to look and got to their feet as soon as they saw the familiar dishevelled figure.

"Good morning, Miss Fielding, good morning, children," he boomed, smiling amiably as the class chorused its reply. "Please sit down and get on with your writing. I must say I am impressed with the atmosphere of industry in this room. It was so quiet as I came in, I thought you had all gone for a nature walk! Now don't mind me. I have just come to see what you have all been doing this morning. Will it be acceptable for me to have a peek at the children's work, Miss Fielding?"

Emma had stood with the children. She felt flustered now, and alarmed. What was he doing here? Did it have anything to do with Charlotte Adams? At least she had vetted the girl's essay earlier. It was a harmless account of preparations for her brother's wedding next month. She forced herself to smile.

"Certainly, Mr Hopwood. We shall be stopping our writing soon and the children will be reading their accounts, but I am sure they will be only too pleased if you will read them first." She got out of her seat and busied herself looking over the shoulders of the infants, pointing out spelling errors and badly made letters. He talked quietly to the older children at the back of the room, including the Adams girls, asking questions and complimenting them on their work. At the end of the allotted time, the children stood in turn to read their essays aloud. Some glowed with pride, obviously pleased to be able to display their skills to the Rector. Others stumbled and blushed, hardly able to decipher their own writing. She hurried these along, stopping some after a sentence or two, embarrassed that he should see the poor quality of their work. She missed out Percy Trench altogether, for both their sakes.

Twelve o'clock arrived and she dismissed the children for their lunch. Most went home. A few sat in the yard with bags of bread and cheese. But the Rector made no move to leave with them. He had obviously not come simply to review the children's work. He cleared his throat, smiled at her rather awkwardly and walked to the front of the room.

"Miss Fielding, please sit down. I will sit here. Goodness, these benches get lower every year! I need to have a quick word, if I may."

❧

Alfred looked across an expanse of green leather and polished oak at the bank manager, a short, round man with shiny head, pasty cheeks and gold-rimmed spectacles which slipped slowly down his greasy nose. He was sitting on the other side of the desk, leaning back comfortably in a large, matching green leather chair, his fingers pressed together in an upside down V, an apologetic smile playing around his fat lips. Alfred had never liked him. Now, though he heard the sincerity of the apology, he saw only that the man was enjoying himself, enjoying the power he could wield over small men like himself.

Mr Dewey had been reviewing the loan for the new project and had decided he was unwilling to advance the final portion unless it was secured against Stonefield House. No, the other property owned by the business would not be sufficient. It must be Alfred's home. His mother's home. Built by his grandfather nearly fifty years ago.

Alfred was horrified. The thought of putting his mother's future at risk was awful, especially after her recent illness. She was recovering now, but her growing frailty was all too obvious. It couldn't be done. He fought to keep his voice steady as his heart banged in his chest. "May I ask the reason for this change, Mr Dewey? My understanding was that our terms and conditions had all been agreed at our last meeting. I have my signed copy here."

The bank manager gave up all pretence of apology and the smile was replaced with a steely look. "Circumstances have changed, Mr Nicholson. The railway…let's just say there have been delays. Its arrival in the town by the end of next year can no longer be guaranteed. The agreement for the loan was made on the basis of the increased demand for housing that the new line would create. If the demand is not there, you may find yourself with unsold or unlet houses on your hands. To put it bluntly, young man, you may be staring bankruptcy in the face if you insist on continuing with your present plans."

"But I've already recruited the men, put orders in for most of the materials. I can't scale it all back now. It's too late!" Alfred's voice rose in panic.

Mr Dewey pasted the reassuring smile back onto his face. "There is no need for alarm, Mr Nicholson. Simply sign the new agreement and the money is yours. I am sure you understand that I must put the interests of the bank first. We bankers cannot throw caution to the winds like you young business men. But, who knows, you may sell your houses after all and I shall be happy to be proved wrong. In which case your home will be safe."

Alfred slumped in his chair. He had no choice. What else could he do? He sat staring into space for a minute. When no miraculous answer came to him, he reached for the fine quill pen the manager was holding out with his pudgy hand and signed his name.

❧

Ten minutes later he was riding at a slow trot through familiar streets towards the edge of town, one hand on the reins as he chewed the nails of the other. Normally he would scrutinise each house that he passed, especially those newly built by rival firms, absorbing every detail – the patterns in the brickwork, the pitch of the roof, the size and proportions of the windows, the quality of the guttering. Today he noticed none of it. His face was set in a tight frown. He wasn't sure whether he was more angry with the manager or with himself. How could he have been so naive, so careless, so *stupid* as to recruit the men *before* he had the money in his hands? Yes, he had been given the piece of paper, but he should have known not to trust that man. He shook his head in disbelief at what he had done. He was a fool.

His mind tracked back and forth between the two options now open to him: use all the money and go ahead as planned, risk everything, including the health and happiness of his own mother, or scale back the project, spending only what was necessary to discharge his current debts. It took less than a minute to decide. He must scale back the project – build a couple of houses, not a street. Bricks, wood, pipes, all the spare materials, must go into storage. He would use them one day. They wouldn't go to waste. But the men? He couldn't put them into storage. No, he had no choice but to dismiss most of them, men who had given up steady jobs to come and work for him, men who had rent to pay and families to feed. His stomach churned with nausea at the thought of what he would say to them. What could he possibly say?

All too soon he arrived at the site. Men were already hard at work chopping trees and digging out stumps, the remains of an old orchard. His father had bought the land twenty years ago. At the time there wasn't the demand for new housing in the area, but he had had the foresight to see its potential. It had once been part of a farm on the edge of the town, near enough to walk into the centre for the market or the shops. Two new factories had recently started up in Wittenbury, manufacturing gloves and conserves, and the railway line from Chatham was to have been extended here by next autumn. There had been no doubt in Alfred's mind that demand for housing would increase enormously in the near future. Until today. He guessed that some fancy lord or other was objecting to the railway passing through his land. A pal of the bank manager no doubt. Now nobody knew what the future held for Wittenbury and for businesses like his own.

He tied the horse to the gate and walked over to find Reg, who was wrestling a tree stump with a horse and two of the new men. He joined them on the end of a rope, heaving and slipping in the mud, sweating and grunting with effort. He was glad of the chance to struggle, to pull against the banker, the railway, his own stupidity. When the stump eventually came free, he felt calmer and more in control of himself. He stood beside Reg, wiping his forehead with his sleeve, watching the other men as they dug and sawed.

"I need to have a word with you, Reg."

The foreman was panting and sweating profusely. "Right you are, Mr Nicholson."

"In private. Walk with me to the gate." Reg looked concerned. They passed a young man sawing branches off a felled tree. Alfred stopped beside him. This was one young man he would definitely not dismiss.

"Harold Carpenter. I'm glad to see you here."

Harold lifted his cap. "Thank you, Mr Nicholson. I'm pleased to be here."

"I shall be watching you, Harold. I've heard good things about you. I hope you'll be able to show us your potential."

"I hope so too, sir. Thank you, sir."

Despite his heavy heart, Alfred gave what he hoped was an encouraging smile and left the lad to his work. He beckoned to his foreman and they sat down together on a nearby log.

"When's Bill arriving with the old shed, Reg?"

"Any minute now, Mr Nicholson."

"Good. Then I'll help him set it up. I think I can manage to bang in a few nails without causing too much damage. Then you and I must sit down and do some hard thinking. I've some very bad news, I'm afraid."

❧

Within three hours the shed had been erected. Alfred sat behind the small trestle which served as a desk, surveying his five square yards of cold, bare office, comparing it ruefully with the luxurious workplace of the bank manager. Immediately he felt guilty. At least he still had an occupation, unlike the men he was about to see. He couldn't put it off any longer. Taking a deep breath, he opened the door and called out.

"I'm ready, Reg. Send the first man in."

The foreman poked his head around the door, frowning at his master. "I wish you'd let me stay in 'ere with you, Mr Nicholson."

"No, Reg – thank you. This is my responsibility and I'll deal with it alone."

"As you like, sir." Reg walked over to a group of men who stood in a huddle a few yards from the shed, shuffling their feet against the cold, talking and laughing in low voices.

Alfred watched them through the open doorway, heartsick at the thought of what he was about to say. As the youngest, a sixteen year old, came towards him, he rehearsed his speech in his head, as he had done countless times already throughout the afternoon. The lad knocked on the door frame.

"Come in, Benjamin, and shut the door behind you please." The fresh-faced young man stood before him, cap in hand. Alfred swallowed hard and began. As he spoke, he watched the boy's face register first shock, then dismay. Feeling a desperate need to finish the thing as fast as possible, he rushed on, leaving no space for reply, opened the cash box and held out an envelope. "Here's a week's wages, Benjamin, for the two days' work you've done. I realise that it's far from adequate, but it's all I can offer. I'm sorry. I hope…I hope you will find more work quickly." His voice trailed away. He hated the sound of it – gabbling, pathetic, as insincere to the boy as the bank manager had seemed to him.

The lad took the envelope, then burst out, "Bloody 'ell, Mr Nicholson! What am I s'posed to tell me ma? She's only got me bringin' in a wage now pa's sick."

Alfred drew his hand across his eyes wearily, avoiding the boy's distressed gaze. "I'm so sorry, Benjamin. Believe me, if I could help you more, I would."

The boy flashed him a furious look, turned on his heels and pulled the door open with such force the whole shed shook. Reg was there waiting with Bill. Together they steered him away from the rest of the men and out of the gate, then turned to fetch the next in line.

It didn't take long to dispatch them. Within ten minutes he had seen all but one of the group. His hands were shaking. His face had grown pale and drawn. A couple of the men had sworn at him. One had remained silent, staring at him with utter contempt before snatching the envelope from his hand. Others had shrugged as if to say, these things happen, it can't be helped, and had thanked him for the week's wages. The worst was a huge, bull of a man who had wept uncontrollably, terrified that his young wife and baby would be sent to the workhouse. Somehow Reg and Bill had helped him out of the shed and sent him on his way. There had been no trouble, though the waiting group must have grown suspicious as the interviews went on. Alfred was almost sorry. Perhaps he wouldn't feel so guilty if they had taken it less quietly.

The last to be sent in was a short, wiry, middle-aged man, dark and close-shaven, a bit like George in appearance. He listened to the speech with barely a flicker of emotion. Alfred passed him the envelope, breathing an inward sigh of relief that it was all over, and didn't see the fist that floored him. A brilliant light flashed in front of his eyes, he felt a searing pain across his nose and cheek and found himself in the corner of the shed, his legs and those of the chair hanging above him. For several moments his mind refused to function. He wasn't sure who he was or what was happening. He heard a commotion of shouting in the distance, then felt hands pulling him upright out of the corner.

"Lawk-a-mercy, Mr Nicholson! I knew I shouldn't 've left you on yer own. Are you alright, sir? No, I can see you ain't. That's a tidy old bruise you're goin' to 'ave there sir, and no mistake. Just let me put the chair to rights and we'll set you down." Reg's kind, concerned face swam before him, drifting in and out of focus. Somehow he couldn't organise his brain and mouth to reply.

"Bill and 'Arry Carpenter 'ave 'old of him still, Mr Nicholson. Should they take 'im to the constable?"

Even through the fog that was his brain, Alfred knew this wasn't what he wanted. He didn't blame the man. He deserved to be hit. He was glad of it.

"No...let...him...go." He forced out the words with great effort, like a drunkard, but their meaning was clear and Reg didn't argue, though he frowned his disapproval.

An hour later, and with the aid of a stiff dose of Reg's

medicinal brandy, Alfred was sufficiently restored to himself to insist that the men went home. He dared not go back to Stonefield House himself until his mother was in bed, so Reg was telling her some story about paper work he needed to finish at the site. He sat slumped over his table, miserable and exhausted, his face and head banging like a blacksmith's hammer on an anvil. The light gradually failed until he was left in complete darkness, staring at the walls of the shed, listening to the rattling of the door in the wind.

What he needed now was a beer and a friend.

CHAPTER 23

As Alfred stood on the doorstep of Forge Cottage, he heard the church clock strike the quarter hour. It must be a quarter after six, he decided. He knocked tentatively. Luckily it was George who opened the door. He didn't think he could cope with a houseful of women fussing over him.

"Don't say a word, George. Just take me to the beer house," he whispered quickly.

His friend closed his mouth, which had opened in a large O. "All right, Alf. I'll just get me coat. Wait round the corner."

They walked across the dark green without speaking and entered the beer house. Alfred was relieved to find that they were the only customers. The place seemed darker and more dreary than ever – just what he needed. They drank their first jug in silence and ordered another. He ran his hand gingerly over his swollen nose and cheek.

"Do I look terrible, George?"

"A sight for sore eyes, I'd say, 'cept you're the one with the sore eye!" Despite the joke, Alfred saw concern in his friend's eyes and felt the fragile dam holding his feelings in check begin to crumble. Tears ran over his bruises as he poured out the story. He made no attempt to stop them. As he finished, he put his head in his hands and stared down at the table.

"I don't know, George. I feel much too young for all this. If my father had lived another ten years I might have been ready, but not now. I'm just not up to the job."

George slapped his hand down on the table, making Alfred jump. "That's 'ogswash, Alf, and you know it! You've been doin' a fine job. If anythin' the business 'as done better since you took over." George's face was animated, his voice passionate. "Folk round 'ere speak well o' you. You've 'ad some terrible luck and made one mistake – *one,* that's all. I know you, Alfred Nicholson. You've got brains and a good nose for business. You done right today, though it don't seem so to you. And you've to get on with it now, my friend…like we all 'ave to."

Alfred wiped tears from his face with the back of his hand and tried a weak smile, which turned into a grimace with the pain. When he spoke his voice was still unsteady. "That was quite a speech, George. Thank you."

George gave him an earnest look. "That's what friends are for, ain't it? We go back a long way, you and I, don't we? Right back to when we was both lads – you so nervous, bringin' the 'orse to the forge on yer own for the first time, me terrified I'd be kicked from 'ere to kingdom come. We've grown into men together."

Alfred nodded. "We have. I've always preferred the company of working men like yourself, George. The boys at my school… well…I never felt like them. But with you it was easy, somehow. We had more in common, both working for our dads, both in trades. That's why it's been so hard to do what I had to do today – I feel I've betrayed men of my own class." He looked at his friend and his eyes filled with tears once more.

"I don't think that's 'ow they'd see it, Alf, and nor do I, for that matter. You've been a good mate to me, but I've always felt you were a cut above the rest of us, some'ow."

Alfred waved a finger at his friend. "Now you're the one talking hogswash, George. I'm only different on account of my school and my mother – making me speak so-called proper English, dress a certain way, eat a certain way. But I hate all that. Under my skin, I don't feel any different from you or the men. Certainly not above them…not in any way."

"Yes, but that ain't what *they* feel – that's all I'm sayin'. To them you're the Master. You're the Boss. When there's difficult things to be done, you're the one to do 'em. They won't like it, but that's life. That's just 'ow things are." George paused to pat the landlord's dog, a black mongrel with lopsided ears, which had abandoned the heat of the fire and laid down at his feet. He straightened up, giving Alfred a stern look. "No point in dwellin' on it, Alf. You can't change nothin' by cryin', that's what my ma always said. Time for another jug, I should say." He lifted a hand to the landlord and the two sat in companionable silence again for a moment or two, enjoying the restorative effect of the beer, before George embarked on a series of amusing and shocking anecdotes drawn from the latest village and family gossip.

Alfred listened quietly, grateful for the effort his friend was making to distract him. The combination of the stories and the beer succeeded in taking the edge off the throbbing in his face and, to a limited extent, the pain in his heart. After ten minutes or so George paused, eyeing his friend as if making some sort of calculation, then continued, "Now, at the risk of upsettin' you further, there's somethin' else I need to speak with you about."

Alfred winced. "Oh Lord. Let me get another round if it's more bad news." The landlord placed the jugs in front of them and Alfred drained his quickly. "Go on then. What's the problem?"

George looked uncomfortable. "I don't know 'ow to put it and I surely don't want to be the cause of any more grief, not after the day you've 'ad."

"Nothing can be as bad as what I've just been through. Spit it out, man."

"Well…no…it's not *that* bad. Just a bit awkward. There's a…a difficulty between your Emma and my family, see, and I think you should know 'bout it."

"Oh? What kind of a difficulty?" Alfred couldn't immediately think how any such problem might have arisen, then remembered with an unpleasant jolt the incident he had witnessed in the playground.

"Er…well… it's our Charlotte – she's been misbehavin' at school."

Alfred nodded. "I know about that, actually."

"You do?"

"Yes, I was there. I called in on Emma, and saw it all happen. She didn't see me, though. I don't want her to know I was there, George. I left just as she was about to…you know…use the cane."

"Oh…well…then you'll know what a little besom our Charlotte is. She deserved to get a whackin'. Our dad would've, if she'd given 'im or our mother any of 'er old lip. But the problem is what your Emma said to 'er. And it got back to Pa and now 'e's gone to the Reverend. 'E thought 'e must. 'E said it weren't right."

"What did she say?" Alfred was genuinely puzzled now. Nothing she had said before he left the schoolroom could have been objected to, especially not by a parent who was anxious to discipline their children, as he was sure the blacksmith would want to do. She was severe, yes, but she had every right to be in the face of such defiance.

"She said she'd 'ave Charlotte taken out o' school. For good. The 'ole village's in a twitter 'bout it."

"Oh." Alfred frowned and ran his hands through his hair. "That does seem harsh. I think I need another drink. What about you, George?"

"Not for me. But you go on, Alf. You've a greater need of it than me." Alfred signalled to the landlord while George continued, "The thing is, it's not just that it were 'arsh, as you put it. It's that she'd no right to say it. It's for the School Board to chuck kiddies out if they're misbehavin'. The Rector most-times, since 'e 'as most dealins with the school."

"Oh Lord. Poor Emma. I'm sure she only said it out of desperation. What do you think will happen, George?"

"The Reverend wouldn't say. 'E's a soft old stick – I'm sure 'e'll think the same as you. 'E won't want to sack 'er. 'E just said 'e'd speak to 'er and to the Board. I'm sorry to 'ave to put it on you like this, old friend. I know you're partial to 'er and it's the last thing you need to 'ear about right now. I just thought you should know, 'case the village tittle-tattle gets back to you. It'll all blow over soon enough, I reckon."

There was silence for a long moment. Then Alfred leant back in his chair and fixed his friend with a determined look. "Well, actually, George, I think you've done me a favour."

"I 'ave?"

"Well, I can see what I must do now."

George raised his eyebrows. "Oh? What might that be?"

"Marry her! Get her out of there. It's not the right place for her. She deserves better than to be slaving away like she does. I'm sure it's just tiredness and pressure that have caused her lapse of judgement."

George looked taken aback. "Marry? So soon? You can't know you're right for each other after such a short time, surely? And what 'bout the business? It don't seem to me to be exactly the best time to be gettin' married."

Alfred's eyes regained some life for the first time since he had sat in the bank manager's office. "Oh, I know she's right for me, though I couldn't tell you how I know. I just know! As for the business, well, this confirms that what I had to do today was the right thing, horrible though it was. I must safeguard the house, for her and my mother. Yes…I feel quite certain now…I shall ask her to marry me."

They both sat quietly for a minute or two, each absorbed in his own thoughts.

George said quietly. "And will you tell 'er 'bout today?"

"She'll hear about it, I'm sure. The whole village will, sooner or later. Yes, I'll tell her. The business is still solvent. It'll be smaller than it would have been, but there's no reason why it shouldn't do well and we can manage on the income I have now. And who knows how things might change in a couple of years? The railway might come to Wittenbury and things could look very different." He paused and frowned. "But I won't tell her or my mother about the house. They don't need to know about that. If I'm careful from now on I can repay the loan once the houses are sold or let and that will be the end of it. You won't tell anyone about the house, will you, George? Only you and I and Reg know."

George shook his head. "'Course not."

Alfred continued, "But listen, George, there's something else. I've been meaning to show you this for a while now, but if I'm going to ask Emma to marry me I have to decide whether I should tell her about it. It's been another horrible shock for me, I can tell you." He pulled the doctor's letter from his jacket pocket and handed it to his friend. While George read, Alfred sat watching the dog, now slumped back in front of the fire, snoring and twitching its way through a dream. George put the letter down and looked back at him, his thick brows knit together in concern.

"Well?"

"Lord, Alf. This is 'orrible."

"You know who it's referring to?"

"Yes – 'course. I always wondered what'd 'appened. 'E must've 'ad a weak 'eart, poor little bugger. But why did it 'appen, do y' know? And what's this 'sec..secon…'?"

"Secondary diagnosis."

"Yeah, that's the one."

"I don't know, George. Something that caused the heart failure, perhaps. Nobody ever talked about it at home. I can't remember any of it, though I must have been eight at the time. I asked Mother about it a few weeks ago, but she got very upset and wouldn't tell me. I was left with the feeling that it had somehow been my fault."

"Your fault? What on the Lord's earth made you think that?"

"Oh, I don't know…her face…the way she looked at me…the way she has always looked at me."

George leant forward, giving him a stern look. "I think you're imaginin' things. You know what you're like – always findin' things to fret 'bout. You've got real worries now, Alf. Ain't they enough?"

Alfred gave his friend a weary smile. "I don't know. Maybe you're right. I wish I could remember what happened. I just keep thinking about him, trying to remember him, picture his face, but I can't." He stopped and looked across the room. "And of course there's the thing about it being hereditary..." He paused again, pulling at his beard.

"What you thinkin'?"

"Well...I think that's why the doctor was trying to reassure Father that it wouldn't be on the death certificate, so that no one need ever know. So it must have been something bad. The letter was hidden so I'm not even sure whether Mother knows the whole story. And I can't ask her now. She's been so ill and it would upset her too much. But what about Emma? Doctor Tucker said I should be told about the 'infirmity' before I marry, so should I tell her?"

"I can't decide that for you, Alf."

"Then, if it was your Sarah. Would you tell her?"

George scratched his beard and thought for a minute. "Yes, I think I would."

CHAPTER 24

Condensation streamed down the walls of the small scullery to join pools of soapy water on the floor. The air was thick with steam and the smell of wet clothes. Cecily and her mother wrestled with a large sheet, lifting it from the copper and feeding it through the wringer, trying not to burn their fingers or soak their feet. Their faces were shiny, their cheeks deeply flushed and the hair at the edges of their caps curled into tight coils in the damp atmosphere. They worked quietly for much of the time, talking only when the job required it.

Cecily was thinking about Aunt Ellen's last hours. If someone had told her six months ago that she would sit at an old lady's bedside for three days, watching her slowly die, she would have been horrified. But as it was, her aunt had faded away and she had felt nothing, not fear nor sadness, just a lonely, empty feeling of inevitability. This is what happens to us all, she had thought. This is where I shall go in the end.

She hadn't attempted to talk to her mother about it. Cecily had always told her as little as possible of her own feelings, guarding her privacy with prickly, short replies if ever her mother tried to probe. She had been bruised too often by her sharp comments, her fears and hurts dismissed with careless ease, or so it seemed to her. So now, when her mother appeared to want a more adult relationship with her, to confide in her and have Cecily share her thoughts and feelings in return, she found she couldn't change. Her childish need to protect herself was too strong. She had retreated into herself since returning from Whitstable and spoken as little as possible to anyone except the young ones and Harry. He was working long hours and it was difficult to find time to be alone with him. Sometimes she felt as lonely as she had done in the cold, musty house beside the sea.

At least her mother wasn't nagging and scolding her as she used to. She had even complimented her a couple of times on housework which would have previously drawn only complaints.

"I think our Cecily's growing up at last," had been her comment at teatime yesterday to her father. "What do you think, Richard?"

"I know she gets more like you every day. She's going to be tall and shapely like her mother, though we all said what a puddn' she was just a few months ago."

"Oh, Pa, stop it." Cecily hated these family discussions in which children's growth and looks, characters and achievements were discussed freely as if they weren't there. Frances had smirked at Tom, though he couldn't care less, she knew.

"No, I didn't mean her *height*, I meant she's much more *adult* now." Her mother had rolled her eyes in exasperation, as she frequently did at her father's inability to immediately understand her meaning.

"Oh, I'm sure you're right, Ruth dear. You usually are." This meant he wasn't really interested in the discussion. It would keep her mother happy, and therefore quiet, to be told she was right.

Cecily had squirmed in her seat and left the table at the earliest opportunity. Now she looked across at her mother who was stirring clothes with the dolly in the copper. The thought that she might resemble her in any way irritated her. Her mother's figure was far from shapely in her view. It sagged and protruded, especially around her middle. She seemed to make little effort with her appearance these days, wearing the same old dresses and aprons, tying her hair in the same careless knot at the back of her head, hair which might once have been chestnut brown like her own, but which was now greying and dull. The thought that her face could one day look as lined and worn as her mother's was distressing.

Her mother wiped her face with her sleeve and pushed stray hairs from her eyes. "Let's get this lot out, Cecily. Have you got the rinsing water ready?"

"Yes, Ma."

"Well, I must say I'm glad to have you here today, what with Dorothy ill on laundry day of all days."

Cecily said nothing. It wasn't the first time her mother had commented that she was pleased to have her home. *She* should be pleased, too, she knew, but somehow she wasn't. After the first happy excitement of seeing Harry at the station, and greeting everyone at the house, she had settled into a strange numb state, where she didn't really know what she felt. It was almost as if her mother was right. She *had* grown up and didn't fit here anymore. As if to confirm that she really was an adult now she had found blood in her drawers yesterday. Her mother had explained everything to her sometime ago in a cold, factual way, including no mention of the strange turmoil of feelings which had accompanied this momentous change. She found the set of rags she had kept in a secret box away from Frances' prying eyes and managed the whole business herself. She hadn't even told her mother yet.

They worked together, rinsing and squeezing. Cecily went out several times for more buckets from the well, lingering each time for a minute or two to breathe in lung-fulls of crisp, clear air. Then back to more washing and rinsing, starching and wringing. It seemed to go on forever. She wondered if it was possible to avoid having so many children and creating so much work. Two children, a boy and a girl, seemed a sensible number to her, not this endless succession of babies that her mother produced. Nobody had confirmed that another was on the way, though the fact that her mother was frequently absent from the breakfast table and became white and drawn with exhaustion by the end of the afternoon seemed a clear indication to her. No concession was ever made to her mother's condition. She thought of Mrs Hopwood and the fuss that was made of her. If you have to have lots of children, then it's clearly a good idea to marry someone with money, she decided.

Scenes from the Rectory filled her mind now, and with them came the inevitable sadness. They wouldn't know that she wasn't still in Whitstable. She must write and tell them. It would be lovely to get another of Mrs Norris's gossipy letters in reply, though she didn't want to hear any more about Mr Nicholson and Miss Fielding. It was bad enough talking to Harry, who was full of praise for his new master and mentioned his name in every other sentence. She couldn't tell him how she felt. It would sound so childish. She supposed she should stop thinking about the past. And she should definitely stop thinking about Mr Nicholson. It didn't do any good. The trouble was, her future was so uncertain that there was nothing else to occupy her mind.

As if reading her thoughts, her mother broke the silence. "I've heard back from Grannie Carpenter today. She's been talking to her grocer and he's agreed to take you on for a trial period, starting next Monday. And Grannie's willing to have you to stay. You'll have to share her bed, but she doesn't mind that."

Cecily was horrified. She loved her Grannie, but she didn't want to live with her and certainly didn't want to share her bed. "*I* mind, though! Why can't I stay here? I can walk to the grocer's. It won't take that long."

"Now don't start making a fuss, Cecily. I thought you'd grown out of all that silly sort of behaviour. You've always known you wouldn't be able to stay. We need your bed. Sam shouldn't be sleeping with Tom anymore. They're both too big. The boys should be in the bigger room now, with a bed each."

All the unfairness of recent months suddenly assaulted Cecily. Her voice became agitated and loud. "Oh, as long as the boys are all right, that's all that matters, isn't it? Why does Harry not have to leave home? Why are Sam and Tom more important than me?"

Her mother stopped her rinsing and turned to face Cecily, her hands on her hips and her face set. "Men come first, Cecily. That's all there is to it. The sooner you get used to that idea, the happier you'll be, for you'll surely not be able to change it. It's just the way things are."

"Well they shouldn't be! It's wrong! Girls are no less clever than boys, or capable or hard working. We deserve just as much as they do!"

"What you deserve isn't what you get in this life, young lady. Besides, I'm not sure how deserving you are after losing the position at the Rectory. You should be grateful that Grannie's been able to secure you another post. You'll go to her Sunday night, ready to start work in the morning, and there's an end of it. Harry will take you. Now take this lot out and hang it on the line, while the sun's still shining."

Cecily knew better than to argue any more. She glared at her mother, gathered up the large heap of wet clothes, thrusting it into the wicker basket, and stomped out of the scullery into the garden. Hot, angry tears ran down her face as she pegged the clothes onto the line. It was yet another blow in what seemed to her a long succession of hurts and disappointments. She didn't care what her mother said, if she had a daughter, she wouldn't treat her like this. The children in her family would be loved equally, boys and girls. She sat down for a moment on the chopping log and dried her eyes impatiently with her apron. No daughter of hers would be cast off like a soiled rag. No she would not.

❧

She didn't take much notice of the letter when it arrived two days later. Something about the handwriting was familiar, but she couldn't place it and quickly dismissed it from her mind. It was addressed to her father and sat on the dresser in the kitchen all day waiting for him to return from the tailor's shop. When he arrived home they were all forbidden to bother him until he had drunk his cup of tea. He sat at the end of the long table with the letter, while she and her mother tiptoed around him as they prepared the evening meal. She had no idea why they must treat him as if he were somehow delicate. Perhaps it was something to do with the mysterious loss of his tailoring business. Tonight he caught her eye as he read, and smiled. When he looked at her warmly like that she could see a likeness with Harry, a kindness and sensitivity in his blue eyes and a gentleness around his mouth. He was a handsome man, who still took great care with his dark hair and beard and wore the smartest clothes he could afford. But most of the time he looked empty, she felt, as if there was hardly anybody there, as if he was hiding under a heavy, blank mask. It made him seem tired and old.

Today, though, his eyes sparkled. He beckoned her over to him. "Come and sit here, Cecy. Or are you too big to sit on your old dad's knee, now?"

"Of course she's too old!" said her mother. "Whatever next! She's a young woman now. Cecily, sit down here." She patted the space on the bench beside her. "What is it, Richard?"

"It's from the Reverend Hopwood. It seems all is not well in the Rectory nursery."

"Not well?" Cecily was immediately alarmed. "None of the children are ill again, are they?"

"No, no, nothing like that. It seems they have an unexpected vacancy for a nursemaid. Reading between the lines, I think the new nurse may have been dismissed."

"Oh…Mrs Norris wrote to me in Whitstable and said that she and Edie were worried that she was too severe. But what's that got to do with you, Pa?"

Her father smiled at her again. "It has to do with *you*, Cecy. The Reverend is asking whether you could return to the Rectory as soon as possible to be their nursemaid. What do you say to that?"

Cecily put her hand over her mouth and felt her heart begin to race. She didn't dare to believe it could be true. She stammered, "Oh…well…"

Her mother interrupted, leaning across the table to snatch the letter, scanning it quickly. "But she can't go! Your mother has just made all the arrangements for her to start at the grocer on Monday. It's much too late to change all that now. We would be letting him down, and Grannie – she's so looking forward to having Cecily live with her. She's not getting any younger, Richard. She needs someone to do the heavy fetching and carrying now."

Her father frowned at her mother. "I think we should ask Cecily what she thinks."

"It's not up to Cecily. An agreement has been made and we should honour it."

"Ruth, the agreement was only for a month's trial. At the end of the month, Mr Gregory may not want her. Not if she's broken too many eggs and dropped too many bags of flour, which we know she's likely to do. Cecily has worked in the Hopwood's nursery. They know she's capable of the work. They wouldn't be asking her if they didn't think she could do it."

"And your mother? What are we to say to her?" Her mother was becoming flushed with irritation. She's not used to him standing his ground, Cecily thought, and felt happy and proud that he was fighting on her behalf for once.

"*I* will talk to Mother," replied her father quietly, "I believe she would feel the same as I do. This is too important an opportunity for Cecy to miss…if it's what she wants, of course." He turned to her and raised his eyebrows questioningly.

"Oh yes, yes please." Despite her determination to appear grown up, Cecily found tears swimming in her eyes. "It *is* what I want to do. I loved working with the children, and I believe I did it well, Ma. I think you would've been proud of me if you'd seen me. I nursed them when they were ill and after, and they grew to love me and I them. I know I can be a good nursemaid. I know I can!"

Her father looked directly at her mother. "Then it's decided. I'll write to the Reverend tomorrow and tell him that Cecily will be at the Rectory on Sunday afternoon, ready to start on Monday morning." Cecily ran round the table to him, flung her arms round his neck and kissed his cheeks, wetting them with her tears.

"Thank you, Pa. Thank you, thank you."

"There, there you silly, no need to cry."

Cecily looked back at her mother, who was sitting silently, her face serious, but perhaps no longer angry. She hesitated, then returned to the seat beside her. She would never kiss her mother. They just never did that sort of thing. But she wanted things to be all right between them. She put her arm through her mother's as it hung limply by her side.

"I hope you *will* be proud of me one day, Ma."

Her mother looked at her gravely. "I hope so too, Cecily."

CHAPTER 25

Sunday was the first of March and a fine day, a good day to be starting a new adventure. The air was still cold, but the sunshine felt warm on her back, birds were singing loudly and she had found a clump of primroses on a sunny bank, all signs, she was sure, that things were going to be better from now on. She walked quickly along the lane, her legs full of impatient energy. Harry walked beside her carrying her old carpet bag, complaining that if she didn't slow down she would have to carry it herself.

"But I want to get there, Harry! I can't wait to be with them all again."

He smiled. "I know, Cecy. But I've got to rest for a minute." He dropped the bag and stretched his arms and shoulders. She stood beside him, watching a flock of jackdaws wheeling over the fields, listening to their "jack, jack" cries and the distant cawing from a rookery. Soon she began to fidget, hopping from leg to leg like a small child.

"Come on, you must be all right by now!" she begged.

"Well, if you hadn't filled your bag with bricks I might have got along faster!"

"They're not bricks, silly – they're books! I found them at Aunt Ellen's and the doctor said to take them. He said no one else would want them. I'm going to read them to Edith. There's a Mr Dickens and two more Mrs Gaskells and a book of poems by Mr Wordsworth. I used to read it to Aunt Ellen. Sometimes it was the only thing that would calm her down."

Harry picked up the bag and started walking again. "Was it really awful for you there, Cecy? You've seemed very quiet since you came back, but I've hardly had a chance to talk to you properly."

"At first it was awful, but then I got used to it. I've learnt you can get used to most horrible things after a while. But I'm very happy not to be there." She looked anxiously across at him. "Though I'm not happy that Aunt Ellen's dead of course."

He smiled back, reassuringly. "Don't worry, I know what you mean. And maybe God knew she needed to die and she's happier too, now."

They walked on past fields and woods obscured by high hedges, which kept the lane in shadow. The temperature began to drop and they increased their pace to keep warm. She told him more about Whitstable, the good things mostly, especially the sea and the shingle pathway, how peaceful it was in calm weather and how exciting in a storm. He said they should all go to the seaside one day, in the summer, on the train – she and Edith and him. He was earning better money now and Mother allowed him to save a little for himself each week. She said she thought that would be wonderful, then smiled at him mischievously and asked if he was sweet on Edith, by any chance.

"Maybe." His voice was quiet and shy. "I would certainly like to get to know her more."

She was so happy herself that she wanted him to be happy too. And Edith. "Then come to Blackford on a Sunday afternoon when we have our half day and you can join us for our stroll around the village. That will give the old ladies something to gossip about!" He laughed and said he would like that very much. They walked on for a while in silence.

The lane began to climb steeply as they entered Cornbrook Woods and they remembered being here that awful day in December when it had snowed and Ernie had been ill. She chatted about the Hopwood children, their illness, her feelings when she was with them. He told her about his new job and his hopes of progress, hardly mentioning Mr Nicholson this time, thank goodness.

Soon they were descending the other side of the hill and

could see the village in the distance. The church tower was still in full sun and beside it the sandstone of the Rectory glowed in the golden light. She was filled with such excitement and energy that she snatched the bag from him and ran down the hill before he had a chance to protest, calling to him and laughing.

As she turned the corner at the bottom of the hill, two figures came into view, walking towards her arm in arm. The low sun shone directly into her eyes and she couldn't immediately see who they were. They passed by, the man acknowledging her with a small smile and nod of the head, the woman ignoring her as she talked animatedly to her lover. Cecily's heart missed a beat. She dropped the bag on the ground and stood, motionless, staring unseeing into the distance as Harry came panting up behind her.

"Did you see Mr Nicholson, Cecy? That's his new fiancée – a Miss Fielding, so the lads tell me. She's a beauty, isn't she?"

Cecily kept her eyes to the ground to hide her burning cheeks and walked on without replying. Harry picked up the bag and caught up with her.

"Cecy?"

"Yes, I saw him!" Immediately she regretted snapping at him, but it was too late. She looked into his eyes and saw that he had understood.

"Come on," he said gently. "Let's get you home. Mrs Norris will have the kettle on the range. I'm ready for my cup of tea!"

❧

Late in the evening Cecily and Edith were snuggled together in Edith's bed, pillows piled behind their backs and the covers pulled up to their necks. Mrs Norris had sent them upstairs early, tired already of their giggling and chatter. The candle flickered beside them, casting long shadows on the sloping ceilings, the golden light reflected in their bright, excited eyes.

"I'm so pleased to be here with you, Edie! You've no idea how lonely I've felt the last few weeks. I really missed you!"

"Me too!"

They grinned sheepishly at one another. Cecily's smile faded suddenly into an anxious frown.

"You don't mind me being the nursemaid, do you, Edie? Only I was under you last year, wasn't I? And now we're sort of on a level, aren't we?"

"Oh no, don't be silly!" Edie laughed. "Course I don't mind! You wouldn't catch me looking after kiddies! Besides I 'ad a small pay rise when the nurse was appointed, on account of all the extra work, I s'ppose, and Fanny's doin' extra in the scullery now, so it suits me fine. No, you old silly!" She gave Cecily a peck on the cheek. "I'm just glad to 'ave you back! Now tell me all about Whitstable. What 'appened to you there?"

There was so much to tell each other and they only had tonight. From tomorrow Cecily would sleep in the nursery for six nights out of seven. She talked about the town, the sea, the house, then tried to describe Aunt Ellen without making her sound too awful. Edith obviously had no such qualms as she painted a picture of Miss Cornwell.

"Me and Mrs N said from the first minute she walked in the door that there was somethin' not quite right about 'er. 'Er eyes were too small and too close together and she never smiled once, not the 'ole time she was 'ere."

"But she can't have been dismissed for not smiling!"

Edith looked grave. "No, it was much worse than that. First the missus and 'er 'ad *words*. Mrs N over'eard 'em one day when she was bringin' tea up to the nursery. She'd never 'eard the missus so angry, she said, and she didn't know what to do, whether to leave the tray outside the door and run, or knock and 'ave the missus shout at 'er for interruptin'."

210

"Why was the missus so cross?" Cecily couldn't help the wave of smug pleasure that washed over her as she thought of the nurse getting into more trouble than she had ever done.

"'Cos the nurse was telling 'er she 'ad no place in 'er own nursery with 'er own kiddies! You can imagine 'ow well that went down!"

"Lordy! I wish I'd been here. What did the missus say?"

"She told 'er to remember who was the mistress of the 'ouse! Miss Cornwell was even more sour-faced after that. Mrs N said she'd worked for some squire's wife in the north of the county who'd wanted nothin' to do with 'er own kids, so our Miss Cornwell'd ruled the roost. She didn't like bein' knocked off 'er perch!"

"But what did she actually do to get dismissed?"

"No one rightly knows, but we 'eard a lot of cryin' from the nursery one mornin' and little Charles came down with a very red mark on 'is face. An hour later she'd packed 'er bags and was gone!"

Cecily looked at her friend, horrified. "That's horrible. How could she have done that? Poor little Charlie! The nurse in Whitstable hit Aunt Ellen once, but I soon put a stop to that. I felt so mad when I saw her, Edie. I wanted to punch her!"

"Did you?"

"No, I just shouted very loud. It was like someone else was inside me – a grown up, important person that the nurse had to listen to!"

"Good for you! You've got a big 'eart, our Cecily. I don't think I would've bothered to try an' protect an annoyin' old lady."

Cecily's eyes lost their sparkle. "I think my heart's *too* big sometimes, Edie," she said wistfully. "It makes me miserable or angry or happy or excited, but I'm never just…well…you know…*calm* and *content*."

"Well, you've nothing to be miserable 'bout now, 'ave you, dear?"

Cecily paused, looking away from her friend and up at the skylight. "No, not really, only...no...it's too silly. I can't even talk to *you* about it!"

"About what, Cecy? Come on, spit it out! You know you'll feel better if you do!"

Cecily looked sheepish. "I think I may have fallen in love!"

"Ohh!" Edith grinned mischievously and took her friend's hand under the covers. "Who's the lucky fella? Did you meet a nice tradesman's boy up in Whitstable?"

"No, I'm not interested in boys, Edie. That's the trouble. He's a man. You know all about him. And he would never so much as look at me and anyway he's engaged now."

"Oh, Mr Nicholson! I always said you were sweet on Mr Nicholson! Oh, poor Cecy!" Edith stroked her hand.

"I know it's ridiculous, but I think about him all the time, and these last couple of months I've felt all...oh, I don't know!" Cecily stopped. She could feel herself blushing and was glad the light was too low for her burning cheeks to show. She couldn't even talk to Edith about her strange longings or her embarrassing outburst in front of Harry today. Her friend continued to pat her hand.

"That *is* 'ard. Everyone falls in love with someone they can't 'ave at some time or other, or so I've been told. But you'll soon get over it, dear. You'll be busy with your work and then, one day, some nice boy'll turn up on the doorstep and you'll think 'e's wonderful and before you know it, you'll be goin' off to get married! That's what I'm 'oping's going to 'appen to me, any'ow!"

"Oh, Edie, I almost forgot!" Cecily's face brightened and she turned excitedly to look at her friend again. "Harry sends his kind regards and says he hopes he can come and meet us for a walk on our half day soon. He says he'd like to get to know you better!"

Edith looked at her, completely at a loss for words.

"Edie? Would you like that?"

"Oh yes…I'd like that a lot! Oh Cecy, do you really think 'e might like me, even though I'm common and don't talk proper?"

"Proper*ly*, Edie. You don't talk proper*ly*. Harry's not the sort of person to worry about that sort of thing. He takes people as they are. You're kind hearted and hard working *and* pretty! Those are the things that would matter to him."

"Does 'e think I'm pretty?" Edith touched her face with both her hands, and pulled some of her fine, dark hair from under her nightcap to examine it in the candlelight.

Cecily smiled at her. "I'm sure he does! Now I'd better get to my own bed. We'll never wake up in the morning if we don't get to sleep soon. I can't wait to see the children again. Have they grown?"

"I expect you'll see a difference in the baby. 'E's walking now, you know and Mrs N swears she 'eard 'im say "mamma" the other day!"

Cecily climbed across to her own bed and lay shivering exaggeratedly until the icy covers warmed up. They both fell silent and soon she could hear Edie's breathing change into sleep. She lay looking up at the half moon in the skylight, picturing the three children. Of course her friend was right. One day she *would* meet a nice boy and then she would have babies of her own. Meanwhile she had a good position in a good household. She was very lucky. There was a lot to look forward to. She turned onto her side and curled herself ready to sleep, sighing deeply in an effort to dislodge the ache which had settled in her heart when she had seen Mr Nicholson, and which had persisted stubbornly throughout the joyful reunions. Despite her efforts, it wasn't the children's faces, or Edie's, or Mrs Norris's that she saw as she drifted into sleep. It was his face, smiling kindly, but with no recognition in his eyes at all.

CHAPTER 26

Alfred examined himself critically in the mirror. His hair and beard were kept in check by regular visits to the barber now and he was making an effort with his clothes. Even with these improvements he couldn't persuade himself that his unremarkable features could be attractive to anyone, let alone someone as beautiful as Emma. He brushed his hair and beard for the third time that morning. There must be something about him that she liked. Whenever he felt insecure about her feelings for him he tried to picture the scene when he had proposed, ignoring his own stumbling part in it – his inarticulate apology for his haste, for the lack of a proper courtship – focussing instead on the obvious delight in her response. She had accepted without hesitation, reaching out for him with dancing eyes and kissing him on the lips. He could still taste the kiss if he shut his eyes. Later, when he had told her about the difficulties with the business, he had detected anxiety in her face, but it had soon passed with his reassurances that his income remained steady and his prospects, in the long-term, good. He hoped desperately that her eagerness to be his wife meant that she loved and wanted him as much as he wanted her.

Marrying her meant everything to him now. The thought that she would soon be his wife had carried him through the past two months. His bruises had healed quickly enough. He had passed them off to Emma and to his mother as the result of an unfortunate encounter with a tree stump in the dark. But he still found it difficult to sleep. Still saw the men's faces as they stood before him in the shed. Still heard with distaste the sound of his own voice offering pathetic apologies and meagre compensation. He could never forgive himself for the stupidity that had cost them their livelihoods. But he knew more than ever now that he had done the right thing. With Emma beside him he had begun to feel truly hopeful about his life for the first time since his father had died.

In the two months since their betrothal they had met often. On Friday evenings Emma and her mother came to Stonefield House for dinner. The meal was always something of an ordeal – making conversation with Mrs Fielding, trying to suppress his irritation at the ridiculous comments his mother made, trying to suppress his longing to be alone with Emma. But the hardship of the dining room was more than compensated for by the evening in the drawing room which followed. He played for them, stealing glances at her face, seeing in her shining eyes her love for him as well as for the music. And sometimes she sang. Then, with her there beside him at the piano, her clear, low voice blending sweetly with his own, he felt that all the essential parts of him were finally united and, for a short moment, his heart was full and content.

Now that the weather was improving they were able to take frequent walks together, too, which had the added attraction of ensuring they would be alone. His desire for her had grown with each meeting. It was difficult for him to content himself with walking at her side, her arm through his, or occasionally holding her hand, if they were out of sight of prying eyes. He longed to kiss her and to hold her close to him, but he was mindful of George's advice. Apart from that one delicious kiss, she had given no indication of wanting to be more intimate, so he held himself back, finding pleasure in their conversations and in watching her beautiful mouth and eyes as she talked, tracing the fine outline of her nose, the soft pale skin of her neck and the curve of her breasts with his eyes, longing for the day when his desire, kept in check for now, would find expression at last.

She seemed increasingly relaxed in his company, especially

now that they had set a date – the first of May, exactly a month from today. She had lost much of her cool aloofness and he was beginning to feel that a very different Emma lay beneath the confident composure which had so unnerved him in their early encounters. He was anxious to relieve her of her responsibilities as schoolteacher and provider as soon as possible, for only then did he feel she would be able to be truly herself. They had never spoken of the unfortunate incident with George's sister. He guessed that the Reverend Hopwood had dealt with it in his usual quiet, discreet way and that the matter was now closed. But she was clearly grateful that she would soon be able to relinquish duties that seemed to him to be quite unsuited to her sensitive nature. He felt happy and proud to be able to offer her and Mrs Fielding his protection and support.

He rifled through the clothes in his wardrobe, stopping at the new dark blue morning suit he had bought to wear on the day he had proposed. He would keep it for his wedding day now. All the arrangements were in hand. Mrs Fielding was to live in the small cottage across Stonefield Road from the house. It had been built by his father more than fifteen years ago and was usually let, but had stood empty for three months, waiting for some essential refurbishment. Alfred had charged Bill with the task of organising the work, the first project for which he was to take sole responsibility. Mrs Fielding would need her own servant, of course, and a girl from the hamlet had been engaged. Alfred felt anxious at the thought of all the additional expense the wedding seemed to be creating, but never doubted that this was the right course.

His mother was delighted, of course. Stonefield House was being prepared for the arrival of the new bride with spring cleaning and sorting and clearing such as he had never experienced before.

"The new Mrs Nicholson won't want to live in a dirty house!" was his mother's constant cry as she hounded poor

Annie from room to room with her latest list of tasks. He was glad to see that the prospect of the wedding had brought new colour to her cheeks and a sparkle to her eyes. Their relationship had improved too. Because he was happier he minded her fussing less and doubted her love less. He began to agree with George that his insecurity had come mostly from his own imagination. Admittedly he hadn't broached the subject of John's death with her again. He had convinced himself that there was no point, that she knew no more than he did, that it wasn't right to upset her now that she was happy. If it wasn't for the necessity of telling Emma about the letter, he might have put the whole thing to the back of his mind and left it there, where it used to be.

He pulled out his next best set of clothes and dressed carefully. Taking a last look in the mirror, he adjusted his hair again and went downstairs. His stomach began churning so that the thought of breakfast made him feel ill. He made his excuses to his mother and left the house for the stable, where Jimmy was already mucking out. The horse was soon saddled and he set off down the lane at a fast canter. He would be very early for her, but he couldn't wait now that he had decided. He had been cowardly in waiting so long. His hand went unconsciously to the jacket pocket where the letter lay. Today he would tell her. It was only fair that she should know before they were married.

~

Emma opened the door to him and blinked in the early morning sun.

"Oh, Alfred. Good morning! You're early – I'm not ready yet." Her hands went to her hair which fell about her shoulders, reflecting the golden light like a halo, he thought. "Come in. Mamma has a slight cold and is in bed. We'll not disturb her. Come and sit in the parlour while I finish my

217

hair. Would you like a cup of tea? Have you had breakfast?"

He followed her into the room, ducking his head to avoid the low beams. "No, no, I'm not hungry or thirsty, thank you." He smiled weakly, feeling as nervous as he had done in the early days of their relationship. "I have something I must talk to you about, Emma."

"Oh, sit down then. I'll be back in a minute. Let me take your coat."

"I was hoping we could take a walk along Denford Lane. It's a beautiful day." The truth was he felt much more comfortable walking and talking. She would put her arm in his and he would feel safe with her near him. He could always think more clearly in the open air and would be less likely to stumble over his words.

She smiled at him. "I've taken more walks since I've known you than I ever did in my life before that! At least it's been dry these past few days and my boots shan't be ruined as they were last week." She left the room, returning in a few minutes with her hair sadly concealed beneath her bonnet and her coat buttoned to her neck.

They walked across the green, turning left by the forge along a narrow lane that led only to a small hamlet and rarely saw any traffic. The sun was warm on their faces. The air was filled with the extravagant singing of spring birds and smelt of new growth and life. She talked animatedly about her week, about the new recruit for the school, a young man, who had visited yesterday, and about the preparations she and her mother were making to leave the cottage. He spoke little, content just to listen.

They passed beyond the last house in the village and she took his arm. "What did you want to talk to me about, Alfred?"

He said nothing, pressing her arm to his body unconsciously, needing her closer, until he felt her pull away from him a little.

"Alfred? What is it?" Her voice had a worried edge and he knew he must tell her now. He had spent weeks convincing himself it would be all right. She loved him and wanted him. This wouldn't change anything. He took a deep breath.

"I've recently found out something about my brother John, which I think you should know."

"Your brother? I didn't know you had a brother! Why didn't you tell me?"

"We don't speak of him at home."

"Is he dead?"

"Yes, he died many years ago, when he was six and I was eight." Alfred looked at the ground as he spoke, dreading the next question.

"How did he die?" She turned towards him, pulling her arm from his. Their pace had slowed and they stopped in a gateway to a field. He leaned back on the gate as he took the letter from his pocket and turned to face her.

"I found this in my father's bureau. I'm not sure if my mother knows about it. I suspect not, and she's been too unwell lately for me to bring the subject up. It's from old Doctor Tucker to my father. I think it was written very soon after John died…" There was a long pause as he looked at her, running his fingers through his hair and beard. "Um…I think you should read it."

"Why does it concern me? I don't understand."

"Just read it, Emma, please." He handed her the letter. She read quickly, her eyebrows knit in a small frown and her eyes squinting against the brightness of the sun on the paper.

She looked up at him anxiously. "I don't understand. What does it mean? 'Heart failure? Secondary diagnosis?' Explain it to me, Alfred, please."

"I think it means he had a weak heart, but I don't know what the 'secondary diagnosis' bit means. I was never told, and I'm not sure that Mother knows, either. I haven't been able to ask her…" He stopped, watching with dismay as the colour drained from her cheeks and her breathing became shallow. She put her hand to her mouth and said nothing. Her eyes stayed on the letter. He felt his heart begin to race and eventually could stand the silence no longer.

"What are you thinking, my love? Talk to me…please!"

She looked up at him and he saw tears well in her eyes. He longed to take her in his arms, to comfort her, but he stayed fixed to the spot, watching her misery, waiting for her to speak.

Her voice, when she spoke at last, was small and broken. "I can't do it, Alfred. I'm…I'm so sorry…but I can't."

He waited for her to continue, to explain herself, but she stayed silent, just looking at him with desperation in her eyes as she wept. He moved towards her.

"What do you mean, darling? What can't you do?"

She began to sob now and he took the letter from her hands and gathered her to him. She didn't resist. They stood together, her head on his shoulder as she wept uncontrollably, his arms around her, holding her tightly to him. Despite her distress and his own anxiety a surge of desire flooded through his body as he felt her pressed against him. He drank in the smell of her, the closeness and warmth of her, and longed never to be apart from her again.

After several minutes she raised her head and pulled herself from his grasp. She took a deep breath, retrieving a handkerchief from her coat and wiping her eyes and nose. Her skin and hair glowed in the sunshine as she looked up at him. He felt he had never seen her so beautiful. Her voice was small, but calm now.

"I can't marry you, Alfred. I'm so sorry." He started to protest, but she shook her head to silence him. "Listen to me, please. I can't bear a handicapped child, I just can't. I know I couldn't love it as a mother should." She paused, looking at him as if weighing up in her mind whether to continue. She took a deep breath. "Sometimes I wonder if I can love any child. The thought of being a mother terrifies me, but to produce a child who was…somehow infirm…" She looked at him, pleadingly, her eyes becoming watery again.

His heart was pounding in his chest now and he fought to keep desperation from his voice. "But it might not happen, Emma. Of course the infirmity, whatever it was, could be passed on, but these things are never inevitable. Our children may not inherit it. I didn't. And John wasn't handicapped. He was normal, intelligent, healthy, until…" His voice trailed away. He could see that he wasn't convincing her.

"I have seen children who weren't…weren't right." She looked away from him across the field. "I know what I'm capable of. I couldn't deal with it, I just couldn't."

He caught her hands, his face contorted with the grief he was struggling to contain.

"Emma, please. I love you. I long for you to be my wife. Every day I think of you and want you. I can't just give you up now."

She looked at him for a long time, a new composure apparently descending on her. "There may be a way we can marry," she said quietly.

His heart leapt with hope. "Oh, yes, we must. I'm sure it will be all right. Our children *will* be healthy. We *will* be happy together, darling, I know we will."

"No, Alfred." She held onto his hands with a firm grip he had scarcely ever felt from her. "No, there won't be any children. I shall marry you only if we can live as brother and sister, if we lie in separate beds and refrain from all those… intimacies…which make a true marriage." She paused for a moment, looking at him intently. "I think I would be quite suited to such a life, in fact. I've no great need of…of all that marriage entails and I wouldn't be unhappy if we never had children. I think perhaps I'm not meant to be a mother. Or a teacher! I'm not very good at it. I don't even really like children!" A small, apologetic smile played across her face – relief, perhaps, at having finally confessed this momentous failing.

He took a step back and dropped her hands. His whole body went cold, even in the growing warmth of the sun. He couldn't believe what he had just heard her say.

"But...but I thought..." He stopped. It didn't matter what he had thought. He had been wrong. He staggered back from her and leant against the gate again, breathing heavily. "No...no." The words came from him in a strangled cry. "I can't live with you like that! I have wanted you for too long, Emma. My body aches for you constantly! It would be torture...impossible!"

He saw her face fall in dismay, perhaps even disgust, but he couldn't worry about her feelings now. It was too late for treading carefully. His voice became more passionate. "And I *want* children, I know I do. I'm happy to take my chance with whatever child God sees fit to give me. I know I shall love it, whatever it may be like, whatever handicap it may have. And I want a wife who wants children too. I...we..." He stopped, seeing her begin to weep again, but he made no move towards her this time. There was a long silence.

"Then we can't marry," she said finally, quietly, through her tears. "Our needs are too different."

"No." He gazed back at her, his face frozen in dry-eyed misery. "We can't marry."

He wasn't sure how long they stood, each looking away, across the field, at the trees, their feet, at anything except the other. A question appeared in his mind and, though he knew he should stay silent, should walk away, he felt compelled to speak.

"Emma...I have to know...Have you...have you *ever* wanted me? For myself I mean?"

She started visibly at the sound of his voice and shrank away as she listened to his words. Her eyes searched the ground by her feet and refused to meet his own. She said nothing.

He slumped back against the gate. "No...I see...So...so why...why exactly did you agree to marry me?"

He waited, searching her downcast face. A breath of wind lifted a strand of hair and blew it across her eyes. She made no move to brush it away. Finally her tear-filled eyes met his. Her voice was so quiet it was almost carried away on the soft, spring breeze. "Forgive me."

He looked away, covering his face with his hand. A sob rose in his chest, but a tiny spark of pride forced it back, kept his eyes dry and his mouth set. He had been humiliated enough. He would not let her see his weakness. Grunting with effort, he pushed himself away from the gate, turned from her and forced his feet to begin the long walk back to the village.

They walked apart and neither spoke. He looked ahead. The birds continued their enthusiastic chorusing, calling for their mates, but he heard nothing and saw only his future, stretching along the road in front of him, bleaker and emptier than any winter landscape he had ever seen. They bowed silently to one another outside the cottage. He untied the horse, mounted and rode away at a slow walk. He didn't turn around.

❧

He had no real recollection of the journey – the horse must have taken him home. Jimmy led it away and Alfred walked straight back out through the yard gate without speaking to anyone. He couldn't go into the house, couldn't face his mother. He didn't know how he would ever face her. There were too many difficult words to say. He had tried to form them in his mind, but they refused to come. None of it felt real.

At the top of Stonefield Road he turned first one way and then another before retracing the route of his early morning walk of a couple of months ago, along the lane and down through the fields towards the woods. It was a very different scene from earlier in the year. The pasture was soft and lush, sheep munched noisily, their lambs sleeping or playing nearby, and hawthorn hedges showed just a faint touch of green here and there. He was normally a keen observer of nature and of the changes in the seasons, but today he barely noticed where he was. He just needed to keep moving. If he kept walking perhaps he could hold back the despair that lay somewhere in his chest, constricting his breathing, pulling at his throat, threatening to drown him.

His feet followed a well-worn path and he was unaware that he was veering from his usual route into the trees. The rushing of the stream grew louder, drawing him into the valley where sunlight streamed through bare branches onto a carpet of celandines and wood anemones. He stumbled over stones and roots, almost falling several times. The path had disappeared, but he walked on towards the sound of the water, catching his clothes on brambles as he waded through the undergrowth. Finally he could see it, just a few yards below him. He slithered down the bank, coming to a stop inches from the water's edge.

As he looked around him, at the stream rushing over rusty rocks and stones, the banks of dappled sunshine, the overhanging branches and the old fallen tree lying half-rotten in the water, the flimsy dam he had built against his grief and pain suddenly gave way, leaving him gasping for breath. He slid from the bank into the water and stood with the icy current running over his boots, his chest heaving with sobs. She had never loved him. Never. He had opened his heart to her, had been willing to give her everything of himself, but she had never wanted it. What had he left to live for now? She had taken everything – his future, his belief in himself, his trust in love and God and life itself. His legs began to buckle beneath him. He staggered across the shallows, slumped down onto the log and sat with his head in his hands, staring into the blackness of a deep pool. Tears ran from his face and were carried away by the stream. For hours he sat, as helpless to ease the pain of his despair as a small child, and completely alone, until the sun dropped below the top of the ridge and darkness stole over the valley.

PART TWO

July 1865

CHAPTER 27

The long windows of the breakfast room were wide open, letting in the sweet air of a fine summer morning. Clementine and David Hopwood ate in silence, each engrossed in a letter. Between them sat Charlie and Will, who were bored. They had eaten their eggs, bitten their toast into pistols and swords, fought with them, until their father intervened, and eaten them. Clementine glanced at the boys over her letter, frowning with disapproval as they squirmed on their seats, poking each other whenever they thought they were unobserved.

"Boys, please sit nicely. You are big boys now and will soon be going to school. Whatever will your teacher think of two such wriggling worms?"

Charlie looked at her eagerly. "When are we going to school, Mamma?"

"Well, we're hoping you may go to school after Christmas, when you're nearly five."

"Which school shall we be going to?" asked Will.

"Papa and I haven't quite decided yet." Clementine gave her husband a meaningful glance. "Have we, David?" she continued, getting no response. He looked up from the letter he was reading.

"What's that, dearest?"

"We haven't decided which school the boys are to attend. Will is asking."

"Oh no, Will." He looked at his sons and smiled. "We'll

talk about that another day. Have you finished now, boys? Would you like to go to find Cecily and your brother and sister in the nursery?"

"Yes, please, Papa." The boys slid eagerly from their chairs. Clementine gave them a reproving look.

"Stop, boys. What do you need to say before you leave the table?"

Two heads of curly brown hair turned towards her, straightening their backs and arms like soldiers on parade as they chorused, "May we get down please, Mamma?"

She looked into the large blue eyes fixed on her with the appealing look they had recently perfected and couldn't help smiling.

"Yes you may. Come here, both of you." Wiping their mouths and fingers with her napkin, she gave them a quick kiss on the tops of their heads and watched them scamper from the room before picking up her letter again.

"I've had a letter from Emma Roberts, dear."

"Oh yes?" David put down his own letter and looked at her over his glasses. "How are they getting on?"

"She's expecting a child and feeling very nervous about it, she says. She's fallen for her first as quickly as I did, poor thing. I'm not sure how suited she'll be to motherhood."

"Why do you say that, dear?"

"Oh, I don't know. You just get a feeling about people, don't you? She never seemed at ease with children and the gossip in the village was always that she was unnaturally strict with her pupils."

He frowned at her. "You know what I feel about gossip, dearest."

"Yes, David, I do know. I'm sorry I don't always live up to your high standards."

He smiled at her indulgently. "What else does she say?"

"Edgar has settled well in the new parish. The Rector there isn't as kind or good natured or eccentric as you are, but

228

then that was to be expected. She and her mother are enjoying having more space in the house. Her mother is delighted about the baby, of course. All in all, she seems happy."

"Good, good." He scratched his head and took his glasses off, looking at her with a worried expression. "I wish I could say the same about poor Alfred Nicholson. Dear, dear, I do feel somewhat responsible for that sad affair."

"What nonsense, darling. How could you have been responsible?"

"Well, I did encourage them, didn't I? I still have no idea what went wrong and the worst of it is he's apparently still not over it, more than a year later." He waved the letter at her. "This is from his mother. She's been unwell herself recently. I haven't seen her at church for months. Nor him. I just assumed he was too busy with his work, but it seems that he's fallen into a state of melancholy and rarely goes out, except to work and on solitary walks. She's very concerned about him and asks if I might speak to him. Oh dear, Clemmy, I had no idea. It seems strange for a young man to react quite so badly to the end of a love affair, doesn't it? Do you think there could be more to it?"

"Who knows? Men and their feelings are something of a mystery to us all, including themselves, I suspect."

"I do hope you don't include your husband in such a judgement!"

"Do you know your own feelings, dear?"

He looked puzzled. "I have no reason to think about them."

She flashed him a triumphant smile. "My point exactly!"

"Well, be that as it may, I shall write to Alfred Nicholson this morning. I've recently applied to the Diocese for a grant to repair the stable roof and I heard a couple of weeks ago that they had agreed to the full amount. It has been in my pile of tasks to sort out, but I have a tendency to overlook roofs and other practical matters in favour of people and wildlife…as you know, dear." He smiled sheepishly as she nodded in agreement. "Well now I have a very good reason to be getting on with it. Alfred can come tomorrow afternoon to discuss the repairs and stay for dinner. Will that be all right, dearest?" Without waiting for her reply he continued, "Meanwhile I shall ponder what other measures we can take to lift a young man from the slough of despond. His mother says he isn't even playing the piano at the moment. I'm sure we can do something to remedy that."

Clementine gave him a serious look. "I shall be glad to help if I can. He's a pleasant young man. I don't like to think of him languishing. But, David…" She paused, waiting for him to look up and give her his full attention.

"Yes, dearest?"

"We really must talk about the boys' schooling again soon. You know my views. With the money Mamma and Papa are offering…"

He interrupted her. "And you know my views about taking money from your parents, Clemmy. I can see no reason at all why the boys should not attend the village school along with all their contemporaries."

She sighed in exasperation. He was impossible. Realising that his mind was elsewhere, however, she decided it would be wise to drop the subject for now. "Very well. We shall have to discuss this later, I can see. I'm taking the boys to see Mamma and Papa this afternoon. They were very impressed last week to see that they are beginning to read."

"I'm sure they were! They are clever little chaps. And Cecily is a good teacher. She's wasted in the nursery, you know."

"Oh really, David! We would have no servants at all if it were left to you. They would all be in the world bettering themselves and we would be left with no one to see to our needs at all! Now I must get upstairs. The children will be waiting for me."

Cecily heard the thundering of small feet on the staircase and waited for the inevitable crashing open of the nursery door as the twins came up from breakfast.

"Good morning, Will. Good morning, Charlie. How are you both this morning?"

"My scab's fallen off!" Will proffered his knee and she examined it carefully.

"So it has. That's good, isn't it? How wonderful it is that knees can mend themselves!"

"Does God do it?" Charlie looked with interest at the new, pink patch of skin on his brother's knee.

"Well, I suppose in a way He does." Cecily ruffled their hair as they stood beside her at the table.

"Now, out of my way, boys, please. Go and help Edward with the Noah's Ark animals. Your Mamma will be up soon and Gracie needs to finish her breakfast."

She turned to the chubby, blonde-haired toddler perched on cushions at the table beside her.

"Let me help you finish that now, Gracie." She tried to take the spoonful of porridge from the child's tiny hand, but met with determined resistance.

"My! My!"

"Hmm…yes, I know you want to do it, but Mamma will be here in a minute. Give Cecily the spoon please." Her more serious tone and slightly severe look had the desired effect. As she spooned in the last few mouthfuls, she surveyed the blobs of porridge on the table and Gracie's pinafore. She was an independent little thing, quite different from her brothers. Cecily liked to encourage her desire to do things for herself, but was sure the mistress wouldn't approve of this new messy self-sufficiency. She mopped the child with a flannel before lifting her from the chair, surprised, as she was every day now, by the solidity of her.

"Goodness me, what a big girl you are!" She scrutinised the fat, pink cheeks for any more signs of porridge, before planting a kiss on them and carrying her to the rug where the boys were engrossed in their game. "There you are, my lovely. Edward, can you find Gracie an animal to play with?"

"Gracie like my ephant?" Edward, sturdy and tall now, with the family curls and large blue eyes, held the toy out for his sister.

"Yes, I'm sure she would. Good boy. Say 'ta' Gracie."

The baby snatched the animal, beaming.

"Gracie didn't say ta!" Edward complained.

"No, never mind, dear. She's just a baby. She'll learn some manners when she's a bit older."

Cecily left the children to their play, hurrying to clear the table and make the beds before the mistress arrived. If she was quick there might be time for her to join in the game on the rug. That was her favourite time, when she had all four of them to herself and could be immersed for a few minutes in their world, a world full of unlikely events and bizarre conversations, where anything you wanted could happen. It was like being a child herself again, a moment of relief from the responsibility and hard work of her position. Not that she ever complained. Not even when the mistress was scolding her. She had no intention of suffering the same fate as Miss Cornwell.

This morning Mrs Hopwood appeared while she was still clearing up and swept little Grace into her arms, kissing her and smoothing her hair. She crooned into the child's ear,

"Here's my lovely one. Oh, I have missed you! Have you been a good girl this morning? Did you eat all your porridge?"

Will leapt to his feet and tugged anxiously at his mother's skirt. "Did you miss me, too, Mamma?"

"Don't be a silly, Will. I saw you at breakfast this morning! Cecily, why does Grace have porridge on her pinafore?"

"Oh, sorry, ma'am, I thought I'd got it all off. Shall I get a clean one?"

The mistress frowned disapprovingly. "Yes, well, I suppose you had better, though I'm sure there's enough laundry to be done already without adding to it unnecessarily. I don't know how you manage to be so clumsy, I really don't. Please be more careful in future."

"Yes, ma'am. Sorry ma'am." Cecily hurried to the chest of drawers at the far end of the room, thinking it would be wise not to tell Mrs Hopwood that Gracie had been feeding herself.

She finished her chores while the mistress sat with the children, reading to them and watching them play, her little girl nestled in her lap. Later it was decided that they needed fresh air. Mrs Hopwood would take Grace in the perambulator to her friend across the green. Cecily would watch the boys in the garden. She hummed happily to herself as she gathered a blanket, toys and books into a basket and led the three children downstairs and out onto the wide, sunny lawns.

The boys ran wildly together, shouting, as little boys do, for no other reason than that they suddenly had space and freedom to run and shout. She spread the blanket in the shade of the horse chestnut tree, watching them with an indulgent smile, until Charlie whisked off his sailor's hat and, shrieking with laughter, threw it at Will. She walked over to him, frowning reprovingly.

"Charlie, stop that! Put your hat on now, please! You know your Mamma wants you to wear your hats when you're in the sun, in case you get sunburnt."

"Like Papa did, when he felled asleep in his garden chair and his face went red as a 'mato?" enquired Will, helpfully.

She smiled at the image. "Just like that! Though we wouldn't say that to Papa, would we, Will? He might not like you to call him a tomato."

"I did call him a 'mato, and he laughed!" said Charlie, reluctantly replacing his hat.

She pushed it more firmly onto his head, wondering, as she often did, why the boys couldn't be dressed in more practical clothes for playing in the garden. Their pretty dresses would almost certainly look grubby and creased by the end of the morning and then she would be in trouble again. She decided she should curb the wild running and suggested a game of hide and seek. It was their favourite game and worked well when she and Edward were the seekers, while the twins went off to hide in the greenhouse, or summer house, or behind the wall of the kitchen garden. When it was Edward's turn to hide, the game was less successful. He could only stay quiet and hidden for a few seconds before leaping out with a triumphant cry of " Here I am!" or, as happened today, refusing to hide at all, shouting "I *did* hided!" his hands clamped firmly in front of his eyes.

As she watched him stamping his little feet, the twins spinning and whining with impatience, she laughed at how impossible they were and suggested taking the balls and hoops onto the lawn. All three boys measured her attention jealously with cries of "You rolled it to him last time, Cecily!" or "Throw to me! Throw to me!" She did her best to share herself out fairly, remembering what it had felt like to watch her own mother lavish attention on the younger ones, while seeming to have no time for her at all. But she had also learnt to be firmer as the months had gone on, understanding that little ones just needed more attention, while older ones must learn to grow up. As Edward's tiredness turned to tears, she didn't hesitate to leave the twins to their game, ignoring their protests and leading him back to the rug under the tree for a story.

After a while, when Charlie and Will had temporarily exhausted their apparently boundless store of energy, they too flopped down beside her to listen. At the end of the fifth story from Aesop's Fables, their current favourite, she closed the book firmly and stood up, brushing leaves and grass from her skirts.

"Time for a drink, boys. Let's go and find Mrs Norris, shall we? Perhaps there's some of her lovely elderflower cordial left. I'm thirsty. Are you?"

"Yes!" all three shouted back and, needing no further invitation, ran for the scullery door.

❧

In the early evening she sat with Edie and Mrs Norris eating supper in the kitchen, a precious thirty minutes of adult time as each recounted the trials and high points of their day. She could always make the others laugh with her imitations of the children, especially Edward, whose experiments with language were a constant delight. She was feeling particularly content today. The morning with the boys had been a largely happy one, if exhausting, and her afternoon had been spent alone with Gracie, sitting under the tree darning while the baby slept in her perambulator, then giving her tea and a bath, before the boys and the mistress returned. It was the kind of day that made her tell herself several times how lucky she was.

It came as a shock, then, to be jolted out of her pleasant contentment by Mrs Norris's news.

"We've to get organised early tomorrow, Edith. The mistress says that Mr Nicholson's comin' to dinner and that he's been poorly of late, so she wants a big meal, to feed him up, she says."

Edith and Mrs Norris discussed the details of the menu for several more minutes before Edith stopped and looked at Cecily.

"You all right, Cecily? You look a bit serious all of a sudden."

"Oh…yes…I'm all right." Cecily hastily swallowed the last few mouthfuls of her pudding. "I'd better get upstairs. The missus'll be waiting."

She bolted for the door, catching sight of the exchange of raised eyebrows between her friend and the cook as she went.

Mr Nicholson. She hadn't thought about him for months. Her pointless, unhappy obsession had gradually faded last year as she had become absorbed in her work and the life of the house. And now there was someone else. Tom, the new baker's lad – the result of Edie's scheming. It had begun one morning in the spring when her friend had called her to the nursery window to watch him as he wandered, whistling cheerfully up the path to the kitchen door. A tall, fresh-faced young man who reminded her a little of her father, always well turned out, even on his everyday round, with carefully combed, fair hair and smart waistcoat and tie. Yes, she liked the look of him, she had to admit. So Edie had introduced him to her at the May fair and they had chatted a little, about their families, their work, the usual sort of thing, and he had bought her some candy floss. Lately he had stopped to talk to her over the gate when she was in the garden with the children, making her laugh and blush. Sunday night discussions in the attic room, for so long dominated by the topic of Edie and Harry, were now, with much giggling, exclusively devoted to Cecily and Tom. Last week Edie had suggested she should invite him to join them on their next Sunday afternoon walk in the village with Harry and had arrived panting and grinning at the nursery door the next morning.

"'E says 'e'd love to come, Cecy! We're goin' to meet 'im on the green at two o'clock. What do you think of that, eh, Missy?"

Cecily couldn't help a huge smile spreading across her face in reply, accompanied by the inevitable blush. It was to be their first proper outing together. She couldn't wait.

Now, as she thought of Mr Nicholson and Tom together in the same moment, her heart sank a little, she had no idea why. Mr Nicholson's face appeared in her mind as clearly as the day she had watched him play in the drawing room of the Rectory. A kind, gentle face. An intelligent, musical face. Like Harry's, but with maturity and depth. Beside him Tom seemed no more than a boy, rather silly and empty headed, though that was not what she had felt about him this morning. She shook her head to clear both of them from her mind, straightening her apron and pulling herself upright at the nursery door. This wouldn't do at all. She was sixteen years old – as good as an adult now. Opening the door, she looked at the sweet faces at the table, all turned expectantly towards her as they drank their bedtime milk. Thank goodness for the children. There was no chance of childish dreaming while she was with them. Time to get on with her work.

CHAPTER 28

Alfred stood on a grassy bank in the hot sunshine looking across at the houses in Orchard Road, named after the orchard they had replaced. High above him he could hear swifts screeching, the sound of summer, a sound he used to hear with pleasure, now a sound he merely noted, as he might note the time on a clock. There are the swifts – it must be summer time.

He often stood here, drinking in the solidity and fine workmanship of the two houses, now almost complete. They were spacious, semi-detached, red-brick villas, two reception rooms, with kitchen and scullery downstairs, three bedrooms upstairs. The sight of them anchored him when his black thoughts threatened to overwhelm him. If he had achieved nothing else, he had built good homes for working folk, homes with dry walls and sound roofs, decent sized rooms and a garden large enough to feed a family. There was no jerry building here. With such a small workforce the work had been very slow, but he had refused to compromise on good workmanship, even with money so tight. These houses would still be standing in a hundred years' time. He took a deep breath. Now he needed someone to buy them, or rent them at a decent rate.

His heart lurched with anxiety at the thought of the solicitor's letter he had received last week giving him three months to pay off the loan, threatening to initiate foreclosure proceedings if he did not. With the railway still at least a year from completion and the housing market in Wittenbury quite stagnant, he couldn't see how he could raise the money by then. He could hear the bank manager's voice predicting bankruptcy and ruin and hated to give the greasy little man the satisfaction of being proved right. But far worse was the thought of his mother. She had been ill for some time and he felt sure that the loss of her home would kill her. Nausea swept over him, his scalp pricked with sweat. He took several deep breaths, forcing himself to think of something else, something practical.

He crossed the road to one of the properties. Harold Carpenter stood in the open doorway.

"How's the plastering coming along, Harry?"

"All right, thank you, Mr Nicholson." Harry lowered his voice. "Though I've had to have a few words with Danny." He indicated a room off the hallway with his head, rolling his eyes. "He's a bit of a slacker, that one, if you don't keep an eye on him. I've told him he'll be answering to Mr Barton if I catch him on his backside again. But we've nearly done with the plastering here, sir. Just the scullery to do. The plumber's finished the sink. All we need now is more warm weather to dry this lot off, then we can get the carpenters back in." He smiled at Alfred. "I'm just off to get some more timber from the store."

"Right you are, Harry. I won't see you later. I've an appointment at the Rectory in Blackford. Your sister works there, doesn't she?"

"Yes, sir. Cecily. She's the nursemaid. Say hello to her for me if you see her. Tell her I'm looking forward to Sunday afternoon." Harry smiled sheepishly, his cheeks colouring a little.

"I will. You deserve an afternoon off, Harry. You've worked like a mule these past months."

"Thank you, sir."

He watched the young man walk past the window as he settled himself at a table in the temporary office in the front room. Harry was proving a great asset to the firm. He sighed, unable to avoid a pang of envy as he admired the lad's energy and enthusiasm. Where had his gone? It was a question he knew he couldn't afford to dwell on. He couldn't feel as he used to, but work was still his salvation. Men, bricks, timber, money, planning, sorting. Thinking only of the next task.

He rifled through a pile of invoices. Over the last year he had learnt to set himself small goals. Anything too large and the anxiety turned into panic. When he had cleared this pile and answered the queries from suppliers that had arrived yesterday, then he could leave for the Rectory. He took out his pocket watch. Yes, he could manage that and be there by four. He dipped his pen and began to write.

⁓

Later he rode out of Wittenbury, feeling irritated in the heat and frustrated by the market day traffic clogging the lane, carts and groups of walkers laden with the day's purchases, all slowing him down. The thought of the visit worried him too. The Rector was bound to ask how he was and where he had been. It would be embarrassing to have to explain his long absence from church. What could he possibly say? That God and church held no meaning for him now? How could he describe his turmoil of feelings to someone who was such a straightforward, faithful, *good* man? Someone who had never appeared to suffer from a moment's anxiety or doubt in his life? Perhaps he was doing the Rector an injustice. His mother had urged Alfred to talk to him on several occasions. But he couldn't bring himself to talk to anyone. Not even George.

He felt sad and guilty that he had avoided his friend for so long. He knew George would be hurt, but his depression had been so profound that he couldn't shake himself out of it, not even for friendship's sake. Dark shadows followed him everywhere, every day, the small one as powerful as ever, sapping his sense of self worth and filling him with shame, and now Emma's too, more distinct than the other, her face, her voice, her being, still in his head and gut, inflicting pain which hardly seemed to have lessened since the day they parted. A few months ago perhaps he had begun to think of her less often and the pangs when he did so had weakened a little, but then had come the news of her engagement to the curate and the heartache had returned, as strong, if not stronger, than before.

The day of her marriage was his lowest point. The memory of it brought a hard lump to his throat. He had hidden in the valley, his frequent refuge, especially in the early days. But even here he fancied he could hear the church bells ringing and the joyful voices of the choir and congregation. He could see her turn to her beloved and smile and say "I do." He knew he was torturing himself and that he should stop. But he could not. He had never come closer to using the knife than he had on that day.

Two miles out of Wittenbury he turned off the lane and onto a bridleway, kicking the horse into a fast canter, relieved to feel the wind on his face. He rode much faster these days, taking risks he would never have contemplated before. A good gallop always helped to clear his head and steady his jangling nerves. Riding hard, walking hard, working hard and sleep. These were his self-prescribed remedies, and sitting down in the valley, when it all got too much. Nothing else was of any help. He had drunk himself into oblivion on several occasions, but always felt far worse the next day. And music – his solace and his joy – it had become grey and meaningless, like everything else.

When he arrived at the Rectory he was breathless, sweating heavily, but calmer. He spoke firmly to himself. Keep the conversation on a professional footing, Alfred. You can manage this. He rode into the stable yard, casting a professional eye over the roof as he did so.

≈

Cecily was doing a jigsaw puzzle with the twins under the chestnut tree. It had been a hot afternoon in the garden and the boys had been fractious. She was glad it was almost time to take them in for their tea and bath. Charlie placed the last piece with a triumphant gesture, completing the steam engine as it roared through the rolling hills, smoke pouring from the funnel.

"Done it!" he cried. "I won!"

"No you didn't! Did he, Cecy?" Will tried to snatch the piece back out of the picture.

"It wasn't a race, Charlie," she said gently, replacing the piece and removing the puzzle from their reach. "We were doing it together. It's a fine engine, isn't it?"

Will tugged at her sleeve. "Can *we* go on a train, Cecy?"

"I don't know, Will, you'll have to ask Papa. Shall we do some reading, boys, just until tea time?" She pulled out the old primer from the bottom of the pile of toys on the rug. It was a dreadful old book, rescued from a set the Reverend had found in his library, a relic of his own childhood, she guessed. The sentences were horribly stilted, consisting almost entirely of two- and three-letter words; the story was non-existent and the engravings few and far between. Yet the twins loved it. They scrambled to be close to her.

"Don't push, boys. There's plenty of room for you both. Shall we read together, or do you want to read on your own?"

"I want to read on my own!" they cried in unison.

"Then we'll take it in turns. Will, you start." She pointed to each word, mouthing it with him.

"The h – e – n…hen is in a b – o – x…box. The pig is in a p – e – n…pen."

"Good boy, Will. That's such good reading! Your turn, Charlie."

She was amazed, as she always was, at how fast they remembered the letters and the words she had taught them.

In fact it seemed now that she didn't really need to teach them at all. They were teaching themselves, working out the words and learning them as they went. It was exciting to watch them, especially as they were so excited themselves. Sometimes she felt a pang of sadness, realising how much she would have enjoyed teaching a whole class of children how to read, but it never lasted long. She was meant to be here with these children, she was sure.

As Charlie worked doggedly through his page she became aware that they were being watched. Just a few yards away, in the stable doorway, stood the Reverend, beaming with pride, with Mr Nicholson at his side. Her heart missed a beat. She focussed even more intently on the child's reading.

When Charlie had finished, his father strode over to them, ruffling each curly head in turn.

"That was splendid, boys. What clever little chaps you are! Mr Nicholson, come and meet my sons. Charlie, Will, stand up and shake hands with Mr Nicholson."

Cecily looked on, feeling as proud of them as if they were her own children, then jumped up in a fluster of embarrassment as the Reverend went on to introduce her to his guest.

"And this is Cecily, our nursemaid, who has been teaching the boys so skilfully. I think she should have been a teacher, Mr Nicholson, but my wife will scold me for saying so, she's so terrified of losing Cecily now!"

She bobbed a curtsy, looking up shyly into the young man's face. Now she was close to him, she was shocked to see how he had changed. His face was thinner than she remembered. He looked tired and pale, older, she thought. Mrs N had said that he'd been ill. Perhaps that was why. His smile was the same, though. Still warm and gentle. She felt her cheeks flush as he greeted her.

"I'm pleased to meet you, Cecily. You're doing a fine job with these boys, I can see. Your brother sends greetings, by the way, and says he's looking forward to Sunday."

"Thank you, sir." She returned a shy smile as she bobbed again.

The Reverend took hold of the twins' hands. "Come along, my dears. Let's go into the drawing room. There is something I wish to talk to you all about."

Cecily began packing up the toys. The Reverend beckoned to her to join them. "You, too, Cecily...and Mr Nicholson. I need you all there."

He strode across the lawn, through the French windows into the drawing room, a boy on each hand, Cecily and Mr Nicholson following close behind. They gathered beside the grand piano.

"Now boys, put your fingers on the keys like Papa. Let's see if your hands are big enough. Mr Nicholson, come and have a look. What do you think? Could we make pianists out of them?"

❦

The large bedchamber was cool after the heat of the day and the ride home. Being on the north side of Stonefield House, above the dining room, it was always far too cold in the winter, but a blessing in hot weather like today's. Alfred sat at his mother's bedside, enjoying the breeze from the open window behind him, telling her about his day. As he talked he looked at her, thinking, as he often did these days, that she had shrunk since yesterday. At this rate he felt that she would soon disappear altogether. Her digestion was very bad and so were her nerves. She ate hardly anything and was often in bed before seven o'clock. He could see that she was worn out, and he felt that he was to blame. While he avoided her during the day, unable to cope with her anxiety as well as his own, he made himself sit with her for a short time each evening. He wasn't always sure that she wanted him there.

Sometimes they could think of little to say to one another and he would leave after just a few minutes. But it helped him to feel less guilty and today she seemed more interested, especially in his account of his afternoon at the Rectory.

"Piano lessons." Her tired eyes fixed on him. "What a good idea. And you said yes, of course."

"I said I would think about it. I've never taught a child in my life and to have two of them, even with the maid's help, seems very daunting. Besides, I'm so busy, Mother. I'm not sure I can fit it in, even if it is only once a week for an hour."

"Oh don't be silly, Alfie, of course you can fit it in. It will do you good, get you playing again. It's such a pity not to hear you play any more after all those expensive lessons your father paid for."

"I know." He grimaced apologetically. "I just don't have the heart for it, though. I'm sorry."

She looked back at him, some of the old determination in her eyes. "I want you to do it, Alfie. I expect they'll give you supper at the Rectory and you could play for Mrs Hopwood sometimes as well. She has a nice voice. I know you'll enjoy it. It will take you out of yourself – just what you need. All this moping at home on your own isn't good for you."

"I'm all right, Mother, really I am. But I will think about it. I'll write to him tomorrow. To tell you the truth, I think this is one of his little schemes. He told me after dinner, when Mrs Hopwood was out of the room, that he's hoping to persuade her of the merits of the village school for the twins, over the expensive school she wants to send them to. He thinks some additional culture, in the form of piano lessons with me, might allay her fears about the lack of refinement at the village establishment. Those were his very words!"

"Well, there's no reason why you couldn't be a good teacher, Alfie, if you put your mind to it."

Alfred winced. "Hmm…I'm not so sure. Though the nursemaid is very good with the children and she'll be there. It might be all right. I'll let you know what I've decided in the morning."

His mother frowned at him. "Do it, Alfie!"

He stood up, kissing her on the cheek before walking over to the door.

"Goodnight, Mother. Sleep well."

"Goodnight, Alfie."

He walked slowly downstairs and into the drawing room, a room he avoided now whenever he could, preferring to sit in his office or his bedchamber. The piano looked sad and abandoned. His father's photograph too. He felt he should apologise to them both. The air smelt musty and he opened the window wide, letting in the scent of warm grass from the garden and the evening chatter of the birds, before sitting at the piano.

He ran his hands over the dark wood of the lid. Perhaps he should agree to do the lessons for a while. If he or the children didn't enjoy it, if he was no good as a teacher, then he could always stop. He had to admit that he had enjoyed his meal with the Hopwoods. Neither had mentioned his absence from church and he felt calmer for some good company. It wouldn't be a problem to find an hour a week towards the end of the day, and for the first few weeks he could combine it with casting an eye over the roofing work, which Bill would be supervising. His mother was right. It would help take his mind off his troubles, especially his growing anxiety about the business. The small, additional income would be useful and his mother would be pleased. He wanted to do something to make her happy for once.

He opened the piano lid, resting his fingers tentatively on the keys, looking out of the window into the garden, where the low sun touched all the roses with a deep orange glow. His fingers traced a sequence of chords, creating a short theme in C minor – suitably melancholy, he thought. He sighed heavily, shut the lid abruptly and went to search for his old music books in the cupboard beside the fireplace. He looked up at his father's photograph. The old man would be pleased to know they were being used again.

CHAPTER 29

It was a Thursday, nearly three months after his decision to become a teacher as well as a builder. He stood at the back door of one of the houses in Orchard Road, looking down the long garden to the newly painted white picket fence and the line of oaks beyond. The garden was freshly dug and completely bare apart from two old apple trees which had been saved from the orchard.

A smartly dressed, middle-aged man stood beside him, also surveying the scene. He had introduced himself earlier – Mr Drake, the new assistant manager of the conserve factory, looking for a home for himself, his wife and two small children. He had a steady income and good references, just the sort of tenant Alfred needed.

"What sort of apples are they?"

"Bramleys, I believe," replied Alfred. "They'll make good pies." He turned to go back into the house. "Well, I think you've seen everything there is to see now, Mr Drake. When can I expect your decision?"

"Well…" Mr Drake rubbed his chin as he cast his eye around the kitchen once more. "It's a lot to pay, Mr. Nicholson."

Alfred spoke in a detached, businesslike voice, hoping that the man could not hear his loudly beating heart or see the desperation in his eyes. "I realise that, sir. But this is a well-built house and worth every penny I should say." He made for the doorway. "I'll be at my desk in the front room, Mr Drake, if you want to take more time to decide. Feel free to wander around the property at your leisure."

"Oh no…I don't need to see anymore. I've made my decision."

Alfred's heart sank. This would be the third client who had turned the property down because the rent was too high. Yet he needed to charge this amount if he was to begin to recover his costs and save his own home. He forced himself to stay silent, though he was sorely tempted to make a lower offer in order to ensure at least some income.

Mr Drake looked at him with raised eyebrows. "So where do I sign, Mr Nicholson?"

⟋⟍

Two hours later Alfred sat on a hard, wooden bench outside the bank manager's office. With the tenancy signed and the first month's rent in his wallet, he had swallowed his pride, a large and unpleasant mouthful, and had come here, cap in hand, to ask for an extension to the foreclosure on the loan which was due at the end of the month. The manager had frowned, shaken his head, shuffled his papers and shaken his head again. Then he had made a great play of needing to consult with colleagues as he considered the proposal. That was an hour ago. Men with large stomachs and pocket watches on ostentatious gold chains walked in and out of the office, while Alfred sat chewing his nails, trying to still his hands and calm his loudly churning stomach. By the time he was finally called back in, he had convinced himself that the answer would be no and hardly heard the words which told him that he had until the end of November, another two months, to pay off the rest of the money. He forced himself to thank the manager graciously and to bow deferentially as he left.

Outside in the street once more he sighed heavily with relief and rode quickly out of town. Although the problem was only postponed, not solved, he felt energy surge through his body for the first time in many months. He turned from the Wittenbury Road onto the bridleway. The route from the site to Blackford had become a familiar one and the horse needed no encouragement to accelerate into a canter. The sky was heavy. Spots of rain blew into his face, carried on strong gusts of cool air. Leaves, ripped prematurely from the trees by the force of the wind, swirled around the horse's hooves. He looked about him, noticing the small changes in the woodlands and the fields with some of his old pleasure. He particularly liked early autumn, with its warm colours and rich, musty smells, its fierce winds to clear your head and sunshine that could still warm your back, before the real cold arrived and all the colour and scent disappeared beneath the ground.

He was looking forward to his weekly visit to the Rectory now. He smiled as he thought of the twins, picturing their identical animated faces and mops of curly brown hair, their wriggling bodies, pursed lips and small tongues playing at the corners of their mouths in fierce concentration. He heard their laughter and chatter and arguments and the terrible music they made, banging the piano keys with their small fingers, apparently incapable of doing anything quietly or slowly. The chaos of their endlessly eager, flitting minds and restless bodies, and the din that they made, should have irritated him. Instead it was invigorating, like the autumn wind in his face. He tried to imagine having children of his own and hoped they would be boisterous and noisy like the twins, not timid and quiet as he had been.

He rode into the stable yard of the Rectory, leaving the horse with the boy. The housemaid let him into the house and took his coat. As he opened the drawing room door he could see two small figures already sitting on the stool, dwarfed by the grand piano, waiting for him. Their eager faces turned towards him, hands flapping excitedly.

"We can play it, Mr Nickson," cried one (he could never tell them apart at first glance).

"We practised every day! Cecily made us!" shouted the

other, bobbing up and down with frustration. "Shall we show you? Can we play now?"

Cecily stood at the side of the piano. He caught her eye and they grinned at one another conspiratorially.

He drew up a chair to the left of their stool. "Yes, I'd love to hear it. Thank you, boys."

The children glanced at one another and at the music, only sixteen bars, a duet for two right hands he had composed and written out for them in giant notation. He counted them in. They took no heed either of the tempo he had set, or of the music in front of them, but set off at a great rate, racing one another to the end of the piece. Charlie won by half a bar. They looked at Alfred and at Cecily anxiously.

She tutted gently. "They can play it much better than that, Mr Nicholson. I think you were a bit excited, boys, weren't you? We've talked about not racing, haven't we?"

He smiled reassuringly at them. "It was a good first try. Now I'm going to count one, two, three, four all the way through and you must stay with me. The winner is the person who finishes at *exactly* the same time as I do!"

The second attempt was better, and the third better still. Finally he was able to stop counting and to play the left hand part with them. The overall effect was surprisingly pleasing. It was decided that their parents should be called in to listen. Clementine and David stood with Cecily and the two little ones, listening with proud attention. When the end of the piece arrived with no mishaps, the adults laughed with pleasure and clapped loudly. The children were exultant.

Alfred looked at Cecily. Her dark eyes were shining and her cheeks pink. She returned his gaze, not with her usual blushing shyness, but smiling steadily and happily. They had achieved this tiny triumph together and for just a moment he felt something wonderful pass between them, a deep recognition of shared joy.

The twins grabbed her by the hands and pulled her

towards the door. "Is it tea time, Cecily? I'm hungry!" "So am I! What's for tea?"

He watched her leave, his heart full.

∞

He rode home later through the blustery darkness. The evening had left him feeling calmer, as it always did – the pleasant conversation over supper, David Hopwood's amusing anecdotes and quiet concern, Clementine's singing and his own playing. To have his music gradually restored to him over the last couple of months had been a profound relief. He had even played the piano a few times at home in the evenings recently, leaving the drawing room door open so that his mother could hear.

He was aware that his calm was superficial. Beneath it lay the usual mixture of anxiety and melancholy, about his mother, his brother, the house, the business, himself, everything. And as the horse trotted home, the sound of its hooves lost in the rushing of the wind in the trees that hung over the dark lane, his fragile sense of peace was swept away by memories of the afternoon and of Cecily, replaced by an unsettling desire to see her again. The thought that he was growing fond of her frightened him. It was absurd. She was just a girl, far too young to become involved with a tired old man like himself. Besides, she had a young man of her own. He had seen them together, last Sunday afternoon on the green in Blackford, when he had finally given in to George's patient letters and had gone to visit him and Sarah in their new home. Cecily and the lad hadn't seen him, they were too busy enjoying each other's company on the circular seat under the old yew. His heart had ached as he watched them there, obviously happy, their heads close together, laughing and chatting with the other maid and young Harry Carpenter. But what else did he expect? She was a lovely girl, with her

252

brown eyes and wide smile, not beautiful like Emma, but full of life and warmth. Young men were bound to be interested in her.

In any case, after his experience last year, how could he ever trust himself to know anything about love? Love seemed to him now to be something destructive, obsessive, self-deceiving. It made the beloved into something they were not and never could be. No, he couldn't fall in love with Cecily. He wouldn't allow it. But he needed her in some way, that much was clear.

As he turned into Stonefield Road the full moon appeared briefly from behind fast-moving clouds, bathing the wall of the yard, the gate and the walls of the house in pale grey light. He loved to see the house in all its different guises, golden at dawn and dusk, shining brightly in the mid-day sun, dull white on cloudy days and now shimmering silver, almost ghostly. This was his home, a part of him. He couldn't bear to think that he might lose it. The moon disappeared as fast as it had come, leaving everything in thick darkness. He strained his eyes to find the latch of the gate and led the horse into the yard. Looking up, he could see no lamp in his mother's window. She must be asleep already. He stabled the horse quickly, yawning as he closed the stable door and walked across to the house.

❧

The following afternoon he sat on the bank of the stream, his hands shaking as he pulled off his boots and socks and rolled his trousers to his knees. He stepped into the water, grunting with the shock of the cold. The larger stones were agony in the soles of his feet as he picked his way gingerly upstream, wading knee-deep until he reached the gravel shallows and the old fallen tree. The pain of the rocks and cold was good. It was what he needed. He sat down on the damp, rotting

253

log, stretched his legs out in front of him and watched the water, parted by his toes into rivulets, run over his long, pale feet. After a few moments his head and shoulders sagged and tears came, an inevitable consequence, he now knew, of coming to this place. A consequence and perhaps a reason too.

After a while, when his anxiety and distress had begun to subside, he sat quite still, his head in his hands, staring blankly at the water as mottled brown and yellow rafts drifted slowly past him. Another long interval passed before he sat up, splashed his face with the icy water and looked around. The woods were quiet. There was very little wind. A blackbird rustled about under a nearby bush, flicking up leaves with its beak. The stream gurgled quietly as it slid by, still low after the dry summer and early autumn. It had been a few weeks since he had last been here. The strange, sad music of the valley hadn't drawn him as it had so often done before, pulling him down to the water whenever his melancholy threatened to overwhelm him. He hadn't felt the need of it lately.

He looked down at his legs and traced his fingers over lines of hairless skin on his shins, remnants of childhood scars. Their origin was a mystery. He had no memory of what had caused them. "You had an accident," his parents had said, and the subject was swiftly changed. In his worst days he had been tortured by a terrible urge to reopen the scars with a knife he had taken from the workshop down to the stream. Tears were not enough then. He needed to see his own blood flowing into the water, as if, by watching it disappear, diluting into nothing, he too could fade away, with all his pain and failure. He had never done it, thank God, stopped only by the thought of his mother's distress if she ever found out. The desire had faded with time. Now it made him sick with shame to think of it. It was bad enough that he needed to come here at all, that he was unable to master his feelings and be a proper man, but that…he must not think about it.

A cool wind began to blow down the valley and he pulled his jacket closer about him, looking up through the trees to the thickening clouds above. The sky grew darker and it was difficult to tell how late it was. He always lost track of time down here. With the fading of his agitation and distress came a growing awareness of the discomfort in his body: feet numb with cold, trousers damp, legs and shoulders stiff and aching. Then he felt drops on his face and heard the growing rush of rain falling on the dry, withered canopy above. It was time to leave. He stood up, sighing deeply, stretched his arms and waded back through the stream to find his boots.

As he sat on the bank, drying his feet with his socks, he knew he must think about his mother now and about the news that had catapulted him backwards into panic earlier in the afternoon. Dr Tucker hadn't minced his words. She was dying. She had a large tumour on her liver. That explained her extreme fatigue over the last months, her recent terrible colour and nausea. She should have come to him sooner. There was nothing to be done except to keep her comfortable. He prescribed laudanum for the pain, which was slight now, but would get worse. Alfred should engage a nurse to care for her. It was impossible to say how long she might live. It could be just a few weeks, or possibly months. She was unlikely to see her sixtieth Christmas.

He had known for a long while that she wasn't well, but hadn't allowed himself to think that she might die. Their relationship was difficult. John's death hung over them as dark as the clouds above his head, and her over-anxious, critical nature was a constant irritation. Yet she was still an anchor to him. What would he do without her? She needed him. She gave everything meaning. The house, the business, what would any of it be to him without her? Hearing the doctor speak of her death as an imminent certainty had been terrible, like a physical blow, winding him, sucking all the strength from his legs, leaving him dizzy and disorientated.

He took deep breaths to steady himself and began to walk back up through the wood to the path at the bottom of the field. He must go to her now. She would be wondering where he was, why he hadn't gone back up to see her after the doctor's visit. He quickened his pace. The rain was falling hard, but he was oblivious to the water soaking through the shoulders of his jacket and running down his face and neck. As he passed behind the cottage gardens of Stonefield hamlet he agonised about what he should say to her. She wasn't a stupid woman. She must know something was terribly wrong. But how much should he tell her? Should he pretend she might be cured, give her some hope? Or was that a cruel deception that would only make her feel worse?

He reached the house and an answer at the same time. Letting himself in the front door, he resolved to tell her as little as she seemed to want to know. If she asked, he would be truthful. If she didn't, he would keep quiet. He climbed the stairs and stood outside her chamber, hoping desperately that his renewed steadiness would withstand the conversation he must now have. He knocked quietly and pushed open the door.

His mother lay back against a large pile of pillows, her eyes shut, her sallow face lined and hollow. It shocked him again to see her looking so old and ill. He felt terrible that he had not called the doctor sooner, that he had listened to her excuses and willed himself to believe them — she was just tired, it was her rheumatism giving her pain, it was something she had eaten, it was "women's trouble", she didn't need the doctor, just a little more rest.

She opened her eyes, looked at him and frowned. Her voice was quiet, completely lacking power, but her disapproval was clear. "Alfie, look at you! You're soaked through! What have you been doing? Where have you been?"

He ran his hands over his wet face and wiped them on his trousers. "I needed some air, Mother, I'm sorry. It's just come on to rain."

"Go and dry your hair and change your clothes, dear."

"I'm perfectly all right…really."

"You'll catch your death and you look a fright. Do as I say!"

He smiled, grateful to her for irritating him and restoring normality between them. "Very well. But you're not to go anywhere! I'll be right back."

A few moments later he returned, clothes dry, hair towelled and brushed back into some semblance of order. He sat down on the edge of the bed.

She smiled weakly. "That's better. What is the time, by the way? I've had such a nice sleep. Is it late?"

"It's half past four."

"Good heavens! So late already." She looked out of the window at the driving rain and back at him, her eyes wistful. "I seem to be sleeping my life away, Alfie."

"It's good for you to sleep… Now…about the doctor…"

"Never mind about the doctor now. We'll talk about him another day. Though…I *have* been thinking that perhaps I should have a nurse. It's too much for poor Annie, now. I'm finding it so difficult to stand and wash myself and…and all that kind of thing."

He let out an inaudible sigh of relief. "That's a very good idea, Mother. I'm sure Dr Tucker has someone he can recommend."

"Oh, no! She'll be loud and overbearing like him."

"All right, I'll make sure she's quiet and overbearing. You need someone to keep you in order, you know, or else how are we to get you to eat and drink properly?"

She wrinkled her nose. Her voice was quiet and apologetic. "It's hard for me to eat, Alfie."

"I know. Don't worry. We shall find someone kind to take good care of you."

"Thank you." She smiled up at him again. "Now go downstairs and have a cup of tea and a piece of Mrs Dawes' tea bread. And ask Annie to bring me some tea too."

"Shall I drink mine up here with you?"

"No...thank you. But you could play the piano for me. That's what I would like. Some of that music by Mr Sh... Sh..."

"Chopin?"

"Yes, that's him. That lovely piece you played at the Rector's Christmas recital, before everything went...oh, well, you know what I mean. *That* piece – it was so beautiful. And everyone else thought so too. Do you remember, Alfie?"

He stood up, leaned over and kissed her on the cheek. "Of course I do. Mr Chopin it shall be, Mother, just for you."

CHAPTER 30

The dusty upright piano inched its tortuous way up the stairs. Charlie and Will stood on the landing looking, large-eyed, through the banisters.

"I fink that man's going to burst soon," announced Charlie in a loud voice, pointing at the over-weight man holding the lower end of the piano.

"Shush, Charlie! That's very rude," hissed Cecily, trying not to laugh.

The top piano mover guffawed. "D'you 'ear that, Archie? 'E's worried your goin' t' burst!"

"So am I, young man! So am I," gasped his colleague, sweat running into his eyes and dripping off the end of his purple nose. "And it won't be a pretty sight, I can tell yer!"

Cecily took the boys' hands and pulled them out of the way as the piano finally reached the landing.

"Thank Gawd for that," said the leading man, wiping his face and hands with his handkerchief.

Cecily frowned with disapproval.

"Oh, beggin' yer pardon, miss. Now, where's this old pianna goin'?"

She and the twins led the way to the nursery while the two men rolled the piano along the landing. Soon it was installed on the wall opposite the doorway, beside the window, where there would be plenty of light for reading the music. The twins hopped and jumped like a pair of new lambs as the men left the room.

"Can we play it now? Can I go first?"

"No, me! I want to go first!"

Cecily produced a duster from her apron pocket. "Neither of you can play it yet. We need to clean all this dirt off first, then a man's coming this afternoon to tune it."

Will began writing his name in the dust on the lid. "What does 'tune it' mean?"

She lifted his hand away from the dirt, pointing to the letters he had made. "That's an 'M' for Mamma, Will. A 'W' for Will goes up the other way, do you remember?" She had started teaching the boys to write their names a couple of weeks ago. Charlie had grasped it almost immediately, and was noisily proud of his efforts, but Will was finding it more difficult. It reminded her of her own struggles with writing. Before embarking on teaching them she had practised her letters secretly on an old slate. She couldn't teach them if she couldn't write properly herself. In the event she was pleased that, with a little effort, she could produce quite a school-teacherly script. It surprised her. Perhaps now that she was a woman – calmer, less impatient – she was becoming less cack-handed too.

"Cecileee! You're not listening! What does 'tune it' mean?"

"Sorry, Will. Um…it means he will make the notes sound right. Bumping the piano up the stairs like that will have made the strings change their notes. The man will have to put them right again." She gave the casing a quick wipe. "But it *would* be fun to hear it, wouldn't it?"

"Oh yes please, yes please." The jumping and hopping began all over again.

She took a key from her pocket and opened the lid. The boys leapt forward and began banging the piano keys in a frenzy. She watched them for a moment, horrified. They were like two wild children from some isolated community who had never seen a piano, let alone been taught to play. She summoned her loudest, most authoritative voice to cut through the jangling din.

"NO BOYS! STOP NOW!"

The children's hands froze above the keys.

"Goodness me! What a dreadful noise! Look at me now, both of you, please."

They turned to her, faces already hot with shame, eyes cast down to their feet.

"That's not how we play the piano, is it?"

Their heads drooped as they shook silently to and fro.

"Whatever would Mr Nicholson say? Or Mamma? It's a good thing she's out this morning, or she might have asked the men to come and take the piano away again." She paused to let the full impact of this sink in. Their heads sunk further still. The trouble was she was beginning to feel sorry for them now, as she always did when they were naughty. She knelt down in front of them.

"Now… let's start again, shall we?"

Silent nodding.

"We'll try your duet. Grandmamma and Grandpapa are coming to hear you play it tomorrow, aren't they?"

More silent nodding.

She settled them on the stool, found the music and counted them in. They played tentatively and made mistakes, too nervous to remember their parts, the overall effect not helped by several badly out of tune notes. After two attempts they all agreed that it would be better to wait until the man had come to put the notes right.

The children went off to find their toys and she locked the lid, installing the key on the top shelf beside the fireplace and settling herself in the large chair in front of the fire with her darning basket. As she sewed she glanced frequently at the piano. It was exciting to have one of their own. Using the grand piano in the drawing room had been proving difficult now the twins were keen to practise more often. They would calm down and get used to it soon.

A little later an exciting idea came to her: perhaps she could learn to play now, too. She had followed their lessons carefully, understood the notation and the location of the keys and had even played through some of the children's pieces herself, secretly, when no other adults were around. It had been quite easy, so far. Too easy almost. Could she ask Mr Nicholson for some harder music for herself? Would he think her impertinent? The thought of displeasing him in any way horrified her. Tomorrow was Thursday. Piano lesson day. Her stomach leapt in anticipation. Should she ask him tomorrow? Nothing ventured, nothing gained, her Grannie always said. Yes, she should. He was a kind man. There was no real reason why he would say no.

She continued darning Edward's small green cardigan, gone through at the elbows. Her sewing was still slow, so that it seemed to her that she could never keep pace with the growing pile in the basket, but the results were usually quite reasonable now. Even the mistress had said so once. And it was quite a soothing job. You could sew and think, she found. Her problem at the moment was that she often found herself thinking about the wrong man.

The man she should be thinking about was Tom. They had spent several Sunday afternoons together now, with Edie and Harry. He was a nice boy and good-looking too, with his lovely fair hair, all smoothed down and parted so sharp at the side of his head. She liked the idea of being seen in the village with him. And he was clearly fond of her, had tried to hold her hand several times, though she had never let him. But they didn't have much in common, she knowing nothing about baking, he caring little for small children, or teaching or music or books. He liked to tell a joke and could make her laugh, but he wasn't much of a talker. They often lapsed into silence and she would look across at Edie and Harry, chatting excitedly with one another, so delighted to be together after their long month apart, and feel that they had something different, something much more real and permanent.

And then she would start thinking about *him* – Mr Nicholson. And dreaming about what it would be like to be with him, to talk to him as an equal, rather than as servant and teacher. She was sure they would share many interests and enjoy lively conversations. They wouldn't run out of things to say to one another. When she thought of him she felt excited. She looked forward to Thursdays eagerly now, feeling impatient when the week seemed to pass so slowly. The other day, when he had looked at her, so pleased and happy, her heart had somersaulted and her legs had gone weak. That never happened when she looked at Tom. Never. She looked at him and merely felt guilty that she was thinking of someone else.

Today, having made the decision to ask Mr Nicholson for some music, she allowed herself to forget Tom for a few moments and let her imagination run free. Today in her dreams Mr Nicholson was teaching her to play. An absurd idea, she knew, but delicious in its possibilities. At first he sat decorously beside her at the piano, quietly instructing and encouraging. Soon he was standing behind her, murmuring in her ear, holding her shoulders as he talked. She progressed quickly. Her talent amazed him. Now he was placing his hands over hers, demonstrating some fingering, now leaning over her to point at the music, kissing her, loving her. Her heart beat fast in her ears. Her cheeks flamed. The needle poised, stationary, above the cardigan.

The sound of the twins squabbling loudly over a wooden steam engine jolted her back to reality. She sighed, put down her sewing, and went over to sort them out.

⁂

For Alfred, too, Thursday could not come soon enough. He had noticed recently how the week between each Thursday stretched further than it used to; this week had passed even more slowly still. Trying to come to terms with his mother's diagnosis, organising a nurse to live in, worrying about the loan as time sped frighteningly fast towards the deadline – it had all been difficult. He longed for the distraction of the children and Cecily, and the pleasant, undemanding evening that would follow.

Today, as the front door of the Rectory opened, he could see the boys waiting for him in the hallway, hopping from foot to foot with excitement. As soon as the maid had taken his hat and coat, they grasped his hands, one on either side, and pulled him up the stairs and along a corridor, shouting in sing song voices, "We've got a surprise!"

They pushed open a door and stood aside with a flourish, grinning with pride as he entered their nursery. There at the end of the room was a large, upright piano and on the piano stool sat Cecily, playing through a piece from one of the books he had given them. She stopped and got up to greet him, smiling shyly. Before she could say anything one of the children blurted out,

"It's *our* piano, Mr Nickson, our very own, but we're not to bang on it, or the notes might go wrong again, and then the tuner man will have to come to make the notes right…"

"…and Cecily will lock it up with her key…She's hided it on the shelf up there, look…" This was said standing on tiptoe, pointing up to the highest shelf beside the chimney breast.

"…and Mamma might take it away again."

"Oh…yes, I expect she might, if you bang on it. But you wouldn't do that, would you?" He looked at them gravely, then turned to Cecily and winked. "Good afternoon, Cecily."

"Good afternoon, Mr Nicholson." She bobbed a curtsy with a smile which lit up her whole face, or so it seemed to him. And there was a definite flush in her cheeks, too, a flush of pleasure he hoped. It made him want to sit with her, to talk to her and spend longer looking at her youthful face and warm, dark eyes. Instead he walked over to the instrument and ran his fingers over the keys.

"Well, this is all very exciting, I must say. When did it arrive?"

"Not this day, but the day before this day," one of them replied.

"Will means yesterday, Mr Nicholson," said Cecily.

Alfred looked at the children and frowned. It always irked him that he couldn't immediately distinguish them as individuals. "Boys, come and stand together in front of me. Stand still, please. Ah, yes, that's better – now I can see who you are. So, Will, have you practised your piece on the new piano yet?"

Will looked worried. "Yes, but we weren't very good, were we, Cecily?"

Cecily ruffled his hair. "Well, no, but that was before the piano tuner came. And this morning the boys have been out with their Mamma buying new shoes, so they haven't had time to practise I'm afraid."

"Well, never mind. We shall start now. But what about you? We saw you practising as we came in."

This time she blushed scarlet. "Oh…I was just…"

He was sorry he had embarrassed her and gave what he hoped was a reassuring smile. "It's good that Cecily is practising, isn't it, boys? Then she can help you in the week when I'm not here. Once we've practised the duet, I think we could all learn the piece that Cecily was playing. It's time we put both hands together."

"Like this, Mr Nickson?" Charlie put his hands together, prayer-like. "We say, 'hands together, eyes closed', before tea, don't we, Cecily?"

Alfred caught her eye and laughed. "Oh no, Charlie, I mean…" He scratched his head, trying to think of a simple way of explaining. "What do I mean, Cecily?"

"Mr Nicholson means we shall play with both hands on the piano at the same time. Perhaps you could show us, Mr Nicholson."

He played a sprightly version of "Hickory Dickory Dock" complete with ascending and descending glissandi as the mouse ran up and down. The boys clapped their hands in excitement.

"Can we play Hickory Dickory?"

He smiled kindly. "Well, not quite yet, Charlie, but one day you'll be able to…as long as you practise. Now that's enough talking. Come and sit up both of you. Let's try this duet."

❧

Later in the evening he sat between Clementine and her mother, enjoying a second helping of Mrs Norris's blackberry and apple pie. He ate far more here than he ever did at home, where the atmosphere of sickness, and now death, took his appetite away. Clementine's parents were a rather odd couple, he thought. Mr Gresham was very tall, with uniformly black hair, quite incongruous with his aging skin, and darting, pale blue eyes. Mrs Gresham was tiny, grey-haired, with a small, rather expressionless face. He was intelligent, talkative, opinionated. She was silent, obviously content to let him speak for them both. Clementine was like neither of them, Alfred decided. Perhaps she was adopted.

Mr Gresham complimented him on the boys' playing – "A triumph" – and expressed hopes that he would play for them after dinner. He was happy to agree. He felt relaxed. Mellow. Like the fine port they were drinking. No doubt partly *because* of the port.

The conversation turned to the knotty question of schooling for the boys and he detected a small, but unmistakable rise in tension in the room. Mr Gresham had introduced the subject, to the obvious discomfort of his daughter, who sat with a tiny frown between her brows and her lips clamped shut. David Hopwood pleaded for a change of topic for Alfred's sake. His father-in-law was dismissive.

"Nonsense, David. Mr Nicholson won't mind us

discussing the boys' schooling, I'm sure. What is your view, Mr Nicholson?"

Alfred felt awkward. "I don't think I'm really qualified to comment, sir."

"Why on earth not? You are obviously an educated man."

"Well…I went to a small private school and know nothing of other schools. But I see no reason why the village school could not offer a good, basic education. I think I would be happy for my own children, if I had any, to be educated there."

David leaned across the table towards his father-in-law. "There you are, Charles. 'A good, basic education.' That's exactly what we need for the boys. And now they are making such good progress under Alfred's expert tutelage, we can be sure they will turn out to be cultured, well-rounded young men like him. He will provide the culture and the village school will give them good experience of the world in which they must one day make their way."

Mr Gresham raised his eyebrows. "Do you mean a world full of common people, David?"

Alfred winced. He was tempted to ask, do you mean common people like my friend the blacksmith, Mr Gresham, and the men who work for me? All those good, skilled, intelligent, hard-working people?

He could see the Reverend frowning too, leaning even further forward. When David Hopwood spoke, his tone was cool, quite lacking its normal joviality. "Common people, as you put it, Charles, are as valuable to God as our dear Queen herself. They only lack the privileges that we have been given – given, I might add, through no merit of our own. Yes, I do think the boys should mix with every kind of person and not only with those of wealth and privilege like ourselves." He sat back and swept the table with an authoritative smile. "Now, I insist that we continue this discussion at another time. It is a family matter. Tell me, Alfred, honestly now, do you think the boys have any musical talent?"

Alfred finished his mouthful slowly as he considered his response. He hated being put on the spot, especially twice in the course of one meal. He couldn't very well say "no", with so much riding on the "culture" he was supposed to be providing for the boys. On the other hand, he couldn't say yes, for he didn't honestly feel that they were particularly talented.

He coughed to clear his throat. "Charlie and Will are very young. I didn't start learning to play the piano until I was twelve years old. They lack the…" He put down his spoon and smoothed the tablecloth in front of him. "…the um…the concentration and…perseverance that comes more easily to older children…so it's difficult to say yet whether they have any special talent." Then he smiled encouragingly at David and Clementine. "But they do have plenty of enthusiasm and energy and seem to be mastering the basics well, mainly thanks to Cecily, I have to say. She has worked hard with them, especially in the last two weeks. And now they have their own piano, who knows what they might achieve?"

"And why is Cecily involved?" Mr Gresham asked. "That seems a very curious idea, to have a nursemaid teach one's children."

Alfred felt his irritation with the man rising. Why did he feel the need to give his view on every aspect of the children's upbringing? Surely it was none of his business. He kept his voice as neutral and even as he could.

"Oh I couldn't possibly manage them alone. You know Charlie and Will. They're like a bag of young ferrets. Cecily keeps them under control and I teach them, though, as I say, she's beginning to teach them herself now, during the week. She's learning the notation and fingering and has even asked me for some harder music, so that she can get ahead of them."

David Hopwood gave him an encouraging smile. "That is splendid, Alfred. I like to think of our staff acquiring new skills. I have always thought Cecily had hidden talents."

"But that's ridiculous. What use does a maid have for a skill such as piano playing?" Mr Gresham turned to his daughter. "What do you think, Clementine? Surely you don't support this? The maid doesn't need to be there at all, as far as I can see. Mr Nicholson should simply teach Charlie and Will individually and Cecily can do what she's paid to do – look after the babies."

Horrified, Alfred blurted out, "But Cecily has to be there!" The words hung in the air for what seemed a very long moment. He noticed a glance pass between Clementine and David, just the very slightest lift of an eyebrow and twitch of the lips. He felt very foolish and folded his napkin with unnecessary attention.

Clementine patted her father's hand. "Thank you for your thoughts, Papa, but I think we can manage to organise our own domestic help. I know it troubles you that we are quite an unconventional household, but really you shouldn't worry. It took me a while to get used to it, but now we wouldn't have it any other way. Would we, dear?"

David Hopwood looked shocked. "Are we unconventional, dear? Surely not! Let's put the lie to that vicious rumour and ask the ladies to retire while we gentleman indulge in some traditional brandy and political gossip. Now, Charles, tell me, what do you make of Mrs Elizabeth Garrett Anderson graduating as our very first woman doctor?"

"Preposterous! Scandalous! Women in the professions – where will it end? Women lawyers? Judges? They'll be giving them the vote next!"

The Rector responded with gusto, defending the lady doctor, of course, and Alfred let out a long breath, relieved to be out of the limelight. He was angry with himself. What on earth made him say something so...so obvious? The Hopwoods would be bound to suspect something now, something that wasn't even happening. But he couldn't deny the strength of his reaction. The thought of her not being there had terrified him. And the fact that he was terrified, terrified him. He decided it was time to arrange an evening at the beer house with his friend. George's calming influence and sensible advice – that's what he needed.

He sipped his brandy and made an effort to focus on the gentlemanly conversation, which continued in a heated, but amiable fashion. In other circumstances he might have found it interesting, but tonight he did not. He hoped they would be joining the ladies in the drawing room soon for piano and song, a much more appealing prospect, guaranteed to soothe his jangling nerves.

CHAPTER 31

On the Monday afternoon of the following week Cecily sat in the nursery alone with Grace. The fire was burning low and the light in the room fading fast, but she was unable to get up to see to either coal or lamps. Grace was asleep in her arms, her flushed face pressed against Cecily's chest, her pale curls stuck damply to her head. Cecily lifted her gently, leaning down to rest her own cheek lightly against the little girl's forehead. The silky skin was hot against her own. She frowned. Her attempts to put Grace in her cot after lunch had led to piteous sobbing. It had taken Cecily more than half an hour to calm her and get her to sleep. She daren't move her now, but she was becoming increasingly anxious about this fever. There had been no sign of it when the mistress had left earlier in the afternoon. Grace had had a runny nose and a cough for a couple of days, which was why she had been left at home. But she was only a little fractious then, not really ill. Cecily wasn't sure what to do and sat softly stroking the child's hair, staring into the cooling embers.

Her thoughts followed their usual well-worn path and she was lost for a while in various scenes involving *him*, herself and, of course, a piano. Grace whimpered and wriggled, obviously uncomfortable in her sleep. Cecily moved her gently into a different position, cross with herself that her mind had wandered away from the child. Edie had lost patience with her too.

"Cecily Carpenter, you can't talk 'bout nothin' sensible 'cept piano music and Mr Nicholson these days," she had complained on Sunday during their evening together in the attic room. "What 'bout your poor Tom? If I didn't know better I'd think you was still sweet on Mr Nicholson and didn't care for Tom at all."

Cecily looked mortified and said nothing. Even in the dim light of the candle she could see the flash of disapproval in Edie's eyes.

"What? You tellin' me you don't love 'im no more?"

Cecily shrugged. "I don't know, Edie. I don't know what I feel. I'm in a right old muddle, to tell you the truth. How do you know that you love Harry?"

Edie smiled then. "Oh…lots of ways. 'Cause I always want to be with 'im. 'Cause I'm not really 'appy away from 'im anymore. 'Cause I love to just look at 'im. 'Cause I just feel at 'ome with 'im I s'pose."

Cecily was silent for a moment, looking at her friend, envious of the certainty that shone from her eyes. "I don't think I feel like that about Tom, Edie. I'm sorry."

Edie waved her hands about in uncharacteristic agitation. "Oh, Lordy! What we goin' to do with you? It's not me you need to say sorry to, young lady. It's *'im*, poor lad. And the sooner the better. Before you break 'is 'eart…if you haven't done that already."

Cecily grimaced. "I know. I've been thinking I'll write him a letter. This week, maybe."

Edie raised a questioning eyebrow.

" All right, this week definitely. I will. I promise."

And so she had. She had tried to make it as gentle and apologetic as she could, but still she felt terrible. She had been selfish, unkind, had used him to make herself feel good with no real thought for his feelings. There was no excuse. But once it was written and posted, she had felt nothing but relief. She couldn't help it. That was how she felt. And since then she had felt free to indulge in her dreams of Mr Nicholson, safe in the knowledge that they would never come true.

Now, looking at little Gracie lying in her arms, she felt

foolish and guilty and longed only to see her well again, toddling and chattering, delighting them all with her sweet smile and affectionate, stubborn nature. She glanced up at the clock on the mantelpiece. It was past four o'clock. She sighed and tutted. Where was Edie? She should be here with Grace's tea by now. Someone needed to fetch the mistress from the tea party she was attending with the boys. The Rector would still be out visiting, no one knew where. She looked anxiously towards the door, willing her friend to appear.

A moment later she was startled by a quiet knock. That was odd. Why was Edith knocking? She waited for the door to be pushed open and the tea tray to appear, but nothing happened. The knocking came again, this time a little louder.

"Come in." Cecily called out as quietly as she could, but still Grace stirred and whimpered. The door opened and Mr Nicholson appeared in the doorway, smiling at her. She felt a rush of pleasure at the sight of his warm face and blushed furiously as usual. He stepped into the room.

"Hallo, Cecily. I hope it's all right for me to come up. Edith said you wouldn't mind."

"Oh, Mr Nicholson, no…of course that's all right. Come in. I'm sorry, I can't get up. Grace really isn't well. I don't want to wake her." She spoke quietly, almost in a whisper.

He took his cue from her and replied in a quiet voice. "I'm sorry. I can see this isn't a good time. I'll come back another day."

Despite her guilt and anxiety of only a moment ago she found herself saying, "Oh no, please stay. At least for a few minutes – as long as she doesn't wake. If she does we shan't be able to hear ourselves." She gave a small, apologetic smile.

"I just came to give you this." He placed a flat brown paper package on the floor at her feet. "You can open it later. I've marked the first two pieces with some fingering. Let me know how you get on. If you like you can play them to me at the end of the boys' lesson – when you feel ready. It would only take a few minutes. The Rector is happy. He thinks it's a good idea for you to learn."

She looked down at the parcel and back up at him. She couldn't help feeling excited. "Thank you. It's very kind of you. I'll look forward to trying them out as soon as Grace is better."

"Oh good." He stood by the doorway and reached out for the handle. At that moment Grace gave a little cry and Cecily glanced down at her. The little girl's breathing seemed to have changed. It was faster, shallower, more like panting now. Cecily suddenly felt alarmed.

"I…oh, I'm sorry, Mr Nicholson, I'm worried about Grace. Could you ask Edith to come upstairs quickly. I think we need to get the doctor."

"Yes, of course. Please don't apologise. I'll go right away. Goodbye, Cecily. I do hope Grace recovers quickly."

"Oh…yes…thank you." She didn't even watch him leave, but bent down to touch Grace's forehead with her cheek again. This time the child's skin was burning.

"Oh Lord," she muttered. "Poor little girl. I think we need a doctor for you now, dear, don't we? Come on Edith… where are you?" She tutted with frustration, then sighed with relief as the door burst open and Edith stood, breathing heavily, at her side.

"Thank goodness, Edie. Where've you been?"

"Oh, I thought you might like some time alone with Mr Nicholson. Sorry. I didn't know Gracie was ill."

"Well, never mind that now. This little girl's hotter than the fire. Please send Peter for Dr Tucker. Then tell him to run over to the Mayhews' house to fetch the missus back. And can you bring me up a bowl of water and a sponge? And some more coal for the fire. And could you light the lamps? And…"

"Yes, yes. Let me find Peter first. Then I'll sort you out." Edith disappeared. Cecily was left alone in the near dark, listening to the sharp little breaths, feeling the heat of the child's head against her chest, where her own heart was still thumping, mostly with anxiety, but not entirely.

∽

The talk over supper in the kitchen that evening was quite different from the usual lively chatter. Mrs Norris' forehead was creased deeply with concern.

"Measles…oh Lor, that's not good, Cecily, not in such a little one. But where could she've got it from?"

Cecily looked anguished. "The doctor said several children at the school have gone down with it this week, including Charlotte Adams' little sisters, Helen and Rose. For the last few Sundays they've come and made a fuss of Gracie while I've been talking to Charlotte outside church. I let them hold her hands and blow her kisses. She loved it. It made her laugh. We all laughed. And now I'm thinking it's all my fault and…" She stopped, near to tears, unable to voice her worst fear.

"Well 'course it's not your fault, dear." Mrs Norris patted her hand across the table. "You couldn't've known they were sickenin' for it. You can't keep kiddies from each other, it wouldn't be right. Though I daresay the mistress'll be anxious to try now. This won't help the Reverend's case for sendin' the twins to the village school, that's for sure."

"We all 'ad the measles," said Edith. "I remember bein' kept in a dark room for what seemed like weeks and 'avin' terrible dreams and bad ears."

"I've had it, too, but I can't remember much about it." Cecily pushed her food around her plate. "I'd better go back up. Sorry, Mrs Norris, but I'm not hungry."

"No, you'll stay here and finish that plate, young lady. I'll not have you wastin' good food and another few minutes ain't goin' to make no difference to them upstairs. And there's some lovely stewed plums for afters. They'll slip down nicely."

"And *I* want to hear why Mr Nicholson came to see you." Edith leaned across the table towards her friend, her eyebrows raised expectantly.

"Oh, not now, Edie, please." Cecily frowned.

"Yes, now! It'll do you good to think of somethin' other than Grace for a minute or two."

"But that's just it. If I hadn't been thinking about him I might have done something sooner or…oh, I don't know. I just don't think I should have been thinking of him at all."

"That's silly, Cecy. It wouldn't 'ave made the slightest bit of difference to Gracie. You called for the doctor as soon as you could. Now, tell me why 'e came to see you!"

Mrs Norris paused, a spoonful of plums hanging in mid-air over a bowl, her eyebrows, like Edith's, raised in a question mark.

Cecily looked at them both. She couldn't help a tiny smile appearing at the corners of her mouth.

"Well?" Mrs Norris put down the spoon. "Don't just sit there smirkin', girl, or we'll all die from suspense. What did he want?"

"He came to give me some music." Cecily paused.

"Was that all?" Edith looked disappointed.

"And to tell me that he will teach me the piano. Just for a few minutes after the boys' lesson. The Reverend has said that he may." Despite her efforts to stop it, Cecily's smile broadened and she blushed scarlet.

There was a long pause while the two absorbed this information, looking at each other and back to Cecily.

"Well, well, well. Our Cecily learnin' the piano from that nice young man." Mrs Norris passed her a bowl of plums. "And…" She turned to Edith with a conspiratorial nod. "I've said several times how much better he's been lookin' these past few weeks, haven't I, Edith? Well, well, well!"

CHAPTER 32

Alfred let himself into the house by the back door and walked through the kitchen, noting with appreciation the cold supper Mrs Dawes had left for him on the table. He preferred to eat in the kitchen in the evenings these days. There seemed little point in shivering all alone at the long dining room table when he could be warm and comfortable here.

He climbed the stairs to his mother's bedchamber and stood for a moment outside her door, continuing the debate which had simmered inside his head for days and throughout the ride home from the Rectory. Should he ask her again about John? Time was fast running out, that much was obvious now. If she died without telling him what had happened, he would never know the truth of either the infirmity which had killed his brother, or his own part in it, the terrible shame that hung over him still. But he couldn't bear the thought of distressing her further. He had told her nothing of the problems with the business. The second new house remained empty. Even reducing the rent had not succeeded in tempting tenants to let it. He had been forced to go, cap in hand, to the bank manager once more, to explain the severity of his mother's illness and to beg that Stonefield House should not be sold while she lived. When the greasy little man had agreed to postpone the date of possession for one month following the date of her burial, Alfred had felt profound relief. Whatever had passed between himself and his mother, he knew he wanted her to die in peace. No, he would not ask her about John.

He pushed open the door. Miss Blackwell sat at his mother's bedside, working a piece of embroidery by the light of the lamp on the chest of drawers beside her. She peered at him through thick spectacle lenses. These, together with dark hair pulled back severely from its centre parting and old-lady lace cap perched on the top of her head, gave her a rather intimidating appearance in complete contrast to her calm, kind and humorous nature.

She smiled at him. "She's been asleep for most of the afternoon, Mr Nicholson. I'm afraid she didn't eat much lunch. The pain was troublesome this morning so she's had more laudanum. It would be good for her to wake up for a while and have a little chat. Then perhaps she'll be able to eat some supper later." She put her embroidery away in a basket at her feet and stood up. "Will you be all right here while I have my supper?"

"Yes, of course. You go down. Thank you, Miss Blackwell."

"I'll be back up in half an hour."

"No, please take as long as you like. I'm sure you need the rest. I'm quite happy here and if I need you I can always call out."

"Very well, sir. Thank you."

She left the room quietly and he took her place on the chair at his mother's side. He placed her limp, thin hand in his own and stroked it for a while, observing her gaunt, yellow cheeks and sunken eyes with fresh dismay as he did every day. Somehow, with a stubbornness he felt he must have inherited from her, he kept alive a healthy, happy picture of her in his head. He knew it didn't help him to accept the reality of the situation, which felt shockingly new each time he walked into the room and actually saw her. But he didn't want to remember her like this. She wouldn't want that either, he was sure.

Her eyes were shut fast and she showed no signs of stirring. He patted her hand.

"Mother, Miss Blackwell thinks it would be good for you to wake up for a while." There was no response. He tried again, louder this time.

"Mother dear. Will you wake up and talk to me for a little while?"

Her eyelids fluttered open with a great effort and she turned her eyes towards him, opening her mouth to speak. When no sound came out he offered her a drink from the spouted china cup which he found amongst the sick-room paraphernalia on the chest of drawers. She sucked weakly, shaking her head after a couple of mouthfuls.

He frowned at her with mock disapproval. "Come along now. You know you must drink more than that or Miss Blackwell will scold me for not taking proper care of you."

She gave him a knowing look, almost a smile, taking more mouthfuls until he was satisfied and put the cup away. He straightened her pillows and covers.

"Are you comfortable now?"

She nodded and replied, almost inaudibly, "Thank you… yes." She gazed at him for a while, then smiled weakly. "You look well today, dear."

"Do I? That's good. I'm feeling better these days, Mother. You were right. It has done me good, going to the Rectory." He smiled at her sadly. "I wish we could say the same about you."

She shook her head. "You mustn't mind about me, Alfie. I'm an old lady. I only wish…" She closed her eyes, overcome with exhaustion. He sat quietly, stroking her hand, waiting. "…I only wish I could have seen your wife and your children." She closed her eyes again and tears slid from beneath her eyelids.

He wiped her cheeks gently with a handkerchief, struggling to keep his voice steady. "I know. I wish that too. But there will be children here again one day, I promise you that." His heart sank at the lie, but he knew it was what she needed to hear. "And I shall tell them all about you and Father and…" He didn't speak the name, but even so it was too late. She opened her eyes and in their darting distress he

279

saw again the terrible pain of losing her precious child.

She struggled to speak. "I have to ask you, Alfie...before it's too late." She stopped for breath once more. His heart began to race as he wondered what she was about to say.

"I know you were only...only a little boy and...and I have tried to...to...I have tried to...understand." Tears ran faster down her cheeks now and he could see her fighting to quell the sobs which rose in her throat. The words were barely audible, strangled by her distress and pain, but he heard them as clearly as if she were shouting.

"I could...I...never...understood why...why...didn't you help him, Alfie? ...Why?"

A long, shocked silence filled the room. It was as if she knew that he could never give her an answer. There was no answer. She shuddered and closed her eyes, slipping into a deep unconsciousness once more. He sat beside her, paralysed with anguish, his breath coming in shallow gasps, his face white as he watched her sleep. The hour ticked by on the old clock on the mantelpiece and still he didn't move. She became increasingly restless, moaning and moving from side to side in her sleep. Suddenly she arched her back and cried out, her eyes wide open, terrified, desperately searching the room. She gripped his hand, crushing his knuckles so hard that it hurt, crying out again and again. He stood up, his heart banging in his chest and went to call for the nurse. Before he had reached the door Miss Blackwell was in the room, moving him aside, reaching for a bottle on the chest of drawers.

"I'm sorry, Mr Nicholson, I think it's best you go now."

He felt desperate. "Can't I help? There must be something I can do."

"No...I don't think she wants you to see her like this. I'm sorry."

His mother cried out again and he left the room quickly, running downstairs to the kitchen, where he fell heavily onto the nearest chair, his legs and hands trembling uncontrollably. He could still hear her, the sound quieter but just as terrible, seeping through the ceiling into the kitchen. He put his hands over his ears and sobbed.

✎

Later, when the house had gone quiet, he tried to eat the supper which had looked quite appetising earlier, but now stuck in his throat. He gave up and instead drank a large glass of brandy, before steeling himself to go back upstairs. Miss Blackwell smiled gently as he pushed open the bedroom door. She put down her embroidery and tiptoed across the room to stand beside him on the landing. They both stared through the open doorway at the dying face, peaceful now, resting on the pillows. She turned to him, her eyes full of concern.

"I'm so sorry you had to see her like that, Mr Nicholson. I have increased the dose now. I hope that will keep her more comfortable. But it does mean the end will come more quickly, I'm afraid."

"It isn't important how long she lives now…I just don't want her to…" His voice became choked.

She took his hand. "I will do my very best to see that she suffers as little pain as possible, sir. I shall make up a bed beside her so that I hear her as soon as she starts to stir. Tomorrow we should send for Dr Tucker. Now perhaps we could both sit with her for a while."

He nodded silently and crept behind her to the bedside where he sat motionless, listening to the quiet tick of the clock and his mother's shallow breaths, until he could no longer keep himself awake.

CHAPTER 33

His mother's dying was neither quiet nor quick. For three interminable weeks she suffered horribly and Alfred suffered with her, despite Miss Blackwell's best efforts to shield him from the worst moments. He hardly moved from her bedside, except when shooed from the room by the nurse. He left all the day to day management of the various building projects to Reg and the world disappeared for him – his work, the Rectory, Cecily, everything. His only reality lay within the four walls of this airless, pain-filled room.

His mother hardly spoke again and then only to ask for water, or more laudanum, or the nurse. There was no comforting reconciliation. Her question lived with him as if those had been her last words.

In the final three days she fell into a merciful coma. The end, when it came, was peaceful. He was hardly aware that she had gone. Thank God, he thought, thank God, thank God. The nurse left him alone for more than an hour to sit beside the still body, drinking in the silence and the peace. He did not cry. When she returned, he kissed his mother's cheek, slipped quietly from the house and wandered, numb with exhaustion, down into the valley.

❧

Two days later he sat with the Reverend Hopwood in the parlour, shivering. Since his mother's death he had never felt completely warm. It was partly that the weather had suddenly become wintry, with a biting north east wind and unusually hard frosts for late November. But it wasn't just the weather. The cold came from within him too, from a core of grief which had frozen in his chest. No tears had come to relieve the pain. Just a terrible ache and this numbing cold. He put another log onto the drawing room fire, drew his jacket closer about him and began to speak.

The Rector sat facing him on the other side of the fireplace, listening intently, his teacup untouched on the small table beside him, his eyes full of kindly concern. Alfred talked about his mother. About her indomitable faith, her love of the church, the hymns, her favourite passages from the Bible, and about the hope she had expressed in her last weeks that she would soon be reunited with her husband. He talked about her love of music, and of the piano in particular, of the comfort she had found lately in listening to him play familiar pieces, especially hymns. He wanted to talk more, to impress upon the Rector the significance of this short life which had slipped away so quietly and left so little trace, but after a while he could think of nothing more to say and stopped lamely, sad with the realisation that words could not express who she really was or even a tiny fraction of what her life had meant.

David Hopwood leaned forward towards him. "Your mother was a good woman, Alfred. Her faith never wavered, not even after the loss of her beloved husband. I have always admired her constancy. She's at peace now, with our dear Lord, we can be sure of that. Did she have a favourite hymn which we could sing tomorrow?"

Alfred replied without hesitation. "Oh, 'Abide with me' – that was her favourite. I have played it for her every day in the past four weeks, even when she was unconscious. I'm not sure I shall be able to get through it tomorrow, though."

"You obviously loved her very much. I can see that. There will be plenty of strong voices in church to carry us through, never fear. And you shouldn't be ashamed of your tears, young man. It's not only the fair sex who have been given the capacity to cry. I'm not ashamed to tell you that I have shed many tears myself in the past three weeks."

Alfred looked at the Rector properly for the first time since they had sat down together. "Oh, I'm so sorry. Have you suffered a bereavement too?"

"No, thanks be to God. But we almost lost our dear, beloved Grace and she is still not recovered. They have all been ill with the measles since we last saw you and she was taken very badly. I can't imagine how a parent can bear the loss of a precious little one, though I know so many who have had to endure it." Behind his misty spectacles his eyes filled with tears as he spoke.

Alfred felt a surge of anxiety and guilt. The Rector had not mentioned John. Perhaps he didn't know about the loss his mother had endured for all those unhappy years. Alfred should tell him, should ask him to include her beloved youngest child in the eulogy. Even a child who doesn't live to adulthood was once a precious part of their parents, weren't they? Something they gave to the world. She gave John to the world, even if it was only for a short time. She deserved this. He struggled with himself, staring into the fire for a long moment. He couldn't bear to feel that terrible shame in front of all those people tomorrow. He was sure they would be able to see in his face what he had done. But there would be people there who had known John – Reg, Mrs Barton, Mrs Dawes. What would they think if his name wasn't mentioned? No, whatever his feelings, it would be wrong not to speak.

"My mother was one such parent, Reverend. She had a son, John, who died when he was six. I'm afraid I know very little about him. He was never spoken of in front of me. I do know that his loss was very hard for her to bear. I don't believe she ever recovered from it, in fact."

The Reverend Hopwood took out a large handkerchief and blew his nose. "I am so sorry to hear about John. I shall of course mention him in the eulogy." They sat silently for a while, each absorbed in his own thoughts. Then he turned to

Alfred and smiled. "Now, which other hymn would she have liked?"

They talked for some time about the rest of the funeral arrangements and about the burial plot his mother had bought several years before so that she could lie beside her husband. When it seemed the conversation was at an end and David Hopwood was preparing to leave, he suddenly leaned forward once more, fixing Alfred with a concerned gaze.

"There is just one thing more that I need to speak with you about, Alfred. I hesitate in the circumstances to add to your concerns, and I suspect Clemmy would disapprove strongly of me talking to you about this matter at all, but I feel it's important. I hope you will forgive me?"

Alfred felt both puzzled and perturbed. "Er...yes...of course. What is it?"

"Please don't be offended if I say this, but both Clemmy and I have noticed your growing attachment to Cecily." Alfred coloured at the recollection of his outburst at the Hopwood's dinner table. There was a pause and he wondered anxiously if they disapproved of the growing friendship, as his mother may well have done.

The Rector continued, "We have also been pleased to see the recent improvements in your health and have concluded that those two circumstances may not be entirely unconnected." Another pause as he fiddled with his spectacles. "So I hope you will understand my extreme reluctance to say what I'm about to say now."

Alfred felt his heart begin to beat more quickly. He wanted to tell the Rector to hurry up and say whatever it was he needed to say. Instead he wiped his suddenly sweaty palms on his trousers.

David Hopwood took a good long while to begin his next sentence and, when he did so, spoke slowly, as if weighing each word. "A few days ago I received a letter from Cecily's father. It seems she may now be in a position to take up a long wished-for opportunity which would take her away from Blackford, perhaps for good. I believe you might share my view that even women, especially talented women, should be permitted to improve themselves if they are able?"

Alfred's face, so recently flushed, began to drain of colour. He gave a slight nod in reply. The Rector looked apologetic as he continued,

"My anxiety is that your feelings for Cecily may influence her to reject this chance for self-improvement. She's so young, still only sixteen, much too young in my view for the commitment of marriage. Too young, possibly, to make the right decision, the decision that will benefit her most in the long term. I have come to think of her almost as a daughter, Alfred. She has become a much-valued member of our household. I want only what is right for her, as I am sure you will understand." He stopped, looking anxiously at Alfred, obviously waiting for some kind of response. When none came he continued,

"Well…I will say no more, now. I have explained my feelings. It is not for me to suggest a course of action for you or to try to influence you further. We hope that you will be able to resume your lessons with the boys as soon as they are completely well…and when you have recovered sufficiently from your loss, of course. They often ask when they will see you next and Clemmy and I have greatly appreciated your company each Thursday evening." He stood up, holding out his hand. "God bless you Alfred. I hope you will forgive me for speaking at such a terrible time. I thought it would be kinder to inform you sooner rather than later, before… well…you understand, I'm sure. Goodbye, then. I shall see myself out. Until we meet again tomorrow."

Alone once more, Alfred slumped back into his chair and sat for a long while, elbows on knees, hands cradling his head. Finally he pushed himself upright with a weary sigh and left the room, crossing the corridor to the small parlour opposite.

His father had used it as an office, but he and his mother had rarely come here, there being no reason to sit in the cold and gloom when the drawing room was so much more pleasant. Now the lack of warmth and light were perfect for its new function as his mother's last resting place before her grave. A dark mahogany coffin lay on trestles in the centre of the room which was lit by a lamp glowing from a corner shelf. A single vase of white roses stood on the window sill. Miss Blackwell sat under the lamp, her ever-present embroidery in her hands. She looked at him with an expression of concern as he sat down heavily, pulling his chair into the centre of the room to be as near as possible to the coffin. He nodded his gratitude as she got up, gave him a small, wordless smile and left the room, closing the door quietly behind her.

He gazed down at the strange face nestling on its pillow of blue satin. In every way it resembled his mother. It was her hair, neatly framing her face, her lips, her chin. Every fold in her skin, every line, mole and whisker, were hers. Yet in some profound and unarguable way, it was not her. For whatever it was that made his mother who she was had gone. He hoped she and the Rector were right – that she was somewhere else now, with his father and with John. He could not believe in heaven or any other kind of afterlife for himself, but maybe he could for her. He dangled his arm over the side of the coffin and stroked her cold cheek lightly with the back of his hand. He began to whisper then,

"Well, dear, this is all very strange, isn't it? You there and me here. I can't get used to it. But you look peaceful, I think. No more pain or grief, eh? No more fretting over me. And maybe you can hear me. Who knows? Just because *I* can't believe any more doesn't change the reality of anything, does it?

"I want to tell you about Cecily, Mother. She and the children and going to the Rectory and the music – they've all been a kind of salvation for me, bringing me out of all that terrible blackness which worried you so much. But I've slowly come to realise that it's mostly being with Cecily that has done it. I think I may be growing to love her, you see. And I think if you had got to know her you would have loved her too. She's not a woman of standing or great beauty like Emma, but she's full of life and warmth. You may not have approved of her, but she would have won you round, I'm sure."

He stopped then, gazing for a long while through the window at a large group of sparrows squabbling loudly in the front hedge. When he turned back to her his voice had lost its steadiness.

"I know she was never mine. She has a young man, a boy nearer to her age. But somehow I still hoped. There was something in her eyes and her smile, when she looked at me, you see. Something that made me think she might love me too, one day. And now it seems I must give her up, before I've even found her. The Reverend is right of course – she's much too young. I don't think I'm cut out to marry, Mother. I just keep getting it wrong. So stupid…stupid…"

His voice trailed away and he slumped back in his chair, his arm resting across his eyes. After a long silence he sat forward and touched her face again, gently searching, as a small child might touch a parent to gain their attention.

"And we never talked about John, did we? I shall never know now…what I did or should have done." Suddenly a sob caught in his throat. "Whatever it was, I've come to ask you to forgive me, Mother."

He stopped and looked down at her, his eyes pleading, full of love and pain. "Can you forgive me?" Silence filled the room and outside, too, the birds were suddenly quiet. It was a silence so profound that it had a noise all of its own, filling his ears, giving him his answer.

The funeral was Alfred's last gift to his mother. He stayed calm. He said the prayers and sang "Abide with me" tearlessly in his strong, baritone voice, hoping, but not believing, that she could hear him. He carried the coffin to the grave and watched her sink into the dark, musty hole, shovelling earth onto her with steady hands. Afterwards, in the drawing room of the Rectory, he spoke with her friends, with George and Sarah, with Reg and his wife and Bill and Jimmy, and with Annie and Mrs Dawes, both teary eyed and stricken. He even drank the tea. He couldn't eat the sandwiches and he couldn't talk to the Rector. But all the rest he did for her. Then, when the mourners had left, he said goodbye to Miss Blackwell, thanking her warmly for her kind and unfailing support, and returned with the servants to Stonefield House. They drove in silence along the lane, the women in the carriage, the men on the cart. The sun was setting behind them and the air was already sharp with the smell of frost. When the horses and carriages had been stabled, he said goodbye to everyone in the yard, firmly refusing their anxious offers to keep him company, and sent them home.

Hearing the click of the gate closing behind them, he walked slowly into the workshop and stood for a while, breathing in the familiar scent of cut wood, putty, varnish and paint, looking around at the benches, the shelves and walls crammed with tools, all vague outlines in the growing dark. His father's tools. His father's workshop. It had never felt wholly his; that was part of the problem. He knew that his father, like his mother, could never forgive him now, but his parents' unhappiness couldn't touch him. They were gone and he was alone. Nothing touched him. He reached into his jacket pocket, withdrew an envelope and placed it on the bench. Then, picking up the nearest sharp knife, he walked quickly back across the yard and out into the lane.

CHAPTER 34

It was a fine, late autumn morning. The low sun had finally crept above the garden hedge and was sparkling on the frosty lawn. Grace was sitting on Cecily's lap in the window seat of the small parlour watching a group of birds just outside the window. Starlings and sparrows hopped about, squawking loudly, fighting over the breadcrumbs that Edith had scattered on the terrace earlier. Usually Grace would be shouting excitedly, pointing and banging on the window. Today she sat watching wide-eyed, but silent, sucking her thumb. It was only to be expected, Cecily reasoned. After all, she had only been completely free of the fever for three days.

"Look, Gracie – birds. Naughty birds, squabbling like children!" She gave Grace's cheek a big kiss, noticing with dismay how it had lost much of its pudginess, and tightened her arms around her small body. "Oh, I have missed you! You've been such a worry, young lady."

She was delighted to have this time with Grace, the first since she had fallen ill. The Mistress had allowed no one except herself and the Reverend to nurse her baby girl for three exhausting, agonising weeks. Only today, when it was obvious that Grace was so much better, had she agreed to leave her in Cecily's care for the morning, while she and the boys took a much-needed break from the house.

Grace wriggled to get down. She toddled over to a heap of toys on the rug in front of the fire. The parlour had become a second nursery while the children were ill. Cecily had spent many days here with the boys, once they were over the worst of their illness, leaving Grace in the nursery with her terrified parents and the frequent visits of the doctor. It had been horrible not seeing her, relying on reports from

Edith and Mrs Norris, imagining her struggling against the infections which raged in her ears and her lungs, always dreading the worst. But now here she was, well again. It seemed like a miracle.

Cecily watched as Grace sat down with her back to the window amongst the toy animals, fingering them listlessly, settling on nothing to actually play with. She began to grizzle, shaking her head to and fro.

"Are you getting tired already, little one? Would you like a picture book? Come and sit with me and we'll look at the farm animal book together."

The little girl continued to cry in a small, high voice and to shake her head. It was an odd movement. Not like her usual unmistakeable 'no', but more of a rocking, as if something in her head was bothering her. Cecily watched her with concern.

"Gracie, come and sit with Cecily." She reached for a book and opened it on her lap. "Look, there's a big pig here, saying 'oink, oink'. He's coming to find you!"

She slid from the window seat down onto all fours and crawled across the floor oinking. Normally this would be enough to send Grace into squeals of delight, but today she didn't react at all, not even turning round to look. Cecily knelt in front of her, looking directly into large, anxious eyes that moved from Cecily's face and away as she rocked. She seemed lost, as if she was searching for something.

Cecily took the dear, baby face between her hands, holding it still as she spoke softly. "What's the matter, my lovely?"

Grace looked back at her and burst into tears. Cecily scooped her up, carrying her back to the window seat, where she soothed her until she was quiet once more. Her first anxious thought was that perhaps the fever had returned, but the child's forehead was cool and her colour quite normal. There was nothing obviously wrong with her now. So where had the bubbly, independent little girl gone, always eager to talk to anyone who would listen to her baby chatter, always happy to play? Perhaps she's still weak and exhausted, Cecily told herself. Her body needs more time to recover, that's all.

She carried Grace upstairs to the nursery and tried to put her down in her cot, provoking another fit of sobbing. When the offer of another picture book was met with silent, thumb-sucking indifference, she sat Grace on her lap on the piano stool and opened the lid. Before her illness, playing the piano had been Grace's greatest treat, causing shouts of excitement as she hit the keys with her tiny fists. Cecily would never let her play when the boys were in the room, for they would complain loudly and bitterly that she should not be allowed to bang the keys – "It's 'gainst the rules!" Today she looked momentarily excited as she began to hit the keys, then stopped abruptly, craning her head to look up at Cecily, her eyes puzzled and anxious.

"What's the matter, lovely? That was right. You were playing the piano nicely. Like this, look." Cecily began to play the piece that was propped on the music stand, the last piece she and the twins had practised together before they became ill. At that moment the door behind them burst open with a great shout of "Gracie! Gracie!"

Mrs Hopwood's voice could be heard in the corridor, "Wait, boys! I told you to wait, didn't I? In case she's asleep."

Cecily looked down at the blonde head nestling against her chest. Grace's thumb was back in her mouth. Throughout the commotion she continued staring at the piano keys, motionless, apparently completely unaware of either her beloved brothers' voices or her mother's. Cecily's hands stopped mid-note. Suddenly it was obvious what the problem was, though it was almost too awful to believe. Her heart thumped in her chest. What should she do? She couldn't talk to the mistress, not with the children here. Forcing herself to smile, she turned Grace to face the boys and her mother. As she suspected, at the sight of them the tiny thumb flew out of her mouth with an excited cry and Grace slid from Cecily's lap, running happily into her brothers' arms. Mrs Hopwood walked in behind them, beaming with delight at the sight of her little girl running and shouting as normal. Cecily could hardly meet her eyes.

❧

Over supper she poured out her anxiety to Mrs Norris and Edith. The cook put her knife and fork together and stared gravely across the table at her.

"Dear, dear. That poor little mite. But are you sure? Wouldn't the master and mistress've noticed if she couldn't hear, Cecily?"

"That's what I thought, Cecy," added Edith, "I'm sure they'd 'ave noticed."

"I think perhaps she's been so ill most of the time, that they put her lack of response down to that. I did at first. It wasn't till she ignored the boys that it really hit me. 'Cause normally she'd have jumped off my lap straight away, shouting and carrying on, she's always so pleased to see them."

Edith frowned. "Maybe she's just feeling too poorly still."

"She didn't even turn her head, Edie. It was as if they weren't there. But when I turned her round to see them, she was off, just like before. And the piano and talking to her earlier in the parlour – she didn't react to any of it. Nothing. And I can see that she knows something's wrong, too. She keeps shaking her head as if she's trying to make her ears work again. It's horrible."

"Oh dear." Mrs Norris sighed and stood up, wiping her hands on her apron. "You must go to the Reverend as soon as they're in bed, Cecily. I think it'd be better to speak with him first, and let him talk to the mistress. You know how upset she gets."

"That's what I thought too. I'll make sure the boys are asleep and then I'll go." Cecily felt sick at the thought of the conversation she must have later and wanted to refuse the large bowl of rice pudding Mrs Norris was placing in front of her, but knew it was pointless – she would be made to eat it anyway.

"Poor Cecy." Edith gave her friend a sympathetic look. "Rather you than me."

❧

The Reverend sat behind his mound of books and papers listening to Cecily, his mouth sagging open with dismay. When she had finished he pulled off his spectacles and lay his hands across his face, muttering from behind them,

"I knew something was wrong. I knew it." He put his hands down again and looked at her sadly. "Parental love can be as blind as any other, Cecily. I can see it now, but I think I just didn't want to see it before. Oh dear…oh dear."

She felt terrible. Just when there seemed to be hope once more, she had taken it away. His eyes were clearly filling with tears.

"Shall I go now, sir?"

"Oh yes…no…" She watched him struggle to keep control of himself. "Stay here for a moment. I shall be all right. We have to consider what to do."

"Doctor Tucker can advise us, I'm sure sir."

"Yes, yes…of course"

"Shall I send Peter for him in the morning?"

"Yes…it's not an urgent matter…send for him in the morning. And we must pray, of course. We must not give up hope. Perhaps it's just a temporary problem. Our good Lord does not send us more troubles than we can bear as long as we stay faithful…"

He stared into space for a long while. Cecily stood

quietly in front of him, waiting. His eyes became watery again and when he spoke his voice was unsteady.

"It is very hard to bear, though….very hard. I would sooner cut off my own leg than see my children suffer, Cecily."

She bowed her head, unable to think of anything helpful to say.

He stood up suddenly then. "Well, I must speak to Mrs Hopwood now. Thank you for coming to talk to me. It will be easier for her to hear it from me, though she must suspect it too, I am sure." He began to walk towards the door and she followed him out. At the doorway he stopped, turning back to her.

"I have never thanked you properly for your tireless devotion to my precious little ones these past three weeks, Cecily. It has not gone unnoticed or unappreciated by either myself or Mrs Hopwood, I can assure you."

She opened her mouth to thank him, but he held his hand up.

"We are also aware that you missed your afternoon off two weeks ago."

"I don't mind that, sir. I wanted to stay here."

"No, I know you did it willingly, but you need a rest now, Cecily – now there is no longer any danger. Besides, there is someone who wishes to see you. I shall write to let him know that you will be free this Sunday afternoon."

He gave her a small, weary smile and turned to walk slowly upstairs to the nursery.

❧

That night she tossed and turned on her narrow bed, quite unable to sleep. Grace's every snoring breath reminded her of the terrible new problem the family must now deal with. She wanted to be able to help. She was sure that she could. Once Grace was completely better they would all have to learn a new way of talking to her, of being with her. Despite her anguish at the thought of the little girl's situation, Cecily couldn't help feeling excited, too. Perhaps this was an opportunity for her to become the teacher she had always hoped to be – a special teacher for Grace. She couldn't bear the thought of leaving her locked away in a silent world, lonely, unable to communicate. There must be ways to help her. She would find out and she would learn. And perhaps later there would be other children like Gracie that she could help. It would be her new important task in life, given to her by God.

Then there was the other matter – the "someone" who wished to see her. Could it be Mr Nicholson? She had thought very little about him in the past weeks, with the constant worry about Grace and the boys needing so much attention. In some ways she had been relieved to have her obsession forced into sensible proportions. Most of it was in her imagination, after all, and had seemed profoundly insignificant and foolish when compared to the loss of a child. Now, though, the thought that he might have asked to see her brought back all the old excitement and nervous agitation. Perhaps he was going to ask her to walk out with him and had written to the Reverend to arrange a meeting, as the piano lessons were postponed. The thought sent shivers of anticipation through her body, re-kindling a strange ache between her legs and in her breasts which had tormented her when she thought of him in bed at night, before the children's illness. She pictured his face, his warm smile, his long fingers on the piano and longed to see him again, to be close to him. Part of her felt ashamed at the strength of her feelings, which had so little basis in reality or reason and which seemed so out of her control. But at the same time they made her feel so…so alive. How many days were there until Sunday? She counted on her fingers – three. An eternity. Thank goodness there was so much else to think about and to do, or she would surely go mad.

CHAPTER 35

Doctor Tucker was no help at all in the matter of Grace's hearing. The Reverend and Mrs Hopwood sat with Cecily watching anxiously as he demonstrated, using a small bell rung at various volumes from various places out of Grace's sight, that she was profoundly deaf in both ears. He could not say whether the hearing loss was permanent. Now that the ears were dry once more, he could offer no remedy that might improve them. He had no specialist knowledge of the handicap of deafness to help the family understand how to communicate with her or teach her to speak. He could perhaps contact an old colleague in Harley Street who might be able to recommend a specialist, but generally he felt, with regret, that they should resign themselves to her remaining deaf and dumb for the rest of her life. The consultation was over in less than ten minutes. He bowed, solemn faced, at the door of the nursery, offering his condolences to a now weeping Mrs Hopwood and presenting his bill discreetly to the Reverend. Then he was gone.

The three exchanged dismayed glances. Mrs Hopwood's weeping deteriorated into sobs and the Reverend took her in his arms to comfort her. Cecily sat with Grace and her doll on the hearth rug, keeping her attention so that she remained unaware of her mother's distress, thinking ruefully that there was at least one advantage to being deaf.

Eventually Mrs Hopwood was able to speak. "Do you think we could afford to see a Harley Street specialist, David? If such a person existed and could help?"

"No, my darling, we most certainly could not, I'm sorry to say." He opened the doctor's bill. "This will prove enough of a challenge to our finances."

"Then I shall speak to Mamma and Papa."

Cecily detected a slight wince pass fleetingly across the Reverend's face, but his reply betrayed none of his feelings.

"Of course, my dear. They would be happy to feel that they could help in some way, I'm sure."

⁂

Over the next three days Doctor Tucker unknowingly did Cecily a great favour, for she hardly thought of Mr Nicholson at all, at least not until she was lying in bed each night trying to get to sleep once more. The doctor's willingness to condemn Grace to a life of isolation and misery as a deaf mute had so incensed her that she became filled with a fierce determination to prove him wrong. Her mind raced with thoughts and ideas about how to teach Grace to talk and about how to talk to her so that she could understand. She had watched several small children learn to speak over the years. No one had taught them as far as she could tell. They just learnt all by themselves. Or did they? She pictured her mother with Ernie and Mrs Hopwood, and herself with Edward and Grace. What were the adults doing while the little ones chattered on in baby talk, making sounds or nonsense words? She racked her brains and pestered Mrs Norris about her babies. She pictured herself and Grace before her illness, Grace pointing and Cecily saying, "That's your *doll*, Gracie." "Do – ," Grace would say. "Yes, *doll*. Clever girl!" Gradually she came to realise that some words were much more important than others in first learning to speak and that babies and adults alike homed in on these words – emphasising them in sentences, repeating them endlessly. Grace had already learnt to say dozens of them – "milk", "apple", "bird," "mine," "no!" and many more. She hadn't always said them correctly, but she had made herself understood and her every attempt had been recognised, repeated and applauded by everyone around her.

"Why do you think she's not talking at all now?" she asked Mrs Norris at Saturday evening tea. "It's not as if her voice or her brain has been damaged, is it? It's only her ears."

"But she can't hear her own voice, remember," replied the cook. "She'll need convincin' that she can still talk."

Cecily grinned, impressed, as she had often been, by Mrs Norris's simple wisdom. She felt excited now.

"Then that's what we need to do! We'll start with all the words she knows already and we'll help her to say them again." She paused, frowning once more. "But that doesn't help her to understand what *we're* saying, does it?"

Mrs Norris raised her eyes to the ceiling. "One step at a time, young lady. I'm sure you'll think of somethin' soon enough. Goodness me, she's like a terrier after a rabbit, ain't she, Edith?"

Edith nodded, smiling. "That's one very lucky little girl, I say. Not only is she still alive, which she shouldn't be by rights, but she's got our Cecy frettin' over 'er day and night."

"Oh, not at night! I've got something else to worry about then."

Edith raised her eyebrows. "Oh yes? And what might that be?"

"It's a 'who' not a 'what'." Cecily stopped, embarrassed.

"Well?" Edith pursed her lips with impatience.

"If you must know, the Reverend's told me that someone has asked to see me tomorrow afternoon… I think it might be Mr Nicholson."

A blush spread across her face and she excused herself, leaving the kitchen hurriedly, but not before she had seen the quick exchange of knowing smiles between her friend and Mrs Norris. She shrugged off her discomfort and walked back upstairs to the nursery, pleased that she now had the beginnings of a plan for teaching Grace, convinced even more than before that this was what God intended her to do with her life.

Sunday was dark and overcast. Grey sheets of drizzle swept across the green from time to time, obscuring the houses on the far side. It was the sort of day when the sky seemed to weigh heavily on the earth below and the lamps must be kept alight even at midday. Cecily was sent with the boys to church in the morning. Keeping them amused, so that they didn't wriggle from boredom from the pew onto the floor, or set the old ladies tutting with their loud whispering, helped calm her nerves about her meeting with Mr Nicholson that afternoon. After lunch, when she had been upstairs to wash, change and brush her hair, and there was nothing left to be done, she sat at the kitchen table biting her lip, twisting her hands together in her lap.

Mrs Norris stood looking at her, hands on hips, frowning in mock disapproval. "Goodness me, stop frettin' child – you're a bag o' nerves!"

Cecily grinned sheepishly. "Do I look all right, though – you know, my hair and my dress?"

"You look lovely, dear, as we've already said – umpteen times."

Edith raised her eyes to the ceiling. "Put an apron on an' come an' 'elp me dry up. It'd be better than sittin' there pullin' yer fingers out their sockets."

At that moment the Reverend poked his head around the door. "We are off now, Mrs Norris. We shall be staying out for tea as usual, so I hope you will all take a much-needed rest. Cecily, your visitor is waiting for you in the small parlour. Please feel free to stay there this afternoon as the weather is so inclement." He gave her a small, conspiratorial smile and disappeared.

Cecily looked at her companions and stood up. "Oh dear, my hands are shaking."

Mrs Norris flapped at her with a tea towel. "Be off with

you, silly girl. Have a lovely afternoon, dear, and be good!"

"I will!" Cecily almost ran from the room, down the corridor into the hallway. She stood outside the parlour door for a moment, trying to steady her breathing, before pushing it open. In front of her, standing beside the fireplace, was her father. He looked up, smiling broadly. She forced herself to ignore the great jolt of disappointment that passed through her body and to smile back as she walked forward to greet him.

He held his arms out to her. "Cecy! It's so lovely to see you again. My goodness, but you are even taller and more beautiful – just like your mother."

"Pa! What are you doing here?" She kissed him on the cheek. He held her tightly for a moment, then pulled away to look at her, his face creased in an enormous grin.

"I've some wonderful news for you, Cecy. Sit down."

Her mind raced. Another Carpenter baby on the way would *not* be wonderful news. What else could it possibly be? She held her breath as they both sat down on either side of the fireplace and he began to talk.

"You remember your Great Aunt Ellen, of course?"

She nodded. "Of course." How could she forget that terrible time?

"Well it seems that she has left me a large sum of money in her will. I've known about it for some time, but the legacy has been in dispute – a distant cousin of hers – so I haven't been able to say anything. But it was all finalised a few weeks ago. Apparently I was always a favourite of hers, though I never knew. I wrote to the Reverend as I wanted to tell you in person. Of course the children have been ill, so I couldn't come before."

"That *is* wonderful, Pa. What will you do with the money? Is there enough to buy a bigger house?"

"Yes, there is – we'll buy one of those fancy new ones your brother's been building. I believe there is still one available. And I can set myself up in business again. I won't make a mess of it this time, Cecy. Your Ma can have all the help she needs and plenty of room for the children. I feel like I've been given a second chance in life."

She looked at his handsome face, still lined, but youthful now and eager. Despite the crushing sense of disappointment still lodged in her chest, she felt a surge of love for him. She got out of her chair to kneel in front of him, taking hold of his hands.

"I'm so happy for you, Pa…and for Mother. It will be good for her to have help now."

"Yes, it will. She deserves some rest, your poor Ma." He looked wistfully out of the window for a moment, then turned back to her. "But I've come to talk about you, Cecy."

"Me? Why?"

"Because I can do something for you now, too."

"I'm all right, Pa. I'm happy here. I love my work."

"I know. And the Reverend speaks extremely highly of you in his letters. We're very proud of you, dear, your Mother and I."

"Mother? Proud of me?" She moved back a little and looked at him askance.

"Yes. I know it's not always been easy between you and your mother, but she feels proud of you too. And she agrees with what I'm about to propose. We both felt bad about sending you here and about what it was like for you in Whitstable."

Cecily couldn't help it. The ancient hurt rose from deep inside her, forcing its way out of her mouth, her voice suddenly high with distress. "But she never said! *You* never said! I felt so…so abandoned." Tears welled in her eyes. "I thought neither of you cared about me. I thought no one cared about me… except…except Harry." She was sobbing now.

He leaned forward and put his arms out. "Come here, my lovely."

She crawled over to him and rested her head in his lap, while he held her, stroking her hair, just as he used to do when she was little.

"That's why I've decided we must do this for you. Because I know you were hurt. And…and I think I was to blame…I didn't stand up…" He stopped, then, looking over her head into the fire with troubled eyes. They stayed silent for a few moments, before he sat upright, sighing deeply, and smiling.

"But that's all water under the bridge now. And after what you went through in Whitstable, I thought it was especially fitting that you should benefit from the legacy. So…" He held her face in his hands and squeezed her cheeks. "How would you like to be a teacher?"

❧

"Teacher training college? My Lor, Cecy – you can be a proper lady now, with yer own money and everyone thinkin' you're someone at last. 'Course you must do it, girl."

They were huddled together in Edith's bed, the candle burning low on the bedside table, rain beating heavily on the skylight above their heads. Edith's eyes were bright with excitement, but Cecily was frowning, chewing her lip.

"I don't know, Edie."

"What don't y' know for goodness' sake? It's obvious. You'll never get a chance like this again, will you? It's what you've always dreamed about. What's to stop you? I don' understand."

Cecily sighed. "I know you don't. I can't explain it, really. It's just I feel sure that I've been given this special job to do – to teach Grace to talk and to help her understand."

"What d'you mean – 'given' a job?"

"You know – by God. You do believe in God, don't you?"

"Well, yes, 'course I do…but as for bein' given jobs…I don' know 'bout that sort of thing, Cecy. That's all a bit too religious for me."

"Yes, and for me. I haven't even really been sure I believed in God sometimes, when I was in Whitstable and when Gracie was so ill. But, now I feel…" Cecily looked anxiously at her friend. "…I feel I *know*, somehow – that that's what I'm meant to be doing. I can't explain it." She shrugged her shoulders and laid her head back against the pillows.

Edith turned to look at her, shaking her head in disbelief. "You're a complicated one and no mistake, missy. And what's your poor Pa goin' to say? 'E thinks 'e's doin' somethin' wonderful for you and your tellin' me you're just goin' to turn yer nose up at it?"

"I know…I know." Cecily chewed her lip even more ferociously.

They stayed silent for a while, each lost in her own thoughts. Then Edith turned to Cecily and took her hands in her own.

"I've got somethin' to tell you too, Cecy. 'Arry came today. And 'e wants me to marry 'im. What d'you think of that?"

Cecily gazed open-mouthed at her friend.

"You're betrothed? That's wonderful news! But why didn't you say? Why did you let me carry on so long about all my worries?"

Edith smiled sheepishly. "Well, we ain't exactly betrothed. Not yet. We've gotta wait till 'e gets promotion. Then we can go to my Pa and ask 'im. So we're not sayin' anythin' to anyone else. Just you."

Cecily sighed. "You're a lucky girl, Edith Penton. He's a good man."

Edith leant over and kissed her on the cheek. "I know. And…I shall 'ave you for a sister. I'm lucky twice." She yawned then and patted Cecily on the hand.

"Well, as for your difficulty, my Ma always says you should sleep on it before you decide anythin' important. So 'op out now and back to yer own bed, girl. Try to stop worryin' – it'll all come right, you'll see. Night night."

"Night night, Edie."

Cecily returned her kiss and climbed out reluctantly, padding across the floor and slipping between her own cold sheets. Edith was soon snoring softly. Cecily lay staring up at the skylight, listening to the rain, now a patter, a soothing sound which usually helped her to relax. But tonight sleep would not come. Her mind was still racing with thoughts of Edith and Harry and with the impossible choice she must make. She wanted it all with equal passion – to be a teacher, her long held dream, and to stay here, where she had found purpose and friendship. And love. They hadn't talked about him tonight – the other reason for her doubts – but he was there in her mind all the time. And in her body, too, aching and longing to see him. It seemed so long since that dreadful evening when Grace had first become ill. With his mother so recently dead, it might be weeks before she would see him again. And after her disappointment this afternoon she couldn't rid herself of the nagging fear that his kindness in bringing her the music and offering to teach her to play had been only that – kindness. Her hope that he might love her too was nothing more than a childish dream.

It was all so confusing. So uncertain. She had no idea how she could begin to decide. Her head began to feel as if it might burst from the pressure of too many thoughts. She plumped her pillow impatiently, pulling the covers more tightly around her shoulders. This wouldn't do. She must try to sleep now. What did Harry used to say to her when she got herself in a state? "Take deep breaths, Cecy. Slow down. Think of something calm and pleasant." Well, she had heard two pieces of good news today. She would think about them. First she conjured a picture of Edith and Harry walking arm in arm down the aisle of the church, the Reverend Hopwood smiling benignly behind them, their families looking on with pleasure as they passed by. Then another picture, this time of her Pa, handsome and proud, and her Ma, in a pretty dress and bonnet, standing outside their new house with the children. They were all starting out on a new life now. Perhaps, as Edie said, her own new life would become clear soon. She turned on her side, let out a deep sigh and closed her eyes.

CHAPTER 36

Alfred's memories of the night of the funeral came to him in unconnected pictures and sounds, like fragments from a half-remembered dream: dark shapes of trees and bushes in the moonlight, a man's voice shouting, twigs cracking and breaking, the harsh breaths of men either side of him, his own voice shouting "No! No!", though to what, he had no idea, the click of the bedroom door latch as he was left alone. There were no events to connect the pictures and no feelings. No pain even, despite the bandages Mrs Barton came each day to change. He only knew that he had wanted to die, but had found that he was still alive.

Since that night (he could not say how long ago it was) he had been powerless to move himself from a half alive, dream-like state, sleeping much of the day, talking to no one except the servants, staring mostly – through the windows at the trees and hedges, or the frost-withered shrubs in the garden, or at the ever changing clouds. He ate and drank when meals were put in front of him, though he never felt the need and only did so to save the servants from more anxiety. He thought very little. His mind was empty, his body leaden with tiredness.

And this is how he might have stayed had Reg not appeared one afternoon, standing in the drawing room doorway, shifting nervously from foot to foot, his cap twisting in his hand. With a huge effort of will Alfred smiled a welcome and offered him a seat. He knew he should ask about the business, about the men, and the myriad problems that Reg must be dealing with alone now, but he couldn't bear to hear about it and hoped desperately that that wasn't the purpose of the visit. As if reading his mind, the foreman, now perched awkwardly on the edge of a chair, launched into a long, reassuring description of the progress of the various building jobs, all of which were apparently going along splendidly without the boss. Alfred sighed with relief as Reg continued,

"Young 'Arry Carpenter's been a God-send, to tell you the truth, Mr Nicholson. I couldn't 'ave done it without 'im. I've had to leave 'im managing several of the sites and 'e's coped marvellous well, sir. So you see, you've nothing to worry 'bout. You just take yer time and get properly well." He paused, drawing an envelope from his jacket pocket and passing it to Alfred.

"Er...I thought you'd better 'ave this back, sir. I didn't open it. I would've done, obviously, if...if..."

Alfred could see the poor man becoming flustered with embarrassment, but curiously felt nothing at all as he took the letter. His memory of writing it was very clear – the day before the funeral, his last words to the world, or so he thought at the time.

"Thank you, Reg. I...I appreciate your...discretion." He leant forward, dropping the letter into the fire. A long silence followed. He looked across at this steadfast rock of a man, always there when he was needed, kind, thoughtful, utterly dependable through nearly thirty years of service.

"That..." He indicated the letter, now curling into ash in the flames."...that was just to ensure that you and the men and the servants were well taken care of."

Reg flushed. "I'm grateful, sir."

"Don't be, please. It was no more than you deserve. Anyway..." He sighed deeply. "...it's not needed now." Another long pause. "So...was there anything else, Reg?"

"Well yes, sir, there was, as a matter o' fact. I 'ope you won't think I don't know me place, coming to talk to you like this..." He cleared his throat noisily. "...but I've been speakin' to Mrs Barton and to Mrs Dawes and we're agreed that somethin' needs to be done and they say I should be the one to talk to you, as I was the one that found you…as it were…sir. And as you've said you won't 'ave the doctor or the Rector or your friend and we're not to speak to them."

Unable to think of anything to say, Alfred nodded for him to continue.

"The thing is…Mr Nicholson, sir…Mrs Barton and I 'ave been wondrin 'ow much you remember 'bout what 'appened, like…before. We think it all might be connected, you see. We think it might be why you've been so weighed down with your…with the melancholy, sir."

Alfred sat up a little straighter. "*Before*, Reg?"

"Yes, what 'appened to your little brother, sir – to Master John."

"I don't know anything about that, apart from something I read in a letter from old Dr Tucker to my father."

"You don't remember nothin'?"

"I wasn't there, Reg, as far as I know."

"But that's just it, beggin' yer pardon, sir – you *were* there."

"Was I? How do you know?"

"'Cause I was the one that found you both – you first, then 'im, poor little beggar. And it was there, by the stream, where I found you the other night, sir…that's where 'e… that's where 'e died. You do remember the other night, don't you, sir?"

Alfred's reply was so quiet, Reg had to lean over to hear it. "No I don't. Not really. Tell me, please."

◈

So, as the sun sank below the hedgerows of the garden, leaving the drawing room lit only by the flickering light of the fire, Reg told him. And he listened, silent and completely still, apart from his trembling hands.

First the story of the night of the funeral. Ten days ago it was, so Reg told him – ten days ago when he had found him, sitting on the tree with the knife. He would never have found him if Mrs Barton hadn't sent him back, when the others had gone home. She knew the master wasn't right, she said. He was much too calm for her liking. Reg had told her about the other times, you see, when he had noticed a knife was missing and how he'd followed him one day, and had watched from the path above the stream, until he was sure he was safe. So she knew what the master was capable of and she had sent him back to the yard, where he found the letter and saw the knife was gone. He took Bill. They ran together, though Bill got there first and saw him first. They didn't realise what had happened till later. The water was so cold, it stopped the bleeding. The master was nearly unconscious, chilled to the bone by the stream and the frosty air, but it wasn't till they got him home, half carrying him up the hill and along the path, that there was all the blood, running onto the kitchen floor and under the table into a pool, and they saw that his lower legs were in shreds. They were frantic, he and Bill. They had never seen so much blood. But he wouldn't let them get the doctor. Shouted at them when they suggested it, he did. Thank the good Lord Mrs Barton had known what to do or…

And after she had sorted him out, and they were sure he was out of danger and had put him to bed, they had talked long into the night, he and Mrs Barton, about what had gone wrong for their master, whom they respected and were very fond of. For they'd known him since he was just a nipper, and he'd always been such a polite and gentle boy, and a good master, generous and fair, and they couldn't bear to see him so unhappy. And they realised that it might be no coincidence that he took himself down to the valley and sat in the very place where that dreadful thing had happened all those years ago. And Mrs Barton said she wondered if it was like a terrible canker deep inside his mind, which had lain there all this time. Maybe he needs to talk about it, she said. You know, Reg, like a wound that needs the air and the sun before it will heal. And they had taken advice from Mrs Dawes, who always seemed a wise and Godly woman, and she had agreed. So that was why he had come.

∽

Reg paused then, looking anxiously across at Alfred in the half light.

"I wonder if I should stop there for now, Mr Nicholson. You look done in, if you don't mind my sayin' so. I can come back tomorra and tell you the rest. It can wait. Why don't you go to bed now, sir?"

Alfred shook his head and motioned with his hand for Reg to continue.

"I'm all right, Reg. Just so sorry…It must have been so…"

"Oh no, sir, I don't want no apologies!"

"Then please, carry on. Tell me about John."

The story of the young brothers was more difficult for Reg to tell. Several times he stopped for a moment, unable to speak. It was as if it had happened yesterday, he said.

∽

The heat of the afternoon sun had bounced off the cobbles in the yard that day and the air in the workshop had been stifling. Reg had felt the sweat running down his face, making his hands slippery as he planed and chiselled. He had been pleased to be asked to go down to the woods to fetch the little lads back for tea. It would be cool there and he could put his feet in the stream too, for a few minutes.

When he first saw the young master running towards him along the path at the bottom of the field he thought he must have lost his clothes or got them wet. He was as naked as the day he was born. Then he saw the little boy's hair, wet, dripping down his back, and his legs, running with blood – a terrible mess they were. He was crying and ran into Reg's arms with such force that they both ended up on the grass. He couldn't catch his breath, poor little lad, what with the crying and the running. It was a good few minutes before Reg understood that he'd cut himself trying to scramble out of the rocky pool and running through the branches and brambles to get help, and that it was John who was really hurt.

It was hard to know what to do then, but when he suggested they should go back home to get help the little boy became distraught, shouting and crying that they couldn't leave John there any longer, not on his own. So he had heaved him onto his back, bloody legs trailing across his jacket, and hurried down to the stream.

What he saw there was still as clear in his mind as if he was standing on the bank today. Beside the log, a newly fallen tree in those days, on a shallow stony shelf, lay John's small naked body, his nose down in the gravel, his arms and legs tucked up as if he were sleeping, while small streams ran into his mouth and nostrils. He remembered the sun on his hair, making it shine like polished rosewood, a dragonfly resting there for a moment before darting off across the water.

Reg could see straight away that he was dead. Draped over him was an untidy heap of clothes, placed there by young Alfred who had tried and failed to pull his brother out of the water onto the bank. Knowing he must get help, and hating to leave him alone in the cold and wet, he had covered him up as best he could, to keep him warm. That was the part that was hardest to tell. Not about John, but about Alfred. He could hardly speak, poor little lad, his chest was heaving so with sobs. He thought he was to blame, you see. He thought he should have been able to help. And he knew that it was too late, though they neither of them said.

Reg dressed Alfred quickly and wrapped John in the rest of the clothes, then carried him up through the woods and the field to his home, Alfred trailing beside him, white faced and terrified. The scene in the house when they arrived was not one he could describe. He would only say that he was there when the doctor came and that he had seen the holes in John's tongue, punctured by his own teeth, during a fit. There was no water in his lungs. He hadn't drowned. His heart had failed, unable to cope with the stress of the seizure. He had probably had a weak heart all along. No one could have known that it would happen. No one was to blame.

⤬

When the story was finished they both sat for a long while staring into the embers, saying nothing. Then Alfred spoke very quietly.

"Why do you think I've never remembered about it all, Reg?"

Reg rubbed his thick beard for a moment.

"I don't rightly know, sir. The 'uman mind's a curious thing. It was terrible what you saw and you believed it was your fault, so it's not surprisin' you buried it deep down inside yerself somewhere. Per'aps it was better for you that way, as a child – not to remember. Only, maybe in the end things are better off in the open where we can see 'em – see 'em for what they are. I know it's not the way of the world, sir, but it's what us country folk believe." He sighed, pushing himself out of his chair.

"Well, I think I should be off now, Mr Nicholson. Let you get some rest. I sincerely pray you may find some peace of mind now, sir – now you know your part in the sad business, and that you did everything a little lad could 'ave done. And I 'ope you'll call on meself and Mrs Barton if ever

313

you feel the need of some company. We'd be very glad to see you."

He let himself out without waiting for a reply.

Alfred sat motionless looking into the fire, his hands quite still now. He retraced his steps back to the valley on that hot summer day. And as he watched the small boy struggle to keep his brother alive as best he knew how, tears began to run down his face.

CHAPTER 37

Clementine and David sat alone in the dining room eating supper. He was speaking gravely, she listening, eyes wide with disbelief and dismay. He had hardly finished before she cried out:

"But she can't go! I can't possibly manage without her, especially not now – with Gracie. Why didn't you tell me about this before? When did you say he came – Sunday?"

"Yes, Sunday afternoon. You were busy with the children and I didn't want to add to your worries, my darling, not until Cecily had had a chance to think about it. I know it's hard, but this is a marvellous opportunity she has been given."

"She has a marvellous opportunity *here*, to look after *our* children."

"But she wants to be a teacher, dear."

"She can teach Grace. She's been working hard with her, encouraging her to use all the words she used to say and it's working. Our little darling said 'no' to me today when I tried to spoon porridge into her mouth. 'No', as clear as a bell!"

David laughed. "That's our Gracie!"

"So how can you tell me it would be a good thing for Cecily to leave now?"

"It wouldn't be until next September, dear, when Grace would be quite a lot older. And, yes, I do think it would be a good thing for Cecily. We cannot just claim her as our own, you know. She has her own life to lead. We must have her best interests at heart."

"I have *my* children's best interests at heart. Really, David, sometimes I just can't understand you." She huffed with exasperation as Mrs Norris walked into the room. Clementine couldn't resist the opportunity to enlist an ally.

"What do you think of this idea of Cecily training to be a teacher, Ada? You don't think she should go, do you?"

The cook placed a pudding bowl on the table. "Oh, I don't think that's for me to say, ma'am. But she's not sure herself, you know. She's so excited about getting little Grace to talk again. I think that's what she really wants to do, but of course she doesn't want to disappoint her father. She's in quite a state about it, to be honest. Talks about nothing else." Ada stood for a while by the door. "Will that be all, ma'am? Only I'm all behind, with Edith ill."

"Oh yes, sorry, Ada. Do go." Clementine rounded on her husband, waving the rice pudding spoon as she served him. "There! She's not even sure she wants to go. There must be something we can do to persuade her to stay."

David was frowning and ruffling his hair, as he always did when he was thinking hard. He muttered to himself, "I wonder…"

"What?" She stirred the rice pudding vigorously, trying unsuccessfully to curb her growing impatience.

"Well…this is only an idea, of course, but Dr Tucker was here today asking after Gracie and he mentioned a school in London where they are trying a new method of teaching deaf children to speak. He thought it might be appropriate for her when she is older. I wonder whether…" His voice trailed away and the ruffling began again.

"Oh, David, for goodness sake! Tell me what you're thinking!"

"It occurs to me that perhaps it might be possible to secure an assistant teacher position for Cecily at this school for a while, perhaps a year, or more. I know some fellows up there from college days who could probably pull a few strings. Cecily's father could use the money he has set aside to support her."

"But how does that help *us*? We want her *here* and *she*

wants to be here, more to the point."

"Well, she could be here in the holidays, dearest. And she would bring back expert knowledge about teaching deaf children that would help us with Grace. And after her training was finished, she could come back and perhaps we could… we could open a small school!" This last thought was accompanied by a triumphant flourish of his napkin.

"A school? For whom?"

His eyes shone with excitement. "For Grace and any other local deaf children. I know of at least one other case in the parish – caused by measles, just like Grace – a bit older, but that wouldn't matter."

"Where would it be – this 'school'?"

"Oh…I haven't quite worked that out yet…perhaps here. Perhaps we could convert part of the stable block. It wouldn't need to be large."

Clementine leaned back in her chair and gazed at her husband. "Well! Whatever will you think of next? I don't know, David. There are so many things to consider. We haven't seen the specialist yet. Grace's deafness may not be permanent, please God. Cecily may not want to go to London. And I would need another nursery maid in term time. It will be extremely difficult to find someone as competent as her."

"Of course…of course. There are bound to be difficulties, but it's potentially a solution which could suit us all. I shall talk to Cecily and to Dr Tucker in the morning."

She frowned thoughtfully. "Well, I suppose it has to be better than losing her for good. And Alfred Nicholson would be pleased about that too, I'm sure."

"Oh…yes…" Her husband's face suddenly lost its glow of excitement.

She looked at him, eyebrows raised, waiting for him to continue.

"Oh dear, Clemmy. I think I may have upset that young

man. He avoided me like the plague at his mother's funeral and has sent word since that he's not well enough for a visit. And it was about young Cecily, too."

"About Cecily? What do you mean?"

He adopted a rather pained expression then, the one he often wore in a vain effort to deflect her anger before a major confession. She pursed her lips and frowned at him.

"David, what *have* you done?"

"Oh…well…I know you'll be angry with me, Clemmy dear, but please try to understand, I was only thinking of Cecily."

"Well?"

"Well…I spoke to him the day before the funeral. I knew that Cecily's father was about to offer her the opportunity to go to teacher training college. I felt it was important that Alfred didn't try to influence her in any way to stay and I told him so. She is so young, and might have taken his feelings for her as sufficient reason not to go."

Clementine drew in a sharp breath. "You've known about this since *before* the funeral and you've only just told me? And what about *her* feelings?" Her voice grew high and loud. "Did you consult *her* before you set about discouraging a match that would be supremely advantageous for her and which I know, from a conversation with Ada a little while ago, she hopes for herself? And what about *his* feelings, poor man? The day before his own mother's funeral – David, how could you? Especially knowing the state of his health over the last year. Sometimes your desire to help others becomes nothing but meddling. Really it does!" She gesticulated increasingly wildly through the speech and with the last word slapped her hand down on the table, making him flinch.

He said nothing for a long while. When he finally spoke, his voice was low, contrite.

"I'm afraid I must admit that you are right, dearest, as you

318

usually are, though I'm not sure that your motives are entirely pure. However, it is clear that I have, as you put it, been meddling in a most unhelpful way and that I must do something to put this right. Do you have any suggestions?"

She thought for a while, then looked at him, her eyes softening. "Well, a letter of apology would be a good first step, including an invitation to dinner – delivered by hand, I think."

"Oh no, dear. I don't think that's a good idea. He specifically said he didn't want me to visit at the moment."

She rolled her eyes. "Not *you*, silly."

He looked puzzled for a moment, then smiled back at her. "Ah, yes…what a clever girl you are, Clemmy!"

❧

Cecily gazed at the fields, still white with frost, at the bare brown trees and the hedgerows as they passed by, and marvelled at finding herself being driven, alone, in a carriage. If it wasn't for Peter's incessant chatter about the latest calamities in his large family, she might almost have felt like a lady. She fingered the letter on her lap, wondering what was so important that he couldn't have been trusted to deliver it himself, and thinking about the conversation she had just had with the Rector. His suggestion for her future had filled her with intense nervous excitement. This was her dream and she could hardly believe that it might come true. But she mustn't get her hopes up – it could still all come to nothing. She told herself that it wouldn't matter, she could stay at the Rectory, looking after the children, teaching Gracie as best she knew how. But she wasn't convinced. Of course it mattered. She had never wanted anything as much in her life – apart from him.

They rounded a corner and, as if reading her thoughts, Peter called out,

"We're nearly there now. That's his house."

He pointed to a white, weather-boarded house sitting back from the lane in a large garden, its walls glowing in the low morning sun. She loved it at first glance. How lucky Mr. Nicholson was to have such a beautiful home, nothing like the little red brick cottage she had imagined so often in her dreams. The carriage came to a halt at the front gate and her stomach immediately filled with butterflies. She had dreamed of a meeting such as this so many times, but now it was here she was scared. It would be strange to see him alone, without the children. Would he be pleased to see her? What would they say to one another? How should she address him now they were meeting away from the Rectory?

She knocked timidly on the door and was greeted by a small maid who showed her along a corridor to the drawing room, a much smaller room than that of the Rectory, more cluttered with ornaments and furniture, but pleasant nevertheless, light and airy, with a large window looking out onto the back garden and an orchard beyond. Mr Nicholson was sitting in a chair beside the fire. She noticed at once how pale he was, dark shadows beneath his eyes. He looked up as the maid showed her in, his face breaking into a wide smile, then stood up, walking stiffly towards her.

"Cecily! How lovely to see you! Come in, please." He held out his hand and she took it, smiling happily, her nerves evaporating in the warmth of his obvious pleasure. He motioned her towards the chair opposite his own. As he sat down she noticed again how stiffly he moved.

"Have you hurt yourself, Mr Nicholson?"

"Oh please, you can't 'Mr Nicholson' me here, unless I'm to call you Miss Carpenter. Alfred, please, or Alf – you can suit yourself. Anything but Mr Nicholson or Alfie. And yes, I had a small accident, but I'm on the mend now. Thank you for asking."

She suddenly remembered his mother's recent illness and death and put her hand to her mouth, horrified. "Oh…please forgive me. I should have said how sorry I was to hear about your mother."

He turned to look out of the window for a moment. When he spoke, his voice was quiet, less steady. "Thank you. It has been a very difficult time. But her death was a blessing in the end, to be honest…for her. I miss her terribly. This house seems much too big for me alone."

"Will you stay here?"

"Oh yes, I think so. I was going to move into the cottage, but I had some good news last week about a family you might know, I think." He smiled conspiratorially.

She looked puzzled for a moment, then laughed, "Oh! *My* family! They're going to buy one of your houses."

"Yes, they are. I'm very happy for them, but it also changes my situation and I've decided now that I shall stay. This is my home. I've never lived anywhere else."

The maid came into the room then, with a tray of tea. Cecily felt very strange, being waited on by a servant, a girl just like herself. It was even more odd when Alfred took charge of the teapot. She didn't know any men who poured their own tea. They sat drinking and talking for a while, about the children, the weather, the house and garden. Then his expression became more serious.

"I've been unwell since Mother died and I've had a lot of time to think, Cecily – about life and what it means and all that kind of thing. You're probably too young to ever think of dying and of needing to find the right path in life before it's too late."

"Oh no, I've often thought of it." She looked at him earnestly. "Especially recently, what with nearly losing Grace and her becoming deaf – I've thought about it a lot."

He looked shocked. "Oh, I'm so sorry to hear that she has become deaf. How terrible never to hear music or bird song or people's voices."

She nodded. "It is terrible. We're all really upset about it, especially her parents of course."

They both stared at the fire for a moment, then he turned back to her.

"And did you reach any conclusion – about the right path for you?"

"Yes, I think so, though I don't know whether it'll be possible yet." Her eyes became bright, eager. "I hope to learn to teach children like Gracie, who can't hear and who haven't learnt to speak. I may be going to London, to a special school there, to become an assistant teacher and learn as much as I can. Then the Reverend says he may start a school here, in Blackford, when I come back – for Grace and children like her."

"So you *will* come back?"

She shrugged her shoulders. "I hope so, if I go...but it's only an idea at the moment." She looked wistful then. "I really hope so...it's my dream."

"Then you must do everything you can to make it happen." He smiled, then looked away to the fire for a moment. When he turned back to her, his face was serious. "And what about your young man? The one I saw you with on the green? Is he a part of your dream?"

She blushed, horrified that he had seen her with Tom, shocked at his boldness in asking. "Oh...oh no. He never was...not really."

She saw the relief in his face and heard it in his voice.

"I'm glad...very glad."

As her eyes met his, so intense and warm, she could hardly breathe for the longing which swept through her body. If only he would reach out to her and kiss her. For a moment, as they held each other's gaze, she thought he might, but then he sat back, eyes still shining.

"I've been thinking about my grandmother these past couple of days," he said. "Nana Nicholson, we called her. She died many years ago and I had almost forgotten about her till the other day. She was an eccentric kind of person – didn't always do what was expected of her, wore strange clothes, very odd hats, had an untidy house, that sort of thing. It annoyed my parents. My father must have taken after his father – he certainly wasn't like her. And I've been remembering how she looked after me when my little brother died and how she used to feed me cake for breakfast and spoonfuls of honey at bedtime and let me run about in the garden with no shoes on or hat. And when I said I wasn't allowed those things she used to say, 'Sometimes, my lovely, we just have to do what makes our hearts sing.' I was only eight. I had no idea what she was talking about then. But I think I'm beginning to understand it now." He gazed out of the window at the frosty garden for a while, then back at her. "So what I'm saying, Cecily, is you must do what makes your heart sing."

She looked at him, a small frown knitting her brows. "But we can't always, can we? Do what we want, I mean. That's what my family have told me. 'Stop making a fuss, Cecily. You can't always have what you want, you know.' And I think sometimes they're right – sometimes you do just have to do things, even unpleasant things. And sometimes the thing you didn't want turns into what you do want, 'cause *you* change."

"Ah, yes, that's very wise. That does happen. It has happened to me. But it doesn't mean you should forget the dreams you once had or stop trying to make them come true."

She thought about this, wondering if he could possibly be right. Could she – *should* she fight for her dreams? Was it just because he was a man that he believed this was possible? Her mother believed that only men got what they wanted in life, but that was clearly not what he believed. And what were his dreams? Was she a part of his dreams the way he was a part of hers?

"What are you thinking?" he asked quietly.

"I'm not sure I can say, Mr…er…Alfred."

"Try me."

She hesitated, fearful of appearing too familiar. "I was wondering…I was wondering what your dreams are. What makes your 'heart sing'?"

"Ahh!" he laughed. "Now you're asking! I'm six and twenty years of age and I'm only just beginning to figure it out. So you're a long way ahead of me, Cecily – a long way ahead. I think for me it's music. I've decided to take my piano playing more seriously, to conquer my nerves and give more recitals and perhaps to do more teaching. I've really enjoyed teaching the twins, the little scallywags. And I have a very promising young man in the company who can take on more responsibility, so that I can work a little less." He winked at her. Then his expression became more serious. "And I have another dream, too… But that can wait, I think…yes, it can wait."

He gazed at her then with such gentle, loving eyes that she found herself struggling to breathe once more. She looked away, down at her lap, and at the letter.

"Oh, I'm sorry, I nearly forgot. This is why I've come – to give you this."

She handed it to him and he read quickly, his face breaking into a broad grin.

He looked up at her, still smiling. "Please tell Reverend Hopwood that actually I think he was right, though I accept his apology of course. And, yes, I will be delighted to come to dinner next week. Can you remember all that?"

"You think he was right, but you accept his apology and you'd like to come to dinner?"

"Yes, you've got it. Thank you… Well, Cecily. I have a young man coming shortly for an interview for a promotion, a certain Harold Carpenter, and I need to get down to the office. Thank you so much for coming to see me. I've really enjoyed having you all to myself for a while, without my two little rivals. And I shall see you next Thursday, all being well, for our first piano lesson. I hope you've been practising."

She gave him an apologetic look and he laughed. "Don't worry. I know you've had far more important things to think about. But you should keep it up. You're very musical, you know."

"I'm not sure there'll be much call for piano playing in a deaf school."

He laughed again. "No, you may be right. But you should do it for yourself. And keep hold of those dreams, Cecily. Don't let them go."

He stood, holding out his hand. She took it, savouring the warmth of his skin, losing herself again for a moment in his eyes. Then they were walking down the corridor and out of the door, he was helping her into the carriage, waving goodbye and was gone.

She pulled the rug up to her chest, hugging herself, and looked out at the clear sky, over the fields and the ridge beyond. Peter was quiet, thank goodness. She only wanted her own thoughts now. She remembered the way Alfred had looked at her, the warmth and love in his eyes. Did she dare to hope that it was love for her that she had seen there? What was it that he had said? He was pleased to have her *all to himself*, without his little rivals. And he was glad that she was not with Tom. *Very glad.* Yes, she dared to hope. She would hold onto this dream too, just like he had said she must. A bubble of joy rose in her chest and she found herself smiling foolishly at a passing field of sheep, munching oblivious, as the frozen grass melted slowly in the low winter sun.

❧

It was difficult to make his escape. Reg was extremely anxious, but he insisted. He needed to go, to lay the ghosts to rest. He would be all right. He would walk slowly, carefully. No, they couldn't come with him. He would be back soon.

Outside the gate he filled his lungs with frosty air and lifted his face to the sun. The interview had gone well. Young Harry was delighted with the promotion, of course. He could think about marrying his young maid, Cecily's friend, now.

And he….he could think about his music. About playing and singing and teaching and everything that made his heart sing.

And about Cecily.

She's beautiful, he said to the sheep, as he walked down through the half green, half frost-white field. And I love her. They eyed him with indifference, continued their loud tearing and munching. He laughed. Wanted to shout out: Didn't you hear me, you old miseries? *I love her.*

He stopped at the edge of the wood, in the long shadows of the trees, listening. The wind was blowing harder now, making the branches creak and crack. A wood pigeon cooed gently above him, before taking off in a loud whirr of beating wings. And afterwards nothing but the soft rush of the water, like a long, continuous sigh.

He climbed awkwardly down to the stream, his legs sore and stiff. Stood on the bank. No taking his shoes off today. No cold shock of water or hard agony of stones. Mrs Barton would not be pleased to see her careful handiwork ruined.

Just standing and watching. And waiting. It took a long while, but eventually he saw them. Sitting on the log, together in the sunshine, in the green, shimmering light of summer, jam jars swinging from string. Laughing. Splashing.

Then the older boy, legs dangling, staring into the dark, still water. Dreaming. Alone.

He looked around, anxiety rising, panic threatening. Where was he? Where had the little one gone?

Ah…there. In the shallows by the roots of the tree, where

the water flowed fast, sparkling, dancing. He was building a dam. Lifting rocks and stones to fill the gaps beneath the tree. Handfuls of gravel, mud. Leaves, twigs, bracken. Face set with fierce determination. Hair shining in the sunlight, like polished rosewood, just as Reg had said. And the dragonfly. A spark of blue iridescence around his head.

He couldn't move. Hardly dared breathe in case he frightened him away, lost him all over again. But he seemed to know, the little boy. For he turned his head and caught his eye and smiled. Large, beautiful brown, smiling eyes. Just like Cecily's.